YESTERDAY'S GONE

Season Four

SEAN PLATT

DAVID W. WRIGHT

STERLING & STONE

To YOU, the reader.
Thank you for taking a chance on us.
Thank you for your support.
Thank you for the emails.
Thank you for the reviews.
Thank you for reading and joining us on this road.

YESTERDAY'S GONE

Episode 19

(FIRST EPISODE OF SEASON FOUR)

"The Darkness Is Coming"

Prologue

EVA FLORES

Duncanville, Ohio
September 2013

EVA FASTENED her 1-year-old daughter into the jogging stroller, kissed Maria on the forehead, and looked up to see the other mothers in the Mommy and Me Pound the Pounds group waiting at the head of the jogging trail that wound through their neighborhood park.

It was a beautiful day, the sun still low in the sky and not yet blazing as it had been through most of summer. A cool breeze blew through the park's many elms and buckeyes, blowing Eva's long, dark hair into her eyes. She stopped for a moment, grabbed a purple scrunchie from her wrist, pulled her hair back, then wrapped it in a loose ponytail as she continued toward the path.

"Hey, sorry I'm late," Eva said as she met the group: 12 women and their children, most with one, except the blonde mom with twin boys. The mothers all stood waiting behind jogging strollers similar to hers, except for Ellen, whose daughter, Bianca, was now 4, and old enough to ride along on her Barbie bicycle.

"Hi, Ellen," Eva said, as the little redhead met her with a giant smile.

Ellen leaned toward the stroller and smiled at Maria. "Aw, she looks so cute in that shirt." The shirt, a light-blue tee, sporting the *Octonauts* characters from Maria's favorite show.

"Thanks," Eva said. "Her grandma bought it for her birthday."

"OK, ladies, are we ready?" Kensie asked.

Kensie, a cute blonde (as short as she was perky) who looked like a former cheer captain, was the group's leader and founder. When they first met, Eva thought she was a superficial bitch. After a year of knowing her, she still did.

Kensie started running, and the rest of the mothers fell in line behind her. Eva's best friend in the group, Lacy, ran up beside Eva, then held her pace as Robbie, her 2-year-old son, babbled from his seat in the stroller.

"Are we better today?" Lacy asked, smiling at Eva.

Eva had been feeling blue for a while and couldn't shake it. It started when Tom's ridiculous schedule started sucking the blood from their lives. She put up with the hours in med school, then again through the hell of his internship, but it was supposed to stop. He promised it would. Yet, after Maria was born things had gotten even worse. Eva knew she wouldn't have the house, or the car, or anything else without the endless hours it took for Tom to earn them, but what good was having all these things when she felt alone more often than not?

She might have been OK with his schedule if Tom would let her get a job. It wasn't that he *forbade* it. He wasn't a misogynist. But he said they didn't need the money, so why stick Maria in a daycare or with some nanny? He even cited studies he'd read saying how children who spend time with their mothers were better adjusted, smarter, and all the other good things you wanted for your kids. Never mind that *she'd* read studies that showed that kids in daycare were often smarter and more sociable entering kindergarten.

Each time they got into the argument, she found herself feeling guilty, like a bad mother for wanting to get away from her child, for just a little each day. Guilt to the boredom: wet cement on broken ankles.

Running kept it from drying.

Eva didn't need to pound an ounce from her body. If anything, her athletic frame could stand to gain a few. Her house had a small workout room, and she used it every day. Her muscle memory was fantastic, and the baby weight had practically melted from her body after Maria was born. The twice-weekly runs gave Eva the chance to bond with some of the other neighborhood women. Problem was, half the time Eva had no idea why she did it. She found most of the women boring, if not altogether insipid, except for Lacy, Donna, and Carol. Samantha, too, but only sometimes. These late-morning runs, despite the quality of their company, helped Eva feel human again, though the feeling was fleeting if it showed up at all. She considered it a sad commentary on her life that running with women she barely cared about was one of the highlights of every week.

Eva loved nearly every moment she shared with Maria. Her daughter was the sweetest, most angelic face Eva had ever known. But Maria was only a baby, and did little to answer her mommy's ambition. She longed for conversation, it didn't even have to be especially deep or meaningful. Eva would settle for anything that helped her feel more alive than merely there.

"So, are we feeling any better?" Lacy tried again.

"Sorry," Eva said, wondering how long her mind had been wandering on her problems. She laughed, feeling awkward. "I'm not sure where my head is. I'm better, I guess. Just tired."

Eva smiled at Lacy, then fixed her eyes to the road, hoping

Lacy would be content to run quietly beside her. Usually hungry for conversation, there was enough happening in Eva's head to make her hungry for quiet. Maybe she'd feel more like opening up after the first lap around the path, when the group started to scatter into smaller groups as they tended to do. Now she craved silence.

Lacy smiled back, silent, holding her pace beside Eva.

A few weeks back, Eva had stumbled into the first truly awful flare-up from her growing depression. There had been flickers before, but nothing like that night. It was horrible. Maria had been a terrific sleeper, ever since a few weeks into her infancy, but one night she started screaming, and then kept screaming with what sounded like night terrors for three evenings straight. Tom was clocking even more hours than usual, and Eva's mother was being an absolute bitch, calling her and running Eva through a ringer of guilt over everything she expected and a few things Eva never saw coming. None of it was particularly catastrophic or even unusual, but somehow the sum total of everything seemed to rattle Eva from the insides. Without warning, she woke on that fourth morning and found it physically painful to get out of bed. Tom left for work, and Eva cried for hours. Maria cried in the crib beside her.

Eva cried while changing her daughter, cried while feeding her, and cried while lying down for their afternoon nap. She cried while drinking her morning coffee, and cried during lunch. She cried while filling her cart at Whole Foods, then again while checking out. There was no sobbing or heaving or nose blowing, only an endless stream of tears that seemed to flow from a busted spigot from early dawn to the ugly shadows of dusk.

She couldn't say anything to Tom, of course, and while Eva would have gladly confessed her every feeling to Maria, and did, her baby daughter could do nothing to help.

Eva's boredom, the sentence served for being a stay-at-home mom, was slowly fermenting into resentment. Being at home was never what she wanted; it was a product of Tom's insistence. A few years before, Eva had been looking toward a future dappled with the blooming fruits of her ambition. She wanted to be an actuary. Certainly not the coolest job in the world, as Tom often reminded her, saying it sounded almost as exciting as cardboard, but Eva was, and had always been, fascinated by risk and uncertainty. To her, being an actuary sounded fun; she would provide assessments of financial security systems, evaluating the probability of events to quantify outcomes so her clients could minimize the losses associated with uncertain undesirable events. OK, boring as cardboard, but her brain would be busy, and it was certainly better than losing years as a maid, chauffeur, short-order cook, and dishwasher.

"So," Lacy asked, after the near silence of clomping Nikes was finally too much. "How was last week's doctor's visit?"

"They tried putting me back on the happy pills," Eva shrugged, "but I said no thanks."

"There's really no shame in taking antidepressants," Lacy said. "Hell, all the moms are either on them, or have been."

"Yeah, I did them for a bit after Maria was born. Had postpartum depression, and Tom convinced me it was best."

"And?" Lacy said, "They helped?"

"Yeah, at first, but after a while I felt like a zombie. I hated it. Besides, it's normal to be down every now and then, right? That's what's wrong with people today," Eva lowered her voice to keep from offending the group, "everyone thinks they have to be happy 24/7. I shouldn't have even gone back to the doc. All he wants to do is put me on pills."

"So," Lacy said, her voice low, "are you OK? Have you considered … *therapy?*"

"Yeah, yeah, I'm fine," Eva said. "And no thanks on the therapy. Been there and done that, too. They want to put me on meds, no different from the other doctors. A big no thanks to that; you guys are my therapy, just getting out of the house and being with adults, you know?"

"Yeah," Lacy said. "Hey, you should come to the cookie swap this Saturday. It should be fun. Supposedly, Deb's going to make those brownies we're not supposed to talk about."

"Yeah?" Eva felt herself wince. "Who's going?"

"Almost everyone? Didn't you get an e-mail?"

Eva frowned, "No, I didn't." She looked at Kensie, and felt a sudden flush of anger.

Why didn't they e-mail me?

This wasn't the first time the group had *overlooked* sending an invitation to Eva. There was a dinner a few weeks ago that she found out about only three days later. She looked around at the other women, and could feel them thinking she wasn't good enough to be with them — as if *she* was the boring one. There had been five or six times (depending on how she was counting) in the past three months when Eva had been left out of something. Each time, Lacy managed to bring it up, making Eva feel like shit. She wondered if it was some sort of passive-aggressive thing and that Lacy was purposely telling Eva so she felt excluded. So she felt like a lesser.

Lacy asked, "You OK?"

Eva snapped, "Why are you so damned concerned about whether I'm OK all the time?"

Lacy looked at Eva as if slapped. "What?"

"You know what!" Eva said, running faster, wanting to flee one of her few friends before she said something worse, or something that she couldn't take back. Like last night with Tom, Eva could feel her temper threatening to spill, and knew it would be even worse than it had been with Tom, yet she could do nothing to stop it.

Maria started crying. Eva ran even faster, but still Lacy caught up.

"Hey, did I do something to piss you off?"

Eva said nothing, her mind bubbling from emotions she

didn't understand. She felt as if all the women were staring at or right through her. Someone up ahead laughed, but Eva didn't see who. *Probably that bitch Kensie.*

"Hello, Earth to Eva?" Lacy said, her voice suddenly like a handful of broken glass.

"What?" Eva replied, stopping with a sudden halt.

While the world around them suddenly seemed to freeze, with all eyes from the other mothers on them, Eva felt a building pressure in her brain, and a shortness of breath. It felt like a panic attack times one hundred.

Maria screamed, though Eva couldn't focus on her now. She was feeling a strong desire to run — run far away. Don't look back, just go, leave everything behind.

"What's your problem?" Lacy asked.

Eva's hands trembled as she forced them down at her sides, trying to shutter her sudden urge to swing at Lacy. She'd never hit anyone before, and didn't know from where her feelings were stemming. She was claustrophobic, as if the bitches were closing in: pointing, whispering, laughing.

Eva's right hand slipped into her right pocket as if working independently from her brain, finger curled around her house key, only peripherally aware of the movement.

"Maybe you should go on pills, Eva! You're acting like a nut," Lacy said, then turned and jogged ahead.

Eva stood, shaking. Then, before she knew what she was doing, she lunged forward. Movement without thought flung her toward Lacy. Eva's hands flew into the air with the key like a sword sticking out from her fist.

Lacy turned, eyes wide in shock before Eva's key found her left eye socket, then twisted the key to unlock an eruption of blood.

Lacy's screams were echoed by the women around them, but Eva barely noticed as she flipped Lacy over and dragged her from grass to asphalt path, and smashed her face hard into the ground, repeatedly, rending her skull into chunks of bone and meat.

Lacy's son, still in his stroller, screamed for his mother. Somewhere in the din, Eva heard her daughter, also crying out. But the pressure in her head swelled, and she had to find relief. Had to stop it.

Eva turned, eyes narrowing on the 3-year-old boy, strapped tight into his stroller, unable to escape, "Shut up, shut up, shut up!"

She leapt onto the stroller, her open mouth tearing at the child's neck. Warm blood flooded her mouth, animal adrenaline shot through her body.

The child's screams were like fuel to the fire in her head. She had to silence them. She arched down to bite again, but as she moved forward, something stopped her.

Hands were on her, pulling her from the child.

Eva fought back: tearing, biting, painting the mommies in blood before some of the women managed to wrestle her to the ground.

"Get off of me!" she screamed, desperate, thrashing, and lashing out.

She had to get up, had to get away, had to silence the screaming children.

Had to …

And then something hit her in the head, hard, stopping the chaos, and slowing things down.

She relaxed, feeling a dizziness overwhelm her. It was almost intoxicating in its promise to silence the din.

As Eva's vision clouded with smudges of darkness, all she saw was her baby girl, crying and reaching out for her.

～

ONE

Michael Blackmore

Lancaster Township, New Jersey
  July 16, 2009

WHEN THE PHONE woke him at 3:15 a.m., Michael Blackmore knew Amber was in trouble again: the sixth sense of a parent.

He grabbed the phone between the second and third ring, trying to answer before it woke Margie.

"Yes?" he asked, not bothering to look at the caller ID. No one but Amber called so late.

He was in the middle of wondering what his daughter needed this time — a ride, money, or maybe bailout on another DUI. She was 22, and at risk of dropping out of college, and crapping her future, if she didn't get it together. For Mike, the line between tough love and support was a high wire. At some point, you had to stand at the nest's edge and watch your child try to stay airborne.

It wasn't Amber. It was Detective Lou Santori, an old friend and former colleague. "Mike?" he said. "It's Lou."

"Hey Lou, what's wrong?"

"I don't know how to say this."

Lou was never short for words.

"What is it?" Mike asked.

"It's Amber … "

Mike felt the lump in his throat. She wasn't *just* in trouble this time.

This wasn't a call for Daddy to come fix another problem, this was a problem no one could fix.

~

MIKE WAS at the rundown motel within 20 minutes. The Atlanta was a seedy joint known during Mike's time on the force as a haven for prostitution and drugs. He stepped out of his SUV, into the sweltering summer night and surreal circus of flashing red lights, yellow police tape, curious onlookers, and officers avoiding eye contact. There were already news vans setting up in the parking lot: media vultures to feast on the morbid.

His gut twisted and spilled, each second an agonizing hour until he found Lou in front of the open door of Room 113.

Lou was talking with three other cops, and stepped forward to meet Mike, eyes urgent.

"Before you go in there, I have to tell you, it's bad."

Mike's heart raced faster, dread in his veins. Guts churned. "How bad?"

"The worst I've ever seen," Lou said. Lou had worked homicide for 16 years. He added, "You might not want to see this, but I couldn't *not* call you."

"No," Mike said, "I have to."

Lou ushered him past the officers outside the room. He had probably explained who Mike was — to those who didn't already know him or hadn't worked with him — before his arrival.

A crime scene photographer was still snapping photos as Lou led Mike into the room.

His daughter was in pieces.

The impact of seeing Amber dead and mutilated like savaged livestock sent Mike to his knees as if someone had swept his feet from beneath him. He didn't get up. *Couldn't* get up.

He could only stare, shock like dirt in his throat.

Amber's naked corpse was splayed on the bed. Crude blood "doodles" desecrated her flesh.

What kind of sick fuck does this to someone?

Her head, cut off, sat on the dresser — a prop — eyes wide, hair pulled into pigtails, lips smeared with garish red, like the Joker.

Mike tried telling himself it wasn't her as his mind flashed through memories that swore otherwise — starting as an infant so tiny and delicate in his arms to a little girl frightened of monsters in her closet at bedtime, staring up at her daddy like a hero who came to protect her until she fell asleep in his arms.

But he had failed his daughter: The monster *had* gotten her.

Thoughts and questions battered his brain until one rose above the others — *why?*

Why my baby?

~

AUG. 14, *2009*
   9:18 p.m.

MIKE SAT at the Lucky Puck's wraparound bar. The NHL didn't start until October, so the televisions lining the joint's walls were broadcasting a blend of old Devils games and other sports to a mostly blue- collar room, interested in drinking, playing pool, and darts, in that order. The place stank of smoke, alcohol, and all the rest of the stuff that soured the air around loud rock and dance music.

Mike feigned interest in the largest of the bar televisions while keeping an eye on the bartender: Derrick Reynolds of Apartment 215 Chauncey Lane, who was working his magic on a gaggle of women at the other end of the bar.

Derrick, whose father, Stan, owned the place, was one of the last people to see Amber alive on the night she died. Her credit card was used at the bar four hours before she was found. Derrick had processed her order and registered her receipt for $23.59.

Though Derrick wasn't a suspect in Amber's rape and murder — plenty of people saw her leave alone — he wasn't forthcoming with police when questioned. There was something Lou hadn't liked about the guy, so he let Mike know.

Now Mike was paying a visit to the bar to see what he could find.

Derrick was big at 6 foot 4 — four inches taller than Mike — and seemed around 240 pounds of pure muscle coiled behind a tight fitting black T-shirt and jeans. While Mike was also 240 pounds, he was soft from sitting on his ass for six years writing his popular series of Denton Cox detective novels. If things went south with Derrick, Mike would be forced into Option B, nestled in the holster under his sand-colored coat.

Mike kept nursing his Bud until the girls at the other end of the bar abandoned their spot in favor of some guys tossing darts. He drew a photo of Amber from his inside coat pocket and slid it on the counter as Derrick approached.

Mike said nothing, waiting to see the bartender's eyes, hungry to see his reaction. Derrick delivered, showing Mike recognition, followed by an immediate attempt to bury a truth in his eyes.

"What's this?" Derrick asked, his voice instantly defensive.

"My daughter, Amber Blackmore," Mike said, still holding Derrick's eyes, "You remember her?"

"Nah, should I?" Derrick asked, pretending to wipe the bar with a dingy, gray rag, avoiding Mike's stare.

"So, you don't remember her coming in here on July 15?"

"Hey, man, no offense, but a lot of people come in here, why would I remember her?"

"Because you were one of the last people to see her alive."

Derrick stopped wiping, and met Mike's eyes. He wasn't bright, Mike could tell, but did wear a sinister intelligence, the sort that knew how to avoid and deflect trouble or, as evidenced by his rap sheet, meet it with violence.

"What you sayin'?" Derrick asked.

"I'm not saying anything, I just want to know what you remember about that night — who my daughter spoke to, if maybe she left with someone?"

"I already told the cops I didn't see nothing. She wasn't a regular. All I remember is that she sat at the bar, drinking, then left after a while. Wish I could tell you more."

Derrick locked onto Mike's eyes, trying his best to seem open and honest. While his eyes and face were selling the lie, his hands, in his pockets for the first time all night, were not.

He was definitely hiding something.

"Listen, I'm not looking to jam you up or anything," Mike said. "I know there's something you're not telling me. Something you remember from that night that you're not saying. Maybe it's something little you don't think matters, but … " Mike reached into his coat again. This time pulled out another photo, of the murder scene, and set it on the counter, " … anything you can tell me, anything at all … "

Derrick recoiled at the image, backing away, his face red and enraged. "Man, get the fuck outta here with that shit!"

"Please," Mike said, slipping the photos back in his coat as he felt the scene getting out of control in a way he wasn't looking for … yet. "Please, I'm her father. I just want answers."

"I told you I don't know shit, now get out."

Derrick pointed at the door. His muscular arm twitched, as if offering to help Mike outside if he wasn't willing to listen.

Mike nodded, then obeyed.

For now.

~

AUG. 15, *2009*
2:15 a.m.

MIKE TRAILED Derrick on foot to his apartment, six blocks away.

He stopped along the way a few times, running into a surprising number of people on the streets, despite the late hour, shooting the shit, and seeming to flirt with more women — though it was hard to hear from 60 yards back. Mike was afraid Derrick would find someone to accompany him home, but despite his gregarious nature and obvious attempts, Derrick somehow managed to make it back to his apartment alone.

The apartment building was a three-story walk-up, run down like most of the neighborhood. Mike hung back on the far side of the street, in front of a small shopping plaza, watching as Derrick climbed the stairs and made his way to a second-floor apartment. He went inside. Moments later, the dark window beside the front door went bright behind verticals.

Though Mike knew Derrick lived alone, it was always possible that someone was staying over. A dark apartment a few minutes before made it less likely.

Mike waited a few moments, watching both street and building, then crossed at a trot.

~

HE DIDN'T BOTHER KNOCKING.

Mike used the bump key he always carried, unlocked the door, and entered the apartment, gun in hand.

The living room was empty. To his right, Derrick laughed out loud. "Fuck you, noob!"

And then the sound of a machine gun firing.

Mike spun, gun aimed, to see Derrick sitting at a desk in the bedroom, his back to Mike, headphones on, playing some war game on his computer.

Mike smiled as he closed the front door, locked it, and made his way to the bedroom. He pressed his gun against Derrick's head.

Derrick, startled, jumped from his chair, spun around, fists curled and ready to strike. He saw the gun, and recognized Mike from the bar.

"What the fuck?" he said, throwing his headphones aside.

"Sit down; we need to talk!" Mike growled.

Derrick looked Mike up and down, eyes seemingly assessing the odds of him actually using the gun or maybe figuring out whether he could wrest the weapon before Mike could fire a shot.

He short circuited Derrick's possible plan by yelling, "I said sit!" then gave him a look that showed the itch in his finger.

Derrick fell back into his chair, some of his bluster and most of the bravado missing from his face.

"Now," Mike said, "you're going to tell me everything I want to know."

"I told you, I don't know shit," Derrick lied.

Mike smacked him across the face. Before Derrick could

rise from his chair to retaliate, Mike shoved the gun in his crotch. "Sit!"

Derrick's eyes went wide, and he swallowed hard.

"Now talk."

"Fine, fine, I'll tell you, but if you tell the cops, or try and get me to testify at a trial or something, I'm not saying shit! You got that?"

"I get it," Mike said, not bothering to tell Derrick that if he found the fucker that killed his daughter, there would be no trial, except maybe for Mike's — if he got caught.

"OK, there's this guy that worked the kitchen at Lucky Puck's for a while. Name was Jim Silva, dude was always flirting with the waitresses and shit."

"OK, and?"

"Well, he up and left a day after the murder. Didn't call in, didn't pick up his last paycheck, nothing. Just vanished."

"What? Why didn't you tell the officers who talked to you?"

"He was working under the table," Derrick shook his head. "I didn't want to make problems for my dad."

"So, you screwed up a murder investigation?"

"I'm not saying the guy did it! For all I know, he just up and quit. It's not like the bar business is known for steady workers. People leave all the time, ya know?"

"I want whatever you have on him, license, address, anything."

Derrick shook his head, "Dad doesn't keep paperwork on people who work under the table."

Mike sighed, "Come on … OK, tell me everything you remember about him. What he looks like, does he have tattoos, significant features, anything that stuck out about him?"

"Stuck out?"

"Yeah, anything odd or different, anything at all — like maybe he had Tourette's, or a limp, or drawl, or something?"

"Now that you mention it, he did have a sorta Southern drawl, but not like a hillbilly. He was an asshole, but almost poetic? He had this expression, said it all the time, though it annoyed the shit outta me and the rest of us. I swear, the guy was like a 4-year-old, saying the same crap over and over whenever he didn't like something."

"What was the expression?" Mike asked.

"Beer-battered bullshit."

TWO

Boricio Wolfe

Hollywood, California
September 2013

"WELL, ain't that some beer-battered bullshit?" Boricio said, nodding toward one of the yellow-jacketed Designers blocking the entrance to Cache, the restaurant where they were meeting Rose's agent.

The Designers were members of some New Age, pseudo-religious cult called the Church of Original Design, sorta big and recently bigger. Boricio didn't know shit about the church, but figured that Hollywood was probably ground zero for the freaks, and had seen five of the yellow-jacketed aberrations since arriving. This particular freak held a periwinkle flier toward Boricio and Rose. "Hello, brother and sister," he said, "have you forgiven yourselves and found your true potential?"

Boricio wanted to find his true potential slopping two knuckles with the Designer's gravy. He could both forgive himself and find his potential fine, and needed no help from Tweety Bird to do it. But Boricio wasn't broken anymore, at least not like he once was, partly because of Luca the Boy

Wonder's fixing, and partly because of his summer Rose. Either way, his fair lady could smell a bristle on Boricio, even if she didn't know his scent had horns.

She squeezed his hand, and he glanced over. Her worried eyes and nervous smile pleaded, *Please don't make a scene.*

Boricio smiled back, then dug deep into a shit-eating grin. "Why thank you, kind sir! I woke up just this very morning hoping someone would offer me various paraphernalia on ways I could start finding my true potential! I will read this over, thrice at least, highlighting those lines that might change me most for a fourth and fifth gander in the 'morrow!" Boricio trailed off as Rose yanked him through the front doors and into the posh restaurant he hoped would live up to its reputation.

"Thank you," Rose whispered behind her, shoving the flier into the belly of her purse. She turned to Boricio. "You could've just said thanks, ya know. We didn't need your hammy Sir Laurence Olivier."

"You ever know me to just move on from anything? I was delighting their enlightenment. We were the best flier-takers all day. I'll bet you the relish on my ratatouille that they're going home to Designer HQ tonight and telling all the other wackos about the nice couple they met, and how they said they'd be highlighting lines on the flier when they got home. Way I see it, you owe me," Boricio teased. "But I'll be a good boy until we're finished with Veronica, especially if you promise I can be a bad boy again when we get back to the hotel."

Rose smiled at him, her cheeks blushing pink.

The maître d' led them down a short set of stairs and over to a table, centered in the middle of a bright dining area, sucking in the Southern California sun from behind wide walls of glass. Boricio tailed Rose, squeezing her hand, soaking in the restaurant's surroundings with a smile.

A restaurant could brag all it wanted, with A's and stars

and reviews across their walls, but only one restaurant in a hundred — if that — knew how to turn a meal into an adventure. Taste mattered as much as experience. A restaurant with swagger was best: balls without bragging, subtle enough to know it without having to prove it. So far, Cache was ticking Boricio's boxes, the vibe seemed right, but the real test would be the food. Decor, music, service, even 200 pages of wine, all of it meant dick if the menu went flaccid.

Veronica Barrow waited at their table, smiling.

"Ah, so this must be the Boricio I've heard so much about," she said, standing. Veronica was tall, at least 6 feet, with a long curtain of fiery-red hair. Rose had said she was in her early 50s, but Boricio would've taken her for a few ball hairs from 40 at most. Apparently chichi hippie agreed with her.

"Well, well, don't you think for a second that our Rose only whispers sweet nothings to you." Boricio took Veronica's hand and managed to wink at both girls as if he was aiming right at them, though Veronica was directly in front and Rose was at his side. He kissed her hand and finished. "She's told me so many things about the 'brilliant Veronica Barrow' I had to start carrying a scroll so I could just unroll it and scribble at the bottom each time Rose felt the burning need to add a new one, which happens every once upon the hour or so." Boricio added his widest smile to the full stop at the end of his sentence, then dropped Veronica's hand as she laughed out loud and started brushing shades of red onto her pretty porcelain skin.

Smells like she knows how to sweat money in tall stacks.

"You know with this much charm, I could get you cast in something just like that?" Veronica snapped her fingers, still smiling.

Boricio said, "You're just being kind, but even if you weren't, I'd like to get into Hollywood same as I'd like to have chemo for fun."

"Boricio!" Rose punched him on the arm.

Boricio pulled out Rose's chair, waited for her and Veronica to both sit, then took his own seat and said, "I'm interested in it for Rose, though, her words are worth buying and turning into pictures with all the purty people and their shiny teeth. So, let's focus on her."

Veronica smiled, said "Of course," then asked about their flight.

Boricio waited for Rose to finish saying it was terrific before he cut in with the truth that it was really sorta awful, his story drawn with just enough color to relax Veronica more than she already was, and soften Rose's shoulders with the promise that her beaux was at his articulate best.

"So, how long are you in town?"

"A week," they said together.

"Boricio wanted to see the sights," Rose said. "He's never been."

Of course, Boricio had been up and down the West Coast, suckling the state's titties from north to south. He learned to leave fry-cooking behind and become a chef out in Napa, though he didn't stay long, moving to Houston and then New Orleans shortly after that. But Rose didn't know that side of Boricio, or most sides for that matter. Not that he wouldn't be happy to tell her; Boricio loved to let his insides outside to play, but he'd never loved anyone before, and was still circling the animal, inhaling its scent and trying to figure it for what it was. If he breathed out half of what brewed inside him, Rose would've run screaming already.

"I'm just a passenger," Boricio said. "Here to keep Rose entertained."

"So modest," Veronica said. "Rose tells me you're a fountain of ideas, and that *The Billfold's* final draft wouldn't exist if it wasn't for you."

"I do tend to ramble," he said.

"He's a genius." Rose said as a well-coiffed gentleman

gently set a sculpted, silver basket of bread at the table's center. She grabbed a piece of bread from the basket, buttered it, passed it to Boricio, then buttered one for herself.

"Don't believe a word, Ms. Veronica Barrow, my genius ain't nothing. Rose is a tremendous listener, and knows how to find a hog in the codswallop. I never shut up, and she never muffles her curious nature. I just give her plenty of codswallop to sift through." Boricio wrapped his arm around Rose. "You've gotta admire a brain like that, someone always hungry to know *why*. Most folks you meet are too busy waiting for their turn to talk, myself included. Rose is always happy getting another turn to listen."

Veronica laughed, her look knowing. "That *is* true," she said.

They circled this and that and about a dozen other topics until Boricio finally got to the hog. "So, the Maris Brothers," he said, swallowing his bread. "Aren't they a part of that whack job Designers cult?"

"This is Hollywood," Veronica said, "Everyone's part of some weird thing or another. Don't let that put you off."

Rose had her mouth half open, but Boricio cut in front of her, not because Rose couldn't speak for herself, or because he didn't want to hear what she had to say, but because that was precisely why she had asked him to come to lunch, and California, in the first place.

"So why the Maris Brothers?" he asked.

"Because they're the best fit for *The Billfold*."

"You make a beautiful echo, Ms. Veronica Barrow," Boricio smiled. "But isn't that exactly the same thing you said about Epic Media? And that was before we booked our tickets to come meet you. So what's changed in six short days?"

"Nothing, really, except that now I know the Maris Brothers are interested. They weren't on my radar before, not because they weren't right, but because they don't take pitches. Don't get me wrong, Epic Media is a *great* fit. Perfect for you, really. And short term, absolutely the right thing, more than anyone in Hollywood. I promise. But the Maris Brothers are something else entirely."

"So, why the sudden interest if they don't like pitches?"

"I wasn't pitching. I was just talking about your project, as one friend to another. I adore *The Billfold*," she turned to Rose, her eyes earnest, "more than anything I've ever repped, and I've been at this a while. I'm sure Jared could see it in my eyes."

"He the tall one or the fat one?" Boricio asked.

"The fat one," Veronica admitted, though Boricio could tell she didn't like the insult's taste on her tongue.

Rose held her quiet, looking over at Boricio with her bright enough with appreciation that he felt compelled to continue. "So, what makes you think these brothers can make a better movie with a fraction of the budget, and why do you think less money is better for Rose?"

Veronica sighed. "I know this is a hard argument. And I'll even admit that it would be difficult to convince me if I was sitting on your side of the table. But these brothers know their stuff. They're already legends on set, and they've only made two pictures. Considering *Dappled* was shot for under a million, looked like 20, and grossed over 100 domestic, and then they topped that with *Wormhole*, which tripled every number, they've already proved themselves the better bet, at least as I see it. Long term, there's no question who you want making your movie. Right now, today, Epic will change your life more. Definitely. They'll give you seven figures for your script, and that's the best deal you'll get in Hollywood. Your movie *will* get made and it *will* make money. It will probably do *OK* critically, and you might eke by with a 65 percent on Rotten Tomatoes. But your next project will be a tougher sell. The Maris Brothers, on the other hand, will hit it out of the park, and your follow-up, *Insanity*, which already sounds fantastic, by the way, will be firmly in a seller's market."

Boricio squinted his eyes at Veronica while listening to Rose's heart make a thumpity thump beside him. He chewed on her words, each sounding like perfect sense to him, as he considered Rose's reaction. The breath in her chest said it made sense to her, though she'd be juggling *he loves me, he loves me nots* with the thought of turning down a right now paycheck.

The table filled with food as Boricio deftly changed the subject, saying they'd need to think on it. The meal was good enough, but not great, which thoroughly disappointed Boricio, shocked to find conversation beating the food. But he was pleased that he liked Veronica as much as he did. She was sparky, and could hold her side of a volley, but what Boricio liked most — what truly mattered — was that she showed respect to Rose and seemed to have her eye on his lady's best interests.

Veronica wanted to pick up the check, but Boricio covered it on his way to the restroom. It's what Rose wanted, and Boricio approved. He liked owing no one anything for anything ever. After the meal, Veronica profusely thanked them for their time, and again apologized for the last-minute change.

They said goodbye at the table, then Boricio took Rose by the hand and led her to an outside terrace where they looked over a koi pond and onto the boulevard.

"So, are you going with the Brothers or the sure thing?"

Rose wrinkled her nose. "What do you think I should do?" She looked at him, her eyes large and wanting. Rose had come to trust Boricio so much and in such a short time. It was an odd weight to carry, and half the time Boricio half expected to drop it.

"I think you have to do what's best for you."

"And what do *you* think that is?"

Boricio hesitated, shifting on his feet. He still wasn't used to his words or opinion mattering, and found himself continuously surprised that Rose seemed so reliant on both. He took her hands and squeezed them tight, loving her with every part the Boy Wonder had taken to fixing. "Stand upright, speak thy thoughts, declare the truth thou hast, that all may share; be bold, proclaim it everywhere: They only live who dare."

"Is that Voltaire?"

"Probably," Boricio said. "Point is you need to be bold because if you're not, you lose. Even in a tinkle fairyland full of phonies and weirdos and cults, it's best to know the game you're gonna play, so you can spin the dice or roll the wheel or do whatever the fuck you've gotta do to make the house go home and hand you your bags of cash on their way out the door."

"You're mixing your metaphors," Rose laughed.

Boricio laughed with her. "Do what's best for *you*, Rose. Do that the right way and you'll get what you deserve. Then you can keep on doing what's best for you for the rest of your life."

"What's best for *us*," she corrected.

He felt punched in the gut with what felt like a smile. "What's best for us," Boricio repeated, squeezing her hands tighter. "Sometimes you have to dribble down court with fuckers you'd love to see fall, but you keep on dribbling. Let's meet the Brothers and hear what they have to say. I can't see any harm in that."

Her smile spread wider. "OK, I'll call Veronica. The Maris Brothers it is."

"Well, yee-fucking-haw," Boricio laughed.

Rose called Veronica. Two seconds after the third ring, Boricio heard her squealing like a happy hog. He leaned over the terrace and looked out toward the restaurant's entrance and the fool passing out his periwinkle fliers. Boricio thought of Brother Rei, and the bullshit he sold back at the compound. He wondered if Tweety Bird was sipping Kool-Aid, too, or whether he was one of the assholes brewing it: another predator feeding on fears and false hopes.

Either way, no periwinkle flier-passing motherfucker could ever know shit about real predators, not like Boricio. The thought smeared a sudden, impossible-to-bury smile, wide across his face.

He couldn't wait for his alone time. They were in a new town, far from home; Boricio could finally play.

It had been far too long since his last purge.

~

THREE

Brent Foster

Clifton, New Jersey
September 2013

BRENT FOSTER WOKE up to the sound of barking dogs —
upstairs again.

Fucking Chihuahuas!

Every time Frank or Nancy left the house, for even a
minute, and then came back, all five dogs went totally nuts.

Brent pulled the pillow down harder over his head,
desperate to drown the incessant yapping. He glanced into the
darkness over at the alarm clock's soft-blue light. It was noon
on a Thursday, but it wasn't as if he had anywhere to be, or
anyone to tend to. Gina had seen to that, sure enough. Brent
did, however, have two freelance articles he needed to finish
— one on tech stocks, and the other on car insurance. Both
paid about half of absolute shit, and neither article held a
flicker of interest, but since his job at the paper was now a
soured memory, he had to take anything he could find to pay
for his basement room, rented from the old couple in Clifton,
New Jersey.

Brent had been living in a goddamned basement ever since his life had gone to hell, which felt like forever ago.

Forever since he'd come back from the other world.

Forever since Gina had looked at him like he *wasn't* crazy.

Brent wished he'd never told Gina the truth. Because the truth seemed more like a fabrication than the lie Sullivan later helped him design for the rest of the world — that he'd blacked out and couldn't remember his many missing months. Despite his cover story, Brent lost everything.

His job was no longer there — *cutbacks at the paper, sorry.*

Gina, not knowing if he'd just up and left or had been murdered, found comfort in the arms of another: Jack Howard, a former friend of his at the paper — *sorry, it just happened.*

If that was all that had happened, Brent might have recovered. He *would* have. If he had accepted his losses, he might still have his son, Ben, in his life.

But Brent got drunk and loathsome, feeling sorry for himself. That was when he made things worse than he could have ever imagined.

He went to his apartment — the one he lost — and picked a fight with Jack. He sent his old friend to the hospital and himself to jail. No matter how many awful things Brent saw in the other world, none matched the horror of his reflection — standing over Jack, his shirt smeared in the same red that dripped from his fists — etching a memory through his son's watering eyes.

Ben was terrified of his father because his father was suddenly a monster.

Jack dropped the charges against Brent — attempted murder, which could've kept him in jail for a long time — but only after Brent agreed to a divorce without shared custody rights to his son.

This is how his world unraveled.

This is how Brent wound up living in someone else's house, feeling like he had moved into his parents' basement.

As the dogs started a fresh round of barking, Brent found himself wishing he'd never returned from the other world, even if it was being overtaken by aliens and quickly destroyed. There was nothing left for him here in this world. Even empty, the other was better.

Sullivan promised assistance, said he'd help Brent get on his feet — just give him some time. But Brent could think of nothing he or anyone could do to fix the mess he'd gotten himself into. Some holes were too deep to climb from.

Brent looked at the clock again. If he started typing, he could probably finish the articles by 6, which would give him plenty of time to go meet Kevin Vaughn, one of his only remaining friends, and hang out like they said they might.

Get up, get your work done.

Brent pulled the pillow tighter over his ears instead, then started snoring.

～

HE WOKE at 9:41 p.m., startled by the length of his slumber. He clicked on his nightstand lamp and found his iPhone.

Brent checked his messages: Kevin had texted him three times, first asking if they were still getting together, and at last, 20 minutes ago, saying, OK, he'd catch him next time — he was headed to his fiancée's, Felicia's.

Brent tossed the phone on his bed and sighed as he looked around the room. The walls seemed even closer than normal. The ceiling hung lower.

I have to get the hell out of here.

Brent grabbed his clothes and headed upstairs for a shower. Fortunately, Frank and Nancy were already in bed. While he wanted company, and the Torrelinis were kind, he needed to get out of the basement, if only for a few hours.

He showered, grabbed his helmet, and headed off on his scooter, unsure where he was going, but glad it was *somewhere*.

~

BRENT WOUND UP driving back and forth outside his old apartment building in Manhattan, wondering what the hell he was doing there so late at night. He looked up at Ben's darkened window. He wished like hell he could go knock on the door and ask Gina if he could see his son and kiss him goodnight.

The pain of being so close to, and yet so far away from, Ben was a quiet murder to his soul. And as the grief deepened its twist in his gut, Brent felt the old anger stirring. The kind of anger that landed him in jail; the kind that cost him his son and the life that went with him.

I better get out of here.

As Brent began to turn around and head back toward home, he spotted a familiar face walking along the street — Stan, one of the 215ers who had died on the other world.

How the hell?

Brent squeezed his brakes, and the scooter lurched to a sudden stop. Stan, who was carrying a paper grocery bag in both hands, looked back.

"Stan!" Brent shouted, waving his hand.

Stan looked at him curiously, as if trying to identify the dumbass on a scooter. Brent took off his helmet, "It's me, Brent Foster!"

Stan shook his head, turned around, and quickened his pace as he headed toward the apartment building entrance.

"Wait!" Brent called out, but Stan ignored him, and raced inside.

Brent pulled up to the curb and was about to get off his scooter and run in after Stan, but then saw the big, giant doorman standing just inside the doorway talking to him as Stan pointed outside.

Brent wasn't sure what Stan was saying, but his instincts kicked in, and he decided he'd better get the hell away from the building before someone called the cops, and he had to explain why he was driving past his ex-wife's house late at night.

And why he was packing an unlicensed gun in a holster under his coat.

As Brent drove back to his house, he couldn't stop wondering how it was possible that Stan was still alive.

He heard the man get torn apart by aliens. He and Melora had both died.

Then he remembered something that he hadn't thought about since Oct. 15.

Stan and Melora had shown him a video from one of the many cameras the 215ers had secretly placed in their neighbors' apartments. The videos had shown people vanishing in black smoke. It had seemed, at the time, that most of the population had vanished in a similar fashion.

However, as Brent later discovered from Ed Keenan, the people of Earth hadn't vanished. The vanishings only took place only on the other world. A lot of people died, but many more just disappeared to who knows where.

Brent, Ed, and the others he'd fought the aliens with, hadn't *vanished*, though. They'd been yanked over.

So it was possible that the Stan, Melora, and Luis he'd met on Oct. 15 hadn't come over from Earth along with him. They were native to that world. How else could they have video recordings of people who vanished if they themselves had vanished? The cameras wouldn't have come with them.

Brent felt as if a light bulb had come on in his head, which suddenly explained everything. Well, maybe not everything, but it did give him hope that the Stan, Melora, and Luis of *this* world might still be alive.

Brent's heart raced with possibility.

Were the Stan, Melora, and Luis of this world also 215ers who had prophesied The Event? And if they were, could they help him find proof he wasn't crazy? Proof he could show Gina? He could never win her back, not after all that had happened. But how could she deny him visitation with his son if he could prove it was all real, that he wasn't crazy?

Not even Gina could be that cruel.

Suddenly, and for the first time in forever, Brent felt purpose.

He raced home, eager to hatch a plan to connect with the 215ers, and reclaim his life.

~

FOUR

Luca Harding

September 2013
  Las Orillas, California

LUCA TURNED his entire body away from his bedroom window and its open blinds. It was too bright outside, and the last place on Earth he wanted to be today was school.

He crawled deep under the covers with his biggest pillow, then hugged it close to his body, and pulled the comforter up high over his head; there was better thinking inside the fort.

Luca wondered if it was still faking if he said his stomach hurt worse than it did. It wasn't stay-at-home bad, yet, but it might be later. It probably would be later. Then again, Luca had been getting the headaches, and they did worry Mom. That might be the best way to play it. Dad was more worried about his stomach aches, and Mom his head. Luca decided he'd know which hurt more once one of them came to check on him.

Luca usually hopped right out of bed and ran downstairs for his waffle, thinking about warm syrup on the way. He took his showers before bedtime, right before he laid out all his clothes. Mornings were supposed to be easy because Mom was always in a hurry, and she hated to be late. Though she didn't like to rush him, Luca could tell by her face when she was feeling impatient.

He stayed under the covers, figuring Mom would be up any minute to check on him since his waffle was probably getting cold. After what Luca guessed was 15 minutes of nothing, he heard footsteps outside his door. Not Mom, Dad; Luca could tell because the footsteps were heavy instead of light, just like the breathing.

The door opened, and Dad said, "Luca?"

It took him a moment to answer. To prove his pain, Luca crawled out from under his blankets, peeling them back down over his body. Still, he said nothing, just looked up at his father with wide and what he hoped were sick-looking eyes.

"What's wrong?" Dad asked, studying Luca.

"My stomach hurts!"

Luca clutched his stomach, over the invisible knives.

"Oh no," Dad said as he sat on the bed and planted his hand at the back of Luca's head. "Are you going to be OK? How long has it hurt?"

"All night," Luca made his voice whiny, but not too whiny since Dad didn't like that.

"All night?"

Luca nodded. "I couldn't sleep well, so I'm really, really tired, too."

"Come on, Son," Dad said. "You just need some waffles."

He slipped his arms under Luca's body, ready to scoop him from the bed like he did when Luca really didn't want to leave it, but before he could tug, Luca cried out, "No, Dad. I *really* don't feel well."

"I understand," he said. "You have a bad case of the *I don't want to go to schools*. I used to get those all the time, I still do now, except it's work instead of school. But same thing, Luca, believe me, I get it. But you have to go to school. Anna has to go to school. I have to go to work. Your mother has to go to work. That's life, we all have jobs. You're fine. I checked on you a few times last night because *I* couldn't sleep, not to mention about 45 minutes ago before you woke up. You were perfectly peaceful, *so*, Son, let's get you downstairs and eating your waffle before your mother wastes it and makes you another. Or, you can tell me what's *really* wrong."

Luca wondered how his father was always able to read him so well, and could tell when he was faking something.

Dad waited. Luca crossed his arms and said firmly, "I don't like school anymore, and I never want to go back."

Dad laughed. "Wow, that's quite a difference. What changed your mind? Have they started serving snake in the cafeteria? That's what did it for me."

Luca laughed, even though he didn't want to. Dad knew how to make him do that. "No."

"Tarantula? It's tarantulas isn't it? They've started putting tarantulas in the tacos?" Dad slowly shook his head as if absorbing horrible news.

"No," Luca said, smiling. "No tarantulas."

"Then what?" Dad held open palms to ceiling. "What could possibly have happened that has made Luca Harding hate school?"

"I just don't want to go," Luca insisted. "I've learned all I need to know."

"Oh?" Dad raised his eyebrows. "Well, in that case, I stand corrected. If you already know everything there is to know, then you're right, and school is clearly wasting your time. We Hardings will have none of that."

"Are you serious?" Luca asked, daring to hope.

"Absolutely."

Luca stared at his father, wondering if this would be the first time he finally outsmarted him. "What's the catch?"

"No catch," Dad said. "I mean it. I'll ask you three questions, and if you get all three of them right you don't have to go to school."

"OK," Luca said, feeling deflated already, knowing Dad's questions would be too hard.

"What's the capital of California?"

That was too easy; California was Luca's state.

"Sacramento!"

"That's right!" Dad clapped Luca on the shoulder. "Hmmm ... can you tell me the difference between *their* and *there*?"

Luca smiled. That was easy, too. Dad was asking him questions a second-grader would probably know.

"The one with the *I* is people and the one without it means a place."

"*Very* good!" Dad leaned into Luca. "Are you ready for the last one?"

Luca nodded.

"What is the square root of three?"

Luca looked at his father with no expression, not at all surprised that he felt suddenly tricked. "That's not fair."

"Why? If you know everything, you should know all about square roots. And three is a teeny, tiny, easy number."

Luca could figure this out. "What's a square root?"

Dad smiled. "It's a number that produces another specified number when multiplied by itself."

"I don't understand," Luca said, determined to get it.

"I'll give you an example. Eight is a square root of 64."

That made sense. Suddenly Luca understood. And Dad was right, three was a teeny, tiny number. He pinched his nose, trying to understand, but it was like his brain wouldn't work. One times one was one, two times two was four, and three times three was nine."

"You have one minute," Dad smiled.

"That's not fair."

"It's totally fair."

"One and a half," Luca said.

"You're going to school, Son. The correct answer is 1.73205080757."

Luca's eyes went giant. "How did you know that?"

"Stupid trick," he said. "Now, do you want to tell me what's really bothering you? I'd love to hear it." He glanced at the clock on Luca's desk. "But we have to hurry. I'll bet the keys on my chain that your mother is already cooking you a second waffle, and if we're not down there before it gets cold she's gonna be mad at both of us. So, what's up?"

He wondered how his dad *always* got him to say and do what he wanted. Luca didn't want to tell anyone about Johnny Thomas, *or* go to school. Now, only a few minutes after Dad came into his room and sat on his bed, he was doing both.

"Johnny Thomas has been picking on me."

"Johnny Thomas?" Dad scrunched his nose. "Do I know him?"

Luca shook his head. "No, because you're lucky."

Dad laughed. "So, what's he doing to pick on you?"

"He calls me names and always makes me feel stupid."

"Uh oh," Dad grimaced.

"What?"

"That means you're letting him."

"I'm not letting him!" Luca cried out; that made him mad.

"Well, I don't mean to upset you, Little Luca, but you kinda sorta are. Bullies only have the power you give them. If you ignore what they're saying, they have no power at all. My best suggestion, ignore Johnny Thomas. Sooner or later he'll get bored and find someone else to pick on, someone who doesn't know how to ignore him."

"I knew you'd say something like that," Luca crossed his arms tighter.

Dad gave Luca an understanding smile, then disappeared. He was gone for two minutes before he came back, according to the clock, but because Luca was curious, those two minutes felt more like 10.

Dad sat back on the bed and handed Luca a comic book.

Luca was excited for a second, thinking the comic would be about superheroes. But it didn't look super at all; it actually looked sort of dumb. The colors were bright, and the drawings seemed sort of babyish.

The title was dumb, too: *Billy Bully*.

Luca looked up at his dad, wearing his not-real smile.

Dad laughed.

"I know it's not exactly *Spiderman*, but I promise you'll like this. Read it on the way to school. You can throw it away when you get there if you want, but I have a feeling you won't. I'm 44 and I laughed a few times, out loud. Hopefully, the book will help you understand Johnny Thomas better, at least enough to ignore him, and maybe understand yourself a little too, enough to know you're doing the right thing. We only have a few minutes before we need to leave for school, and we're already late for getting downstairs, so before we go, do you want to hear my super-fast advice for dealing with bullies?"

Luca rapidly nodded, dying to hear.

Dad pulled him closer. "Look, Luca, I'm not going to lie to you. Bullying sucks, and unless you're a bully yourself, and sometimes even if you are, most kids go through it at one time or another. You've already done the smartest thing by telling someone. You can always ask your parents or friends to help you — there's safety in numbers — and know what you're going to say before you say it." He smiled. "In fact, if you want, we can practice scenarios when you get home from school. Would you like that?"

Now smiling, Luca nodded.

Dad clapped a hand on his shoulder. "Be cool and control the moment, don't let the moment control you; don't show

Johnny Thomas that you're sad or mad or anything else. Ignore him, walk away; don't make it worse."

Luca threw his arms around his father, suddenly not feeling very sick. "Thanks, Dad!"

Dad told him to hurry, then Luca leapt out of bed quickly got dressed, ran downstairs, mowed through a still-hot waffle — Luca saw two in the trash — then ran outside to the Maxima behind Anna and read his new comic as Mom drove them to school.

Dad had helped Luca feel better, and so did the comic, but he still spent the whole morning dreading recess and gym, because he was sure Johnny Thomas would make his move. All the advice in the world couldn't give Luca the super powers he needed to stand up to the school's biggest jerk, who, despite his big, giant, bullying mouth never seemed to travel without his two big, stupid bully friends, Gus and Kiyor, behind him.

Luca made it through recess because he followed the first part of Dad's advice: Control the moment, don't let the moment control you. He sat midway up the school's front steps, reading his *Billy Bully* comic. It was pretty dumb but kept him smiling anyway. Johnny Thomas and his stupid bully friends kept looking over at Luca, probably making fun of him and his comic, but they never approached him or said anything at all.

Gym was an even bigger worry than recess, so Luca tried not to be scared as the bell rang for fifth period and he changed into his shorts and T-shirt. Luca wished he had told his dad about Johnny Thomas the night before so that he would have already had time to practice what he would say, but since he didn't, Luca ignored the bully as best he could. That worked at recess, and all the way through the time they played soccer, probably because there were so many other people around. But then the bell rang, and gym ended. Everything inside Luca knew trouble was coming.

He ran into the locker room as fast as he could, faster than he ran when playing soccer, hoping to get in and out before Johnny Thomas or any of his stupid friends saw him. Luca grabbed his backpack and clothes, then ran out from the gym and across the hall to the bathroom in Building E that no one ever used. He went into a stall and changed, happy that it was almost sixth period science and that he had almost made it through the day.

Tonight he could practice with Dad.

Back in his regular clothes, he stepped outside the stall, and the bathroom door swung open — Johnny Thomas stood in the doorway, sneering between Gus and Kiyor. All three stepped inside, blocking Luca's exit.

Luca stared at the boys, trying not to be scared and wondering what he should do. Before he could decide, Johnny Thomas was right in front of him, yanking the backpack from his shoulder. With the backpack in his hands, Johnny pushed Luca to the floor.

Laughter echoed in the bathroom.

Luca figured he'd wait it out, ignore the bullies until they left, but then Johnny Thomas started rifling through his backpack, and laughing hysterically once he found the *Billy Bully* comic Dad had given him. The fact that they, these bullies, were handling the comic his father had given was awful horrible.

Luca tried not to cry; it was the hardest thing he had ever had to do.

Laughing so loud it was nearly a scream, Johnny Thomas ran around the bathroom waving Luca's comic over his head, bellowing through his laughter: "Poor little Luca, Luca Crybaby, doesn't want to get bullied by Billy anymore."

Then, Johnny Thomas did something that made Luca hate him even more than he already did; he went to a stall, dropped the comic into a bowl, and peed on it, still laughing. He left the stall and said, "Your *Billy Bully* comic is in the shitter where it belongs," then shoved Luca back to the ground and walked off laughing.

Luca found his courage and yelled, "Why are you picking on me?"

Johnny Thomas turned and met his eyes. Luca was sure Johnny was going to hurt him, maybe even kill him right there, and nobody could stop him.

Johnny leaned in, sneering, his eyes full of a hate Luca couldn't understand, "Because you're a little faggot, and I don't like you."

Johnny punctuated the comment with a swift punch to Luca's balls, sending him to his knees crying out in pain.

The boys all laughed as the bell for sixth period rang, then left Luca balled on the floor, crying.

∾

FIVE

Mary Olson

Fairfield, Colorado
    September 2013

MARY STOOD in front of the classroom watching as the eighth-graders studied her. She was up next — career day — just as soon as Paola's teacher, Lindsay Slater, finished introducing her.

Paola was in the third row back, refusing to look up at her mother. She was probably still mad about the previous evening's argument, or maybe embarrassed that her mom was speaking next. If she was trying to make Mary feel like an intruder in her classroom, it was working.

There was a time when Mary's baby girl loved spending time with her mom, loved when she had showed up at school for lunch every so often, or helped out with after school activities. Now Paola was 13, and growing ever more concerned with boys and her social standing in the school's neatly divided cliques. The last thing she wanted was to be seen with her mother.

Mary knew this time would eventually come, it had, in

fact, been approaching before The Event when Paola was just 11. But when they returned home from the horrible world following Ryan's death, something had shifted. They were closer than ever, and Mary had hoped it would stay that way. They were each a rock for the other, recovering together from their shared nightmare and the transition to a new life in North Carolina briefly, then off to Colorado when Mary decided Paola needed a school that understood her, and she needed a school of her own.

Mary thought the events of the other world might have short-circuited Paola's inevitable "I hate my mother" phase before it took, but it seemed to merely delay it. Now it was hitting hard with vengeance.

Standing in front of the class on career day was odd enough without Paola's anger rolling from her body in waves. Mary couldn't help but compare herself to some of the other parents: lawyers, surgeons, police officers — careers that required degrees and daily heroism. She was an illustrator, someone who drew pictures for a living and was lucky enough to make a ton of money doing so, doing the same thing many others could do, and arguably better than her. Mary didn't *feel* like a role model. She couldn't suggest that children follow her example, particularly when there were so many starving artists pursuing dreams that were slowly broken by reality, working jobs they hated to support ambition that thinned as struggle elasticized. Because of Mary's own lean years, and her maternal instincts, she wanted to tell these kids yes, follow your dreams, but be smart about it. Have a Plan B. She wanted to tell them to take the other parents' advice: Stay in school, go to a university, get a job and a guaranteed paycheck. Be safe.

Paola's school specialized in creativity and believed in dreams. That's why she pulled the plug on North Carolina right after getting there, to give Paola the same opportunities, or at least an environment to foster artistic growth rather than squash it underfoot like schools in the system. To stand in front of the class and preach anything other than "follow your dreams" was hypocrisy, and Mary simply couldn't have that.

"And now," Ms. Slater said, "here's Paola's mom, Mary Olson, a greeting card designer and illustrator."

"Hi, class," Mary said, stepping into the center of attention. She felt awkward, standing with wobbly knees, smiling brightly at Paola's class as she walked to the front and thanked Ms. Slater. She looked out at the room, hoping Paola would look up, then trying not to feel horrible when she wouldn't.

Mary smiled again, half the class smiled back. Paola wasn't one.

"How many of you like to draw?"

Most of the smiles raised their hands, along with two of the frowns.

"How many of you would like to draw for a living?"

Most of the smiles raised their hands again.

Mary wished she had prepared something to say, rather than going on intuition like always. Or that Paola would look up and let her know she wasn't alone, or at the very least not an intruder making her daughter feel stupid. But in a room of 34 kids, Mary had no one, so, like always, she opened her mouth and went with her gut.

"Whether you want to make a living as an artist or not, knowing that there's already an artist inside you can help you get more out of any career." Mary looked around the room, already feeling better. She took a step forward. "Whether you're a doctor, a fireman, or a writer, creativity helps you do your job better because creativity is the ability to put things together in interesting ways. Creative people see the world full of solutions waiting for discovery."

Mary stared at the top of Paola's head, willing her to look up, but her daughter's head stayed down.

"We all tap our creativity in different ways. Some people are born with an artist's eye; some musicians have perfect pitch, and some writers can string words together like brushes of color on a canvas. I doubt they'll ever be able to teach talent, but there are countless ways to train what's already inside you. Everyone has an artist in them, waiting to be found. One of the best things anyone can ever do for themselves is listen to the people in their life who want to draw that from inside them."

Paola looked up, but just for a flicker, as if she couldn't help it, then looked back down. It was enough. Mary finished her talk, feeling better than she expected, earning smiles and applause from Ms. Slater, parents, and even most of the children, including two of the frowners.

Two more parents spoke after Mary, a judge and a soft-spoken man with white hair who owned a janitorial supply company, then everyone lined up for pictures, each child with their parent.

To Mary's tremendous relief, Paola only grimaced a little.

FOLLOWING CAREER DAY, Mary ran a few errands, then went back to school to pick up Paola. She got into the car, mumbled "Hi", then turned on her iPhone, chose a song, and buried buds inside her ears.

Oh no, you are not going to keep ignoring me, young lady.

Mary grabbed the end of Paola's cord and yanked the buds down to the console.

"What the hell, Mom?!"

Mary stayed firm, turning the engine and backing out from the school lot. Once on the road, she said, "We're going to discuss last night."

"I told you, there's nothing to talk about, Mom." Paola's eyes were out the passenger window.

"It's not *nothing*, Paola. You need to listen to me because I'm your mother and I have a job to do."

"Your job doesn't have to be constantly managing me, *Mom*."

Mom was a knife.

"I'm not managing you, Paola. I'm *helping* you."

"No, Mom. You're not. You think you are, but I don't need to be *managed* 24/7. You don't need to tell me to throw my socks in the washer every single time!"

"Are you kidding me?" Mary put a thousand pounds of effort into muting her temper. "You have failed to put your socks in the washer 100 percent of the time that I've *not* mentioned it, *Paola*, and I'd be fine with the socks, really, if that's all it was. I wouldn't care at all, *if* I didn't also have to remind you about your homework, your manners, your coming down for dinner without me calling for you a dozen times, or your media time — all of which scratch the surface of the many, many things that you *need* to be reminded of."

"EXACTLY!" Paola bellowed. "You manage me about EVERYTHING. You tell me when to brush my teeth!"

"You had *six* cavities!"

Heaving, she growled, "We were on another fucking world!"

Mary gasped.

Paola often screamed, but never cursed.

But her daughter was right. They *were* on another fucking world. And they'd lost Ryan — Mary's ex, and Paola's father. And while Mary had somehow been able to cobble a semblance of normality together for them, it seemed sometimes more illusion than reality.

An illusion that the slightest aggravation threatened to unravel.

Mary gripped the steering wheel and drove the rest of the way home in silence. Paola grabbed her cord, plunged it back into the bottom of her iPhone, then cranked the volume loud enough for Mary to hear.

Despite her best efforts, there were some things Mary couldn't fix. At least not alone.

~

MARY STOOD at the kitchen island, spreading veggies across the cutting board as Paola came downstairs and walked past her mother to the fridge, grabbed a bottle of water, then went to the living room, and flicked on the TV.

Mary smiled.

Paola rarely watched TV any more — she was always on her computer. So her being in the front room was her way of slowly opening the door for Mary.

"You want to help me?" Mary called out past the island.

Paola turned around, leaning over the back of the couch, "Whatcha makin'?"

"Nothing fancy. Just cucumber salad."

"Sure," Paola said.

"Thanks," Mary smiled. "Do you want to start the water for pasta?"

"OK," Paola said. She grabbed a pot from the hanging rack above the island. "This one big enough?"

"Perfect." Mary watched as Paola brought the pot to the sink and turned on the water.

Mary grabbed a cucumber, then her Consigli knife, and pressed down.

Paola finished filling the pot and carried it to the oven. "You know," she said, "If you didn't nag me all the time I would want to do the right stuff more."

Mary kept chopping. "That's never worked before."

"Let's try it. Just for one week. You can … "

"Shit!" Mary screamed, looking down and seeing the deep gash in her left index finger.

Paola ran to her, "Are you OK?"

Mary grabbed a paper towel and squeezed it tightly

around her finger, breathing in and out, hoping the injury wasn't as bad as it felt — like she'd cut through to the bone. She squeezed tight, trying not to freak out, not in front of Paola. "Yeah, yeah, I'm fine. Can you get the first aid kit?"

"Yeah," Paola said, sprinting up the stairs and returning moments later with the white, plastic box — red cross on the front.

Paola set it on the counter and flipped it open, then Mary grabbed the peroxide and went to the kitchen sink. She rinsed the wound; it wasn't to the bone, but the slice was deep enough to leave a chunk of her finger barely hanging.

"I need stitches."

"Let me see," Paola rushed toward her mother, bandage wrap in hand.

Paola winced when she saw the wound. "Does it hurt?"

"Not too bad," Mary lied. It did, but she didn't mind the pain so much as the thought of missing the best of her finger.

"Can you wrap it up so I can run to the all-night clinic?"

"Here," Paola said, taking Mary's hand in hers. Mary watched as Paola leaned in closer. The tip of her tongue stuck out like it did when she was concentrating. The look in her eyes, and the urgency Paola flew upstairs with, were touching. A knot formed in Mary's throat, she tried to keep her eyes dry.

"OK," Paola said, taping the bandage and meeting her mom's eyes. "Let's go to the doctor."

"No, you don't have to go," Mary said. "I don't know how long I'll have to wait, and I'm sure you have plenty to do."

"No," Paola said firmly. "I'm going with you, Mom. Don't argue." She unscrewed a bottle of Tylenol and handed two pills to Mary, followed by a bottle of water from the fridge. "Take these."

Mary smiled, took the pills, then hugged Paola, "Thank you, Sweetie."

Mary held their hug, feeling the iciness between them thaw. "OK, let's go," she said.

AFTER SITTING in the waiting room for nearly an hour, Paola could take it no longer. She approached the reception window, knocked, and asked, "How much longer will it be? My mom could lose her finger!"

The receptionist was a heavyset, older woman with short, red hair, who seemed like she was doing her best not to snap back at Paola. "The doctor will see your mother as soon as possible," she said. "But we have to take patients on a first-come, first-served basis."

The receptionist shot Mary a look, somewhere between apology and agitation. Mary shrugged meekly, lightly embarrassed; she didn't know what Paola was going to do until it was too late to stop her.

Paola sat, fuming. "That's just stupid. They should allow emergencies ahead of people who are just sick."

Mary looked up, meek smile still on her face, this time making its way around to the waiting room's other occupants and settling on an old man waiting for his wife, who'd gone back 15 minutes before. The old man either hadn't heard Paola, or was too entranced in the news broadcast above the receptionist's window to care. Some crazy story that had been looping on every channel all day about a woman who went nuts and attacked her friends while jogging.

"It's OK," Mary said, "They'll see us soon enough."

As if on cue, the nurse, a tall, young man with bright-blue eyes and blond hair stepped out, "Mrs. Olson?"

"About time," Paola muttered as she grabbed her iPad and stood, following Mary into the back. They passed the old lady paying her bill and were directed to an open door. Mary was surprised when the nurse didn't weigh her, and figured he must've heard Paola bitching, and wanted to hurry things along.

Mary sat on the examination table. Paola took one of the room's two chairs.

"So, you cut your finger?" the nurse said, reading the paper Mary filled out while waiting, now in an open manila folder resting in the man's hands.

"Yeah, I was cutting a cucumber and sliced right in. I feel so stupid," she laughed. "It doesn't hurt anymore, though. I took two Tylenol."

The nurse then asked her if she was feeling any symptoms other than the slight pain, what medication she was taking, and a few other questions before leaving her and Paola to wait for the doctor. Mary repeated that she felt no pain and that she had taken Tylenol. The nurse said the doctor would be with them shortly, then left the room and closed the door.

As they waited, Paola was drawing something on the DrawCast app, though Mary could barely see what it was. Paola had been drawing since she was able to hold a crayon, often when sitting beside her mother as she worked, filling reams of 8 1/2 by 11-inch printer paper. Mary wondered if Paola's interest in art would survive high school, or if she would find something else. She was already talking about the drama courses offered at the school, and the possibility of being an actress. Mary figured acting was an even longer shot than artist, but never discouraged her daughter's interests. She tried hard not to be *that* sort of mother, and had, for the most part, succeeded.

The doctor knocked on the door, then entered: a thin woman, maybe in her early 40s, with dark hair and darker circles adding weight to her eyes. "Hello, I'm Dr. Farniss, how are you doing tonight?"

Mary held up her bandaged hand, "A bit klutzy, sliced my finger good. I think I need stitches."

"OK," Dr. Farniss said looking down at Mary's file and confirming what the nurse had written.

"Let's take a look, shall we?" Dr. Farniss took Mary's hand

and began pulling the tape. Mary watched as the doctor unraveled the dark, red-splotched bandage, cringing in anticipation, loath to see the wound.

The doctor pulled the last of the bandage away, confused. Mary's eyes went wide. Her cut was gone, replaced by a tiny, pink scar. Her breath caught in her chest as the doctor brought Mary's finger closer for inspection.

"When did you say you cut yourself?"

"About an hour and a half ago," Mary said, baffled.

Paola stood up then came over. "What's wrong?"

"It's healed," Dr. Farniss said, eying Mary skeptically. "Did you put anything on it?"

Mary, without even realizing she was going to, lied.

"Well, I put some cream on it, though I don't remember what it was, something a friend told me would work wonders."

"I'll say," Dr. Farniss said.

"Maybe it wasn't as bad as I thought," Mary almost whispered, feeling Paola's confusion over the lie.

Mary hoped Paola wouldn't say anything to contradict her.

"Well," Dr. Farniss said, "I guess you don't need stitches after all."

"I feel so silly, Doc. I'm sorry to have wasted your time." Mary was in a hurry to flee the doctor's office — before she started asking questions. Fortunately, it was late, and the doctor looked ready for a bed, keeping her from inquiry.

"Well, just keep an eye on it, and call us, or your regular doctor, if there's any changes, OK?"

"Will do, Doctor," Mary said, thankful when she opened the door to leave.

As Mary stood and met Paola's eyes, the doctor turned around, "Mrs. Olson?"

"Yes," Mary said, suddenly certain the doctor had decided she needed some answers; this was just too weird to let go.

"If you think of it, can you call the office tomorrow and

let me know what kind of cream you used? I'd love to check out anything that works this well."

"Sure," she lied, "first thing tomorrow."

~

BACK IN THE VOLVO, heading home, Paola finally asked, "It was me, wasn't it? I healed you? Just like Luca healed people."

"I don't know," Mary said, though that's definitely where her mind was wandering. "Maybe it wasn't that bad."

"Yes, it was that bad. I saw it, Mom."

"I don't know," Mary said, her voice unable to hide her agitation, or fear.

Because they both knew what had happened when Luca had healed others: He aged, rapidly.

Mary looked at Paola in the car's dark cabin, thinking she *did* look older.

No, no, it's just my mind playing tricks on me. Stop it, stop it now before she figures out what you're thinking.

Paola asked, without fear, "Do you think I did it? Do you think I can heal people like Luca?"

"I don't know," Mary said. "It was different when Luca did it. He went into a trance or something. You didn't do anything like that. You barely touched my hand."

"He also aged," Paola said, flipping down the windshield visor mirror and studying her face.

"Stop it," Mary said, "You didn't age. And besides, Luca aged years, and while I know you'd love nothing more than to get your learner's permit, you're still just 13."

Paola looked closer, squinting in the mirror, then looking at her hands. "You don't think I aged at all?"

"No," Mary said, clinging to her string of lies.

~

SIX

Sullivan

Black Island Research Facility
September 2013

SULLIVAN STOOD outside the glass cell, deep in Black Island's bowels, staring at the woman as she lay fetal on the cot. He fastened the seal on his yellow biosuit and glanced at the man standing beside him, looking down at a computer tablet and swiping through the file.

"What's her name, again?" Sullivan asked Dr. Simpson.

"Eva Flores."

Eva was the first person in the past six months' seemingly random outbursts of violence whom authorities had managed to take alive. Sullivan was following his gut, which said this was somehow related to the alien infection, The Darkness, that Boricio Bishop had brought into this world when their world was overtaken.

He suspected that Boricio Bishop was gathering forces, could *feel* it. Sullivan wasn't sure how he was doing it, or of his endgame. If it was a takeover, like the aliens had done on his home world, Sullivan had yet to see any supporting evidence.

No visible infections, no mass, unexplained disappearances reported, no corpses piling the streets.

Yet, Sullivan, who had been touched by The Light, could feel a connection to The Darkness, could feel it here on this world, could sometimes feel its thoughts.

It was here and searching for the vials, Sullivan knew that much. The vials containing the alien in its purest form had crash landed on this world the same as the other. While on Sullivan's world, the government had used and tested the vials on Black Island, this world's version of Black Island seemed not to know anything about the vials.

It seemed as if they'd either never been found, or perhaps discovered by someone else who was keeping them secret. Sullivan spent his first months bringing Black Island Research Facility up to speed and explaining everything to them. They sent teams to Alaska, searching the crash site, but found nothing.

Some suggested that the vials weren't even on this world. That just because the vials had been on the alternate Earth it didn't mean they were here as well. While Sullivan believed this was possible, he thought it unlikely. The Darkness would not be here, otherwise. It needed the vials in order to grow stronger. It was, in its current form, too weak to spread as it had on the other world.

Sullivan looked at Eva, and knew she was somehow connected to The Darkness. He'd felt The Darkness thinking about her after The Event happened. The Darkness had seemed concerned about her, though Sullivan wasn't sure why.

"You ready?" Dr. Simpson asked.

"Yes," Sullivan said, punching a code on the wall beside the door.

The door slid open, and Sullivan stepped through.

Eva looked up, her eyes red and swollen and leaking. Her left arm was cuffed to a metal rung in the wall above her cot.

She bristled as Sullivan stood three feet away, moving his eyes from his clipboard to her. "Do you know your name?" he asked.

She nodded, seemed to consider the question for a moment, then said, "Eva, Eva Flores."

She looked so broken, something inside Sullivan softened. He looked down on her kindly, asking Eva what he already knew. "What's the last thing you remember?"

Eva shrugged.

"There is no wrong answer," Sullivan promised. "Just say the last thing that seems clear in your mind. Not a maybe, but a certain memory."

It took Eva another minute to find her voice, then she said, "I remember buckling Maria into her stroller. I was going to jog with my Pound the Pounds group down the trail through our neighborhood park."

"Anything else?"

Another second, then, "It was pretty. The sun was bright, and the day was breezy."

"Do you remember running?"

Eva scrunched her nose as if trying to pull a thought from somewhere deep.

"No," she finally said. "I kissed my daughter on the forehead, tied my hair in a scrunchie ... then nothing."

Sullivan colored the blanks in her memory, but Eva was screaming before he finished, calling him a liar and many things worse. Sullivan waited for her to calm down, then set a reassuring hand on her shoulder. He looked in her eyes until he saw that she knew his words were true, then asked for permission to continue. Eva swallowed and nodded.

"Do you know this man?" Sullivan pointed to the glass and Dr. Simpson standing on the other side, holding a tablet against it. On the tablet was a picture of Boricio Wolfe, since they had no photos of Bishop. The image was doctored to show Boricio Wolfe bald, and wearing an eye patch. His eyes had been muted to an intelligent blaze rather than the one that gleamed with Wolfe's insanity.

Eva studied the tablet, then after a minute slowly shook her head. Sullivan could tell she was lying. Could *feel* it.

"Are you sure?" Sullivan pushed.

Eva looked at the picture again. She shook her head, this time faster. Scared.

Sullivan said, "We know you're lying, Mrs. Flores." She said nothing, but her haunted eyes widened. He continued. "Unfortunately, we won't be able to release you from custody until you're straight with us. That means you won't be seeing Maria or your husband."

"I'm so sorry," Eva said, her voice cracking to splinters. "I don't know who that is, I don't know what you're talking about." Eva Flores started sobbing. "I don't remember anything."

Still calm, Sullivan took a step toward her. "You're lying," he repeated. "And as long as you continue to lie, we must consider you a danger to yourself and others. I'm sorry."

Eva started to shake, softly at first, then her body fell into a horrible rhythm of violent bucking. As Sullivan fell a step back, Eva lunged at him, then growled and screamed as she slammed herself against a dam of air and the chain cuffing her to the wall clanged against the cot as she fell back.

Eva then yanked harder against the chain as Sullivan backed away farther from the rage, keeping his eyes fixed on hers. She yanked harder and growled louder, screaming in a curdle as her shoulder dislocated. She slobbered and snarled and chomped, lurching forward like a dog on a chain.

Eva then pulled hard so fast and hard, her arm ripped from its socket, and she was suddenly on Sullivan.

He fell back to the ground, drowning in panic as he tried pushing her from his body. The biosuit made it difficult to fight back. She was a demon unleashed, gnashing her teeth as if they were fangs and bearing her nails like claws.

She punched through his helmet, shattering the glass face. Sullivan screamed as shards collapsed through the mask. Even terrified, he felt thankful for his glasses, sparing his eyes from the lacerating glass falling into his flesh.

Sullivan lost his scream to a horrible choking as Eva's mouth wrenched open, as if pried wide by the devil, and black, wet ropes of flesh billowed out from her mouth like tentacles searching for Sullivan's.

He twisted his head away, looking for Dr. Simpson — no longer in sight.

"Help!" Sullivan cried out as The Darkness moved closer to his mouth. It touched his lips. He closed his mouth, clenching his teeth, desperate to keep it from infecting him.

The door opened, and a hot blast of fire swallowed Eva in a blaze. Fire spread to the front of Sullivan's suit. He rolled, trying to douse it. Eva's screams filled the chamber, echoing with her personal wail and the alien shriek he had heard too many times.

Ed Keenan stepped toward the woman, flamethrower in his hands, driving her back. Dr. Simpson ran in beside him and sprayed Sullivan's suit with a fire hydrant, smothering the flames.

Sullivan stood, staring as the woman, now a dark husk in the fire, fell to the ground.

Keenan stepped out of the chamber, closed the door, and looked Sullivan up and down.

"Shit," Keenan said, shaking his head. "You were right."

Sullivan, for once, found no pleasure in victory.

He watched as the last of the creature's skin ripped into ashy, black crinkles, wondering how many more were out there, hiding in humans.

∼

SEVEN

Luca Harding

Luca sat in the back of the Maxima, silent. Anna sat beside him, relentlessly trying to get him to talk or play. She was holding her stuffed "Boo" — supposedly the cutest dog in the world — along with a second, tinier Boo. The two stuffed animals were having a long conversation that consisted of nothing but baby talk blended with the occasional barking. She was trying her hardest to get Luca to join her. Sometimes he would, but he had to be in the mood, and right now he wasn't at all.

Luca was depressed, and didn't like how Mom kept glancing back at him in the rearview, so obviously worried. He wondered if Dad had told her anything about Johnny Thomas, or if she was just worried because she could see the upset all over his face.

Luca hated Johnny Thomas so, so much, but was still surprised when, for only a second, he wished Johnny would die.

Dad was home when Mom pulled into the driveway, which meant Luca's afternoon would be awful, not because Dad would be mad — he wouldn't be — but because he would ask what had happened at school with Johnny Thomas, and Luca would have to tell him, even though he didn't want to.

Sure enough, Luca had only taken a single lick from his Fudgsicle when Dad asked, "So, what happened at school? Anything you want to talk about?"

Luca looked for Mom or Anna, but they were nowhere in the dining room or kitchen. Dad smiled and nodded, understanding like he always did, then went over to Luca, wrapped an arm around his shoulder, and led him upstairs to his bedroom. He eased Luca to the bed, then sat beside him, like he had been that morning.

"So?" Dad said.

Luca took a minute to chew, wondering if he should tell a half truth or a whole one, then opened up and let everything spill.

"I tried not to let them bother me, Dad. I read the comic at recess, and stayed on the steps. I didn't even play with Mason, since I knew Johnny Thomas and his stupid friends, Gus and Kiyor, would bother me. I even made it through lunch and gym. Then, after soccer, I tried to get out of the locker room as fast as I could so there wouldn't be any trouble. I grabbed my clothes then went to the bathroom across the hall and got dressed, but when I was leaving, Johnny Thomas was there. So were Gus and Kiyor."

Luca's voice cracked, his lip quivered.

"And what happened?"

Luca broke down. "They took the comic and put it in the toilet. Then Johnny Thomas peed on it."

Dad's jaw twitched. Luca could tell he was trying to stay *not mad*. He knew that even if Dad lost it, he wouldn't be mad at him. He pulled his son toward him, then held their embrace, rocking back and forth until Luca stopped crying. Once soothed, he said, "You're OK?"

Luca nodded.

"All that stuff I said this morning, that's good advice. But I have some other advice, too. Would you like to hear it?"

He nodded again.

"Never allow yourself to be bullied, Luca. Sometimes, the best way to deal with a bully, the *only* way, is to take them down. Sometimes, if a bully's picking on you, the best thing you can do is to make a tight fist, then hit them as hard as you can, right on the bridge of their big, fat, bully nose in front of a crowd of kids and without any teachers around. With most bullies, you'll only have to do this once."

Luca cried some more, but only because he was happy and knew his father was right. He was a little scared to fight, but excited to be tough and not run away. "Thanks," he said.

Dad smiled. "Anytime, Son. Wanna practice after dinner?"

"What," he asked, "things to say, or punching?" Luca couldn't help but laugh; it was tiny and felt good when leaving his mouth.

"Both," Dad said. He stood, tousled Luca's hair, then left the room.

The rest of the evening was better. Anna came in just before dinner, hungry for Luca's attention. They played with Boo, and Anna even let Luca have the larger puppy. They did baby talk and barking for about 10 minutes until Luca was ready to end it, then Anna talked him into playing for another 10 minutes, this time My Little Pony, which he pretended to mind, though Luca didn't really mind at all (and never did). He still didn't know what Dad had told Mom, but she made hot dogs and hamburgers — Luca's favorite — even though it wasn't hot dog and hamburger night, so he figured she *had* to know something. After dinner, Luca went outside with Dad, and they practiced saying things and punching.

Luca felt better than he had in days. Still, as he slowly drifted to sleep, his thoughts returned to where they'd been in the car:

Life would be so much better if Johnny Thomas was dead.

LUCA SLEPT, cycling through many dreams that he didn't understand.

He was him, but not him.

Anna was her, but not her.

Mom and Dad were them, though they weren't his parents at all.

Nothing made sense.

Everything was black, then white.

There were too many colors, then nothing at all.

There was a terrible car accident, the worst kind; it left a long, yellow car crumpled like foil on the roadside, where Luca kneeled in damp grass sobbing, wiping his eyes, all alone. His parents and sister looked like smashed pumpkins in the burning car a few feet away.

Luca woke screaming, terrified and covered in sweat.

He lay in bed, nursing his whimper, unsure if he was still sleeping. He felt some of the dream's nothingness follow him back to the waking side.

Some of the feelings from other Anna and Mom and Dad (*and other Luca*) felt so real that they scared him from bed.

He slowly shoved his terror down, past his throat and chest and stomach, until it was near his toes. Then he wiggled them away, tore the covers from bed, and plopped his feet onto the carpet. Luca crept toward the door, stepping on a Lego on the way and biting into his lip to hold the scream in his mouth.

I want Daddy.

He crept out into the hall and felt like praying when he saw the light in Dad's office. Luca slowly walked the hallway, trying not to run, then opened the door at the end and spilled yellow light into the mostly black hallway, then slipped inside his dad's office.

A man sat in Dad's tall office chair, but it wasn't his father. The man was old, and stroking the head of a large husky.

Luca was still terrified, but felt happy to know this wasn't real; he had to be dreaming.

"I'm dreaming, aren't I?"

The old man smiled, stroked his beard, then looked down at the dog, who whined. The man smiled at the dog, and the dog smiled back. Then he turned back to Luca. "Well, yes, of course."

Luca swallowed. "Who are you?"

"My name is Will. Do you remember me?"

"Should I?" Luca asked. Every cell inside him said he absolutely should.

I know this man.

"No, I suppose not," Will said.

Luca stood through the silence, waiting for the old man to say something else. But he said nothing. Luca was about to ask the old man how he knew him, and why he was in his house, or at least inside his dream, but before he could say anything, the husky opened its wide jaw and made words instead.

"What about me?" the dog asked, startling Luca.

He fell back three steps until he was standing in the doorway. Even in a dream, the talking dog seemed odd, and like Will's smile (and the other Anna and Mom and Dad) it seemed eerily familiar.

The husky whined again, then added, "Do you remember me?"

Luca didn't, until he did.

Suddenly, with more certainty than he had ever found in a dream, Luca *knew*. For a second he saw everything, then the everything disappeared. It left a name on Luca's lips. He said it out loud before his brain took it away. "Dog Vader?"

"Yes," the dog said. "But you can call me Kick."

The everything returned to take it all away.

Luca's world disappeared.

The boy opened his eyes in the pitch black of his bedroom, terrified.

EIGHT

Marina Harmon

Malibu, California
September 2013

MARINA STOOD ON THE PIER, staring out at the setting sun and leaning into the cool breeze as it whipped at her long, blonde hair and sent a cold chill stirring inside her. She lifted her hand and took a sip of hot Starbucks, allowing the warmth to do its work, and give her a spark of the energy she burned through too fast.

She liked walking out to the pier every so often. It was worth it for the sunset. There was something calming about the sea, and the sun dipping down to claim it. It always brought peace to her mind.

This evening, however, the setting sun only reminded Marina of the phrase that wouldn't leave her mind.

"The Darkness is coming."

It had been her father's final words, a message from the Great All Seeing two years before.

She'd been waiting ever since for her own message from the Great All Seeing, ever since she'd taken over the Church of Original Design. Her father, the late self-help author J.L. Harmon, had first heard the Great All Seeing then founded the church in the 1980s. While Marina had been meditating daily as instructed, she had yet to receive a message from the Great All Seeing herself.

Before, the being had only spoken to her father. It was through J.L. Harmon that the being's messages were interpreted and passed out to their followers. But now, two years after his death, Marina was feeling the pressure — of both heading the multinational, multi-billion-dollar church at age 37, and for delivering the Great All Seeing's messages to their eager followers.

Some within the church had even called for her removal, saying that she was no prophet. No leader. And if she were being honest with herself, and her fellow church leaders, she would agree. Hell, she didn't even believe in the religion a few years ago.

While she'd been the church's vice president for four years, and the face of the religion for the last two, Marina wasn't comfortable with the church's many aspects of management, nor the politics of running it, especially when it came to dealing with the church's leaders in other states and countries. It was too much, and at times, it felt that perhaps this was The Darkness the Great All Seeing had warned of. If Marina failed to navigate her position's politics, she was doomed to crash upon the rocks.

The last thing she wanted to do was disappoint her father in whatever his next form would be. Marina wanted Daddy to be proud whenever she met him again, wanted him to know she wasn't the fuck-up she'd been in her 20s. That she'd found her way back to the light and true way of being.

Marina's phone rang. She reached into her pocket, hoping it was her boyfriend, Steven. It wasn't. Instead, it was the agent Veronica Barrow.

She considered letting the call go to voice mail, but hadn't heard from Veronica in a while and was curious why she was calling, hoping that someone in the church hadn't done something stupid to leave it with another black eye.

Marina took a deep breath and picked up the phone, "Hello."

"Marina! How are you?"

"I'm good," Marina said, inviting no banter, wanting Veronica to get to the point. Fortunately, Veronica was a blunt woman who preferred not to dawdle, but would, if she had to, for the sake of politics. Hearing no need for banter, she said "Hey, I need a favor."

"What is it?"

"I need you to give your blessing to a writer I work with, Rose McCallister. The Maris Brothers are interested in optioning a book she wrote, *The Billfold*, and I know they consult with you before working with anyone ... to see if the potential partner meets your standards. I want you to vouch for her."

"You know I can't vouch for someone I've not met."

"Well, that's why I'm calling. I want you to meet Rose, and the sooner the better. I want you to see how amazing she is. I want you to give her your blessing."

"I don't know," Marina said, not wanting to add another meeting to her already full schedule. "I need to check with Carrie. When do you need to know by?"

"She's only in town for a few days, so the sooner the better. Please, Marina, this book is a scorching-hot property. The Maris Brothers will hate themselves if this book goes to Epic."

Veronica was suave enough not to finish her following thought: They'd be even more pissed if they learned that Marina could have brokered the deal, but didn't. Marina normally had little patience for power brokers and influence peddlers, but Veronica was good and Marina liked her — she was a loyal rarity in Hollywood, and had helped more than a few Original Design members by quashing some ugly incidents that had happened through the years.

"OK," Marina said, trying not to sigh or seem inconvenienced. "How about lunch tomorrow, my house?"

"Perfect!" Veronica said. "We'll see you then. Thank you, Marina."

"You're welcome," she said, then killed the call. She texted her assistant, Carrie, to let her know of her lunch plans.

Marina checked her voice mail to see if Steven had called, then hung up disappointed.

They had planned to meet for dinner at the Bouchard down the road at 8 p.m., but Steven was supposed to call once finished with his meetings for the day.

He had joined Marina's church six months ago, entering her life at the perfect moment, as if sent by fate to help her manage the day-to-day she found so tiresome. Marina had met Steven at an ayahuasca ceremony, introduced to her as "especially enlightened" by their mutual shaman, Master Puissant. She was amazed at how quickly they had hit it off.

In many ways, Steven was too good to be true, and despite a life of privilege, Marina wasn't used to feeling so happy. She had never met a man she could be with for longer than three months. People had a way of disappointing her, especially men.

Marina had never met anyone like Steven, a self-made millionaire who earned his fortune on a few, smart dot com businesses that he sold before the bubble burst. He now spent his spare time as an angel investor. His business acumen was the sharpest she'd seen since her father's. He was handsome, charming, and — most importantly — in no way intimidated by her as so many other men had been. Instead, Steven seemed genuinely curious about both her and her church, which he'd known little of before meeting her, and only from what he was told by Master Puissant.

It was rare that Father allowed outsiders into their fold,

and would never have sanctioned her whirlwind relationship with Steven, let alone his involvement in the church as her right-hand man. But Marina's new beau had taken to the church and its beliefs as quickly as they'd taken to one another.

It wasn't as if he was perfect; Steven was working through plenty of issues: abandonment stemming from his lack of a father, anger from his childhood, and other unspoken demons that haunted his soul. Steven claimed that Marina, and the church's Restoring Sessions, had helped him heal his most open wounds — had, in fact, saved his life.

That kind of honesty and raw exposure was rare, particularly in men who had accomplished so much in their life. But with her, Steven said, he no longer felt fear.

Where is he?

The phone finally rang with Steven on the other side.

"Hey, Honey, where are you?" Marina asked.

"Sorry — my meeting with Gerald ran long."

"Anything I need to worry about?" she asked.

"No, and remember, you pay *me* to worry about the little things — so you better not be paying me for nothing."

"You're right," she said. "So, are we still on for dinner?"

"I'm on my way," he promised, then kissed his receiver before leaving the line.

Marina took a sip of coffee, and returned to her car, tossing the empty cup into the garbage on her way. She climbed in the back of the car, then told her driver, James, where they were headed.

She slid into the limo's seat, and tried to soften her mood. Even though she was on her way to see Steven, she couldn't shake the ominous feeling bristling her body as she stood on the pier.

The Darkness is coming.

~

Epilogue

IT stood in front of the bathroom mirror staring at *ITS* face, wondering if perhaps *IT* hadn't altered *ITS* appearance too much, made ITSELF *too* handsome.

There was something *IT* had liked about Boricio Bishop's rugged looks, the scars, and the ruined eye. Boricio was handsome and ugly at once — a rare feat that had managed to both woo and intimidate at will. But after a few months of living in Boricio's husk, *IT* had decided the scars and patch didn't allow *IT* to blend in as *IT* needed to.

Also, too many people knew Boricio Bishop's shell.

So *IT* changed his face, fixing the eye, removing the scars, and allowing himself to again grow hair — blond, this time — short and closely cropped.

Now *IT* was known as Steven Warner. And with Warner's good looks, and Boricio's sharp wit, *IT* had become even more powerful and persuasive, working to take over the church from within.

IT wouldn't make the same mistakes *IT* made on the other world.

This time, The Darkness would bide *ITS* time, gather

forces, and find the vials that would tip the scales in *ITS* favor before taking control of the planet. This time the right way.

While The Darkness had won the battle on the other world, it was ultimately a Pyrrhic victory, leaving The Darkness with nothing to feed off of once the humans were consumed.

IT smiled into the mirror, perfecting *ITS* authenticity before leaving the bathroom and joining Marina for dinner.

Steven Warner leaned in and kissed Marina softly on the lips.

She smiled, "What was that for?"

IT said, "For all that you've given me."

TO BE CONTINUED ...

Episode 20

(SECOND EPISODE OF SEASON FOUR)

"Old Friends"

Prologue

WILL BISHOP

The Alaskan wilderness
1978

WILL Bishop stared down at the laminated map, pressing it to the frozen tundra. Ice licked its bottom as he tried making sense of the map, clashing with what he saw below.

"That cave ain't on the map," he yelled through his full ski mask, shouting to his unit's men through a howling wind.

Renny looked back and forth, trying to make sure they were still looking south. "Shit!" he stared down the slope. "Think he's in there?"

"Only one way to know," Will said, folding the map and shoving it back into his thick jacket. He looked at his unit's other five men, each hunched under their 60-pound Yukon packs, worn from three days spent searching for their missing pilot.

The pilot, Lt. Joshua Harmon, of an Air Force scouting plane, downed in a whiteout six days back, was missing from the site, probably having walked off from the crash and a mostly intact plane. The pilot's locator was malfunctioning, so following a failed attempt by a team with dogs, Will and his unit were sent to find him.

Though Will wasn't the unit's commander — that would be Renny — he was the unit's psychic, and the primary reason for them conducting a ground search rather than canvassing the terrain from above. Will's abilities didn't work nearly as well from the sky, but the ground paved a neat path for his instincts to follow. But it was hard to focus when he could feel the unit's doubt and annoyance with him increase with every hour they didn't find Harmon.

To make matters worse, a blizzard was approaching. If they didn't turn back and head to base soon, they'd have to stay in the cave or dig igloos and hunker until the storm passed. Judging from their last call into headquarters, it could be 48 hours before another plane could reach them — one rescue operation to serve another.

As the unit drew closer to the cave's open mouth, visibility was shredded by a wall of blinding white. The storm had moved faster than they expected.

"Come on," Renny urged the group forward.

Will focused on the colorful jackets ahead, blue and red in a sea of white, as Renny led them toward the cave.

The cave was wider up close, large enough to fit their unit two times wide. Roman aimed his flashlight along the ceiling, then to the cave's rear. Though wide, the cave wasn't more than a few hundred feet deep.

"Hey, anyone in heah?!" Roman shouted. His Brooklyn accent echoed, but was barely audible over the wind's scream.

"Well," Roman said, looking at Renny and Will, "looks like our pilot ain't here."

"Wait a sec, guys." Otis walked toward the cave's rear, "Check this out."

They all followed, lights on. Each beam settled on the same discovery: a hole in the ground, vomiting wide into an endless pit of nothingness.

"Hello?" Renny shouted down.

They cast their lights into the hole, trying to pierce the gloaming. The black was so black, and the pit so deep, their lights were but drops of rain in an oil barrel.

Renny looked at Will. "Well, Sparks, you got anything?"

Will hated Renny's new nickname for him, but if Will said anything the name would stick, and he wanted it gone, like all of Renny's idiot nicknames before it.

"I dunno," Will said, closing his eyes to concentrate. "Lemme see."

Will's mind floated from his body. He reached out, into the darkness, searching: *Hello? Lt. Harmon?*

Will waited, his mind open like the pit.

The men around him shifted, impatient. Their thoughts were accidental drizzle in his head: They didn't think Harmon was here; they were annoyed, wondering when the blizzard would blow over, wishing they hadn't followed Will into nowhere. A few thought they might die, freezing to a stupid death in the gut of a cave.

Will tried barring their thoughts, reach deeper into the open mouth, when suddenly he felt someone below … staring *into* him.

Harmon?

Nothing.

He couldn't shake the feeling that something was prying into his mind.

As many times as Will had peered into others' thoughts like open medicine cabinets, he had never felt someone on the other side looking back. It was cold, a horrible slither that poured ice water inside his skull.

Will tried to sever the connection and return his attention to the unit's men, but whoever it was wouldn't let go.

Not whoever — *whatever.*

The whatever, Will was suddenly certain, wasn't human.

A shrill, almost digital scramble crackled through the

howl. Then it was a whistle in his brain, exploding into shards of pain throughout his body.

Will thought his soul would crack; death sounded OK.

He fell to the ice, screaming as he clutched his head.

Tears froze on his face and bit him hard. Suddenly, the wind howled as it stormed the cave, as if the blizzard was searching for them. The harder it beat his unit, the louder it howled.

Men screamed. The ground shook, then collapsed.

WHEN WILL FINALLY CAME TO, he was in a bright-blue room.

No, not a room, but deeper in the cave.

His head pounded through clouded thoughts. He stumbled onto wobbly feet and saw the rest of his unit standing and staring, eyes as wide as their mouths.

Will was about to ask them what in the hell they were looking at, then saw his shadow. The light was behind him, yanking their attention.

He turned, slowly, then saw it: a box the size of a phone booth, black and metallic. Strange glyphs dotted its surface, oozing the same bright-blue light that seemed to hum all around them.

The air quivered like a mirage; energy thrummed in a low drone and caromed the cavern in echo.

"What is it?" Norberg asked. Blue smoke plumed from his mouth — despite his full ski mask — like hot breath on a freezing day. Each word floated in a wisp, then, like a match lit to the smoke, turned into blue fire before fading away.

"Whoa!" Otis said, then saw it from his own mouth.

While the men took turns speaking, experimenting with various words and sounds, and watching like awed children as every breath danced with a physical manifestation, Will felt the prying return.

It was coming from the box.

What are you? Will thought.

The weird, alien sound — like digital distortion — was back: communication without a language he could make out. Will turned, trying to discern the cave's depth, and to hopefully see if there was another way out. He saw light from the cave above, where the ground had crumbled. It was hard to tell how far they'd fallen in the darkness, particularly with the light coming from the box, but it seemed like they might be able to climb out without much of a problem.

"I don't like this," Roman said, his voice shaky like the air. "We gotta get outta here. Feels like the walls are closing in!"

"Relax," Renny said, "we can climb out. Get some pictures of this thing, first."

"No!" Roman said, "No, we can't tell anyone about it!"

"What?" Otis asked.

"There's something wrong here, I don't know how I know, but I can feel it!" Roman stared around the circle of men. "Can't you?"

The men looked at one another, shrugging their shoulders, all except Will, who agreed — there was something seriously wrong.

Will spoke, "Can anyone else hear it?"

"Hear what?" Renny asked. "I don't hear anything."

Renny often ignored Roman, who tended to blow everything out of proportion, but Renny respected Will and his gifts.

Will had to back Roman up.

"I hear this hum," Will explained, "something like a voice, but digitally scrambled, like it's trying to talk. Nobody else hears it?"

"I do," Roman said.

"Yeah, right," Otis laughed. "You ain't got the sparks!"

"No," Roman said, hands out and pleading, "I *do* hear it! And I don't like how it sounds! I can feel it … in my head, crawling like a roach, all twitching and shit. This isn't good, guys; we need to get the hell outta here. Now!"

Renny looked at Will, "You think we should leave?"

Will looked at Roman; his eyes were already haunted. Will wasn't frightened, but he was anxious. He agreed. "Yeah, I think we should leave."

"And not report this?" Otis asked, "You're kidding, right? This could be some Russian spy shit, or alien technology, and we're just gonna pretend we didn't see it? I don't think so."

Renny looked at Otis and Roman, then turned to Will. "Otis is right. We need to document this."

"No! Nobody's documenting shit!" Roman said; his gun was drawn from nowhere. Though his gun wasn't aimed at any of them, his posture made it clear he would shoot dissenters.

"Whoa!" Otis said, "Calm the fuck down, Rosetti!"

"No, I see bad shit. This … this *thing* … it ain't right. Can't any of you see it?"

"See?" Will asked.

"Yeah, I'm seeing things, stuff that ain't right. You don't see it?"

Will shook his head, not sure if his abilities were letting him down, if Roman's had grown, or if the man was simply losing it. Of their unit, Roman had bitched the loudest about their assignment; the harsh weather had clearly cracked him.

"I don't *see* anything," Will said. "What do you see?"

Roman screamed, "Get out of my head!" He raised his gun and fired at the black box.

Three things happened at once: Renny screamed, "No!;" the thing that was prying in Will's head screamed, sending a sharp pain through his skull that sent him to his knees; and Roman fell, dropping his gun and clutching his head.

Roman *hadn't* been lying. It was in his head, too.

A flash of white light drowned everything, like a detonation, but without any sensation of heat or pain. One minute they were in the cave, then, the next, they were above ground in the blizzard, with the cave missing.

What the hell just happened?

Will looked around at the men trading stares. Roman stood, shaking, gun dropped in the snow.

Renny decked him.

~

NINE

Brent Foster

Manhattan, New York
September 2013

BRENT STOOD outside the apartment door, nervous, hoping like hell he wasn't making a mistake.

From the other side he heard a muffled TV — a good sign he hadn't driven all this way to find no one at home. It was 7:30 p.m., later than Brent would have liked to come, but he'd slept late after finishing his last two articles. He couldn't fail his clients; repeat business kept him from starving.

He looked at his phone's screen and matched numbers on the door: *516.*

He glanced up and down the enclosed hallway, which reminded him of his former apartment building's halls: narrow, dimly lit, and desperate for fresh carpet and paint.

Stop stalling. Knock!

Brent knocked, hoping he was right and would see Luis alive.

It felt like an eternity since he was forced to watch Black Island Guardsmen murder an infected Luis; few nights settled without Brent staring into the memory. His heart pounded as he waited for the door to open. He felt odd, hanging so many hopes on Luis being alive. It wasn't as if this Luis, if he were in fact here, was *his* Luis. The man he had known — his friend — *did* die on the other Earth. And he was never coming back. This Luis, assuming Brent's theory on the 215ers was correct, had no clue who Brent was.

Still, Brent felt a flickering joy at the chance of seeing Luis. When no one answered, he knocked again, louder, his eyes on the glass peephole in the center of the door, eye level. Brent thought he saw movement behind the glass, but couldn't tell for sure.

A moment later, a man's voice. "Yeah, who is it?"

Brent couldn't be sure if it was Luis or not.

"Luis? It's me, Brent Foster."

"Who?"

Brent repeated, "It's me, Brent Foster," even though he knew that name meant nothing to this Luis. Saying his name as if Luis did know him seemed a decent ploy that might get him to open the door.

"I don't know any Brent Fosters."

Brent stepped back, trying to show as much of himself as he could to the peephole viewer and reveal himself as a harm- less guy. He decided to take a chance, and say something that might make zero sense to this Luis. Because if it did, it would be impossible for him to keep the door closed.

"We met on October 15, 2011," Brent said.

Silence …

"Luis?" Brent said after a moment.

The door opened, and the man — it was Luis, or rather his twin on this world — stepped into the hall, gun drawn and aimed at Brent. He looked up and down as if he expected federal agents to start charging towards them at any moment. "Who the hell are you?"

"My name is Brent Foster. We met on October 15. Well, I met another version of you. A you on another world."

Luis stared at him, expression still confused and cautious, in that order.

"You were with Stan and Melora, part of the 215 Society, I believe you called yourselves. Any of this ringing a bell?"

"If this is a joke, it ain't funny," Luis said.

"I swear to God, I'm not joking," Brent said. "I need to talk to you, I don't have anyone else. They all think I'm crazy. Listen, Luis, I know about the dreams you had — the ones about the world ending on October 15."

"The dreams didn't mean anything," Luis said. "They didn't come true."

"But they did. Me and several other people were snatched from here and wound up in another world, identical to ours. Nearly all the people on that world either vanished or died. There were aliens — these big, ugly, black things that infected people. I know it sounds crazy as hell, but you, the you over there, told me a lot."

As Luis stared, Brent shared details gifted to him by another version of the same man: dreams, his daughter, a wife dying of cancer. He watched as Luis's eyes filled with water. His chin trembled, slowly losing a battle to crying. Brent wondered if the tears were from joy in knowing he wasn't crazy, or liquid fear to think he had escaped the prophecy of October 15, only to have Brent knocking with the truth that he hadn't.

"Daddy?" a girl called from behind. His daughter — *Gracie!* — who had vanished on the other world, and whom Luis had missed so much.

"Stay inside, Honey!" Luis snapped before she reached the door. He closed it, but kept his gun firmly on Brent.

"Why are you here?"

Brent said, "I was gone for six months, and my wife thinks I'm nuts. I was told not to tell anybody what happened, and for the most part I listened, but I've lost everything — my wife, my son, and my job. I need to talk to someone who would know I wasn't lying. You and I were good friends over there. I trusted you with my life. Hell, you saved me. I'm assuming I can trust this version of you, too. Please, I just want to talk. I know you must be at least a *little* curious about what your dreams really mean."

"Meant," Luis corrected Brent. "I haven't had the dreams since October 2011 came and went with nothing around it. I was hoping to keep it that way."

"I'll tell you everything you want to know," Brent said. "And I'm hoping you can help me."

"Help you what?"

"Get my life back," Brent said.

"Okay, let's assume you're not insane, we can talk," Luis said through a deep exhale that sounded like he'd been holding something in. "But not now, and not in front of my daughter. Give me a call later, after 10, but before midnight, okay?"

"Thank you," Brent said. "I knew I could count on you."

Luis looked like he wanted to say something back, but only nodded, then said, "Talk to you later," and went back inside.

10:40 *p.m.*

"JESUS, that is the craziest shit I've ever heard," Luis said once Brent finally finished detailing everything from the moment he woke on October 15 to when the other Luis was killed by the Black Island Guard, then everything that followed, all the way until he was back in Ben's bed, exhaling beside him.

"Do you believe me?" Brent said, not wanting to ask, afraid Luis might think him crazy, like Gina.

Luis said nothing for a while, adding to Brent's apprehension. If Luis didn't believe him, Brent wasn't sure he had any chance with the others. Stan had been friendly enough on the other world, but the Earth-Stan ran when Brent tried to talk to him. And the other Melora was icy to start with, Brent had no reason to expect a warmer version on this world. Luis was his best — his only — hope: his friend. If one Luis trusted Brent with his life, Brent had to believe this one might, too.

Finally, Luis said, "Yes, I think so. But I'm not sure what good that will do you. I mean, *you* were there, not me. All I have are a few dreams that never came true."

"That's why I want to talk to the others — Stan, Melora, and the other woman who didn't make it."

"What do you mean the other woman who didn't make it?"

"On the other world, when I met the 215ers, it was the other you, Stan, and Melora. They said there was another member of the group who was supposed to meet them and wait for The Event. But she never made it."

"There's no other woman in the group. But there is a man. And he didn't make it, either."

"What's his name?" Brent asked.

Luis hesitated before answering. "Roman Rosetti, but his name don't matter," Luis said.

"Why's that?"

"Because you're not gonna be able to talk to him."

"Why not?" Brent asked.

"Because on October 14, he walked into a veteran's administration building and opened fire, shooting six people before turning the gun on himself."

"Jesus!" Brent whispered. "And? He's dead?"

"No, he ran out of ammo, oddly enough. Before Roman could reload, he was tackled. He's locked up in Harrison Psychiatric Hospital, last I heard. We tried to visit, well, Melora did, but they wouldn't let her see him."

"Why do you think he did it? It must've had something to do with The Event, or the dreams, right?"

"I don't know," Luis said. "Roman hasn't been right for a while, ever since his wife killed herself six years ago. I mean, he was already messed up from his time in the Air Force, so this pushed him over the edge. He started talking about black helicopters, aliens, government agents following him, tin foil hat shit … well, it seemed tin foil hat at the time, anyway."

Air Force? Maybe he knew more about the aliens than just some dreams.

Brent's journalistic wheels started spinning as he thought back on people he could contact for help getting to Roman. He had interviewed the hospital's newest director, Mindy Benson, when she first took the job three years ago. They had hit it off, and she had reached out to Brent for a number of features. He wasn't sure he had enough juice to see Roman, particularly since he was no longer a reporter or in any way valuable to the director, but he could certainly ask.

"Tell me, Luis, if I could get us in there, will you go with me? Would he talk to me with you there?"

"I don't know," Luis said. "He was kind of in and out of our group, never really opening up all that much. I don't think he trusted us. What do you think he can tell you?"

"I don't know, but my gut says if anyone knows something, it's him."

~

TEN

Ed Keenan

Black Island Research Facility

ED AND SULLIVAN stared into open laptops as they sat at a long table in the bright-white light of the main communications room, waiting for Frank Bolton, the Black Island Research Facility Director.

Bolton was the man who arranged for the expunging of Ed's crimes the Agency had trumped up, in exchange for helping Sullivan track the alien threat. Bolton was in his early 50s, short and built like a brawler. His rock-like shoulders bookended a stone-cold, *don't-fuck-with-me* stare. He never minced words and called shit like it was: exactly why Ed liked him. After dealing with too many silver-tongued bureaucrats in the Agency, Ed couldn't stand the politics of bullshit.

Though Ed liked Bolton well enough, he couldn't trust the man to honor old deals once Ed fulfilled his job's duties. Which was why Ed played it safe and moved his family — Jade, Teagan, and Becca — into a safe house in upstate New York that nobody knew about.

Bolton stepped into the room in his crisp, black uniform,

which, despite the man's general ranking, bore no decorations and declared no honor: black and utilitarian, same as any other Guardsman.

"So, the shit's hit the fan, eh, gentlemen?" Bolton said, taking a seat opposite them.

"Yes, Sir," Sullivan said. "We have our first documented infection. We're culling everything we have on Mrs. Flores to see if we can trace her point of contagion."

"And her child? Husband?"

"Both were quarantined on Level Four, but neither shows signs of infection."

"And the other women with her in the park?"

"Also quarantined, along with their families. We don't expect any positives."

Bolton sighed, "OK, the press is having a fucking field day, suggesting everything from biological attack to homegrown terror from a sleeper unit of soccer moms. We need to find this Boricio Bishop. Have we got *any* leads, at all?"

"No, Sir," Sullivan said. "We're monitoring all communications and all closed circuit television for any sign of him, but we're at zero hits."

"So he's just out there infecting people and there's nothing we can do about it?" Bolton asked.

"We're doing everything we can," Sullivan said. "And this is the first person that we know is infected. The other cases we worked showed no change to the bodies, so we had no actual proof linking Bishop to this."

"Until now," Bolton reminded him.

Ed sympathized, seeing Sullivan sitting empty handed beside a man used to commanding answers with a snapping finger. Ed had seen many men in Bolton's position get petulant when their underlings didn't stuff their hungry bellies with the answers they wanted yesterday. To Bolton's credit, he was either managing his stress well and trapping his rising anger, or truly in charge of his emotions. While he was short with

Sullivan, Ed had seen men like Bolton go completely unhinged, batshit ballistic.

While Bolton's patience was a deeper well than other men's, it wouldn't be long before that well ran dry. Men like Bolton didn't only expect answers, they also had to *provide* answers to someone higher up the food chain. And those people, in Ed's experience, were far less patient.

Earth's Black Island wasn't the same agency as the other world's. While this organization was also part of Homeland Security, it hadn't benefited from the alien technology as it had in the other world. This Black Island was designed as a biowarfare research facility, with four levels rather than seven. Neither the facility nor its staff, comprised more of scientists than actual Guardsmen, were prepared for a full-scale alien invasion or outbreak of infected. The pressure was on Bolton to head this off before involving the military.

Once the military was involved, keeping the information secret would be impossible: The people of Earth would know there were aliens among them. Mass panic would tear society to pieces.

"OK," Bolton said. "We picked up a communication last night on the computers, and I need you to follow up. Someone you both know: Brent Foster."

Ed felt Bolton's eyes on him, weighing his surprise.

Bolton punched his laptop's keyboard, and played a recording 0f Brent speaking to someone Ed didn't know. The men were discussing Black Island, the aliens, and someone Brent referenced as the 215ers. They were also discussing a man named Roman Rosetti, a former Air Force member who went on a shooting spree before being committed to a psychiatric hospital.

The recording ended, and Bolton's eyes met Sullivan's. "I thought you said we could trust these survivors to keep their mouths shut. This man sounds like he's doing the opposite. Do I need to remind you of the mess this makes for us?"

"No, Sir," Sullivan said.

"I need you two to take care of this," Bolton said.

Ed swallowed, "Take care of?"

"I want you to find out what Brent Foster knows, then kill him. And the man he was talking to. Name's Luis Torres."

"Whoa, whoa," Ed said, "I didn't sign on to kill anyone."

Ed looked at Sullivan, who seemed equally surprised by Bolton's directive, but was silent.

Bolton responded, the first bit of anger tinging his voice, "We have a deal, Mr. Keenan, predicated on you helping us do whatever must be done to eradicate the threat. I don't need to remind you that we secured your freedom from some fairly serious government charges, do I?"

"What part of not reminding me is this?" Ed asked. "I said I'd help, yes. That was before you had me killing innocents."

"Please," Bolton said, "don't insult me by acting like a whore with last-minute scruples. You are a paid killer, Mr. Keenan, the only thing that's changed is your master."

Ed stood, "Excuse me? *Master?*"

"Sit down!" Bolton thundered, his face red.

Ah, there's the anger. The well is shallow, after all.

Ed refused to sit.

Bolton glared at him, "Let's not kid ourselves, Mr. Keenan. You're here not out of the goodness of your heart, nor because we wiped your slate clean and made you a 'free' man. You're here because we found you. And we found your family. And you've nowhere to run, do you? It would be a shame for something to happen to Jade, Teagan, and her baby."

"Are you threatening my family?" Ed said, trying to throttle his own rising anger before he leaped across the table to see how tough Bolton actually was.

"I'm only telling you what you already know," Bolton said. "You've seen how this works. Don't make *me* the bad guy. Your time in the other world has made you soft if you can't see Foster's clear and present danger. I never wait for cracks in the foundation to worsen. I take care of them *before* they spread. We could roll in with a team of operatives and snatch all these people up, but I prefer discretion, and we'll need you to find out what they know. You're still good at that, right?"

Bolton didn't wait for an answer. "So, you will do as instructed, then get the rest of them."

"Rest?" Ed asked, swallowing.

"Yes, everyone who came back. I want you to find them, get whatever info they have, then kill them. Discreetly."

"And if I say no?" Ed stared down at Bolton, his face settling back into its calm facade.

"We both know you won't," Bolton said.

The fucking bastard was right.

~

ELEVEN

Rose McCallister

The murder inside her head had been working for hours.

Rose didn't want to meet Marina, even though it was the biggest opportunity she had ever had. Her head hurt too much. She wanted to crawl under the comforter and sleep for several more hours. Rose had begged Boricio for "just 15 more minutes." He was hesitant, knowing her ways, but finally gave her the quarter hour, after she promised to be a good girl and get out of bed when it was time, but now, a full hour later, Rose was determined to prove that some promises were born to be broken.

"Time to rise, shine, and bring God your glory," Boricio said, sitting at the edge of their hotel bed. "Kick those covers in the face, and give 'em bloody noses. You've important people to meet today, and you're running thin on seconds."

"No," Rose said, or moaned, then turned toward the window and pulled the comforter tighter around her body.

"Well, ring around the Rosie," Boricio said, like he always did when trying to talk her into something she didn't want to do. Except this time there was no talking after he started. Instead of finishing his sentence Boricio reached into bed, scooped Rose out from the comforter with a hand slithering up under her waist, then draped her over his shoulders like dry cleaning and carried her into the bathroom. Boricio kept holding Rose like a sack as he started the water, then planted her on the ground and started undressing her, though not at all like he normally did.

Rose tried to fight, but only barely and mostly for fun since she and Boricio both loved the banter, and it usually gave her energy, which at the moment she needed more than anything else, besides a nuclear bomb to soften her head's relentless pounding.

With her clothes in a puddle, and Boricio smiling and waiting, Rose stepped into the shower and let the hot water beat her into waking up enough to ignore the throbbing in her head.

"Another headache?" Boricio asked.

Rose couldn't see his face through the shower curtain, but could picture it easily enough: his furrowed brow and twitching nose, bothered if not altogether angry that her headaches had been growing worse for a month without more than a few minutes of reprieve at a time. Rose didn't want to admit it, especially an hour away from meeting Marina and the Maris Brothers at Marina's home in Malibu, but most days Rose felt physically incapable of lying to Boricio.

"Yes, and this one's especially bad. It's just starting, but I can already tell I'm going to want to die in another hour, you know, right when I'm supposed to be at my charming best. How much will Veronica hate me if I reschedule?"

"You know you can't do that," Boricio said. "You can't let this slip, Rose Red. You've gotta grab this fucker by the neck and choke it 'til its eyeballs pop from its face and get all squishy."

Rose shampooed her hair. "So violent this morning! It's still early and you're wanting me to give my covers bloody noses and choke the eyeballs from my opportunities."

She laughed. Boricio was always so … colorful.

"Look, Rose, it's simple," Boricio peeled back the curtain, poked his head inside the shower, looked Rose up and down, from her big, pink nipples to her tiny toes, giving her a blush all over, then pulled his head back out and finished the thought. "Today is one of those days when anything *can* happen, and something sure as a big shit after a chili dog will. And what might happen in the hotel room ain't near the same thing that'll happen outside. Now I know your head hurts, sweet blooming Rose of mine, but you can't stay in bed and sleep off this chance. You'll hate yourself forever."

Like always, Boricio was right. But that didn't mean Rose was happy about it.

"And why won't you come with me again? You know I feel better when you're with me."

"Well of course *you* do," Boricio peeked his head back inside the curtain as Rose rinsed her hair, "but that's because Boricio's all special sauce. Still, special as I am, I'm also smart enough to know when I'm a use and when I'm a waste. Today is your show, and I'm in the way. They want to meet the woman who wrote *The Billfold*, and I had nothing to do with that. If anything, I was a distraction, sucking on your tiny toes like I do, distracting you from your writing."

Rose pouted as she stepped out of the shower and towel dried her hair. "I know you just want me out of the hotel because you have some hot date coming in here while I'm away."

Boricio laughed, then made one of his horribly off-color jokes: "Nah, baby, you know you're the only woman who can satisfy me. I'd never cheat on you. But I can't get away with murder with you watching, so I'm waiting for you to leave so I can go downstairs and find me a victim; waiting on you to leave so I can commit some truly unspeakable acts."

Rose half laughed because she didn't know what else to do when Boricio was so … odd. She pulled on her panties and a smart looking charcoal skirt, already laid out, then continued getting ready, staying topless for Boricio.

A second later her man was wearing *that look*, and sidled beside Rose at the mirror. "You look like you're keeping Victoria's secret in that skirt," he said.

Rose laughed, knowing exactly what Boricio wanted. "Thanks."

"Mind lifting it up for, oh I don't know, four or five minutes? Maybe less."

Rose said, "No," even though she meant yes. She would happily lift her skirt, lower her panties, and let Boricio knock the migraines from inside her. But before she could play, her phone buzzed with a text. She picked it up, looked at the screen, then showed the text to Boricio. "Gotta go," she said. "Veronica's waiting downstairs."

"OK," Boricio shrugged. "Your loss. I was planning to lay my healin' hands all over your sweet body, kill that headache."

Rose laughed again, touched up her makeup, put on her bra and top, then quickly finished, kissed Boricio on the cheek, went downstairs and through the lobby, and climbed into Veronica's silver Lexus, waiting outside just past the valets.

"Why so pale?" Veronica asked as Rose slammed the silver door shut.

"I feel like shit," Rose admitted. "But I'm here to play ball, I promise. No one has to know I feel run down by a bus but you. Just tell me what to say and I'll say it. This stuff all stresses me out so much, I just want it to be over. I don't even *care* who makes the movie anymore."

"That's ridiculous," Veronica said. "Of course you do. The Maris Brothers will knock this out of the park, then after they do, you can write whatever the hell you want forever, OK? Trust me."

"I'm in the car, aren't I?"

"That you are," Veronica said, then pulled away from the hotel and drove the remainder of the way to Marina's playing

XM softly in the background and leaving Rose to nestle her pounding head against the soft, leather seat. Veronica spoke only through the commercial breaks, punctuating each with a fresh promise that all would be fine.

Rose tried rubbing the stress from her temples, trying to believe Veronica, telling herself that everything would be fine, and over soon. Marina lived in Malibu in what wasn't just the biggest house Rose had ever seen, it was easily bigger than the next three piled together. Veronica's Lexus was taken by a valet in front — *how many visitors did she get?* Then they were led into a large foyer and asked to wait. Rose expected a long pause, taking several minutes seemingly designed to feel the weight of Marina's importance, but the interlude lasted only a minute. Marina met them almost immediately, took Rose's hands in hers, and kissed her warmly on each cheek as if she'd known her forever and was grateful for their reunion.

Marina led the girls into a gorgeous study, with a long wall of glass looking out onto a tennis court, pool, and lush gardens — the Pacific must have been on the other side — then gestured for Rose to sit on a plush, white-leather sofa beside Veronica. Marina sat in an overstuffed chair across from them.

After a few minutes of shockingly natural small talk, Marina bluntly said, "So, Rose, the Brothers will be here shortly. In the meantime, I'd love for you to tell me what you think of Original Design."

Rose was grateful that she'd refused Marina's offer for a drink, surely she would have lost a swallow to spit. She didn't know what to say, and had no idea how to answer. She only knew a little about the Church, or *cult* as Boricio insisted it was. She didn't want to say anything false — Rose wasn't wired to pretend — but also didn't want to insult Marina, nor did she want to jeopardize what could be an amazing future, starting with the Maris Brothers.

"Honestly," she looked directly into Marina's eyes. "I don't know *what* to think. I don't know much about the Church at all, other than the same rumors everyone's heard, and I'm smart enough not to trust those. I have an open mind, and would love to learn more, but do have my own ideas about faith and spirituality — I'm sure you got at least some of that if you've read *The Billfold* — and am not really looking for anything to join or believe in."

Marina gave Rose what looked like a well-practiced smile. "I hate to admit it, but I've not read *The Billfold*, yet. I only just heard about this meeting and didn't want to scan it. I trust Veronica's judgment completely, though, and I'm sure if she thinks it's right for the Brothers, it is. I promise I'll read it if things go well between us." Marina uncrossed her legs, shifted in her seat, then crossed them the opposite way. "I do want to make certain that you understand our religion isn't a cult, and that it's in no way 'wacky.' In fact, I would argue that even if we're among the world's smallest, our religion is the best because unlike so many others, we have science behind us."

"Science?" Rose raised her eyebrows. She felt Veronica, nervous beside her.

"Yes, of course," Marina nodded. "Science. You'll never find the Church of Original Design's true beliefs in the rumor rags. But it's a fact: Our religion is founded on research that no one wants to discuss because it conflicts, rather violently, with so much of what western science *chooses* to believe, even though their beliefs have been proven wrong time and again."

Rose tried to hold her smile as she shifted in her seat.

"Man is made up of mind and body, but no one outside of our Church seems interested in The Current — the force between the two. If you can understand The Current, then you can understand the Universe. Most Original Design funding is spent in understanding this, which is why our centers have some of the best brain and recovery research in the world."

Rose's head felt like it was about to burst; it was a melon

beneath a hammer, and hurt enough *before* she started trying to hold a non-judgmental expression.

Marina laughed. "I can tell what you're thinking, and I promise, it's not bullshit. I don't need to convince you, and I could talk all day about the science, but I won't. I'm not trying to get you to join the Church, Rose, I simply want to prepare you. If the Brothers want to work with you, which it seems like they will, it's in our best interests to give you some background so you're not overwhelmed or weirded out. And what's better than background?" Marina smiled, then answered herself. "Proof, Rose. Proof is better. I have no secrets, and love to share; if you have questions, I have answers. We still have a few minutes before the Brothers arrive, might I suggest using a few of those minutes for proof, and letting me help you?"

"What do you mean?" Rose felt her forehead beading with sweat. She wished Boricio hadn't stayed back at the hotel.

"Well," Marina uncrossed her legs and folded her hands. "Do you have any problems? Troubling pains you've been unable to get rid of?"

Without thinking, Rose admitted, "Yes, I have the worst, most crippling migraines." She swallowed and added, "I have one right now."

"And they won't go away?"

"No," she shook her head. "I've had them on and off all my life, but they've recently come back with a vengeance."

"Would you like me to take your headache away right now, then make sure it will never return?"

Joking, Rose said, "Do that and I'll sign my membership papers before leaving this room."

"That's not what I'm trying to do." Marina stood, laughing, and held out her hand for Rose. "Come on, follow me."

She crossed the room to a door behind her desk, swiped her thumb across a small pad on the wall beside it, then stepped through the doorway and gestured for Veronica and Rose to follow.

Rose looked at Veronica hesitantly. She nodded and Rose followed. If Boricio had been with her, there was no way in hell he would've let her go into the room. But Boricio wasn't with them, and Rose didn't want to offend her host and potential business partner. She trusted Veronica as much as she trusted Boricio, at least when it came to stuff like this. She figured she was at least safe from a brainwashing.

The room was sparse, and seemed to have no materials other than glass and steel. In the room's center stood a thin metal chamber with a small oval window at the top. The doors were parted as if in invitation. Rose thought it looked like something from *Star Trek*.

"Five minutes in there," Marina pointed to the tube, "and you'll never get a headache again."

Rose stared at the tube, then at Marina, speechless.

Marina smiled. "I know it seems impossible to believe, but it's true, Rose. This is science that no one else has because so few people are willing to believe in miracles, even if they're the sort that can be easily explained by science. And unfortunately," she added with a sigh, "our government is in the business of preventing us from sharing."

Rose didn't ask what Marina meant, even though she wanted to know. Instead she said, "How does it work?"

"When we have more time, I'll be happy to give you a longer explanation. For now, let's just say it fixes what's broken inside you."

Rose looked from the machine to Marina, then back to the tube, raising her eyebrows. As if to answer her unspoken objection, Marina said, "The simplest explanation: The machine finds the cells in your body most in need of repair, then repairs them."

"What's it called?" Rose whispered, meaning to ask in a normal voice.

"The machine is called The Capacitor; it fixes your Current."

Veronica appeared in the doorway, and said, "It's completely safe, Rose."

Even though a part of Rose was terrified, most of her was awed, excited, and curious. She stepped into the chamber as if pulled, then planted her back flat against the plush interior and folded her arms across her chest as instructed. The doors closed, and she heard a whir, like magnets, Rose thought for some reason.

The chamber filled with brilliant-blue light and spun her thoughts until they circled euphoria.

Before the whirring, Marina told Rose the treatment would last five minutes. But it didn't feel like five minutes to Rose. It felt like a year somehow compressed into seconds.

Time meant nothing when everything else felt so *empty*.

Rose was blank: All she could see inside herself was an endless swath of nighttime, stars doused from her sky one at a time before twinkling back by the twos, brighter and more brilliant than before, clotting black with glittered intensity. Outside her mind and inside the chamber, which had gone from rather narrow and perfectly small to roughly the size of a sprawling meadow, bright-blue sparks crackled and leapt from her skin.

When the chamber doors finally opened, after five minutes or forever, Rose felt more whole — more aware — than she had ever felt before. She had a deep and sudden need to see Boricio, almost an ache, then that feeling faded into a placid calm and turned her headache to a distant memory.

"How do you feel?" Marina asked, beaming as the chamber doors parted.

Rose had no idea how to answer. She wanted to say, *better than I've ever felt in my life, like I've died and gone to heaven, unreal,* or any other of a thousand superlatives, but what she felt was too good to be true.

"I don't know," Rose said, working not to stutter. "Did you guys put some kind of drugs in the air?"

Veronica giggled and shook her head no. "It's amazing, right?"

Rose swallowed and nodded, not knowing what to do or say or think. She had no idea if the feelings in her mind and body, and The *Current* between them was real, or whether it was a placebo designed by lights and wizardry inside the chamber — a magician's trick — and Marina's power of suggestion.

Marina took Rose by the hand and led her out of the small room and then away from her office. "Don't answer now," she said. "It's too soon. Your body will want to process what's happened, and your mind requires time to settle around its newly repaired cells. Your body will accept this more easily than your brain. But don't worry," she took Rose's hand in hers, "everything *will* get easier to understand. And believe me, you'll never want to live without The Capacitor ever again. Fortunately, now, you won't ever have to."

Rose was still silent, shuffling on her feet without any clue what to say in response to Marina.

"It's okay that you don't know what to think," Marina said, reassuringly. "It would be far odder if you did. I'd take offense if you were to blindly believe, and would wonder about your character; faith is empty if never questioned."

They ascended the stairs, walking toward a second-floor meeting room where Marina said they would meet the Brothers. Just outside the room, they ran into the siblings approaching from the other direction. Because the Brothers didn't like to be photographed, Rose had found little while searching online, other than a few photos taken away from the set, and mostly from far away. She was startled when she saw them, though it took her a few, long seconds to figure out why.

In the few photos she had seen, one of the brothers — she wasn't sure which — was a *bit* heavy, if she was being kind. Boricio, on the three occasions Rose had found a picture said, "Reason there aren't more pictures of fatty-fatty fat fat is that most photographers get sucked right into his gravitational pull right after they're snapped," "At least that motherfucker never has to worry about getting kidnapped," and "Think those are Double D's?"

Now, standing before her, both brothers were model-thin. The difference was striking: Rose wondered if that was the work of the machine.

Could you nuke fat cells like that?

Is this what being rich means in the 21st Century?

The brothers were pale, strikingly so, with almost-white hair, despite being in their early 20s, and piercing, blue eyes.

The Brothers were also nothing like Rose expected: They were calm and soft-spoken, overly kind and well-mannered. One never spoke over the other, always waiting for what Rose thought seemed like exact turns. One would ask a question, then wait for Rose to respond in full before the other brother would follow up. The length of each question seemed the same, almost precisely. Most odd, it seemed that the brother sitting on the left — or was it the right? — asked logic-based questions while the other one seemed more focused on creativity.

By the end of the conversation Rose's head was swimming, and she could barely tell up from down. She certainly couldn't tell the Brothers apart.

"Would you like something to drink?"

"Sorry?" she said, feeling pulled into a daze by her ankles.

"Would you like something to drink?" the Brother repeated. "We're going to go down to Marina's office for a few minutes, just the three of us. Would you care for something to eat or drink while waiting?"

"No, thank you," Rose shook her head.

Her world moved at half speed as the Brothers followed Marina from the meeting room and back into the hall, leaving Rose alone with Veronica.

"Well?" Veronica said.

Rose looked at her agent, silent.

"Well?" Veronica tried again. "What did you think? Amazing, right?"

Rose could remember almost nothing from the last hour, and only knew it had been that long because the small clock on the corner desk said so. She remembered leaving Marina's office and then running into the Brothers at the end of the hall. She remembered excitement and bubbling energy, but couldn't draw a single line between her thoughts or memories. Rose did remember, however, that yes, it was quite amazing.

"Yes," she said. "It was amazing."

As Rose spoke to Veronica, her fog slowly lifted. By the time Marina returned to the meeting room — without the Brothers — Rose was giddy, smiling ear to ear and eager to hear the good news she knew would be coming.

Marina beamed, holding her arms wide. "They're thrilled to be working with you, Rose," she said. "*The Billfold* is the Maris Brothers' next official project. They'll be announcing it once all the contracts are signed next week. If you can stay a bit longer?"

"Of course, I can stay!" Rose said, excited, hoping Boricio wouldn't mind.

Rose wanted to explode in excitement, and while she and Veronica talked a lot on the trip back to her hotel, she was saving her best words for Boricio.

She couldn't wait to share the good news with him. She pictured him in the hotel room, waiting anxiously for her return.

~

TWELVE

Boricio Wolfe

With Rose finally gone, it was time for Boricio to beat his id into submission.

He had a quiet covenant with himself, set into place after swapping the dead world back for his old and frisky one, after he'd been supposedly fixed by Luca the Boy Wonder.

But Boricio wasn't *really* fixed, though he was a bitch and a half better than he had been before, and pigs in a blanket cozier with the demons who'd not bothered to stop wrassling inside him. Finally, Boricio had learned the *right* way to feed them.

Before all the shit that went down with that whole other world, Boricio was indiscriminate with his purging. But not anymore, he'd gone from bomber to sniper.

While Boricio had always been careful enough to never get caught, he was also never worried. Now he was obsessively careful, his purging had to stay invisible.

Fortunately, Boricio had never been prone to the weaknesses of other serial killers. For one, he never kept souvenirs, because mementos were for pussies. What sort of sick fucker kept ornaments to commemorate a purging? You put 100 random motherfuckers in a row, and 99 would agree that

Boricio was a sick fucking duck. But Boricio said beer-battered bullshit to that: *Sick* was keeping shit after a kill.

Nor had Boricio ever stuck to patterns or taunted the authorities with cryptic messages. That bullshit about killers playing cat and mouse with the cops was just an excuse to get handsome actors waving plastic guns in well-lit shadows. Why the fuck anyone would ever want to play games with gumshoes was a fucking whodunit to Boricio. There was a *right* way to do it: purge, change the mother fucking channel, then return to regularly scheduled programming later.

You wanna prove you're smarter than the cops, don't get caught.

But not getting caught didn't mean you couldn't have fun at the playground. Boricio wasn't the sort to leave a merry-go-round unspun, and there were plenty of ways to make merry at the scene of a purging. Doodles were a laugh, so was makeup. Sometimes he'd put costumes on people and dress them as famous characters. Other times, he'd not leave a whisper. Point was, you kept shit random, from your methods to victims.

And while Luca had made it so Boricio actually felt compassion for people, for the first time in his life, he didn't — and couldn't — turn off Boricio's need to hunt and purge: an itch that only grew worse the longer it was left unscratched.

While Boricio couldn't get rid of the itch, he was far more selective in who he chose to hunt. He picked people who deserved it, the assholes and dickheads of the world who just made shit worse for everyone — in other words, people like Boricio once was.

So, he tightened up his game, was more careful than ever.

Wanting a woman for more than her slippery fish was a new thing for Boricio, but it was true and he knew it like the billow of his own breath. Rose was deserving of his fiercest protection, even if that protection was from the knowledge of what he was. There wasn't much in his life that he truly cared for, but Boricio would bloody his knuckles to keep his most sacred holy. Right now the order went: Boricio, purging, Rose.

Boricio went back into the bathroom, unbuttoned his pants, plopped his already hard cock into his open palm, wrapped it tight, then after 40 or so seconds of squeezing and jacking, blasted a half billion itty, bitty Boricios onto the porcelain, imagining he was cock-sprinkling Rose, just like they liked it.

It was good to free seed from his system, prior to a purging.

Boricio assessed his volume of man oil, nodded, then looked up to the mirror and ran his hand through his hair, admiring his smile without vanity — no different from admiring the gleam on a blade.

He went to the fridge, grabbed a $1,000 bottle of goddamned water, cracked the cap and swigged, thinking that life was a giant load of spunk, with him drinking an expensive bottle of water from an expensive room, without leaving a body behind. He finished swigging, then dropped his empty into the trash and stepped out into the hallway.

Boricio smiled as he closed the door behind him; It had been too long since his last hunt. The trip to California was exactly what he needed. Now that Boricio was living with Rose on Paddock Island, it was harder than ever to purge. This trip came at a perfect time for both Rose and Boricio. She'd seal a deal, he'd flush his system and a couple of fuckers.

He walked the lobby then left the hotel, crossing the street to the Marriott across the way. Hotel bars were perfect for hunting, just not his.

Boricio went to the bar and ordered a Jack, neat. He sipped, wondering if his morning adventure would take him an hour or six, and wishing it didn't matter. But it did. Boricio didn't want Rose missing him, at least not for long. He wasn't a dog, and Rose wasn't the sort to hold a leash, but she was human, and a girl, which meant Boricio could only stretch his absences so far.

Purging was different than it used to be for Boricio. It had never been easier, or more rewarding, provided he had the time to settle into the job and get things done right. However, there was a new wrinkle to his post-fixed-by-Luca life.

On occasion, Boricio suffered blackouts. He'd just pass out, only to wake a few minutes to a few hours later. So far it had happened twice, and oddly both times during his purges, but he was lucky enough not to get caught either time. He hadn't told Rose about the blackouts because he didn't want her worrying, or more closely monitoring him for his safety.

That wasn't the only weird thing to happen since Luca "fixed" him.

Every now and then, Boricio could *hear* stuff. Wasn't no way to explain it other than that. It was like he could hear how others were buzzing, sometimes in colors displayed in auras around them, sometimes he could hear their thoughts, other times he could see their memories. People were opening up like a book to Boricio, always read and maybe bled. It wasn't a sense that was always on, but it seemed especially heightened during his hunts, as if nature enhancing him for purging.

The heightened senses seemed to always lead him toward the perfect subject; victims who were asking for it, stuffing so many ugly secrets inside them.

Everyone had secrets. When purging, Boricio was drawn to the worst. Depending on whether it was a sound or a sight or a scent that caught his attention, Boricio would get different glimpses into the evil the victim had done, their offenses surfacing with varying levels of clarity. The two clearest Boricio had seen so far was a man who had killed one girl-friend and a pair of hookers; he got away with all three murders, but hung the memories proudly in his mind's foyer, so he could see them each of the thousands of times he passed each day. The other was a woman, so broken after drowning her baby, she wore her bleeding emotions like an apron on her withered body. Both were excellent kills, leaving Boricio's soul feeling freshly showered.

Evil was indiscriminate, and Boricio didn't give a dick about gender one way or the other, at least not anymore. Before his fixing, Boricio preferred honeypot to bratwurst, but then he met Rose and it mattered not at all. The purging was a secret to keep, good and plenty. The scent of sex meant nothing.

Boricio knew how to hide his killing fine, but had no desire to start keeping the sort of secret Rose would be able to smell, and, much to his surprise, found he didn't want to. Boricio had no need to wax his candle anywhere else. Rose waxed it fine. He wanted only to calm his itching. For the first time ever, killing was almost an honorable profession for Boricio — cleaning the world.

Boricio sat for almost an hour and half, and was nearly about to swap bars since it was stupid to stay in one place too long, when he finally found what he was looking for.

Boricio had already let a pair of smaller fishies swim off. One was a horrible cunt of a woman: in the hotel cheating on her husband, paying for the room with money embezzled from her school, and wearing a stolen dress from Nordstrom's. The other guppy wasn't too different, just a husband instead of a wife and stealing from his father's account instead of a school. Boricio considered paying a visit to both, but his instincts said he could do better, he'd waited this long after all. His instincts were true; a second before Boricio emptied his glass with a final swallow, he saw his subject: a short, balding man who liked to diddle kids with his diggler.

The Diddler's body burned bright-red, and would until Boricio muted his hue forever to black.

The big, wide world won't miss this asshole a bit.

Boricio finished his Jack but stayed in the bar. He ordered

another one, then waited through another 40 minutes after the crimson-colored cocksucker disappeared from the lobby and into an elevator. Boricio wasn't sure what he was doing upstairs, but knew as a matter of goddamned fact that it was something worth getting a head removed from his shoulders.

When the Diddler stepped back into the lobby from a bank of elevators Boricio hadn't moved his eyes from once, he sifted through the asshole's mind, happy to find that the Diddler was dumb-fuck enough to think about missing a payment on his Infiniti FX35 earlier that morning.

Boricio left the bar, jogged down to the hotel garage, careful to avoid security cameras, climbed inside the back of the Infiniti, and waited for the Diddler.

The drive was short, though Boricio wished it was shorter since the cocksucker wasn't just a pedophile, he actually listened to the same crap as his victims — bands with pubeless punks. They made two lefts and four rights spread across what the predator's guess said was about three and a half miles. Boricio stayed tense throughout the drive, ready to strike if Diddler was stupid enough to sense him and search in back. Fortunately, One Direction kept the Diddler engaged enough to not notice Boricio, all the way from the airport hotel until he killed his engine 15 minutes later.

Boricio waited until five minutes after his door slammed, then peered up from the backseat at a house that was as nice as the Diddler's Infiniti. After another five minutes staring at the front porch, Boricio thanked the gate at the start of the community, figuring it was the reason the Diddler didn't lock his door or set an alarm. He climbed from the cabin, shut the door, and shot like a blur from the SUV to shadows beneath a green awning, over to a giant wall of bright-pink bougainvillea, and finally around to the side of his house.

Boricio peered into Diddler's window and saw him staring ogle-eyed at his widescreen. He crept low, circled around to the kitchen, then helped himself into the fuckface's house, like he had helped himself into so many houses before.

Boricio watched Diddler for nearly 10 minutes, that was about nine longer than he was usually willing to devote to assholes, but there was something so mind numbingly pathetic about Diddler, sitting by himself, watching TV with his hands in his pants — the fucking Disney Channel — that Boricio was near hypnotized. Finally, he stepped out into the living room, walked straight to the coffee table, grabbed the remote from in front of a startled Diddler, turned toward the screen, flipped it to black, then spun back to Diddler — who'd not found any words — and hurled the remote hard into the fucker's face.

The long, rectangular hunk of plastic smacked the asshole hard in his nose, right on the bridge. Though still too dumfounded to say shit, Diddler screamed as if implements of death were dipping deep into his pucker.

Boricio looked at Diddler and, disappointed that the fucker wasn't bleeding, leaned toward him, grabbed him by a fat handful of hair, pulled his head up from the couch and his face toward him, then launched his fist between the asshole's eyes, aiming for the same bridge that wasn't broken by the remote. Boricio kept pounding, over and over until both the bridge and his knuckles were sticky with crimson.

Fuck. Gonna have to explain that to Rose.

"What do you want?" the asshole was sobbing, already seconds from begging for his stupid, worthless, cocksucking, bullshit-of-a-cunt-hair life.

You've already said adios, now I'm gonna get you to sing it.

"Well, well," Boricio sat on the coffee table. He grabbed a box of Kleenex, sitting a half foot from where the remote was sitting a minute before. He handed Diddler a clump of tissues, said, "Wipe yourself off," and turned toward the TV, noting the time. He reeled back toward Diddler, then smacked him hard on the head just because.

"You're damned lucky," Boricio snarled.

"You're not going to kill me?" Diddler asked.

Boricio laughed, thinking how funny it was that even though he'd said no such thing, the asshole knew what was coming. That's what happened when you spent most nights lying awake, wondering when the inevitable would knock on your door.

Boricio laughed harder. "Oh you're deader than the fucking shake weight, but I can't afford to take nearly the time with you that I'd like. So we're gonna have to make this quick. You do get a chance, but that chance won't dictate whether you live or die. We're gonna decide, the two of us together, exactly how much pain you're gonna live with before leaving God's blue marble."

Diddler stared up at Boricio as if trying to understand him — who was this strange and horrible man who had broken into his house and was going to kill him? Boricio leaned forward, laughed into the asshole's confusion, then head-butted him, because it felt so goddamned fantastic — up high to keep the bruises from Rose.

"OK, listen, cunt hair, you get one chance and one chance only. Like I said, I'm in a hurry. My girlfriend — peach of a lady and a Tarantino of talent I surely don't deserve — is probably waiting for me back at our hotel. She just went to meet with the Maris Brothers." Boricio tried making eyes with Diddler, not caring a hair on his sack if this nugget impressed him, but curious to see if it did. No luck: Diddler was still clasping at his head and trying to see, whimpering through the splayed palm that cradled his face.

"Well, anyway," Boricio said, his voice back to casual, "I've gotta run. But I'm not the sort of man to leave a job anything less than finished, so I'm looking for an excuse to trim my chore list. You tell me why you deserve to die, now I don't need to know all the details you sick, fucking fuck, just enough to hear you admit what you and I both already know, *then* I need a reason why you deserve to have the Grim Reaper get to you quick, rather than turning afternoon into night while making you bleed from your dookie hole. Do ya dig?"

Diddler cried.

Boricio head-butted him again, this time harder, then screamed into his face. "I said, do ya dig?!"

Diddler whimpered, "Y-yes … "

"Why do you deserve to die?" Boricio asked.

For a long minute Diddler cried too hard to make any words. Boricio let him sob since it was part of the show. Then, when tired of the simpering, Boricio started thinking about his own experience with men raping his childhood in one way or another, then grabbed the cockweasel by another clump of hair, this one at the back of his head, and dragged him off of the couch, across his house, and into the bedroom. Boricio dropped him like a sack by the side of his bed and slammed a boot heel into his gut.

The one thing Boricio hated about purging on the road was that most times he had no access to his tools. But Boricio bent down and did it the old-fashioned way, pulling the middle digit from the Diddler's right hand and bending it back toward his wrist until there was a horrible snap, followed by a shrieking, muffled only by Diddler's deafening scream. Boricio reached up to the bed, shook a pillow from its case, wadded it up and shoved it into Diddler's wide-open, and still-screaming, mouth, told him to "Shut the fuck up before I fill your mouth with my shit," then grabbed his left hand and made the other middle finger match.

"I'll break every bone in your body the same goddamned way," Boricio said, "and make you listen to *Muskrat Love* while I do it if you don't start talking. You satisfy me, and you can ask any number of the bitches Ol' Boricio's left breathing, I'm pretty easy to satisfy, and I'll kill you quick. Otherwise, I'm drawing blinds and we're hunkering down."

Somehow, Diddler found his voice through the sobbing. "Because I hurt people."

"What?" Boricio asked, leaning in as if he couldn't hear.

"I deserve to die because I hurt people … children."

The final word cracked the man's voice into something awful. Boricio said, "Got a reason I should make it quick?"

Boricio had heard it all before, and expected more of the same from Diddler — any number of reasons why the indefensible was worthy of defense: the same bullshit that had victims spending lifetimes trying to understand what couldn't be understood, and long lifetimes hoping that one day they would, praying for answers if they were stupid enough to believe in a God, telling themselves over and over like fucking Rain Man that it wasn't their fault, often while loving the fucker who did shit to them, thinking that maybe they brought it on themselves somehow.

Instead, Diddler surprised him. "I don't deserve you to make it quick. Please, Demon," he begged, "make me suffer."

Boricio had a speech cycling through his mind, all about how he would be doing the world a favor, ridding the planet of a dirtbag, but Diddler disarmed him. All Boricio could think to do was give the cunt hair what he didn't want.

He kneeled down, wrapped his arms around Diddler in a chokehold, stood straight, snapped the asshole's neck on his way to standing, then dropped him into a pile on the floor.

Boricio searched the fucker's place until he found his stash of kiddie-porn — it didn't take long since Boricio had a decent handle on how most monsters thought — then opened the box and dumped it all over Diddler's dead body. Boricio cleaned up any evidence of his being there and on his way outside, slammed into a wall of white, right as he opened the front door. Something slithered in between his ears and started screaming.

Boricio fell to his knees.

No, not again, he thought as he blacked out.

~

WHEN BORICIO OPENED HIS EYES, the sky outside the half-open door had already traded blue for gloaming. Boricio lay there blinking, trying not to be scared that he'd blacked out again during a purging. That was the sort of shit that could get him caught, dead, or worst of all, make him lose Rose.

Tic-tac-toe, three in a row, your momma got shot by a G.I. Joe.

A car motor rumbled outside. Strong beams from a headlight bathed the house in light.

Fuckity fuck fuck.

Boricio leapt to his feet, heart racing. He slammed the front door, ran to the rear of the house, slipped quietly out the back, hopped the first fence then another two after that, and didn't stop running until he left the residential neighborhood behind him and was bathed by the bright light of a major L.A. street, scoping his surroundings to figure location.

He had to get to the hotel, and explain shit to Rose.

As he thought about what he'd say, Boricio wondered if he'd managed to keep his prints off the Infiniti while he was hiding inside it. He thought so, but couldn't be certain. And there was no way in hell he was going back to the scene of the crime.

Boricio hoped his carelessness wouldn't come back to cost him everything — not now that he had a life worth clinging to.

~

THIRTEEN

Steven Warner

Marina wanted Steven to turn his attention from the TV back to her, wanted him to nibble at her ear, fog warm breath onto her neck, or put his mouth all over her, whispering sweet promises as he slid across her skin.

But *IT* couldn't: *ITS* eyes were fixed to the moving pictures, just as they had been since the story of the murderous woman first broke. Since then *IT* couldn't shift *ITS* eyes from the screen, or the bloodbath behind it.

The woman was just another bored housewife, until The Darkness claimed her, worming *ITS* way into her body, then nested to grow stronger by the breath until *IT* was ready to summon her, and *ITS* growing legion.

The footage was gruesome, the news cut back on little, wanting to grab viewer attention, even if their overtures were earned only through gore.

It was as if Steven's body was hypnotized through *ITS* fascination: this one story meant so much, maybe everything. If *IT* wasn't careful, the world, and all of *ITS* plans might unravel. *IT* had made so many mistakes before, on the other world, the dead one, but a new planet meant new opportunity; *IT* didn't have to make the same mistakes again.

This planet was *ITS* for the taking, so long as *IT* didn't make any mistakes — like letting things out in the world that *IT* didn't, or couldn't, control.

IT was obsessed with the story, hungry to know more, to know everything, but *IT* couldn't afford for Marina to know, couldn't afford for her to find out, or smell what *IT* was.

"Turn off the TV, Stevie," Marina said. "I'm much more interesting."

"Of course you are," *IT* said, then picked up the remote from the nightstand, aimed it at the screen, smothered the picture to black, then tossed the plastic onto the carpet and rolled over into a hover above Marina.

"Nothing is more important than you," said Steven's mouth.

That was mostly true. Marina was essential to *ITS* plans. But the story of the woman, Eva, was important, too. *IT* just had to know how she'd broken free. She had been one of the 315, one of *ITS* chosen, and was supposed to have been *ITS* to command. But Eva, the woman who was once part of The Darkness, had broken away, she had grown unstable, become a liability rather than an asset.

IT had felt Eva when she snapped and killed her friend in the park. *IT* had felt it almost as if *IT* had murdered the woman. However, and most disturbingly, *IT* wasn't able to seize control over her, *ITS* connection severed.

Eva was one of many such people *IT* had lost control over recently. While most of the incidents had not made the news, an increasing number were — people snapping and committing acts of horrible violence.

IT started trailing kisses across Marina's body, nibbling at her ear like she wanted, like she *always* wanted. *IT* lifted her gauzy top to suckle her nipples. She exhaled, lightly bucking beneath *ITS* mouth, purring as *IT* spread kisses and kept her humming.

While *ITS* host body, Steven, followed the routine with

Marina, *ITS* mind, or the alien part of IT, couldn't stop thinking about Eva.

IT was slipping, losing control. If *IT* did nothing *ITS* power was threatened.

The thought brought a sudden flare to *ITS* body.

The kind *IT* didn't quite know how to control.

IT snarled, then bit Marina, lightly on her shoulder, just enough to make her yelp, squeal, and purr for more. She'd mistaken *ITS* rage for passion. Humans were so ignorant when it came to knowing things.

In a second, *ITS* temperament shifted, *IT* felt more like *ITSELF*, less like IT did when masquerading in Steven's shell; *IT* felt more like the entity IT was, alive and born to consume.

IT thrashed, suddenly aggressive on top of Marina. *IT* grabbed at her gauzy top, ripping it from her body as she rattled and squirmed under Steven. *IT* was suddenly hungry to quell the hunger wafting from *ITS* host body like a stink. Pleasure hummed from Marina's mouth; guttural craving quivered from her body involuntarily, jolting up toward *IT*, craving satisfaction.

"Fuck me, Steven," she growled. "Hard."

"My pleasure," *IT* said.

Then *IT* attacked her, satisfying something inside Steven by ravishing Marina, planting kisses almost with malice, biting rather than nibbling at her nipples, then tearing creamy panties down her ass and over her ankles and positioning himself between her legs — *IT* had no underwear to shed, already naked, as *IT* preferred to be as often as possible — and started thrusting *ITSELF* into Marina as if trying to punish her.

It should have been too much for her body, how *IT* pounded, but it was exactly what she wanted, what she needed. Marina proved it with her every shudder, scream, and whimper. She tried crying out for him, using the name Steven, but was so deep in her pleasure, she could only mutter and groan.

IT made mad, almost violent, love to Marina — not that what *IT* did was anything like love. Once finished, when *IT* should have been exhausted with *ITS* host's body so thoroughly spent, *ITS* mind started to crackle.

IT left Marina passed out and breathing heavy on the bed, then went into her office to watch her Confessionals.

The Confessionals were a huge source of curiosity for *IT.*

IT had been watching them for a while, sometimes with Marina's knowledge, though mostly without, and never grew tired of the … entertainment. The Confessionals were semi-well known among the Church, and critics of it. The sessions were supposedly designed so sufferers could unburden their souls, much like with a priest, but the Church of Original Design did something with their Confessions that Catholicism did not: They recorded the sessions and kept them in clearly labeled files. Ostensibly, they did this to "evaluate ticks" and "mine truth from a candidate's face." In reality, it was done because secrets were the world's best currency when shopping for loyalty. While Marina was more or less ignorant of the Confessionals' use, *IT* had seen the truth in the heads of her inner council, and knew how the videos were used in the past, before Marina came into power.

IT clicked Play on the first QuickTime Confession, and watched as a miserable wretch of a woman filled the screen. She had a long face like a horse, her stringy hair falling in a straight curtain around her homely face.

The horsewoman, Catherine Munn, according to the file name, looked at the Confessor with her large, empty, eyes and said, "Most people who meet me think that I have a great life, and I suppose I do, in a way. I have a family and friends. A husband. We don't have children, yet, and I don't want them. My husband does, two at least, and knows I don't. It's affecting our relationship. I won't make a good mother."

The horse shook her head, held her temple, and continued with a sigh, "Parenting is a burden, and I'm *not* a happy person. I've struggled with depression for years. Besides, I'm in love with my ex and have sex with him all the time, even though I have to beg him sometimes. He has a girlfriend and thinks we should stop. It's only a matter of time before my husband and I have kids I don't want, all to keep living a lie I wish would finally end. I'm so miserable, I feel like I'll never be happy again."

Most humans would have probably thought the Confession sad, but *IT* saw the video as pathetic; stupid humans who didn't know how to be happy or use what they had to get what they wanted. The horse woman was one of a billion, feeling the same things that they all did, perhaps in a slightly different shade, not knowing what to do with her stupid, tiny, little feelings.

She wasn't unique. She wasn't original.

She was pathetic, a waste, of no use to *IT* at all.

And as *IT* thought, a smile spread onto Steven's face.

The horse woman might not be of any use, but surely there were plenty of files from people who would be. The Church's Confessions had recorded some of the worst of the worst. Marina told Steven about some of them, people with the blackest baggage: cheaters, criminals, sexual deviants, and predators — people *IT* could worm *ITS* way into, then stay close, nested until needed. *IT* could find people closer, easier to stay connected to. Easier to control.

Everyone wanted power, longed for it even if they didn't realize it, and *IT* was now in a position to give it away. *IT* would find these people yand give them positions in the Church of Original Design.

Then *IT* would no longer need Marina at all.

~

FOURTEEN

Paola Olson

Paola sat in the back of her first-period class, barely staying awake while Mr. White droned on for three million years about world history that no one cared about. Paola often wondered what the people in her class, or her teachers who claimed to know so much, would think if she told them about her experiences on the other world. It would probably be hilarious; no one would believe her, and she'd be in a world of crap.

Sullivan had come to their house and warned them to keep quiet — for their own good. Paola wasn't sure what he meant, but her mother seemed to get it, and told Paola that this was more important than any secret ever. "If you tell anyone, people will come and take us away, forever. We'll never see each other again."

Paola kept the secrets to herself. It was hard, throttling her longing to scream it. It was hard pretending she didn't know something so special, and harder pretending that her dad wasn't dead; having people think he was a jerk who abandoned his family — rather than a hero who gave his life to save them — was torture.

As Mr. White rambled, with half the class pretending to pay attention, Paola felt like someone was staring at her. She turned, surprised to see Harry on her left. She met his eyes, and he quickly looked away, pretending to study Mr. White instead.

She felt a warm flush, followed by butterflies.

Oh my God, is he checking me out?

Harry was one of the cool kids, a skateboarder with a long, blond wall draping his tanned face. He had cute dimples and a killer, confident smile. Paola had spoken to Harry twice so far this school year, both times he seemed bored.

She turned her eyes down to her desk, waiting to look back up, then dared a glance.

Holy crap, he is looking at me!

She looked back down, her heart pounding, fighting the urge to giggle. Paola hated how she laughed when nervous, at least around boys. She wished she could be confident like Brianna Collins, her most popular friend; Brianna had a way of turning any boy into a quivering mass of silly stupid.

Paola sat through class intensely aware of her every movement. She tried to be cool, tried not to look at him, tried not to giggle, tried not to bite her nails, tried to just be *normal*. But it was impossible when the cutest guy in your grade was staring at you.

Why is he looking at me?

She casually brushed her fingers over her face, just to make sure it wasn't a giant, new zit or stray booger that had grabbed his attention. That would make sense. Guys like Harry didn't like drab brunettes like Paola, they liked pretty, blonde cheerleaders with big, perky boobs.

She watched the clock, eager for the bathroom where she could check her face, then find her best friend, Tracy Lin, and tell her the news.

The bell sang. Paola reached beneath her desk, grabbed

her books and stood. She was in such a rush to get out of the class that the moment she stepped from her desk, she dropped her books — right in front of Harry.

No!

She bent down, quickly, eager to grab her books, but bumped her head hard into Harry's on her way.

If Paola could melt she would have.

Instead, she was forced to awkwardly stare as Harry held up a hand, and said, "I got it," then gathered her books, and returned them to her, smiling.

I'm such a dork!

"Thank you," she said, smiling back, then turning her gaze to her shuffling feet.

"You're shy," he said. "That's cute."

Harry was very forward; that made Paola want to run and vomit.

This conversation is NOT happening!

"Thanks," she said.

Thanks? I just thanked him for saying I'm shy and that's cute? I'm so stupid!

"I mean, for the books," Paola said, even though she had already thanked him for that.

I've got to get out of here before I say something worse. I'm stupid and frozen.

Harry spoke before Paola could thaw. "Did you do something different with your hair?" His head was cocked sideways like he was trying to figure it out. He looked Paola up and down. Her flaws felt like they were growing. She crossed her arms over her chest, which *had* seemed bigger this morning, though she couldn't tell if it was monthly bloating or a growth spurt ... *or a supernatural spurt from healing Mom!*

"No," she said, surprised that Harry had noticed anything different about her at all. Before today, she could have come to class bald, and he wouldn't have seen the shine on her head. "I mean, maybe a few weeks ago, I don't remember."

"Looks good on you," he said, smiling like a dream.

"Um, yours, too."

You did NOT just compliment him on his hair! You idiot!

"Thanks," he said. "OK, see ya around, eh?"

"OK," Paola said. She turned and fled, barely keeping herself from a run.

BY THIRD PERIOD, Paola had been asked by five people if she had grown, or changed something about herself. Terri Pantorelli asked if she "got new tits?"

After third period, she waited in the girl's bathroom until the bell rang for class. Paola wanted a few minutes of alone time with the mirror, to see if she could see the same thing that others had.

Paola leaned close, staring at her reflection and searching for change. She thought she looked different, but it was hard to see small changes when you stared at yourself every day. She wasn't sure if she was seeing real changes or just subtle shifts provided by her imagination.

Though Paola *felt* different, she couldn't be sure that she was. She stared with no expression, then lost her frozen face to a smile as she thought of a way to test her hypothesis.

PAOLA SNUCK out of school and caught a bus before lunch. Fortunately, nobody on the bus seemed to notice that she was skipping school as she rode three miles to the nearest hospital.

She had never been to the local hospital, and had no idea where to go once there. She entered through the large doors which read *Emergency* in large, red capitals, then stepped into a giant lobby filled with at least 20 people. Patients were lined at the front counter, checking in.

Paola didn't want to check in, so she took a seat as far from the counter as she could, trying to blend in with a woman and a young boy, around 5. He had a red face and tired eyes, leaning against his mother and staring blankly toward the reception desk.

She wondered what was wrong with him, and if he made a good candidate to experiment with. If she *was* going to age, Paola didn't want to find someone so injured that she risked aging a lot, so a sick person might be perfect, but at the same time she didn't want to risk harming someone else, especially a child.

Paola looked around the waiting room, searching for the right person.

She saw a man who was as yellow as a pepper and a woman who looked nearly green. Everyone else in the waiting room was a varying shade of pale or miserable. There were no clear clues for Paola to follow, no way to know what waiting patients were suffering from, or what her risks might be if she tried to "heal" them.

She felt stupid, and for a short moment wanted to go. Then, after ruling out everyone in the waiting room, Paola felt her mother's determination, dug her heels into her decision, and decided to get up and wander the hallways, maybe find someone who fit the bill better. Several sets of doors led to different parts of the hospital. Paola studied them to determine which she could easily slip through without drawing attention. She wasn't sure how much trouble she could get into sneaking around a hospital, but figured it had to be quite a lot — certainly enough to make her mother furious.

She watched as a pair of women was called through the busiest set of doors, and went to try those.

Her legs were shaky as she made her way toward the doors, feeling like every eye was stuck to her skin, and that at any second a hand would fall on her shoulder — a nurse or doctor demanding to know what she was doing.

As Paola reached the doors a man yelled from behind her, "How much longer do we have to sit here? My boy is hurt, bad!"

From the front desk, "Sir, please sit down, we'll see you as soon as we can."

Paola looked toward the desk and saw the man, but not his boy. She scanned the room until she saw what she hadn't before: in the corner, sitting by himself, a boy of 7 or so, crying, wrapping his leg with a blood-soaked towel.

"This is bullshit," the man said, "I want to speak to someone in charge."

The woman at reception, a large woman who probably didn't take much from anyone, tried telling him to sit, but the man refused. Suddenly, a security guard stepped around the counter and began speaking to him. Paola strained to hear their exchange.

The father continued to yell, and Paola watched the boy, sitting in obvious anguish.

She approached.

He looked up at her, eyes red and still crying.

"Are you hurt badly?" Paola asked, feeling like it was maybe a dumb question, considering the evidence.

The boy nodded, sniffling.

Paola looked back to make sure the kid's dad wasn't looking. He was still arguing, with both the receptionist and the security guard, his voice growing louder. Paola hoped he didn't get himself into trouble.

"Can I see it?" she asked.

The boy nodded, and unwrapped his towel to a horrible break; bone jutted from the front of his leg, right beneath his knee.

Paola winced, feeling his pain twist into her guts as if she had suffered the injury herself.

"Oh, God" she cried out, unable to hide her shock at the boy's horror. She was surprised the kid wasn't screaming his throat raw — his injury reminded her of some of the worst she had seen … over there.

Paola looked back, saw the father still arguing. She didn't have long before someone noticed her, or the dad returned to his seat.

She met the boy's eyes, "Do you want to feel better?" she asked. Paola wasn't sure if it was hope or instinct, but she *knew* she could help him.

The boy flinched as Paola's hands hovered near his gaping wound.

"I'm not going to touch you," she whispered, her palms inches above the white bone bulging through his bloody flesh.

Warmth spread through her body, and her eyes instinctively closed. As a dizziness stirred inside her, Paola felt like a swaying boat rocking back and forth in stormy seas. She fought to stay steady, afraid she would accidentally brush against the boy's injury.

"Hey, what are you doing?" the dad yelled from behind her.

Paola heard him running toward them as she fought her dizziness, refusing to open her eyes or turn around until she felt like she was done healing the boy.

Her heart pounded like a jackhammer as panic filled her like blood.

"What the … ?" the man cried out.

She opened her eyes, turned to see him, frozen and staring wide-eyed at his son.

Paola turned, slowly, her heart in her throat, and looked down to see what the boy's father was startled by.

The bone was gone, and the boy's bright-pink flesh looked like new skin over a healed wound.

Oh, my God, I did it!

"How … how the hell?" the man said, stunned, stammering on his words.

"She fixed it, Daddy!" the boy said, pointing at Paola.

She found her feet, then ran, as if there were bleakers behind her.

~

FIFTEEN

Mary Olson

Mary stared at the tree on her monitor, wondering if it should be burnt orange rather than leafy green. She was adding finishing touches to her latest line of greeting cards — the best of her life, and also the easiest. Her new stuff was admittedly darker, and had been since her return to work, but Mary's clients — mostly museum gift shops and high-end boutiques — had never loved her art more. She referred to this latest batch of drawings, her most abstract by far, as *Screaming Trees*. They were composed of smudges of color, smeared in bursts above rigid trunks. Mary stared at the tree some more; the more she stared, the less she liked green.

She selected the trees' green layer on the Cintiq and began to go over the color in orange. It was immediately better, though now she would have to adjust other layers with light and shadow effects to harmonize the orange. The extra time would be worth it. Mary would always rather take longer and inch closer to perfect than put out something she wasn't in love with.

She was in the middle of erasing stray marks when the phone startled her, buzzing on her desk. She picked up her cell, stomach churning at the number: Paola's school.

"Hello?"

"Mrs. Olson?"

"Yes?" Mary said, dreading whatever was coming.

"This is Mrs. Waddell from Kingswood Country Day. Is Paola home?"

"Um, no, she's at school … isn't she?"

"No," said the voice. "Not since fourth period."

Mary turned to the clock. It was well into seventh, Paola's last class. "And you're just now calling?"

"Sorry, Mrs. Olson, we're short staffed and … "

Mary cut her off, hating excuses. She didn't spend $15,000 a year for short staffed. "Are you saying you don't know where my daughter is?"

"No, which is why I'm calling, Mrs. Olson. Is there a chance somebody else picked her up, or maybe she left early with a friend?"

"How the hell should I know?" Mary said, looking around her living room as if something might point her toward Paola. She leaped from her chair and ran up the stairs, into Paola's room, just to make sure she hadn't come home and gone to bed without telling Mary, as unlikely as that seemed.

Paola wasn't in her room.

Mary's heart pounded faster; her breath became shallow.

Her mind flashed back to the Drury, when Paola had wandered off in the middle of the night and had been infected by The Darkness. She and Desmond had found her at death's door. Paola probably wouldn't have survived without Luca.

What if it's here and has come for her again?

Mary ran her hand over her face, squeezing her cheeks and then her eyes, wondering what she should do. This wasn't like Paola at all. Sure, she tested boundaries, but this was different. Mary couldn't imagine her doing something so drastic without a good reason.

What if something happened to her?

What if she started to age in class, or worse?

Oh, God.

"What's the last class she was in? Did you speak to the teacher? Did you talk to her friends?"

"Her teachers, yes," the woman said, "but not her friends; not yet. We'll get on that right now. Is there someone we should ask specifically?"

Mary tried thinking of Paola's friends, but the girl hadn't made too many since they got here. She listed the few to hit her memory, and apologized for not knowing more, feeling Mrs. Waddell's silent judgment.

"We'll call you back soon," she said. "Meanwhile, you might want to call some friends, or maybe the police."

Mary thanked Mrs. Waddell, then hung up, sitting at the edge of Paola's bed, paralyzed with indecision. She wanted to get in her car, go out, and search for Paola.

But what if she comes home while I'm out?

Shit.

Mary was grateful for their move to Colorado; the girls needed a clean break from their past. But it had yet to feel like home. As she grazed the phone's side with her finger, running it from top to bottom, Mary realized she had no one to call. As she wondered if she could feel more alone, Mary heard the front door open downstairs.

She leaped up from Paola's bed and ran toward the hallway, eager and frightened, praying that Paola was OK.

Mary froze at the top of the stairs, staring down to the front door with her eyes saucer-wide and jaw to the carpet. She dropped her phone. It fell as if in slow motion from her hand, bounced two steps, then spilled through a slat on the banister. It crashed to the floor and shattered to pieces.

Paola stared back at her mom, sobbing. Mary's precious 13-year-old was gone: in her place, a woman she did not know.

~

~

EPILOGUE — **Roman Rosetti**

MANHATTAN, *New York*
1994

ROMAN SAT IN THE DARK, cradling a bottle of Jack Daniel's in one hand, and his service pistol in the other.

The phone was on the bed. He watched it … waiting.

Roman had called and left messages for three of the four other men in his unit — the men who had all shared that *something* in Alaska so many years ago. Whatever they touched had somehow enhanced their lives, all except for him.

The *something* had left a famine inside Roman, a deep ravine of shadow that dragged him down into its horrible depths whenever he was alone, trying to sleep, or live any sort of normal life.

It waited — a forever-present voice in the back of his mind, poisoning his thoughts, and everything he tried to touch or dared to love, filling him with an unending dread that could only be defeated through self-medication, and only for minutes at a time.

The pills and alcohol had finally stopped working. Roman's life now circled the abyss, inching closer to the bottomless pit by the day. Roman could feel the others, the rest of his unit — Renny, Otis, Will, and Norberg — out in the world, living their happy fucking lives and forgetting all about him.

Roman wondered why none had called him, not ever. If he felt them, they must have felt him, too. They must have known his pain, or at least had some idea. Did they still hold grudges, for shooting at the thing which had blessed their lives and cursed his? Did they feel guilty? Or worse, pity, for him?

Is that why they're not calling back?

I should just do it. Screw goodbyes. Not like I owe them shit.

For some reason, Roman couldn't do it, not without letting at least one of his old unit know *why*. He wasn't sure if he wanted to explain himself simply to tell *someone* what he was feeling, or if he wanted the men to feel guilty, as if they were somehow responsible for what had happened to him.

When Roman used logic, rather than the years of bitterness, to think things through, he knew it wasn't their fault that Jenny left him. It wasn't their fault that he couldn't hold a job. It wasn't their fault that his only friend in the world now was the old man behind the counter at the liquor store, a guy named Joe. Fuck if Roman knew his last name.

No, it was that *something's* fault. Whatever it was they found. Or whatever it was that *found them.*

It had changed everything, without rhyme or reason, or the slightest of cares. It had taken what was once a minor, manageable, depression and turned it into something destructive enough for Roman to burn through nine shrinks and God-knew-how-many antidepressants trying to just make it through the day.

The other guys grew stronger, leaner, smarter. They even had a bit of extrasensory perception, allowing them to see things every so often. Like Will always could, even before. The men saw nothing so grand as winning lottery numbers, but the *something* had somehow peppered their lives into something better. Yet, whatever they found in the cave hadn't improved Roman; it ruined him instead. He also sometimes saw glimpses of the future, but only the bad stuff, the *worst* stuff. Stuff no one should see: murders, rapes, bombings, and the rest of the horrors that haunted the blackness behind his drawn lids.

His visions might have served as a gift to mankind, if Roman were able to identify, find, and stop such atrocities from happening before they did. But alas, the visions were a curse, because he was never given a clear enough picture to stop anything.

Roman was always too late, and the visions constantly grew worse.

He *had* to tell someone else from his unit, to let them know that he did try to live with it, and had tried to help. He just wasn't strong enough.

Roman had called all the men except one. Will Bishop was left.

He took a swig of Jack, then set the bottle on the nightstand beside the dim, lighthouse lamp, which cast the room in the shade's amber glow.

He dialed the number from memory, even though he'd not called Will in a long time, if ever.

The phone rang five times.

No answering machine.

Fuck it. I can't wait any longer.

Roman decided to hang up and silence his life, before he again chickened out and woke for another miserable day in the morning.

As he went to hang up the phone, he heard a voice on the other end.

"Hello?" Will said, his voice a million miles off, and yet somehow *right there.*

Tears streamed Roman's cheeks at the sound of his old friend.

"Will?" he said, barely able to bury emotion as it splintered out from his broken voice.

"Roman?"

"Yeah, buddy, long time no see," Roman said, trying to work his way from casual to, "I'm going to kill myself and this is why." He opened with small talk, asking how Will was, what he was up to. Seems Will had finally found someone, which was good. Even though Roman wasn't keen on queers, he liked Will, and figured he had no reason to give a shit what two people did under their own comforter.

Roman listened to Will for a while, trying to find the right opening to bring up what he was meaning to do. But Will wouldn't shut up. He kept rambling. First about his boyfriend, then about the book store they owned, and then on and on about current events. It was almost as if Will wanted to talk about anything but Roman.

What the hell, bro?

Roman tried to interrupt, to bring the subject around to the bad times he'd been having, and his ultimate decision.

Will stopped him. "I know what you're thinking of doing."

"What?" Roman said, surprised, even though he probably shouldn't have been. If any of them could see into his thoughts, it would be Will, who had psychic abilities *before* they found the thing in Alaska.

"Listen, Roman, I don't know what to say that will make things better. I can feel your pain. I was about to call you, in fact, I felt your pain so intensely that I knew I had to call, but then you called me. You can't do it, man. You can't kill yourself."

Roman tried to respond, but instead cried a pathetic-sounding mewl. He felt like a pussy, shaking his head and wanting to say sorry for crying. He couldn't make words, though.

"It's OK," Will said, his voice soft, comforting, reassuring, like a father, even though they were close in age. "But you're going to feel better. Trust me."

"What do you mean?" Roman asked, "Did you see something in my future?"

Will paused, maybe considering his next words carefully in case Roman could smell a line of bullshit delivered. "I didn't see anything, specifically," he said. "But I *feel* it. I feel things will change for you. Soon."

"I wish I could believe you," Roman said, squeezing his hand around the gun, bringing it up to his temple.

I should do it right now — let him hear me shoot my brains out. Let him live with that! See how happy his life is after that!

Instead, Roman asked something he didn't know was inside him, though it bubbled to the surface so fast it had to be there all along.

"Do you ever think about going back?"

"Back where?" Will asked, though Roman figured he was playing dumb.

"To Alaska, to find that thing."

"No," Will said. "I think it was good that we *couldn't* find it again, *and* that we didn't report it."

"Why?"

"I think you know why. We saw something bad inside it, both of us, buddy, something we couldn't tell anyone about. Hell, you *did* shoot at it, and it knocked us clear the hell outta that cave, right?"

Roman laughed, forgetting how good it felt to have lightness inside, even if only for the length of a cough.

Will laughed, too. "Shit, you were crazy as hell back then, man. Remember that time you banged that lieutenant's wife, then sent him the Polaroids just to rub it in his face? You were an Everest of balls."

Roman kept laughing, suddenly feeling stupid for holding the gun.

Will said, "It feels good talking to you, buddy."

"You too, Will."

They talked into the wee hours, until laughs turned to yawns and Roman's bottle was empty. He finally let Will go, and after he hung up, stared at the phone, and his gun, which had found its way to the nightstand.

Roman decided not to kill himself.

He had a better plan. He wasn't sure how he could do it, and it would likely take a while, but Roman knew with a sudden and unflappable certainty: He had to go back to Alaska.

He had to find the something that had ruined his life.

TO BE CONTINUED...

Episode 21

(THIRD EPISODE OF SEASON FOUR)

"Victims"

Prologue

MARINA HARMON

October 19, **2011**
   The J.L. Harmon estate

MARINA STARED at the doorknob to her father's bedroom, trying to summon enough energy to reach out, grab it, and twist.

Just go inside, shut off the camera and end this nonsense!

He died on Oct. 15, just as he'd predicted years before. A video camera had been stationed in his room the past four days, recording and broadcasting live on the web, where his followers and naysayers alike waited to see if his prophecy would come true.

Marina's father had sworn he would rise again, two days after his death, with a message from the Great All Seeing. While he may have predicted his death years in advance, which she had to admit was an eerie coincidence, Marina did not think he was some prophet who would rise from the dead. He was only a man, who had manufactured a religion that had fooled too many people … Marina included.

And now she was left with his billion-dollar empire, in

charge of leading a religion for which she had no faith. It was as if her father, who knew of her doubts, had claimed the last laugh — he'd saddle her with his legacy, forcing her to fake her way through the rest of her life. He probably figured that even if she didn't give a damn about his legacy, she was too smart to walk away from millions of people willing to hand over their money, tax-free, and in perpetuity.

As she stood at the door, trying to summon the courage to enter his room and kill the charade once and for all, her rage began to boil.

I don't need his money. I ought to go in there and turn to the camera and scream the truth. "My father fooled you all. You've been duped. All of you. Victims of fraud."

She could take his estate and set up a fund, pay off anyone who wanted their money back, until his well went dry. Marina didn't care, she just wanted to finally be finished — done being the daughter of J.L. Harmon. She didn't want to live her life in the spotlight — her every move, her every romance, her every failure serving as fodder for the press and critics of the Church.

He's gone, and now I'm finally free.

She reached out for the doorknob when Dr. Phillips suddenly appeared at the end of the hall.

"Marina," he said, "what are you doing?"

"I'm going to check on Dad. See if he's back yet."

"We have monitors on him," said her father's longtime personal doctor, "And staff downstairs monitoring 24/7."

He stared at her like a vulture afraid his prized, golden goose was getting eyed by an eagle. The old man wore dark circles that only made his brown eyes look beadier, and *hungrier*. She couldn't wait to close the Church, fire the "good doc" and every one of the sycophants who had leeched off her father for years.

Marina knew she'd be vilified for her plans after her father was finally declared dead, once and for all. The worst part was that nobody would ever recognize her actions as kind, they would see her as a bitter daughter, never understanding the countless sacrifices she had made when returning to California, helping her father when he first fell sick five years ago. Marina could have done anything with her life. She had dreams of using her years of school to manage an ad firm, but shelved those dreams to help her father further his own.

But nobody would ever know.

Hell, he didn't even realize my sacrifices.

Marina met the doctor's eyes. "I can't go in and see my own father?"

He stammered, not used to anybody, let alone Marina, turning his questions back on him. She waited, watching him stew in between the desire to snap at her and the caution … just in case her father did return. Father would not take kindly to reports of Dr. Phillips being abusive to his daughter.

She wondered if he truly believed her dad was coming back. Sure, the others on his payroll probably did, but Dr. Phillips was a man of science, instrumental in many of Father's scientific and technological breakthroughs with The Current, but not one given to talk of miracles and prophecies.

"Yes, you may see your father," he said, as if granting permission. Marina didn't bother to remind him that she didn't need it.

No, there'll be a time to get forceful, and probably in five minutes or so. But right now, I need to get through this as argument free as I can.

She turned from the doctor, and her hand finally found the doorknob. She turned it, then stepped inside. The doctor tried to follow, but Marina stopped in the doorway, blocking his entrance, met his eyes, and said, "Yes?"

He looked back and forth nervously, realizing he'd overstepped his bounds.

Marina waited for him to leave.

With the doctor gone, she entered her father's bedroom,

closed the door, and softly turned the lock to keep the man from her intentions.

Father's bedroom seemed about as cold as it could get without refrigeration. The room was all white — a pristine ode to cleanliness, order, and minimalism, and took the entire third floor. The room had no furniture, except for the California King and the large chair beside it.

A sprawling window ran along the western wall, opening to the sea, a cliff below.

Marina glanced at the tripod-mounted camera to her left as she entered his room, wanting to turn off the video feed and cut prying eyes from her father's deathbed. But first, Marina wanted to spend a few minutes at his side, before his minions stormed the room and tried yanking her away. Once she set the wheels in motion there was no going back from her plan. They'd probably call the police, not that she thought she'd be breaking any actual laws by killing a broadcast and giving her father's death a shred of dignity; if it wasn't too late. But who knew what her father's men were capable of?

She sat in the chair to his right, grateful that her back was to the camera. She didn't want the vultures seeing her tears as she looked at her father. Other than his skin's ashen appearance, he looked sleeping more than dead. She reached out and touched his hand as it rested at his side, above the white comforter.

His skin was icy to the touch, another indication giving truth to the lie that he was only sleeping.

As Marina stared at his face, she felt her anger dissipate, replaced with regret — regret for things she'd never have the chance to tell him. Not just the things she was angry about regarding the Church, but also kind things: thanking him for being a loving father despite his busy schedule; thanking him for rising to the job when her mother died on her 5th birthday; and thanking him for not forcing his beliefs upon her and letting her choose her faith, even if he did pull on her guilt strings to get her to help him at the end. There were so many horror stories of powerful fathers who abused their children through either actions or neglect; her father may have been a confused man, blinded by warped beliefs, but he was also a loving dad who allowed Marina to fumble and find her way.

He'd been better in recent months, thanks to the machine, which had cured the illness that left him perpetually tired. She never thought he would actually die on Oct. 15. Had she truly believed the prophecy, Marina would've said all the things she'd meant to — would never have held back. Even now, as he lay dead, she didn't believe the prophecy. If anything, Marina figured one of two things happened — either faith that he would die killed him, a self-fulfilling prophecy, or he killed himself to turn prophecy true. Perhaps the "good doctor" had even helped, a matter that Marina would be looking into soon enough.

Either way, her father was gone, and he would never hear the words she longed to say.

Marina squeezed his hand and whispered so the cameras wouldn't hear her, "Thank you, Daddy."

His fingers tightened around hers.

Marina jumped up from the chair, startled, staring down at her father's inert fingers. She looked at his hand, motionless on the bed, thinking for sure she must have imagined his grip tightening around her fingers. She told herself that it had to be some sort of muscle spasm. She wasn't sure how long people still moved after they passed away, but four days seemed *unlikely*.

As Marina stared at her father, leaning closer, searching for any sign of movement at all, she felt suddenly foolish, like everyone watching the feed's live stream was seeing her and laughing. She imagined the Internet haters making mash-ups of her jumping back, inserting all sorts of stupid stuff into the video to make her, and her family, look even crazier than their public image already suggested.

She turned to the camera, and locked her gaze, deciding once and for all that she'd had enough. It was time to pull the plug.

Marina walked toward the camera and leaned in, looking for the button to stop the recording. Then she heard a voice behind her: her father.

"Marina?" he said, his voice raspy, dry.

No, it can't be.

She turned, slowly, certain she was imagining her father's voice as sure as she'd imagined him squeezing her hand.

But she wasn't.

His eyes were open, and he was staring right at Marina, repeating her name.

"Daddy?" she asked, voice quivering as her heart found new ways to hammer.

〜

SIXTEEN

Dan Konig

Chicago, Illinois
   September 2013

DAN EYED the clock at the front of the Shoe Emporium thinking that it wasn't possible for time to move slower. He had two hours left on his shift, then life would change forever.

Tonight, Steph would have a C-Section, and their daughter would be brought into the world. Steph had wanted to have their baby the "old-fashioned way" — though not so traditional that she went without medicine — but the doctor convinced her that the C-section was the way to go because of prior complications. This was their third attempt to have a child, and the furthest Steph had made it — eight months and two weeks.

His stomach churned in anticipation and dread.

They were hours from change that would last forever. He tried telling himself he was ready, though he had no idea how true that was.

When they first started trying, five years earlier, Dan had a better job, drawing decent scratch at a construction firm. But two years back, the housing market took another dive, and Dan was suddenly unemployed, having to take whatever job he could get — an assistant manager gig at Shoe Emporium for $11.40 an hour. Not exactly the stable foundation to start a family. But when Steph got pregnant, accidentally even though she was on the pill, what could he do? He wasn't about to tell her to abort their child.

They'd figure a way.

Just like they'd always done before. Just like his own dad had done.

Two months ago, when Dan finally realized that Steph had an excellent chance of going full term, he admitted to his father that he was scared shitless.

"I'm not making nearly enough, insurance will kill us, and I don't know what we're gonna do. I'm not ready."

His father, not usually one for warmth or reflection, surprised him with advice. "If we all waited until we were 'ready,' nobody'd ever have kids. That fear will make you a good father. You're worried, and that means you care; you'll do whatever you need to."

Tears welled in his eyes as Dan thought back on their exchange.

"Jesus, Dan, you turning pussy on me," Gary said, returning from lunch.

"Just thinking about tonight."

"Yeah, I'd be crying, too, man," Gary joked. "Your life is *over*! That's why I'm never gonna knock any of my chicks up."

"No, you're never gonna knock any chicks up because you can't get laid," Dan said, laughing.

Gary looked around, "Damn, it's dead in here. What's up with that?"

"I dunno," Dan said. They made commission on shoes sold, down time was never good for employees. "I let Brianna go home early. So it's you and me until Jeff comes in at 5."

"Fucking Jeff," Gary said. "You should hear what he did last night. He was closing and … "

A woman entered the store, pushing a stroller. Dan made the sign to "cut the bad language, there's a customer in the store."

Gary went into the back to clock in.

Dan smiled at the young mother, a cute brunette who looked a bit like Steph. She was pushing a little girl, around 2. "Hi, can I help you?"

"Hi, do you have girl toddler sneakers, preferably in Velcro? Maybe with Dora or something cute?"

The little girl looked up to Dan, big, blue eyes, and an adorable smile. Looking at her, and how cute she was, made him that much happier about his approaching fatherhood.

The little girl said, "Dora?"

"No, I'm sorry, we don't have Dora," he said, not wanting to break her heart. "But we do have some Disney Princess shoes."

Dan looked at the mom and said, "Let me show you," as he walked around the counter and headed towards the right wall of the store.

Suddenly, an impossible sound thundered over the horrible dance music the store played on a loop — gunshots.

For a moment, Dan thought he must've imagined the sound, or that maybe it was something else, like a car backfiring or maybe someone messing with the mall's public address system.

Then a second sound ripped that notion away: many, many screams.

Dan looked out the glass storefront, across the way to the food court at hundreds of people running in every direction.

He saw the shooter: a man dressed like a cop.

"Oh, my God!" the mom said, eyes wide and darting back and forth, searching for somewhere to run.

Gary came running from the back of the store, saying, "What the fuck?"

His cursing mattered not at all.

Dan's heartbeat sped up as he grabbed his cell and called 911.

The dispatcher came on, asking for his emergency.

"I'm at Middletown Mall, and there's a man shooting people!"

The dispatcher asked for details as shoppers raced toward the shoe store.

"Shit, he's coming!" Dan said, putting the phone in his pocket as he saw the man walking through the mall like he was strolling the park, raising his rifle, and shooting in semi-automatic bursts as if playing *Grand Theft Auto*.

Don't come here, don't come here.

Dan watched in horror as a group of young women raced toward the store as if Dan was handing out bulletproof jackets. The gunman slaughtered all three, killing them yards from the entrance.

The little girl in the stroller screamed, as the mom yanked her from the seat and ran toward the stock room.

"Yeah, come back here," Gary said, ushering the woman back as if it was his idea to give her and her child sanctuary.

Dan was frozen in place, watching, unable to believe what he was seeing. The gunman was looking around as if searching for his next target. Dan stayed there, half hidden behind a display of sports jackets, not daring to move and attract the man's attention.

If I stay here, maybe I'll blend in, and he'll look for someone else.

The gunman looked straight at the shoe store's window, not even 90 yards away, staring straight at Dan.

Shit, shit, shit.

More gunshots — a cop on the other end of the food court, taking shots at the attacker.

The gunman turned around to fire at the cop, Dan seized the moment to race into the back of the store.

Dan entered the storage room, slammed the door behind him, and locked it.

He called out, "Gary?"

"Back here!" Gary said from somewhere in the back of the stock room.

Dan couldn't see him beyond the 20 rows of tall shelving. He was about to call out and ask where they were when gunshots ripped through the door behind him.

The girl and mother screamed. Dan spun on his foot, nearly slipped, then raced along the aisles, ducking into one just as the door burst open.

Dan froze in his spot, near the front of the aisle where he would be easily spotted if the gunman turned right and started walking.

Shit.

Dan's heart was racing, so loud he was certain it must've been echoing throughout the otherwise quiet stock room.

The room was dimly lit, but offered few hiding spots and no back door. The only way they could avoid the gunman was to stay hidden on the other side of the shelving long enough to sneak back to the front of the store, or until the gunman gave up looking for them.

In other words, shit was not looking good.

Dan heard the man's footsteps, boots, coming towards him.

Fuck!

Dan considered running to the end of the aisle, where he could turn down another one, or hide at the end and stay out of the gunman's line of sight. The end of the aisle was 40 feet off, and may as well have been a mile. If Dan ran, he would surrender his location.

So, he stayed still as the man continued toward him.

Turn down another aisle. Turn down another aisle.

The man kept coming.

He fired his gun, six quick shots.

In the back of the room, the little girl screamed. It was muffled, probably under the mother's hand, but loud enough to broadcast location.

The gunman turned down the aisle beside Dan's and started running toward the back of the store.

Dan froze, not sure what to do. He could probably make it back out into the front of the store and get away. But at the same time, he couldn't just leave Gary and the mother and little girl back there to die.

But what the hell can I do? I don't have a gun!

Dan heard running up one of the other aisles, and the little girl screaming. They may as well have painted a target on their backs.

Dan heard the gunman turn and start back up the aisle, looking to head them off.

He had to do something.

He looked at his hands, then at the tall shelf in front of him and ran at it, hands out, hoping he could send it toppling onto the gunman.

Dan heard the mom and girl run from the stock room, and smiled. He saved them. He couldn't believe it.

The shelving had tumbled, taking the next two rows with it. Dan heard the man scream as he was buried under shelving. He wasn't sure where Gary was, but Dan didn't care quite as much about his safety as the woman and her child. Gary could handle himself.

He ran, eager to join the woman and her kid, and run as far as they could from the chaos until more cops showed.

Dan reached the doorway and felt an explosion of pain in his back as the gunman fired several rounds into his flesh.

Dan went down in an instant, face down, unable to turn and see the gunman shaking the shelving loose and stepping toward him.

Dan heard the boots approaching, and begged God to spare him so he could see his little girl born.

Please, God, don't …

God didn't answer his prayer, though.

The gunman then did his best to make sure Dan could complain to God personally, and shot him dead.

~

SEVENTEEN

Mary Olson

Mary lowered her foot on the Volvo's gas pedal, increasing her speed to exactly as fast as she dared without getting stopped. The trip should have taken 15 hours, but she was hoping to make it in fewer.

Mary was exhausted. They would've booked a flight, but she would've been hard pressed to pass Paola off as a child when she looked to be in her mid-20s. No way she could've gotten on a flight without ID. So, they drove through the night and into the next day, eager to hit California and get help from the one person who might be able to help them — Boricio.

Paola slept in the passenger seat, looking so little like her 13-year-old daughter that Mary couldn't stop crying. Her little girl was gone. In fact, Paola was wearing Mary's favorite blue dress and black shoes. Mary didn't expect to be sharing clothes with her daughter for at least another three years.

But just like that, her little girl was gone, and Paola's childhood was snuffed to nothing.

At first, Mary didn't know what to do after Paola had come home and told her what happened at the hospital. It wasn't as if she could call the doctor and say, "Hey, my daughter just aged 10 or more years after magically healing some kid."

While Mary wasn't a cynical person, usually, she was just suspicious enough of the government not to go waving a red flag and alert them to supernatural changes in her daughter. She could picture Paola spending years in a lab, probably on this world's version of Black Island.

No way in hell Mary was going to let that happen.

She had cried for most of the night after Paola fell asleep, scared and praying her daughter wouldn't age another day in fewer than 24 hours. Mary told her to sleep in bed beside her, so she could keep an eye on her, not that Mary had any clue what in the hell she would do if the poor thing started aging in front of her. It wasn't like she would be able to wake her and stop it.

But it was far better than the alternative — going to sleep and risking the possibility that Mary would wake in the morning to see a woman her age, or older, laying beside her. If that happened, Mary would lose her mind. She was barely able to maintain her scant sanity as it was, trying her best to act like everything was OK ever since their return from the other (dead) world, if only for Paola's sake.

This sudden, unexpected horror made everything worse. Mary tried not to let her fear or tears show; Paola was already scared. No reason to decay the girl's already fragile state. Mary said she'd make some calls. She'd call Sullivan, maybe try to find Luca, or something, to see what they should do.

Paola suggested they call Boricio. "He'll know what to do."

Mary laughed at first, but as she watched Paola sleeping beside her and considered her scant options, Boricio started making sense.

So, with Paola snoring in her bed, Mary crept back downstairs and called him for advice.

"Don't you dare take her to a doctor, or those pill-pushing

butchers'll throw her in a lab quicker than you can flush your civil rights down the shitter," Boricio said. "And don't tell Sullivan either. Least not yet."

"Then what the hell do I do?" she had asked. "I'm scared."

Boricio, as usual, was unflappable, telling Mary to relax, just bring Paola there; they'd "figure shit out."

Mary was never the type to lean on a man for support. She never asked, nor expected, much from Ryan, especially during their separation. The closest she had ever come to needing someone's help, male or female, was Desmond, but when she needed him most, even he was unable to save her or Paola from the freaks at The Prophet's compound. She was murdered, then saved only because Luca and Boricio intervened and saved them.

So calling Boricio, a murdering psychopath who had made Mary's skin crawl from the moment she met him, was difficult. But he'd proven himself in the heat of battle. And besides, Luca had also fixed something inside him, changing Boricio, changing him into something that sort of resembled an *almost* nice guy; a nice guy who seemed to care deeply about her daughter.

Mary had called Boricio a few months back when the cops could do nothing about the sexual predator who had been creeping on Paola. Boricio was *pissed*, practically begging Mary to let him at the fucker.

Mary was shocked by how protective Boricio had been of her baby girl. It was touching, a feeling she never thought she'd associate with a man like him. She had to beg Boricio not to do anything. She wanted to handle things the "right way," without any risk of getting him in trouble. Mary was glad that she told Boricio to stay out of it, because a week or so later, the pervert was murdered. The cops had come to her house, asking questions. Fortunately, she had an alibi.

She asked Boricio about it that night, right after the cops

left, wondering out loud if he had come to Colorado and paid the man a visit.

"You didn't even tell me his name. How would I have done that? If I had," Boricio laughed, "I sure as hell wouldn't bury my pride. I'd declare it to the cops, say yes siree, it was me with a yee-haw, now where do I go to collect my medal and vanilla milkshake?"

Mary laughed, though a small part of her wondered if Boricio was lying. "Are you sure?" she asked. "I won't tell anyone if you *did* do something. Hell, I won't tell Rose, *will* buy you a milkshake, and *might* give you a medal."

"I had nothing to do with it, Mary, I swear," Boricio said. "But from what you said about the guy, it sounds like he probably made himself a thicket of enemies. You said he did time in prison? You know guys in prison don't like kiddy diddlers, right? They probably put a hit on him or something the minute he was cut from the bars; what I would'a done."

It was because of that honesty and dedication to her and Paola that Mary had called Boricio rather than Sullivan. While Sullivan had the scientists at Black Island at his disposal, Mary couldn't be certain they wouldn't want to shove Paola in some cell and study her for the next 20 years.

So, she went with her gut, which Mary always trusted more than logic, and knew Boricio was the right man to confide in. She wasn't sure if he could actually help, but simply speaking to him, someone with the confidence of 10 men, if not 10 times that, made her feel immediately better.

Boricio invited them to "hurry their asses," and "get the fuck out to 'Fornia,'" since they were staying an extra few days. Mary was sure seeing Boricio would help Paola, and maybe, she hoped, he could help her find Luca.

They hadn't heard from the boy since before their return. Mary wasn't even sure he'd made it back, or what he would look like if he did since he was an old man the last time she'd seen him and could even be dead by now two years after that.

She'd asked Sullivan about Luca, but he said he couldn't tell her anything — state secrets and all that.

But if Luca *had* made it back, perhaps he could heal Paola again, or at least help her manage whatever it was she was doing, since they seemed to suffer from a similar affliction.

Mary looked at her speedometer, saw she was going 15 over the speed limit and lightened her pace, checking the rearview to make sure no cops were flashing lights behind her.

She was good. She looked over at Paola, eyes moving fast beneath her lids. Mary wondered if she still dreamed the dreams of children, or if her daughter was now consigned to the nightmares that came once childhood fled without looking back.

~

EIGHTEEN

Boricio Wolfe

"Well, don't you look like Colorado's been your sugar daddy!" Boricio said, whistling as he looked Mary over, head to toe.

He stepped back from the hotel room door. Mary glanced over to Rose, then back at Boricio. "You have no manners, Boricio Wolfe. Your girlfriend is standing right there!"

Boricio turned to Rose, winked, then looked back at Mary. "That she is, and thanks for reminding me, not that I needed the memo, but it's not like you can ever be told the sun is shining too many times. And you don't have to worry about Rose seeing me admiring another good-looking woman — she knows I'm not blind and is damned appreciative I'm not. My eyes work well enough to know when my lady's in need of a smile."

Mary and Rose laughed together, then Paola, who shouldn't have looked like a woman at all but certainly did, stepped through the doorway and smiled at Boricio.

"Well, Paola Olson!" Boricio cried out, unable to hide his stupid grin. "That *can't* really be you!"

Paola stepped inside their room behind her mom, tentative.

Boricio yelled, "None of that timid shit, you come over here and give Boricio a hug!"

Paola smiled, almost as if she couldn't help it, then eased by her mom — standing like a statue in the way — and fell into Boricio's welcome.

"Well, grins and tits, Sister, how in the long hallways of hell are you doing?"

"You mean besides getting a full scholarship to the Luca School of Premature Aging?" Paola tried to smile but couldn't quite make it. "I guess I'm fine."

"Aw, that ain't nothing." Boricio waved his hand. "We've seen crap that didn't make a dingle berry of sense and escaped odds smaller than the drip off a dick tip. This is shit to be flushed, Sister, Boricio gives you his scout's honor your little *Freaky Friday's* just temporary."

Boricio winked. Mary took a turn smiling like she couldn't help it. Paola smiled wider. Rose looked at the three of them curiously, like someone only partly in on the joke.

Boricio had told Rose everything about what had happened on the other world, except for all the stuff about him being a serial killer, and of course the miscellany and whatnot that went with it. He held nothing for later, except for the dirtiest details she never needed to hear. There was a part of Boricio that wanted to say it out loud since keeping anything from Rose was like crushing a flower in his pocket. But there were some things a good woman wouldn't understand, or be too open-minded about, and murder was one, if not the biggest.

Fortunately, Rose *was* open minded about all the rest, and willing to believe in a way that wasn't quite natural. Boricio loved his Morning Rose, and didn't for one curly cock-hair of a minute think he could live beside someone for the rest of his life, however long that might turn out to be, without being straight as a level about all the beer-battered bullshit that had gone down on some other fuck of an implausible world. He was grateful for her ear, even though at first she thought he was fucking with her. But Boricio was convincing, even when speaking about aliens and magical boys who could jump in your head n' fix you up. Rose might have kept on thinking he was yanking her chain like he yanked on her nozzles, but then they drove to North Carolina and met Mary and Paola, the Rory and Lorelei of his little adventure, and stayed with them for a long week of impossible stories. Every one of 'em matched, down to the dirtiest details that went missing from the yarns. Rose moved from incredulous to awestruck.

"It's so good to see you," Rose said as she hugged Mary, then Paola, before leading them both toward the sofa and grabbing a pair of thousand-dollar water bottles from the mini-fridge. They all got to talking straight off, and it wasn't too long before Rose got to doing what Boricio worried she would, but had given a goddamn and a half to hoping she wouldn't.

"I think I have a solution for you guys," she said, without any preamble and holding too much promise in her voice. "This might sound a bit weird, in fact I'm sure it will, and I wouldn't believe it if you told me and I hadn't seen … or done it for myself. But after all you guys have been through … over there … you might have an easier time accepting the impossible."

"Rose," Boricio said, cutting her off, and hoping to steer her toward a topic that didn't include hoodoo voodoo Hollywood juju. "Luca's our closest thing to a sure thing, without needing 1.21 gigawatts of whatthefuck."

Rose spun from the girls to Boricio and gave him the only look in existence that could zip him, a look no one else in the world could ever even try. The look shut Boricio up, put him in his place, and made him *want* her *right fucking now*.

"Okay, Sweetie," he said.

Mary laughed, and was joined by Paola. Mary made a sound like a whip cracking, and so did her daughter.

Boricio said, "Yeah, laugh it up, Ladies! I'll have you know, it ain't about being whipped, it's about showing respect," then he left the living room with a series of grumbling mumbles and sat over by the mini-bar, plopping both feet up on the countertop, leaning back in his seat while Rose finished her pitch.

"It isn't official yet, but it looks like I'll be doing some business with these guys named the Maris Brothers, up-and-coming directors who are really big in The Church of Original Design … they'll be making *The Billfold*."

Mary and Paola shifted in their seats, uncomfortable like they should be.

"I know, I know" Rose said, responding to their dubious looks. "I thought the same thing, and yeah, I know, it sounds like I'm drinking the Kool-Aid. And you can totally think that, but I really want you to at least hear me out, I think you should. I might have just the solution for Paola, and that is why you drove all night to get here, right, for help?"

Paola said nothing.

Hesitantly, Mary said, "Go on."

"The Church believes in something called 'The Current;' they think it's a force between mind and body. They have this machine that's supposed to repair your cells, or something, and well, I went inside the machine, it's called The Capacitor, and there were all these blue sparks and things while I was in it. Then it stopped doing whatever it was doing, I got out and my migraines were gone."

"Power of the mind," Boricio said, "it's a beautiful thing."

Rose ignored him. "I've been having these really awful panic attacks. And now they're gone, too."

"You are what you decide to be," Boricio muttered, leaning toward the mini-fridge to grab himself another thousand-dollar bottle. "Hell, The Church ain't even original, they stole that 'force' shit from *Star Wars!*"

Rose rolled her eyes, and Boricio winked.

"What was it like?" Paola asked.

"It was a metal chamber, long like a bullet, with a tiny window at the top. The inside was nice, really plushy and soft."

"Like a coffin," Boricio offered.

"No," Paola said. "I mean, what did it *feel like* … when it worked."

"Oh," Rose paused in thought, then after a moment said, "It was dark, until these blue lights started sparking from my body. It felt like there were a thousand bulbs lighting inside me, all at once. Then that thousand lit into something more like a million, and the machine stopped. The doors opened, and my headaches were gone. I've felt amazing since. Better than ever. I feel like I can see better, hear better, taste better, and best of all, *really* start to understand the world around me." Almost hesitantly, she added, "I feel like my eyes have been opened."

"I dunno," Mary said, again shifting in her seat, this time ever so slightly away from Rose. "I've kinda had my fill with cults what with the compound and stuff."

Before Rose could defend the 10-ton mountain of batshit crazy that was The Church of Original Design, Boricio said, "Ha, Rose, you'd tell the Maris Brothers, Marina Harmon, and every other citizen of Crazy Town to fuck off, too, if you had ever spent any time at the Ole Ponderosa with Brother Rei and his crazy 'Prophet.' Mary's right, The Church *is* a cult, and the problem with cults — every single goddamned one of them — is that they're all confusing madness with mission. The Church, like Brother Rei, is juggling juju with nuts."

"Boricio!" Rose said, sharp enough to shut him up and get him wondering when it was bedtime.

With Boricio's pie hole shut, Rose turned back to Mary.

"I understand how you feel," she said. "Totally. And I felt the same way. I'm not asking you to do anything you don't want to do, or that would in any way make you uncomfortable. But you did ask for help, and I truly believe this might be what you need, or that at the least it's worth looking into."

Mary's eyes softened.

Rose continued, "Even though they use the word 'church', Original Design isn't a religion, at least they don't seem to be. I wouldn't say they were a cult, either. It's more like a self-help group, with science behind them. And yeah, of course, I can hear the words as I say them and am plenty skeptical about some, maybe even most, of it, but I've been in the machine and the machine works."

Boricio said, "1.21 gigawatts," so low only he could hear it.

Mary looked at Rose, her face painting many pictures at once; she clearly appreciated Rose, her suggestions, and her desire to help, but had been through too much horrible shit to take a crap and not look for the corn inside it, and you'd have to be blind, deaf, and drool-bucket stupid to not see that The Church was leaking crap at the seams, magic machine or no.

Mary stared for what was likely a minute, though to Boricio — waiting for alone time with Rose — it felt like a long, fucking hour.

Finally, she spoke. "I just can't, Rose. Thank you, really, so much. But I have to listen to instinct, and mine's saying no."

Rose opened her mouth to respond, but Paola cut her off.

"I want to try it."

Mary and Rose turned to Paola, both silent.

"I'm too young to look this old," she said. "There are too many things I've never done: fallen in love, sang a song and posted it to YouTube, tried food I can't even pronounce … "

"I can help you with that last one," Boricio offered.

Her face pained, Mary turned to Boricio, desperate. "What do you think?" She swallowed then added, "I trust you."

And there it was, three women staring at him, all three

trusting Boricio with eyes and expressions alike, odd as if his ball sack had started brewing gold bullion. Boricio wanted to say *fuck that shit,* and pipe bomb the entire "Church" to the old, dead world where it likely belonged, but even more than his anger at the machine, and feelings that it might be pulling his Morning Rose in for a ride, he wanted to please her, and help the Olson Twins. Besides, as low as odds might be, Boricio had been wrong before, and *could* be wrong again. This might be one of those rare times; he was a world from convinced that the machine worked, but couldn't argue with Rose's improvement. Still, he saw explanations as easy: Mind over matter could accomplish near everything; Boricio knew that like he knew this his devil's smile could push a parishioner's panties to her ankles.

He grinned. "Why not give it a shot? At worst, nothing happens and we laugh while we piss on 'The Church.' You ladies go, take care of whatever you need to. In the meantime I'll start snooping, see if I can't locate Luca the Boy Wonder."

~

NINETEEN

Steven Warner

The J.L. Harmon Estate
   September 2013

STEVEN SAT on the floor of the meditation room, naked, feeling the early-morning sun kissing his skin. One-way glass ran the length of the wall, opening out to the ocean.

As *IT* grew more comfortable in *ITS* human skin — no easy feat considering *ITS* contempt for the species — *IT* felt the connection thinning with the rest of *ITSELF*, The Darkness, spread among the people *IT* had infected.

IT had become greedy, such a human weakness, and tried spreading too quickly. In doing so *IT* risked losing *ITS* connection and control of the humans who hosted *IT*.

IT blamed *ITSELF*.

IT hadn't expected the human hosts to resist, let alone be aware of, The Darkness inside them. *IT* had chosen them because they were weak, or filled with hate and easy to infiltrate. *IT* hadn't realized that for some people, weakness and hate were temporary states. Once they started stitching their lives back together, some part of their brain, a part even they weren't aware of, began fighting back. However, most humans were ill equipped for such mental and psychic warfare. They didn't know what was inside them, or what was "wrong" with them, so their instincts to fight back when no enemy could be seen were turned into violent urges, manifesting toward others, and in some cases, themselves.

Sixteen had snapped so far, most killing others before turning their confused fury out on themselves. One had drawn way too much attention, killing more than 80 people in a massacre which was all over television. So many acts of violence in such a short amount of time benefited nobody and only weakened *ITS* overall power.

Fortunately for *IT*, The Darkness died with the hosts, forever undiscovered. But now, one of *ITS* hosts had been captured, still alive, and brought to Black Island, which meant that *ITS* enemies knew *IT* was here, robbing IT of *ITS* advantage of working in the dark. Now IT would have to speed up *ITS* search for the vials.

To that end, *IT* had managed to find a host inside Black Island Research Facility who might soon give *IT* an advantage. While the humans might know *IT* was here, they did not know *IT* was already among them, nor did they yet have the technology to find the infected among them.

IT had to be smarter, though, more strategic when choosing hosts. Otherwise, *IT* would never survive, let alone thrive.

Finding The Church of Original Design had worked brilliantly. Already, *IT* had found 24 people to infect — both within the organization and among The Church's members — deeply flawed subjects, ripe for the plucking.

Another human truth: When people were lost, they would beg for someone or something to turn their lives over to, knowing that any answer, even the wrong one, was better than the dull ache of simply not knowing and being lost.

IT had found Marina quite by accident, the most fortunate accident since *ITS* crossing to this world.

One of the people *IT* had nested a part of *ITSELF* inside, a man named Peter Eccles, was a high-ranking member of The Church. Through Peter's perception, *IT* picked up a strong sense that Marina was somehow touched by The Darkness. So, IT figured she might lead IT to where the vials were stored on this world.

So, "Steven Warner" entered the picture, rising to become Marina's head of security, in hopes of finding her connection to The Darkness and the vials. *IT* had considered infiltrating her, however *IT* was unable to for some reason *IT* wasn't quite sure.

Once *IT* grew closer to her, *IT* realized that she hadn't been the one who'd been touched by The Darkness, at least not directly. Instead, if his religious teachings were any indication of the truth, it was The Church's founder, Marina's father, J.L. Harmon, who had been in contact with The Darkness. But he was dead and buried, along with his secrets. *IT* had sifted through many minds in The Church's inner circle, including Marina's, but so far none had known of the vials' existence, leaving their location an absolute mystery.

Still, this was as close as *IT* had come to them so far, so Steven stayed around. Soon, *IT* realized that The Church was fertile ground for building *ITS* army once the time came to move to the next phase, but *IT* had to be careful in *ITS* selection of people; some in The Church were strong-willed and could prove tough to control. The last thing *IT* wanted was to lose command of a host so close to *ITS* home.

For now, *IT* built slowly, using The Church's newfound popularity with the "resurrection and prophecy" of J.L. Harmon to position ITSELF for the right moment when the vials were discovered. Then, nothing could stop *IT*.

IT stared out at the window, then closed *ITS* eyes, trying to connect with *ITS* other parts to see if anyone had yet stumbled across someone *It* could use to find the vials.

It focused on the collective memories gathered since *ITS* last meditation, rapidly sorting and sifting through memories like files on a computer, searching for anything which stuck out as particularly unusual or useful.

IT was inside the memories of a homeless man, Kenny Watkins, who was standing outside a hotel by the airport, when *IT* saw something that brought a low and rumbling tremor to Steve's body.

The tremor rolled, shoulder to toe, then left *IT* with chills.

No, it can't be.

He's here?

IT slowed the memory, inspecting it closely, to be certain. A man who looked just like him, or rather the man he'd been before, Boricio Bishop. This was his Earthly counterpart: Boricio Wolfe.

Boricio Wolfe, the murderer turned protector to Luca Harding, had been touched by The Light, had it flowing through his blood, which made him a looming threat.

Why is he here?

Is he searching for me?

On one hand, *IT* was curious to know more. On the other, *IT* wasn't so strong that IT could allow a human emotion, such as curiosity, to lull *IT* into complacency.

IT should — must — eliminate the threat early.

IT reached out into the world to find *ITS* closest hosts.

IT shared Kenny's memory with the others, and with it, a message:

Find Boricio Wolfe, and kill him.

❧

TWENTY

Brent Foster

Brent sat at the computer, staring at his latest freelance assignment, which wasn't even close to finished, while he held the phone in his right hand, waiting for Lara Andrews to answer. He was going out on a limb calling his former colleague, but if anyone could help him get into Harrison Psychiatric, it was her.

He'd tried to get a hold of the hospital's director, Mindy Benson, but she was conveniently out of the office and not returning his calls. It was sickening how so many so-called friends — or at least acquaintances who pretended to be so nice to him — while he had been working at the paper, turned out to be ghosts when he needed them most.

He hoped Lara wouldn't turn out to be another ghost. She was an investigative reporter with a pit bull's tenacity and a bloodhound's instincts to follow a trail, and she knew plenty of people on the inside of Harrison, following an exposé she did on the place a few years ago, prior to Mindy Benson coming on, which led to massive reforms and greatly improved working conditions.

Lara picked up on the fifth ring. "Hello?"

She sounded out of breath. It was Friday morning, and

there was a good chance Lara had just finished her morning jog before going into work.

"Hey, Lara, it's Brent, Brent Foster," he said, not sure what number or name showed up on caller ID when you used a cheap, pay-as-you-go cell phone.

"Oh, hey, Brent, how's it going?"

"Good," he said. "How's the paper?"

"Same as it ever was, long hours, little help, and a battle of who could care less between bosses and readers. And you, how are you doing?"

"OK," Brent said, trying not to sound as depressed as he'd been feeling through his most recent stretch of forever. "Working freelance, which alternates between writing awesome stuff that I actually like and a ton of other stuff that's too sucky to mention, so, in other words, pretty much the same, minus the health insurance."

Brent laughed but knew it sounded hollow, then since Lara wasn't one he needed to waste small talk on, he got to the point, "You still tight with anyone at Harrison Psychiatric who can pull some strings?"

"Depends on what strings need pulling, and why; what's up?"

"I've got a lead on something big, something I can't talk about yet, but I swear I'll give you first dibs if it pans out. But I won't have anything unless I can get in and talk to a patient there."

"Did you already try?"

"No, but someone I know did. They're not letting anyone but family talk to this guy, and unfortunately, he doesn't have family, at least that I know of."

"Who's the guy?"

Brent paused. This was where Lara would either tell him to fuck off, say that she wasn't getting involved, or sign up immediately. Not only did Lara know the patient, she had been the first to interview him after the shootings.

"Roman Rosetti," Brent said, bracing for impact.

For a moment, Lara was silent. When she spoke her voice had shifted to serious. "What's this about, Brent?"

"I can't really say, not yet."

"Bullshit, Brent. It's not like you're asking me to set up an interview with the school janitor. You want my help to see Roman Rosetti, I need to know what in the hell is happening."

Brent sighed, looking at the computer screen and the work he was in no rush to return to — another meaningless SEO article on some shitty product some company was hawking to people wanting to get rich on the Internet. He knew he could trust Lara with anything, but couldn't be certain he could tell her the truth about what happened on Oct. 15 — not without her thinking he'd lost his fucking mind.

But if he was going to expose Black Island at some point, he had to tell someone who could help him. Right now, Lara was probably the only person who had the cache to tell the story.

"OK," Brent said, "but you have to hear me out before thinking I belong in a padded cell beside Rosetti. And you can't tell Jack."

He knew Lara hated Jack as much as he did, though for different reasons, since Jack hadn't stolen Lara's wife, but rather screwed her on a story that went south and nearly got her fired.

"Fuck him," she said. "Whatcha got?"

"It's a story I'd rather tell in person," Brent said. He needed to see Lara's face in order to know how he should proceed, and just how much to tell her. He was more persuasive in person than on the phone. And something told him he'd need his every drop of persuasion to win her over. "Can we meet somewhere today?"

"I've got some interviews this morning and a staff meeting in the afternoon. How about after work? Say, 7, my place? You remember where I live?"

"You're still in the same apartment?" he asked. He'd hung out with her a few times back when he first started at the paper and she was showing him the ropes. They were good friends, and might have been more if he hadn't been married to Gina. He always felt like Lara had nursed a small crush on him, but never once acted on it, even after his divorce.

"Same place," she said. "See you at 7?"

"See you then," Brent said hanging up the phone, feeling a lot closer to something big, and in no mood to write his damned articles.

~

TWENTY-ONE

Michael Blackmore

New Jersey
    September 2013

MIKE SAT at the table across from Margie, chewing through yet another silent dinner.

As he sliced into his steak and stared at the pink juices spilling across the white plate and into the potatoes, he wondered how many more dinners they'd sit through until finally deciding to kill the charade their marriage had become.

He glanced up at Margie and noticed she was staring to her left and out their front window. He wondered if she was staring at the tire swing dangling from the maple's lowest branch. While it wasn't the same tire that they'd once pushed Amber from — in what seemed like another lifetime ago — the new rope and tire hung from the same branch on the same tree, making it too easy to flash back on happier times.

Times before long, silent dinners.

"So, how's Gail?" he said, asking about Margie's friend that she'd gone to lunch with earlier.

"OK," Marge said, looking at Mike, or through him, then down at her plate. "How's the book?"

"Going slow," he said, though saying he was slow was like saying a 30-year-old Lincoln got shitty mileage. Mike was stalled, and couldn't find his story. He was on the sixth book in his Detective Jacob Solomon series, and was running close to his deadline. He wasn't even halfway through. While he'd earned some grace with the publisher because of strong sales and a core audience eager for the next book, this was the second time Mike had found himself running late on a book. The last one was 19 days behind deadline, and the publisher gave him hellfire, talking about shelf space they'd lose, author interviews lined up that they'd need to reschedule, and advertisements they'd have to scratch.

In actuality, the publisher didn't cancel a thing. They'd designed the schedule with some cushion, telling Mike the manuscript was needed three weeks earlier than their hard deadline. So, Mike probably had an extra two or three weeks beyond the month he thought he had left now. Still, he didn't want to push things to the last minute, or piss off his publisher. His numbers were good, but publishers were under their own stress, trying to stay relevant in the era of e-books. He'd already seen a few mid-list authors get dropped by the same publisher.

"I'm sure you'll pick up your pace," Margie said, not asking for details on the book, why he was going slow, or if maybe he wanted to run some ideas by her. Once upon a time, she was his biggest fan and eager to read every story he had to tell. Those days were dead. Now she wanted nothing to do with his violent books.

"There's enough *real* bad things in the world without wanting to read made-up tragedies," Margie had said a few months earlier when Mike tried to bounce an idea off her.

He couldn't argue with her reasoning. Even though she never saw the crime scene photos, or had to identify Amber's dismembered body, she had been devastated by their daughter's murder. Amber's passing had also been the death of her happiness, and their marriage.

He sipped his wine and stared out the window, following Margie's attention: the tree and the tire swing, spinning in the cool evening breeze, as if a ghost were riding.

AFTER DINNER, Mike helped with the dishes, thanked Margie for making a delicious meal, then kissed her on the cheek. She smiled, sighing as she rubbed her temples and announced yet another migraine. "I'm going to go lay down, do you mind?"

"Go ahead, Honey," he said, kissing her on the head this time. Truth was, Mike was perfectly happy to spend the night without sitting like a zombie in front of the TV watching mindless sitcoms for two to three hours until Margie was finally ready to start hugging the pillows. While the sitcoms gave her comfort, reminders of happier times with fictional happy families and friends, they did nothing for Mike, but remind him how much time was slipping away night after night. Every moment wasted in front of the TV was another he wasn't doing what he knew he needed to do.

As bad as he felt thinking of it this way, Margie's headaches were often gifts to him — treasures of time which ushered his work forward, albeit slowly. However, the definition of "work" had changed in the past few months.

While Mike started out most nights attempting to write something, he often surrendered after a half hour or so, eager for a return to his search. He was obsessed with finding Amber's killer; with no leads, Amber had become just another cold case that would never be solved, at least not by the cops. The only way the killer would ever see justice was if Mike nabbed the bastard himself. He wasn't looking for the sort of justice you found in a courthouse, either. No, this would be a father's justice — the only kind that could ever fill the void left by Amber's death.

Through his law enforcement contacts and private investigators he'd hired since Amber's death, Mike had built up a profile of the killer, and had even linked two other murders to the same man, even if the police had shit.

Usually, when Amber came up with friends and family, people expressed surprise that the cops weren't any closer to finding her killer. Having been a cop himself, Mike was anything but shocked. People carried the odd notion that the police and FBI had these massive databases tracking every murder, linking similar crimes and searching for patterns. It might be like that on TV and in the movies, but in reality, agencies were fractured, databases limited by budget cuts, and law enforcement crippled by disparate systems from one department to another. And then, of course, you had ego and politics, both of which undermined any efforts to share information in a better or more logical way.

Crimes were usually solved despite technology, and by officers who put in long hours, often off the clock, working cases until they were closed. While his former colleagues had put in the hours following Amber's death, eventually they had to move on.

Mike was bitter at first, pissed that nobody seemed to care as much as he did, but then he saw it as the blessing it was: If nobody else was looking for her murderer, perhaps he could find the man first. And if Mike killed the man, there was a greater chance he'd get away with it if nobody knew who he was, let alone his connection to Amber's death.

Mike opened his e-mail and saw a daily report from Franklin Weatherly, one of the private eyes working for him, compiling information he found on police websites, public information searches, and in newspapers around the country.

Most days, Weatherly had little to offer, but today's report featured a subject line that immediately jolted Mike to sitting: *Sexual Predator Found Murdered, Drawings in Victim's Blood Discovered on Body.*

Mike read the file — details of an open case from two months before, about a man named Hank Carol in Fairfield, Colorado — a sexual predator who was found in the woods, beheaded, his head placed between his legs. Doodles covered his body: *Pervert, Pedo,* and *Short Eyes.*

The use of the term "short eyes" led police to believe the man had been killed by someone who'd spent time in prison. Carol had spent three years in prison for sexually assaulting a child and got out early for "good behavior," so there was a good chance he'd made an enemy on the inside who found him on the outside — or had someone else find him on the outside — and exacted revenge. Another suspect in the case, though only briefly, was a woman, Mary Olson, who had filed a report against the man after Carol had approached her daughter at a bus stop a month prior. Since the pervert had done nothing illegal, and technically didn't violate terms of his parole, the cops couldn't do anything except tell Mary to file a restraining order against the man so he wouldn't come near the child. Mike wondered why the man had no stipulations in place already not to go near children.

Why force someone to file a restraining order just to keep him from their kids?

Mrs. Olson was cleared, though, since she had an alibi and the cops didn't like her for the crime. If it was hard to find the dedication or resources to solve murders of innocents, you could bet your last dollar most cops weren't about to put in overtime trying to solve a child molester's murder. With no other leads, the cops dropped the investigation. Mike was damned sure they hadn't looked for other crimes that involved a beheading and drawings on the vic's body.

If this is my guy, why did he target a pedophile?

Did they meet in jail?

Mike sighed, cracked his knuckles, and leaned in closer to the monitor.

Is this my killer?

The only way he'd find out: visiting the only lead he had, Mrs. Mary Olson.

~

TWENTY-TWO

Boricio Wolfe

The women talked for seven fucking years.

Boricio wouldn't have minded since he liked all three of the women making the hotel room smell so purty, but he was still waiting for alone time with Rose, which got him wanting the Olsons to get started on a good night's sleep in the adjoining room. Mary was so exhausted and sick with worry, her bloodshot eyes looked like they were about to roll from her haggard face.

"You should get to bed," Boricio suggested, both because he ached to see Mary so tired, driving 15-plus hours was murder, and because if Mary went then Paola would follow, and with Mary Kate and Ashley out of their room, Boricio could put his pecker someplace cozy.

"You're right," Mary stretched herself to standing, yawning on the way. "I do need rest." She turned to Paola and held out her hand.

Paola took her mom by the wrist and lowered her limb. "Not yet, I'm not really tired. I think I'll stay up and talk to Boricio and Rose for a while."

Mary's disappointment was red on her face, Boricio's felt blue. "You sure?" she asked.

Paola shrugged. "This new body agrees with me, I guess. I feel like I could run a mile. Besides, I slept in the car."

"OK," Mary turned to Boricio and Rose. "Well then, I guess it's good night."

They each swapped an adios, then Mary disappeared and left Boricio with one more body to empty from the room before he could bump fuzzies with his Morning Rose.

"So, is this your first time in California?" Rose asked, delaying Boricio's pleasure.

Paola nodded. "Yeah, we were always going to come out 'someday,' back before … everything. Even after Mom and Dad split, we all said that we would come out to Disneyland together one day, but that never happened."

"What do you think of the Golden State so far?" Rose asked.

Paola shrugged. "Not much to think, yet. This is the only place we've been so far. Mom drove so fast I barely saw anything outside the window. And we only stopped three times for gas and to pee. I guess I'll know better tomorrow." She paused, then added, "Is this your first time here?"

Rose nodded. "Yes. Not exactly my scene, but I'm excited about how everything's going so far. We've already been here longer than expected, though, and I hate that we're still by the airport, but I don't want to change, I just want to go home."

"How much longer are you staying?"

"Until sometime next week. There are a few things we have to settle and sign and all that not-too-fun stuff, and I do want to stay long enough to see you get in The Capacitor." Rose looked over at Boricio then back to Paola. "I know *he* doesn't buy into it, but you'll see. I bet it fixes you without you having to look for Luca."

Worry flickered across Paola's too-grownup face. "I hope so," she said, swallowing. "I think I made a big mistake … going to the hospital like I did."

"You'll be fine," Rose reassured her, patting the top of

her hands. "I'm sure Veronica can get us in to see Marina, and I'm sure Marina will take great care of you once we do."

"If not, I'll turn her face to marmalade." Boricio was surprised he said it, so were the girls.

Rose said, "Boricio!"

Paola laughed.

Rose turned from Boricio back to Paola and took her gently by the hand. "Sorry about that, Sweetie. He's certainly incorrigible, but we both know Boricio would never hurt a fly."

Paola's eyes widened with surprise. Fortunately, Rose's were cast down as she stood from the couch.

"Be right back," Rose said. "I've gotta use the ladies' room."

Silence hung until the bathroom door closed. Boricio scooted from his chair to Paola and said, "Ixnay on the urder-may," in a hushed but urgent whisper.

"You mean she doesn't know?"

"What the hell do you think I'm gonna say? That woman in there loves Boricio like you wouldn't believe, and that's keeping me stitched in ways Luca couldn't fix. You think I'm gonna piss it to the wind? No way," Boricio shook his head, knowing his face was uncharacteristic with worry. It had never occurred to him that either Mary or Paola might threaten his beans. "What am I supposed to say, 'Hey, my sweet Morning Rose, while you pick the petals from that daisy and recite today's *He loves me, he loves me nots,*' I should probably let you know I used to be a serial killer."

"Boricio!"

Boricio growled in a whisper, "Well, I'm sorry, Kitty Cat, but you can't expect me to say shit about dick, if it'll make my lady leave screaming."

"You've gotta tell her," Paola said. "Secrets that big have a way of coming out, eventually. At least if you tell her, you're revealing the secret on your terms and giving yourself a chance that everything will work out."

"Really?" Boricio said, smiling. "Did you tell Mommy Dearest about your little phone call to me? You tell her how you asked me if I could 'take care' of that perverted pecker-head since you were afraid that Mary Mary So Contrary was gonna do something to get the Olsons in trouble?"

"No," Paola shot back, and scooted forward on her seat toward Boricio. "And don't you dare, either."

Boricio zipped his lips and hurled an invisible key through the window. "Hell, I won't say shit, but I thought you just said secrets were for spilling. Goose and gander ain't swimming together, eh?"

Boricio grinned as Paola's brow furrowed in frustration: cute when pissed.

The toilet flushed.

Paola's frown got worse, she looked like she might cry. Boricio realized that while the girl looked like an adult, and an awful lot like Mary — who could give shit as well as she could take it — Paola wasn't as tough, at least not yet. She was still a kitty cat, like Luca had been.

"I'm just fucking with you," he whispered as Rose headed back over to the couch from the bathroom. "Three can keep a secret, if two are dead, or one's Boricio. I won't say shit."

"OK," Paola said, laughing as Rose sat beside Boricio.

"OK, what?" Rose asked.

"I was telling Paola to pound stones on anyone looking her way, cross-eyed, funny or otherwise. She was always pretty, but a girl, now she'll be whistling Dixie whether she means to or not, and that might give some ungentlemanly fellows the wrong error in judgment. I'm saying our girl here, in her mama's body, needs to be ready to jab."

"Actually," Paola laughed, "he said I have to *beat them until they look like bruised bananas.*"

Rose laughed. "That sounds like Boricio."

Boricio laughed because it sure as shit did.

They talked for another few minutes, until Paola yawned three in a row and proved her body wasn't as infallible as she had believed. Midway through her fifth, the adjoining door parted, and Mary stepped through it. "I left my pillow in the car. And I can't sleep without it. I'm gonna go downstairs and get it."

Boricio said, "This is Lost Angeles, where fuckers don't know shit about cock."

"What does that even mean?" Mary asked. "If you're going to corrupt my daughter with your vulgarity, you should at least make sense."

"It *means*," Boricio said, "that the locals here are less forgiving than the hayseeds where you live."

"Hayseeds?" Mary sighed. "We're in a nice hotel with security everywhere. I'll be fine: I've dealt with aliens."

The absurd drew laughter. Rose said, "Oh, just let him go with you. He likes to feel like a guard dog. Makes him special."

Mary sighed again, said OK, then told Paola she'd be right back and left the room with Boricio.

"She's a helluva junior, Mary, Mary," Boricio said as they walked down the hall. "And everything'll be fine. Don't waste sleep on worry."

"You really think so?" she turned, setting her eyes into Boricio's as if his opinion weighed pounds. They stepped into the elevator and rode it down.

Truth was, Boricio didn't know, had no fucking idea. He wasn't worried; same stuff inside him that guided his purging helped him see, hear, and smell what he needed, it kept insisting everything was peaches and titties.

"I think everything will be fine *if* we find Luca. *And* I promise to find him."

The elevator doors dinged into the garage. "How can you promise that?"

He shrugged, smiling. "Because I'm Boricio."

Mary laughed, but before the sound left her mouth three people — two men and one woman — started walking toward them from the far side of the parking lot. One wore a mechanic's uniform, a young man with droopy eyes and messy hair. The other guy was a giant skinhead in a tight black tee — almost painted on —hugging his fat. The third was an older woman wearing a waitress's uniform: three opposites in equal approach.

Boricio felt the beer-battered bullshit immediately, but couldn't stop it fast enough, and was too late to connect the dots.

One of the people, the woman, reached into her dress and pulled out a knife, then charged toward them, screaming.

The skinny guy drew a crowbar from nowhere and swung it at Boricio.

The big man ran at Mary, hacking a machete.

Boricio stepped in front of Mary.

～

TWENTY-THREE

Brent Foster

Brent arrived at Lara's apartment at five before 7, anxious, uncertain how she'd accept what he had to say. Lara was about as no nonsense as you got. While they'd gotten along great, she wasn't exactly a creative type. While most reporters, ones Brent knew, anyway, were just biding time until they finished that novel they'd been chipping away at for a decade or so, Lara didn't care to write a book. She didn't even read books, unless it was nonfiction, and usually only then if it was somehow work-related.

Brent kept imagining how she'd respond when hearing his crazy tale of other worlds, aliens, and secret government forces on Black Island.

There was a good chance she'd think he'd lost his mind, in which case he'd be heartbroken. Not just because it was yet another person who didn't believe him and he was running out of people to call friends, but also because Lara was someone special to him, even if they'd never been romantic. They had a bond, and he didn't want to break it by coming off like a weirdo who needed a room beside Roman's.

He knocked on her door, despite not having a clear narrative to tell her yet. He'd wing it and hope for the best.

There was no answer, so he knocked again.

A moment later, he heard locks sliding open, chain being moved, and the door opened inward. Rather than greet him at the door, Lara was behind it, just out of sight. Brent thought it odd, but stepped into the apartment anyway.

He saw blood on the floor in the living room.

He turned to leave, but instead found a gun in his face. Behind the gun, Ed Keenan.

"Stay put or I will shoot you," Ed said, pushing the door closed and locking it with his free hand.

"What did you do to Lara?" Brent asked, looking around the living room. While he saw a lot of blood, he didn't see a body. "Where is she?"

"I had to take care of her," Ed said — ice cold.

"Take care of? You killed her?"

"I didn't kill her, Brent. You did. You were told to keep your mouth shut! What part of *keeping your mouth shut* means calling the newspaper? Or to tell perfect strangers about Black Island, huh?"

Brent swallowed, metallic fear on his tongue. He couldn't believe Ed had killed her — had killed Lara. He was stunned, short of breath, and feeling as if he'd been kicked in the gut and nuts at once. He was about to vomit.

Knees wobbly, Brent moved toward the wall and leaned against it, sure he was about to pass out.

"Who else did you tell?" Ed asked, clearly agitated.

Brent didn't answer. Instead, he said, "When did you start working for Black Island?"

"I'm asking the questions," Ed said, "Who else did you tell?"

"I tried to get a hold of you," Brent said, trying, in a not-so-subtle way to remind Ed that they'd been friends at one point, "to find out how you and the girls were, but Sullivan said they couldn't find you."

Ed shook his head, "Who else did you tell, Brent? I need to know."

"Why are you doing this, Ed? Why are you doing their dirty work? You're better than this."

Ed charged at him, bringing the butt of his gun against Brent's head before he had time to register what was happening, or defend it. The pain was thunder in his skull, sharp, devastating. He spilled to the floor.

Brent looked up, feeling woozy, seeing double of Ed and everything else, not sure if he was going to pass out or die.

Brent asked, "Are you going to kill me?" but never heard the answer.

～

TWENTY-FOUR

Sullivan

Sullivan took the ferry from Black to Paddock Island just before sunset, eager to get a few drinks in him, and turn the Black Island Research Facility to memory for at least a few hours.

He ignored the nicer restaurants suggested by some of the Island scientists, deciding to eat at Joe's Fish & Chips instead.

He took a table in the back near a large window that looked out over much of the island. He ordered fried shrimp and French fries. He wasn't too hungry and figured if the servings were big he'd make appetizers his meal. He waited for his food, nursing a frosty mug.

Beer tasted more or less the same as on his world, which was good. Some foods were different. Apples here ranged from sweet to bitter. On his world they were all sour, especially the red ones. Sullivan wondered how so many things could be the same, from people with "twins" to buildings to corporations, all following the exact same paths on both worlds. It made Sullivan ponder the infinite possibilities, but when he came across a difference, like the apples, or a person the opposite of their counterpart, or simply different, like Ed Keenan, he realized the impossible number of variables. Sullivan's head would swim and then hurt; he'd start wishing he'd never crossed over.

One similarity on both worlds: an annoying virologist named Alex Wan, who had shadowed Sullivan whenever possible. Wan was one of those people with the need to engage in small talk, and never shut up. Worse: Wan was one of Black Island's best scientists, so it wasn't like Sullivan could have him fired for annoyance.

Sullivan did his best to avoid Wan, particularly in his off hours, hard to do when both men lived on the island's base. As he looked outside at the homes, he wondered how hard it would be to find a rental. A place of his own where he could go to at night and not have to worry about running into Wan.

The waitress came by with two overflowing baskets of food that smelled deserving of their grease spots. She was cute, reminded Sullivan a little of Amy.

He wondered what Amy's counterpart on this world was like. Was she married? Did she have a child? Sullivan had looked into his own counter. He died in a car accident at 19 — another interesting difference in the worlds. Long before he would have met Amy, gotten married, then separated, or lost her forever on Oct. 15.

Sullivan couldn't look her up now. Not when they had the alien threat to deal with. Bishop had already come over, infected a few people they knew of. God only knew how many more there were, ticking bombs waiting to detonate, or ... get triggered.

Sullivan had to think, help keep this world from being destroyed like his. If they could locate the vials, or find and kill Bishop, then, and only then, would he look for this world's Amy.

He wondered if she was happy, and had to fight the urge to stray down the path of what-ifs and could-have-beens.

He took a fry from the basket. Too good for ketchup. Not so, salt and pepper.

Sullivan looked around the bar, watching the island locals, laid back, mostly well-to-do, genuinely nice to one another. Sullivan hadn't felt so comfortable in forever.

Yeah, I'm definitely living here.

Sullivan was about to call the night perfect when he saw the last person in the world he expected, or wanted: Alex Wan.

What the hell?

Sullivan buried his face in the menu, hoping to avoid eye contact, and that Alex would be led to the other side of the restaurant where they wouldn't run into one another. No such luck.

Wan bypassed the hostess and headed straight to Sullivan as if he was looking for him.

"Hello, Mr. Sullivan," Wan said, "Mind if I sit with you?"

Jesus. What am I going to say? No?

"Sure," Sullivan said, "go ahead."

The waitress came by, suffered through Wan's painful small talk, as Sullivan started chewing through his food as fast as he could, eager for an excuse to leave. Wan kept him talking, ordered two rounds of drinks, and nailed Sullivan to his chair.

After Sullivan finished his final beer, Wan stared through the window in a rare and sudden silence.

Good, maybe he's as bored as I am.

Sullivan was waiting for the waitress to look over so he could get the check and leave, but she was busy hustling drinks and food to a table of 20.

"Be right back. If she comes back, can you ask for the check?" Sullivan said, excusing himself to the restroom as he pushed his chair out.

He stood, surprised to find himself tipsy. It had been a long time since he'd had anything to drink, but was still surprised to be feeling drunk on just three beers.

As Sullivan stood, he slipped. Wan reached out to grab him and hold him up.

"Whoa," Wan said. "You OK?"

"Yeah, I'm ... "

And then Sullivan wasn't fine.

~

SULLIVAN WOKE up lying on the ground. It was dark out. Waves sloshed nearby.

What the hell?

He sat up, head aching and dizzy. He sat on the shore — Black Island in the distance — still on Paddock Island.

The last thing Sullivan remembered was feeling tipsy after dinner, then slipping. Wan caught him.

Wan! Did he leave me here? Why?

"Hello, Mr. Sullivan," Wan said from behind.

Sullivan turned. Wan stood behind him, as if he'd been waiting.

"Why are we out here in the middle of nowhere?"

"We were waiting for you to wake up, Mr. Sullivan," Wan said. His voice was absent its normal giddiness, its normal matter-of-fact tone.

"What's going on?" Sullivan asked, standing, still dizzy. "Did something happen?"

"Oh yes, something's happened," Wan said, stepping toward Sullivan as if in conspiracy.

Sullivan was confused, uncomfortable, wondering if the man was about to make a pass at him, or worse.

"You've been looking for me, Mr. Sullivan. I figured I'd come to see you."

"What do you mean looking for you?" Sullivan realized that he wasn't dealing with Wan, just as he said it.

Wan backed him toward the ocean, "You think you can hide from us, Sullivan? We have people everywhere." It's smiled. "You will be so much more useful to us in finding the vials."

Sullivan's foot hit the surf. He had two options: run around Wan, or turn and dive into the ocean. Swim away. He wasn't sure if Wan, or Wan's alien-infected body would overpower him in the water, where he'd be even more helpless.

Before Sullivan could move, Wan's hand shot out and grabbed him hard by the neck. Sullivan brought his arms up, trying to break free from Wan's grip. Wan's hold was too tight — he lifted Sullivan to his dangling toes with superhuman strength.

Sullivan kicked, hard, into Wan's chest, face, and arms — none of it affecting the infected man. Finally, Sullivan's boot knocked Wan's jaw loose. Wan screamed and dropped him.

Sullivan hit the dirt, then scrambled to stand. Before he got even three steps, Wan leaped on him, flipped him over, and shoved him into the ground, lowering his bloodied, broken face to Sullivan's.

What was left of Wan's mouth opened further, and the black alien fog poured from one maw, trying to enter another.

Sullivan gritted his teeth and twisted his neck, not allowing the thing to enter his mouth. He'd seen the aliens infect too many others.

It didn't enter his mouth.

The alien poured into his nose and choked him with Darkness.

～

Epilogue

*October 19, **2011***

   The J.L. Harmon estate

MARINA STARED in disbelief as her father sat up in bed, rubbed his eyes, and looked at her, slowly blinking.

"Daddy?" she whispered, choking on both words and breath as she ran to his bedside, stopping short of throwing her arms fiercely around him, afraid she might hurt him.

He opened his arms and pulled her closer into a giant hug with surprising strength, especially for a man who had been dead for days.

"How?" she asked, "I thought you ... "

"Weren't coming back?" he asked. "You didn't believe me, did you?"

Marina pulled away to meet her father's eyes, expecting him to appear wounded by her doubt. Instead, he smiled, "It's OK, Honey, I might not have believed me either. How long have I been ... *gone?*"

"Four days," she said, sitting beside him on the bed, holding his hands and feeling the warmth flooding his flesh.

"Ah, so I was full of shit," he said. "I said two days, didn't I?"

Marina laughed, staring into his eyes, wondering how it was possible, how he'd come back. Again, she asked, "How?"

The doorknob rattled, followed by a knock. Dr. Phillips: "Mr. Harmon?"

Marina remembered the camera feed, watched not just by people on the Internet, but also by the people downstairs. They wanted to get into the room, probably run tests, find out what prophecy he'd been told to deliver. But first, Marina wanted — needed — to say what she'd almost lost the chance to say forever.

"Tell them to wait, please," she begged.

"Hold on, Doc, give me a few minutes with my daughter."

The doctor said nothing, probably slinking off with his tail between his legs.

Marina stood, went to the camera, and hit a button to stop the recording.

She then returned to her father, tears in her eyes, "I thought I lost you, Dad."

"It's OK, Honey, I'm back. I had to come back to bring the message from the Great All Seeing. Can you turn the camera back on?"

"Yes, but first I want to say some things I thought I'd never get a chance to say again."

"OK." he took Marina's hands in his as she sat back on the bed. "Go ahead."

"First, I want to say thank you for raising me after Mom died. I know you were scared, and it couldn't have been easy to do alone. You did a helluva job."

"Thank you," he said, wiping tears from his eyes.

"And I'm sorry for any grief I gave you during my 'wild years.' And for all the horrible boyfriends I dated."

"Even that Vinnie kid?"

"*Especially* Vinnie," she said, smiling through an eye roll. "Ugh, he was such a jerk. Anyway, I also wanted to … "

Suddenly her father's eyes went spooked. Marina turned, expecting the door to have burst open behind them or something, but there was nothing.

Her father started shaking, his face burning red.

"Dad?" she said, sudden fear in an icy current through her veins. "Dad?"

He pointed up and behind her.

Marina turned, desperate to see what he was pointing at, but all she saw was the camera.

"Turn it on," he said.

"Why?"

"Turn it on!" he shouted, his words collapsing into coughs.

She ran to the door instead, opened it, and screamed, "Doc! Something's wrong with my dad!"

The doctor ran into the room, saw her father pointing, and saying, "Turn the camera on," over and over between coughs.

The doctor, turned on the camera rather than running to her father.

"Help him!" Marina screamed.

Once the camera was on again, the doctor rushed to her father's bedside, feeling his head.

"You're burning up, Josh."

Marina's father ignored the doctor, pushed him aside, and stared at the camera with a gaze so severe it sent chills like snakes through her body.

"I've come back with a message," he said, coughing into his hand. Blood sprinkled the sheets. Marina ran forward to try and help him, though she didn't know what she could possibly do.

He pushed her aside, staring into the camera, intent on finishing his message, "The Darkness is coming. The Great All

Seeing has showed me how close it is. Fix your Current now, for Darkness is coming to claim us."

Her father coughed again, and more blood spewed from his cracked lips; the dark-red spatters were thick, relentless, a certain and too-colorful sign of a second death only so many seconds away.

"Doctor, help him!"

Her father began to violently shake, like a seizure amplified by an electric current through his entire body. He jerked his head back hard into the headboard, repeatedly, each time leaving a deeper, more sickening crunch.

"Daddy!" Marina screamed, throwing herself between the headboard and his head, trying to stop him from bashing his skull into squash.

But it was too late.

He slumped into Marina, looking up at her with wide, scared eyes. Blood gurgled from his mouth.

"I'm sorry I couldn't save them," he said, though she had no idea who he meant by "them."

Four days after passing for the first time, Josh Harmon died again in his daughter's arms.

TO BE CONTINUED …

Episode 22

(FOURTH EPISODE OF SEASON FOUR)

"Bullies"

TWENTY-FIVE

Boricio Wolfe

By the time Boricio realized what in the fuck was happening, he had a holy trinity of bullshit approaching at once.

Right in front of him, some gash of a waitress wielding a knife, yanking it from her apron like it was a pad and a pen and she was waiting for Boricio to snap for biscuits and gravy. A fat fuck who looked like a skinhead version of Ralphie May was swinging a machete like he was hacking sugar cane, and an Ichabod Crane-lookin' cocksucker, whistling air with a crowbar.

Boricio stepped in front of Mary and said, "Trust me?"

Like she has any choice.

Her swallow was almost louder than her words. "I trust you."

"Good, then stay the fuck back."

Boricio charged off from Mary, headed for the fat fuck with the machete first. The fucker swung. Boricio ducked, falling hard on his ass in front of Ralphie May. He kicked up with his right leg and collapsed the fat fuck's left knee, bringing him down in a scream. He dropped his machete, and Boricio grabbed it, and thrust the blade up into the fucker's gut, twisting the handle as he wrapped his left hand around the asshole's neck, picked the fat fuck up somehow, and spun himself behind Ralphie's giant body just as the crowbar and knife both hit it.

The crowbar landed with a wet-sounding squish — awful enough to draw a smile on Boricio — as the knife hit his flesh with a sickening THUNK!

Boricio cried out, "Yee-haw!" from behind Ralphie, to let Mary know he was fine, then yelled, "Get behind the fagmobile!" meaning the Mini-Cooper, the closest car to Mary.

Even with a machete decorating his chest, Ralphie kept growling. Boricio stepped back, dragging the fat fucker behind him, still using his giant body for cover with surprising strength, then a few feet away pulled out the machete and plunged it back in, repeatedly until the fat fuck stopped squirming on the ground.

Boricio smiled at the remaining pair, daring a quick stare around the garage, more worried that someone else would step into their skirmish than he was about losing his life to either of the others, both still staring at Boricio with eyes as empty as any he'd ever seen.

He wanted to take out Ichabod next, but the waitress came on him faster than Boricio anticipated. He ducked under another whistle of her blade, this one slicing a hunk of his hair, sending it fluttering like a feather to the ground as he swatted the waitress' hand with the machete, severing it at the wrist and delivering both it and her knife to the asphalt.

He turned toward Ichabod, plunged his machete straight through the wobbly gobbler's heart, then froze when their eyes met. In an instant, Boricio was deluged with images, coming from the Ichabod fucker like a broadcast:

A man stared into the mirror, his eyes red and milky as he shoved the barrel of a Magnum under his chin — behind the curtain of a foot-long beard — and pulled the trigger, sending chum from his freshly opened skull into an arc of red slop, erupting from his head like a volcano onto the wall behind him as his vision turned black.

A woman leapt onto a baby carriage, opening her mouth like a shark to tear into a baby's neck. A huddle of women yanked her away, but she gnashed and tore at them like an animal as they wrestled her to the ground.

A man screamed his way through a department store, flooded with shoppers, through the store's bottom floor filled with shoes, up one escalator then another, and into a top-floor lingerie department, waving a hatchet and dropping bodies as he ran, until he was finally felled by a guard who lost his life leaping on top of the monster.

The atrocities were all connected, and each somehow strung to the bullshit before him. Boricio knew it as fact because the truth was bleeding from the trio's connection and out of Ichabod's eyes.

Boricio cried out again, this time in an icy fear he wasn't used to, then stopped Ichabod from breathing with a twist of his blade, and pulled it out to give the gash of a waitress what she had coming.

Three more swings, then bodies lined the ground in a row.

"You OK?" Boricio called out to Mary.

She shook her head, peeking up from behind the faggot mobile, then timidly stepped out in front of it, shaking.

"What … happened?"

Boricio tightened his grip around the machete's handle, sweating, his heart racing, and mind still more concerned about someone else joining the fray — good, evil, or otherwise — than anything else.

"I don't know," he glanced around, "but I'm feeling all sorts a shit that ain't making sense."

"What do you mean?"

Mary sounded more scared than Boricio had heard since the dead world. He swallowed, still looking around. Seeing nothing, he turned back to Mary. "I don't know," he said, searching for words, trying to explain. "It's … "

After too long of nothing, Mary said, "It's what, Boricio?"

He swallowed again. "*IT'S* here."

"What do you mean, 'it's here?' *What's* here?"

"No, Mother Mary, not it's, *IT'S:* Whatever IT was we thought we left behind, *IT'S* back, here, on this world. And *IT's* after us, sure as a second season of a show called, *Rich People Fucking.* The three of them," he waved his machete at the bodies. Ichabod twitched, and Boricio plunged the machete into him again, like spiking a football. "They're all connected … somehow … and they're targeting us, as in you and me, or at least me."

"How can you know that?"

"I just do."

Mary looked like she was killing a scream. "So what now?"

"First," Boricio said, "we've gotta get rid of these bodies."

"How are we going to do that?"

Boricio laughed, a wicked, cracking guffaw. "Do I ask you how to make blueberry muffins?"

"No," Mary said. "And I'd probably have to ask you anyway. Paola says I shouldn't try to bake."

Boricio pointed to a Chevy Tahoe with Utah plates. "That one, we're gonna shove 'em in the back for now."

"What if the driver leaves?"

"Then we're in more shit than the crap we're in now, but we've got seconds to do something, sister, and not a lot of choices in our bowl. We need to buy time, but it ain't cheap, and the price is climbing by the minute. We'll stash the cadavers, go upstairs, grab the girls, and get the fuck out of this hotel. Fortunately, I don't see any cameras here, so maybe we're fine. I'll get these stiffs to the Tahoe while they're still soft, you make sure I'm not dripping. I'm counting on you to clean up after me."

"With what?" Mary asked, sounding uncharacteristically helpless.

"You'll figure it out." Boricio reached down, flung the waitress over his shoulder like a bag of nothing, then went to the Tahoe, broke in — American cars were easy as fuck — and tossed her into the back. He went back for Ichabod, lifting the man like he, too, was nothing, then finally Ralphie May. The fat fuck was bloodiest and required Mary's help.

After the bodies were stashed, she gestured toward Boricio, then to herself. "We can't go in there like this, we're covered in blood."

"No shit, Watson," he said, already making his way down a long row of cars, peering through windows one at a time until he found what he was looking for and helped himself inside the car, this time by breaking a window, then grabbed a suitcase from the back.

Two minutes later they were both changed and walking through the hotel, Mary in clothes that were way too big, and Boricio in clothes that were way too small. They matched, with Boricio's small, purple shirt saying *SOUL* and Mary's large one saying, *MATE*.

Mary said, "What if we run into the soul mates these belong to?"

"Then we'll have to kill them for not knowing when shit's stupid."

Mary surprised Boricio by laughing.

A minute later Boricio slid his keycard into their room door and opened it wide. Parted halfway, Rose said, "I was getting worried …"

Before she could finish her thought, Rose was looking from Mary to Boricio and back, calculating.

"I'll explain everything on the way," Boricio said.

Rose said, "On the way where?"

Paola, suddenly frantic, cried out, "Are you okay, Mom?" Then, "What happened?"

"Dealing with dead bodies wasn't a part of tonight's agenda," Boricio said, like he was talking about emptying garbage, "so we need to get the fuck out of here 15 minutes ago."

"Bodies?" Rose said, "What are you talking about? What's going on, Boricio? Are we in danger?"

Boricio waved his hands like it was nothing.

"You watch too much TV. This ain't nothing. We're not disposing so much as fleeing."

"Fleeing?"

"Tell her it's okay," Boricio said to Mary.

Mary said, "It's not, okay," then turned and set her hand on Rose's shoulder. "We'll explain everything as soon as we can, but right now, Boricio's right. We have to get out of here and don't have much time."

Boricio looked over at Rose, and for the first time realized he was moving too fast to think on shit proper. His lady's bottom lip was quivering, and though he hated to admit it, his Morning Rose was shaking like a dog in the rain.

Boricio stopped, forcing himself to think smarter, stronger, and more for her. He turned to Rose, gently planted one hand on each of her arms, then turned her toward him. "You trust me, Baby?"

She nodded, slow but there.

"Have I ever let you down?"

After a second's hesitation that Boricio didn't like, she shook her head.

Not missing a beat, he said, "That's right, Ring Around the Rosie, and I'm sure as shit not about to start. All that stuff that happened to us on the other world, well it's followed us home, and if we don't get going right this minute, it's gonna keep on following, and might just drag us into some fucked up sorta Hades. We've gotta go, all four of us, and that means you gotta come, because I can't bear to think of waking tomorrow and not seeing you with me, okay, Baby?"

Rose swallowed, nodded and said, "Okay." It sounded like

it took everything inside her to nudge the words from her mouth, but it would have to do.

"Good girl," Boricio smiled, then turned so he could see all three girls at once. "OK, we're outta here in five, take only what's necessary. If you can't fit it in the first trip down, it ain't worth taking."

"We only made one trip up," Mary said. "We'll be ready in two."

Boricio winked. "Blue ribbon with a gold star for Mary!"

Rose said, "But we can't leave, Boricio. I'm signing the contract in a few days, and I need to bring the girls to Marina's. We have to help Paola!"

"We *are* helping her, but we can't get to fixing whatever needs fixing if we don't get her, and us, to safety first. You understand?"

Boricio waited for Rose to nod, then added, "And of course we'll take care of your contracts, we just need to stay in L.A. — that's not a problem, there are plenty of rooms in this city, and at least half aren't booked by whores, so we'll find something post haste. But this hotel right here's a no-go, which means we've gotta relocate A-fucking-SAP. Once we're safe and in a new spot, I'll go out and get us some guns."

"Guns!" Rose cried out, eyes dilating from scared to terrified.

Boricio was about to explain to his Morning Rose why guns weren't a luxury when Mary practically did it for him.

"No problem," she said, then disappeared into her room, returning seconds later with a duffel bag.

Boricio eyed it as she entered, a good idea what he'd see once she unzipped it. "Damn, Girl," he said, "and you said you only made one trip?"

"Even if I had two, I wouldn't have left this one for a second."

Mary plopped the duffel onto the bed, then unzipped it to a carnival of pistols, knives, and first aid supplies.

Boricio whistled. "Da-yum, Mary Mary, that's enough to take care of your little lamb, and a whole goddamned flock! Though it would've been nice if you had one down in the garage!"

Mary looked at Paola, then back to Boricio, finding a smile on her way. "Yeah, but I figured I was safe with my big guard dog," she winked at Rose. "As for the guns, Desmond taught me well: Always be prepared."

"Ya done good, kid," he said, laughing as he tousled Mary's hair.

"Thanks."

Rose was a hazy shade of white.

Paola said, "When are you gonna tell us what happened downstairs?"

Boricio promised: "The minute we get the fuck outta here."

They gathered their things, left the room, then went downstairs and crossed the lobby, pausing for seconds at a story on the TV about some mass shooting at a school. Boricio felt a flash of memory, as if it, too, had something to do with the bullshit going on tonight.

They walked by the Faggot Mobile, then the Tahoe — which had no attention on it — and over to Mary's Volvo.

Despite Boricio's promise to tell Rose everything the second they got in the car, they drove for 15 minutes before anyone whispered a word.

~

TWENTY-SIX

Luca Harding

Luca sat on the bleachers staring at his gym classmates as they were having fun playing soccer. He wanted to play, too, but yesterday Johnny Thomas threatened to "kill him" in today's game.

While Luca didn't think the bully would actually murder him, he did think it highly likely, if not certain, that Johnny Thomas would use soccer as an excuse to hurt him. He could plead to the coach, "Sorry, I didn't mean to break Luca's arm. It was an *accident.*"

So, Luca lied to the coach and said he'd left his gym shorts and shirt at home, when in truth he had hidden them in his locker. Luca felt bad lying, suffering a knot in his throat that got thick as he told it, so big he was sure the coach could probably see it.

Coach Carmichael was a heavyset, sunburned man in his 40s with thick, sun-bleached blond hair, who, depending on the day, could either be the most intimidating man in school, or the funniest. He was always nice to Luca, which made him feel even guiltier every time the coach looked over at him in the bleachers.

The only other people in the bleachers were Andy Daniels

and Trevor Banks, polar opposites on the popularity scale. Andy was the quiet, fat kid who never dressed out, and who didn't seem to care if he failed the class. He was lost in his own world, reading books and drawing pictures of monsters in his spiral notebook. Trevor was one of the more popular kids in school, tall and athletic, but also super-laid back. Cool. Trevor was one of those kids who everyone — from the jocks to the rich kids to the comic book geeks — seemed to like, especially girls.

Trevor also said he'd forgotten his gym clothes, which had made Luca's fib seem all the more obvious, like the two had concocted the lie together, even though Trevor had barely ever spoken to Luca, except for one time when he asked if Luca minded him cutting in the lunch line.

Though three of them sat in the bleachers, they couldn't have been sitting farther apart if they'd tried.

Andy sat on the bottom row, Luca in the middle, and Trevor up top, leaning back against the rails, staring up at the clouds and thinking about whatever it was cool kids thought about. Luca glanced at the field and saw Johnny Thomas staring at him. Luca quickly found his feet, not wanting to make eye contact.

Luca had so far managed to avoid whatever Johnny had planned on doing to him, but he couldn't avoid it forever. He couldn't "forget" his gym clothes every class. And there were still several other times during the school day when Johnny could hurt him, even if it wasn't a sanctioned "accidental hit" during soccer. Eventually, Luca would have to do what his father said: end the torment by standing up to the bully.

In theory, it made sense. Fight back. Don't be a wimp. But in practice, Luca was terrified. Bullies didn't play by the rules. When Luca was younger, the most he had to worry about was someone pushing him off a slide or something. But Johnny was crazy, and there was no telling what he was capable of. Johnny was the same kid who, last summer, found a rabbit on the side of the road and started stomping it, laughing the entire time like it was a skit on *Incredible Crew*. Though Luca hadn't seen the rabbit incident, he'd heard the story from enough people to know it was true.

Something was seriously wrong with Johnny Thomas, and whatever that seriously something was, it scared Luca inside out.

He heard footsteps on the metal planks behind him, and turned, surprised to see Trevor standing over him, looking down.

"This seat taken?" Trevor pointed to the empty spot beside Luca.

Luca was confused, both by Trevor's question, and that the cool kid was asking to sit beside him. He shook his head, "Um, no."

"Cool," Trevor said, dropping down beside Luca and landing on the empty seat. "So, forgot your shorts, eh?"

"Yeah," Luca said, the lie back to swelling in his throat.

"Bullshit," Trevor said.

Luca was stunned. "Huh?"

"I said bullshit, you didn't 'forget' your shorts. I know why you're sitting here."

Luca gulped, not sure where this conversation was going, nor whose side Trevor was on. Luca had seen him hang around with Johnny Thomas, but Trevor was one of those kids who hung around everyone. Luca didn't know if Trevor was one of the usual jerks and bullies that Johnny hung out with. The only kids Luca knew for sure were in that group were Gus and Kiyor, but it was always possible that Johnny had found a new recruit.

Trevor pointed at the field, and straight at Johnny Thomas. Johnny wasn't looking in their direction, but Luca was terrified that the bully would turn and see them, then think Luca was talking about him.

"Don't point," Luca said, almost desperately. "He'll see you."

Trevor laughed. "Let him, I don't give a shit what he thinks. Fuck Johnny Thomas."

Luca was both shocked by Trevor's cursing, and also relieved that he didn't seem to like Johnny Thomas at all. He'd never seen Trevor have a problem with anyone.

Trevor kept pointing at Johnny, and Luca was sure that at any moment he would turn around and see him. Fortunately, Johnny was in the center of the pitch with his eyes on Gus, who was on the opposite team and trying to get the ball to Johnny.

Gus lost the ball out of bounds, and everyone on the field turned toward the sideline. Just then, Johnny looked up and saw Luca and Trevor sitting on the bench, Trevor's finger still wagging toward him.

Oh no!

Trevor smiled, and waved at Johnny. Under his breath he said, "Hey, bitch. Yeah, we're talking about you … about what a small dick you have, and how you jerk off with tweezers … to pictures of your sister. You fucking pussy."

Luca couldn't help but laugh, even though he was certain that Johnny would know Luca was laughing at him.

He looked down, trying to wipe the smile from his face, whispering, "Stop, you're going to get me killed."

"He ain't gonna do shit," Trevor said.

"Apparently, you don't know Johnny Thomas," Luca said, risking a look back at the field to see that the bully was no longer paying attention to them, Johnny's eyes back on the action, following the ball.

Thank God!

Trevor looked at Luca. "Why you so afraid of him?"

"Oh, I don't know, maybe because he's bigger than me, stronger than me, and totally crazy? Those all seem like good reasons. He also likes to pick on me, just because, and a lot more than most kids."

"He's just a bully, man, you stand up to him once, maybe twice, he'll turn and run away like a little bitch, trust me!"

"Easy for you to say!"

"What do you mean?"

Luca shifted uncomfortably, not wanting to say the wrong thing and accidentally insult Trevor. "Well, you're big and strong, and everybody likes you. You don't have to deal with bullies."

Trevor laughed. "Well, yeah, I don't have to deal with bullies now. But last year, when I lived in Chino, I didn't fit in either. And some assholes decided they'd make my life hell."

Luca leaned forward, surprised that there was ever a time when Trevor didn't fit in, especially if that time was just one year ago.

"It wasn't until my brother taught me to fight, and I stood up for myself, that things finally changed."

"I don't have a brother," Luca said. "Just a little sister."

"Well, what about your dad? Can't he teach you?"

"I don't know," Luca said, not bothering to explain that his dad *did* teach him a bit. "I don't even know why I have to learn how to fight! Can't people just get along? What happened to everyone leaving everyone else alone? I feel like if I start fighting, it'll never end. Like I'll always have to fight someone trying to mess with me."

Trevor shook his head, "No, no, no. It doesn't work that way, not for people like me and you. It's not like you're in a gang and need to prove yourself, or playing a video game where you have to fight mini-boss after mini-boss until you get to the big, bad boss. You just stand up to a guy like Johnny Thomas once, or, like I said, twice, since *some* thick fucks don't get the message first time around, and you clock that bitch right in his face and he'll leave you alone for good."

"I don't know," Luca said, looking back at the field, watching as Johnny ran fast and knocked into Hector Esposito hard, then yanked the ball from his hands. As Hector fell to the dirt, Johnny laughed too loud. Coach didn't even blow the whistle.

Trevor said, "You might not believe this, but most bullies are just secretly scared, little cowards. Usually they're being bullied by someone themselves, and are looking for victims weaker than them so that they can take out their frustrations, and maybe feel a little stronger. If you stand up to them, then you're taking their fuel away. If you're not scared, then they'll find someone who is."

Luca was impressed by how much Trevor seemed to know. He was so much smarter than Luca expected. While he certainly didn't think Trevor would be dumb, he hadn't expected him to sound like his dad, saying so many things that made so much sense.

"What you're saying makes sense," Luca said. "And even my dad said I should stand up to Johnny. But I don't know … I get scared whenever I think about it."

Trevor looked Luca up and down, then smacked a hand on his back like they were longtime pals. "How would you like it if I taught you how to fight?"

"Huh?"

"Since you don't have a brother, and your dad is probably old like mine and forgot what it was like to be a kid. Let me teach you."

"I don't know," Luca said, even as his mind trailed off imagining a few dreams coming true: Trevor training him, Luca beating Johnny up, him finally being left alone. Then Luca saw the nightmare that dared to ruin his dreams: him getting in over his head, overconfident and unprepared for a real, actual fight with Johnny. The kind that left him bloodied and scared, humiliated.

"Or … " Trevor said, laughing, "You can keep being Johnny's personal punching bag. I doubt he'll get bored, not if you just keep on standing there and taking it. Admit it, man, that's *got* to be getting pretty old, right?"

"Yeah," Luca agreed. Daring to dream, he turned to Trevor. "So, how would you teach me? And when would we do it?"

"Wanna meet after school, at Barker Park?"

Barker Park was across the street from the school, a fairly large park with a nature trail and several bike paths. It was also on the way home for Luca, who rode his bike to school on Wednesdays because his sister stayed late and Luca didn't like waiting around for Mom to come pick them both up.

"I wouldn't have long. I told my mom I was going to run by the comic book shop, and I'd be home by 4:30. Would 20 minutes be enough?"

"Oh yeah, I could teach you some basics in 20 minutes, no problem. Then we can meet again another day, if you want. And I can teach you some more."

"Thank you," Luca said, then risked asking something he thought might anger Trevor. "Why are you doing this? I mean, why help *me?*"

"I don't know, maybe I see a little of myself from last year in you, and want to help. But also, I'd just love to see the surprised look on that fucker's face when you punch him in the nads. That, my friend, will be priceless!"

Luca laughed, feeling an oddly confident swell in his spirits.

Maybe he would stand up to Johnny Thomas after all; he could end the bullying, impress his new friend, and make his father proud.

~

TWENTY-SEVEN

Michael Blackmore

Mike sat outside of Mary Olson's house, watching for any sign of the killer … or anybody.

It was morning, and the house, along with the tree-lined street in the gated community, was quiet.

From his research, Mike knew Mary was a greeting card designer and worked from home. She had a 13-year-old daughter named Paola, probably in school. Mary was separated from a man named Ryan Olson, declared missing in 2012. Mike wondered if the man he was looking for might be somehow responsible for Ryan's "disappearance." Maybe she shacked up with the killer after he took care of her ex.

Mike had long ago stopped being surprised by murderers conniving their way into the lives of normal women, even having long-term relationships and starting families. He wondered how broken someone had to be if they were willing to let such evil into their lives, because there was no way at least a part of you wouldn't know. Human instincts were too strong, even if most people chose to ignore them. It could be that the woman had no idea her new man was a cold-blooded killer until after she'd fallen for him, but at any rate, she probably would've suspected that *something* was up.

While movies and the media liked to play up how serial killers managed to blend into families and neighborhoods, with the tired phrasing, "He was a quiet man, we never suspected anything," that was rarely the case, at least in Mike's ample experience. When it came to serial killers, the only people who didn't know something was wrong were those who didn't really know the murderer. Anyone who spent any amount of time with a serial killer usually knew something was off with them. They might not suspect the person's pure evil, but if they were paying any attention they had to know *something* was wrong.

So, it confused Mike that decent people could allow themselves to ignore those warning bells so often, and made him wonder if it was a different sort of instinct, stronger than the first: an instinct to turn their eyes from the truth, to stay alive and maybe safe, thinking that one monster might help them to keep others away. Mike also wondered if Mary was just such a woman.

Of course, it was possible that Mary Olson was ignorant of this particular monster, or that she didn't know the killer at all, and he was following a dead end. The only way to know for sure was to get out of his car and knock on her door. He reached over to the passenger seat and grabbed a bouquet of roses and lilies he bought from the grocery store for the ruse he planned to use if any neighbors happened to see him.

Mike approached Mary's house, eyes on her windows as he mentally prepared himself to drop the flowers and reach into his jacket for his gun if necessary.

He looked up and down the street and saw an older woman two doors down, pretending to check her mailbox. Mike knew she was scoping him out. He smiled and waved, she quickly looked away as if she hadn't been watching.

He continued up the stone path and knocked on Mary's large front door. There were windows on either side, displaying the spacious interior. Mike could see clear to the back of the house and into the kitchen, but saw no sign of anyone home. The TV wasn't on, and the house was silent.

He rang the bell and continued to wait.

Nothing.

Mike decided to visit the old lady down the street to see what she knew.

Before he reached her door, she appeared at her doorstep, "Yes?" she asked.

From her expression and hand to hip, Mike could tell she was a suspicious type, who wouldn't think twice about calling out bullshit if she got a whiff of it.

"Hello, Ma'am," he said waving his hand and smiling, "I've got a flower delivery for Mary Olson, but she doesn't seem to be there. Do you know what time she's usually home? I hate to leave them on the doorstep because these lilies are thirsty, and they'll die if it gets too hot; there doesn't seem to be any decent shade out front. I could leave them in back, but she might not see them and the customer didn't leave us with a phone number."

The woman relaxed. "No. I think she works at home, so if she's not answering, she might be out running errands or something."

"OK," Mike said, looking up the street, and coming up with a lie. "One of the neighbors said she lives with her daughter and that sometimes there's another guy there, do you know when any of them come home? I don't need to give them to Mary, just someone at the house."

The woman's brow furrowed, "I don't think anybody else lives there. It's just her and her girl."

"Really?" Mike said, trying not to oversell his ploy. "Neighbor said he saw a skinny guy with longish, dark hair, early 30s. Really good-looking, but a bit crude?"

"Oh," the woman said, her face turning sour, "*him?* No, he doesn't live there. He's a friend of hers, from out of town. Rudest man I've ever met."

He laughed, pegging the woman as a born gossip. "Really? What happened?"

"Mary's daughter, Paola, she came to my house one day asking to borrow a cupcake pan so she could make something as a surprise for her mom. So I lent it to her, no problem. But a week or so went by, and she didn't return it. Now, normally, I wouldn't care, I have plenty of pans and don't mind lending stuff to neighbors, but this was my favorite pan, cooked stuff just right, nice and brown, never burnt, and nothing ever sticks. I really should've gotten more, since now you can't find them. So, anyway, I went over to Mary's to ask for my pan back, but Mary and Paola weren't home. Instead, this ... *man* ... answered the door, and said Mary wasn't home, but I could come back later. He seemed nice at first, smiling, and he was even wearing Mary's apron. I told him I just wanted to get my pan back, because I had to bake something for a church func-tion that night. I described the pan to him, and he said he was in the middle of using it, but if I could come back in an hour he'd give it back. Problem was, I didn't really want to wait an hour, so I told him, and he got really rude with me. He asked me what was up my ... well, I don't want to repeat what he said, but let's just say he had a sailor's mouth. Just awful. Nobody should talk like that! I left, without my pan, and at that point I didn't even want it, not after *he* touched it."

Mike laughed, playing along. "Wow."

"So, anyway, Mary came over a few days later and brought me my pan. I told her how rude her gentleman guest had been to. She apologized, then I told her that I was shocked, both that she would associate with such a foul human being, and that she'd allow her daughter anywhere near him. He's disgusting. But she said, 'Oh, that's just Boricio, he's really sweet once you get to know him. He's just a bit eccentric.'"

"Boricio?" Mike asked, wondering if this was his killer's name. "What kinda name is that?"

"I don't know," she said. "I'd never heard it before, but it sounds dago, and the way he talked made me think of a redneck Italian."

Mike ignored the woman's blatant racism. "Wow, sounds like a class act. So, he doesn't live there? After that story, I'd hate to run into the guy."

"No, I forget where she said he's from. I think New York, which would figure, with that mouth of his."

Mike laughed again, then looked back down at the flowers, "OK, well thanks for your help. I'll maybe wait a few more minutes and see if she comes home. If she doesn't, could I come back and leave the flowers with you? I've an awful lot of deliveries today and I'm not sure I can get back on this side of town before dark."

Mike gave the woman his most pleasant smile.

"Certainly," she said, smiling back.

"OK, thank you." Mike went back down her walkway holding the flowers.

He approached a few more neighbors before returning to Mary's with the same ruse. One of the neighbors, an older man named Winston, told Mike he thought Mary might be out of town. He'd seen her leave the morning before, or maybe the day before that, he wasn't sure, and he'd not seen her Volvo in the driveway since.

Mike thanked the man then returned to his car and waited, hoping it wasn't in vain.

After 10 minutes, he couldn't wait any longer. It would be too suspicious, hell it probably already was for a "flower delivery guy" to be waiting around rather than leaving. If he stayed much longer, his cover would be blown and someone might call the cops.

Mike returned to Mary's doorway, took a quick look around to make sure he was still unseen, then slipped to the side of the yard and into the back. His car's windows were tinted dark enough that anyone looking from a distance wouldn't notice he wasn't still in it, which gave him some time to do what he had to.

He went to the home's rear, glad to see that her house backed up to a wooded area, and therefore he didn't have to worry about neighbors behind her spotting him.

He went to the rear sliding-glass door he had spotted when standing at the front, then looked up and down in search of alarm contacts. He saw none.

Mike was also pleasantly surprised that there was nothing in place to secure the doors. He was two for two and feeling confident as he palmed the glass with both hands and pressed, then lifted the right door from its track and slid it open. Once inside, he pulled a cloth from inside his pocket and wiped his prints from the glass, then slid the door back into the groove to erase any sign of his entrance. If he could find what he was looking for — something that might lead him to Boricio — he wouldn't have to discuss anything with Mary. The fewer people he spoke with, the thinner his trail to Boricio's inevitable murder.

MIKE FOUND what he was looking for sooner than expected, in Mary's laptop.

Just as her house wasn't guarded by alarm, her computer wasn't password protected. He was three for three. Mike did a search for the name "Boricio" and came up with nothing. He saw that Mary didn't use her computer's mail program, which meant her e-mail was likely browser based. Whether he could check that or not depended on whether Mary's browser was still signed in to her e-mail or if she stored her password on her computer unencrypted. Given the sorry state of security in her house, it was quite likely.

First, he decided to search through her computer's images. While none were named or tagged Boricio, or any derivative of, Mike found what he was looking for within minutes — a picture of four people, Mary, Paola, Boricio, and a woman who looked to be Boricio's girlfriend.

"Bingo," Mike said.

The image looked too much like the sketches of the suspect in his daughter's death. Too similar for coincidence.

Mike saved all of Mary's images to a flash drive, then clicked on her browser and began looking for anything relating to Boricio.

Unfortunately, her e-mail account's stored password didn't work. She must've changed it and not updated her browser. The first miss in his search so far.

He wondered if Mary was out of town. And if so, had she gone to visit Boricio? He checked her apps and found a personal finance application button, which, if she used it and synced it with her bank account, would update regularly to reflect her credit or bank card charges.

He clicked it and was thrilled to see Mary's bank card history show up. He saw hotel and restaurant charges in L.A., from one day before.

Everything in Mike told him to come back another time and talk to Mary after she got back, until a tiny voice inside him prodded:

What if she's with him? This could be your only chance.

Throughout Mike's career as a cop, he had learned to trust his gut above all else. He wasn't about to stop.

It was time to continue his road trip.

Mike wait until he was far away from Mary's house before calling Margie to explain that he'd be on the road a little longer. Fortunately, she was used to his occasional road trips that he usually used for field research.

As he stuck Mary's laptop under his jacket and left her house, placing the flowers beside Mary's back door, Mike thought of his daughter again.

Soon, Honey. Soon, I'll make everything right.

TWENTY-EIGHT

Mary Olson

Malibu, California

BY THE LOOK on his rosy cheeks, Boricio had slept like a baby. The rest of them slept horribly.

Mary hadn't felt so on edge since fleeing the Drury that awful October past, then fearing for her life through every second of the long, hard winter, until Desmond led them to temporary solace at the Alabama farm.

Rose was clearly terrified, but didn't want to talk about anything, preferring — or maybe even needing — to pretend that nothing had happened before her meeting with Marina. But as much as Rose wanted to pretend that her horrible reality didn't exist, the truth was a blushing ache all over her face.

Boricio had returned to the hotel to "take care of the bodies," whatever that meant, and he had done it for all of them, which horrified Rose in a way Mary could only imagine, but not truly understand. Mary had known both versions of Boricio, both before and after Luca's fixing, and didn't think there was anything about him that could surprise her.

But Rose had known Boricio only as her lover. Mary was grateful for his earlier version, because it was that version who no doubt saved her life the night before, and would no doubt help her find an answer for Paola, if Rose's machine failed to work.

Mary felt for Rose, thought she could practically hear her heart beating as they drove the coast toward Marina's — even if she could buy Boricio's reasoning that the bodies he buried were only dead because they were infected by some sentient monster from "who-knows-where-in-the-fuck-all," and Mary wasn't sure she did. Rose was clearly afraid that it was only a matter of time before they traced the bodies back to Boricio, then, of course to her.

Mary would be happy to reassure Rose, relay more of the horrible stories from the dead world that made Mary fear the police less than the living evil from that other Earth, the monster who swallowed her daughter, holding her prisoner until Luca had saved her, infecting her mind and turning her into an empty shell, or perhaps a marionette with pure evil as puppeteer. Mary would be glad to tell her *why* she trusted Boricio, despite his homicidal tendencies, though Rose obviously didn't know much about those, if anything at all.

Rose clearly wanted none of that, wanted to know nothing, so she held her eyes to the window as Mary drove, following her cell phone's directions and doing her best at pretending the night hadn't happened. She would have to deal with it soon, after leaving Marina's. Until then, Mary figured, Rose would be keeping her mind on the dotted line.

Sick as he was, Mary felt an irrefutable comfort from Boricio. She wished he was with them now, riding shotgun in the Volvo. Someone or something was after them. On the dead world *It* had invaded Paola, and Mary worried that *It* might go inside her again. Mary was haunted by that constant thought, ever since last night's events.

What if It knows where we are, because It can see inside Paola, after having been inside her before?

Mary wished she was more like Rose, able to shut off her mind and simply not think about the creeping evil, but that wasn't how she was wired. Mary would find a thought, and gravitate around it like a moth and flame, even if the flame threatened her sanity.

She wanted Boricio for protection, and friendship. Even though she had Paola riding in back, Mary barely knew Rose, and felt odd going with her alone to meet the leader of a well-known, and oft-ridiculed cult. She had a hard time believing she wouldn't see Marina as thoroughly full of shit, and didn't want to offend Rose if that was the case. If Boricio was with them, he'd say what she was thinking without Mary having to, since she was sure it wouldn't be far from what he was thinking himself. Boricio never had problems telling it like it is. Mary would think it, he would say it, and save her the embarrassment of an unnecessary scene.

All three of them had asked Boricio to go, but he was barely awake and in need of some shuteye after disposing of the bodies.

They pulled up to Marina's house — the J.L. Harmon Estate — and though Rose had prepared her and Paola for what they would see, Mary was unable to stifle her awe.

"Wow," she whispered, turning to Paola in the seat behind her.

"No kidding," Paola whispered, putting a lump in Mary's throat, not from the words themselves, but because Mary still wasn't used to her 13-year-old (baby girl) daughter looking as though she could legally drink.

They had approached the three-story house from behind, driving along a gorgeous stretch of dry and sandy Malibu beach, then behind a waterfall, and past what looked like an acre of lush landscaping before pulling to a stop in front of a sprawling palace. Everything about the house was giant: columns, windows, doors, and view.

Mary looked up to an upper floor window and saw a man looking down, no not looking, *staring*. An icy chill flooded her body, starting at the base of her neck and slithering low past her waist.

She tried to be like Rose, ignoring the stare as she slammed the Volvo door, greeted by a valet before they were led into the house and asked to wait in a sprawling foyer.

Marina showed up in fewer than five minutes, smiling wide as if there were cameras at the door.

Mary had seen Marina on TV, but was still surprised by her in-person beauty. More than just pretty, Marina was gorgeous. She looked freshly scrubbed, her cheeks lightly blushed, long, honey-colored hair piled high on her head. She turned to Rose, kissed her once on each cheek, said it was wonderful to see her, then turned to Mary and Paola, waiting for her introduction.

"These are my friends, Mary and Paola Olson," Rose said, then turned back to Marina. "You helped me so much with my migraines, and my anxiety — which I hadn't even told you about — that I was hoping you could help them as well. Thanks again for seeing us. Their problem is ... *special.*"

"Of course," Marina smiled, seeming pleased. "That's why we're here."

Marina didn't ask what their special problem might be, she just led them through the foyer and into a breathtaking study without any walls, just a single partition of glass running the length of the room and opening out to a pool, tennis court, and gardens so lush they made Desmond's yard in Warson look like a desert.

Marina gestured for the three girls to sit in an oversized, white sofa, then she sat across from them and crossed her legs. "So," she said, "what seems to be the trouble?"

Before Rose could answer, Mary said, "I'd rather not say."

"You'd rather not say?" Marina raised her eyebrows, then without waiting for Mary's response added, "Then how can I help you?"

"I don't mean to be rude, Ms. Harmon, but I'm not sure what to think about … any of this … and as much as I'd love to believe, I would have an easier time if I wasn't telling you what sort of problem you were trying to solve."

Instead of getting defensive, Marina smiled and said, "Go on."

Mary held Marina's eyes. "From what Rose has told me, your machine is called The Capacitor, and it fixes something you call The Current, which you believe to be some sort of metaphysical stream that exists between mind and body, is that correct?"

Marina smiled. "Roughly, yes, but it's really not *quite* that simple."

"Well," Mary continued, "if that's *basically* it, then I think you *might* be able to help us."

Marina sat for a long minute, ignoring Rose as she looked from Mary to Paola and back, several times. Finally, her face slightly tensed, she said, "Very well then, follow me." Marina stood from her overstuffed chair, then crossed the study to a door behind a long desk and swiped her thumb across a pad beside the door.

The door opened. Marina stepped through it, then turned toward the girls and motioned for them to follow. The new room was mostly bare except for a long tube with a small window at the top.

Paola said, "Isn't anyone going to ask me what *I* think?"

Rose was silent, Mary stuttered. Marina said, "Of course, Dear, I'm so very sorry. What *do* you think?"

Paola looked at the machine, then at Marina. "I don't care *how* it works, I just want to know if it can hurt me."

"Of course not." Marina shook her head. "If it could hurt you, we would never allow you inside it. It's possible The

Capacitor won't do anything to you at all. I've seen that happen plenty, though I believe even then it's delivering results we cannot see. Because The Capacitor works by repairing your cells, and improving The Current between mind and body, there's no way it could possibly cause your harm. It's either good, or nothing."

"How can you be sure?" Paola asked.

Mary thought that Paola seemed uncomfortable, but wasn't sure if her discomfort was because of the giant house, the stranger who owned it, the religion that bought it, or the odd, magical machine that could somehow promise the impossible.

"Well, Dear, you know what they say about death and taxes, right?"

"No," Paola shook her head. She was too young to worry much about either, though she had more experience with the first than she should have.

"It means that nothing is certain. Intuition, yes. Inspiration, yes. But certainty, no. You can *feel* that something is true, but you can never *know* it for sure, even if it's right in front of you. Proof can lie. If you begin with certainties, you'll end up with doubts, that's why it's better to start with doubting and leave with belief."

Paola seemed uncertain.

"Are you sure about this?" Mary asked her daughter.

"Even if it *might* help me, then yes. I don't think I really have a choice. I mean, what do I have to lose?"

Mary didn't want to answer with any one of the hundred things *she* thought could go wrong. Best not to add to her daughter's apprehension. If Boricio was right, and this thing was a fancy placebo machine, she didn't want to load her daughter with negative energy.

Marina said, "You have nothing to lose. If The Capacitor does nothing, then it does nothing, and I'm sorry it couldn't help you. But you don't have to worry about whether you believe in it, or joining our Church or anything like that. I'm offering it as a courtesy because of Rose. However, I will add that this experience is available to so few, almost no one, it would be an absolute shame to have such opportunity at your fingertips, only to turn your back on it."

Paola was quiet, still thinking.

Marina added a final thought, "Sometimes, when opportunity knocks, you can't hear it because your heart is beating too loud. It's okay, I've been there before." She leaned forward and took Paola's hands. "Trust me."

Mary bristled not wanting Marina to coerce her daughter into the machine, but before she could speak, Paola said, "I want to do it, I'm ready right now," all in a single exhalation.

Paola stood, stepped toward The Capacitor, and eased herself inside; Mary thought the plush fabric behind her daughter's back made it look like a coffin.

Paola might not have had questions, but Mary did. "What happens now?"

Rose still stood vacant beside them, likely maybe she was finally thinking about last night's events.

"Nothing really," Marina said. "We close it with you inside, then open it back in five minutes."

"There's nothing to set? No dials, no readouts, nothing like that?"

"No," Marina said. "Nothing like that: It isn't that type of machine."

"I'm ready," Paola said, again, in case it wasn't painfully obvious to everyone.

Marina set her hand on the door but before she could close it, a man entered the room.

Marina looked up. "Steven!" she said, as if both surprised and happy to see him. The man smiled, turning to each of the girls and running his eyes across them, smiling as if in study. Mary recognized him as the man who'd been in the upper floor window staring at them. She wondered if he was one of the higher-ups in the cult, or Marina's boyfriend, or both.

Marina asked, "What do you need?"

Something flitted across his face, undeniably odd, a sort of shocked recognition. "Nothing," his smile widened, as if to bury discomfort. "I can see you're busy, of course I can wait."

He turned, then left the study without another word.

Marina turned back to Paola. "Sorry about that."

"It's okay," she said, then repeated that she was ready.

As Marina closed the door Mary felt another chill, feeling like she'd seen the man somewhere before.

TWENTY-NINE

Steven Warner

IT was anguished, sorting too many thoughts inside *ITS* mind.

Ugly, haunting, horrible, real.

Inescapable.

Confusing.

Last night had gone horribly.

IT had sent ITS minions to erase the disturbing presence of Boricio Wolfe, but plans unraveled, after barely starting. The man was stronger than *IT* had remembered on the other world when they'd faced one another before.

IT had failed.

IT had underestimated what was required.

IT had allowed others to do the work *IT* knew *IT* must now do *ITSELF.*

The biggest surprise wasn't Boricio, it was that the hunter wasn't alone: the woman Mary was with him — the woman whose daughter had hosted *IT* through the breath of an evening, back in the other world, before *IT* found the shell, John.

In the midst of *ITS* meditation, an ugly scent had invaded *ITS* nostrils. What was first sensed the night before had come nearer; so close that *IT* knew the smell was somewhere other than in *ITS* mind.

Then *IT* realized the scent was coming from outside: the woman, Mary.

And she wasn't alone.

The last time *IT* had seen Mary, she was pregnant. *IT* could sense that she'd lost the baby after returning to Earth. Her sadness cloaked her in a dark aura.

With her, Mary brought the girl, her daughter, Paola. Such a tender mind; too tender to host one such as *IT.*

The girl's scent was somehow different, not just older — though she was certainly that — but altered, transformed by The Light.

IT considered the memory — a file inside *ITS* mind — then soured at the recall of the man child, Luca, hosting The Light, raising his own army against him on the other world. Though the attempt failed, it had wounded *ITS* strength.

IT opened *ITS* eyes, uncrossed *ITS* legs, then stood, slipped on a robe, and went to the window, peering through the glass and out onto the midnight-blue Volvo as it pulled up to the drive and idled in front of the valet.

The woman, Mary, looked up, and for a second *IT* wasn't sure if she recognized *ITS* presence. *IT* continued to study her, feel — nearly bask — in her discomfort. No, *IT* decided, she had no clue who he was, only that there was something she *should* be feeling.

Humans were vapid, so unaware of their world. Such a diminished ability to be mindful, too often occupied by what they lacked, rather than seeing what was there before them.

Moments later, *IT* heard Marina on the other side of the door, preparing for the visitors; the visitors who had been to the other world.

IT thought how unfortunate it was that the man, Boricio Wolfe, wasn't with them. It would be ... convenient ... to eliminate all threats at once.

These humans weren't just survivors from the other world, they'd all been touched by The Light. It made them stronger, and more resistant to *ITS* influence. *IT* had to dispose of them before they could gain influence, before they, and The Light wherever it was hiding, raised an army against *IT*.

Why are they here?

Have they come to destroy me?

IT left the mediation room, went downstairs to Marina's study, crossed to the far side, then pressed *ITS* ear to the door.

"Are you sure about this?" The woman, Mary, asked her daughter.

"Even if it *might* help me, then yes. I don't think I really have a choice. I mean, what do I have to lose?"

Marina was selling the girl on the machine.

The girl was quiet.

Into her silence Marina said, "Sometimes when opportunity knocks, you can't hear it because your heart is beating too loud. It's okay, I've been there before." A pause, then, "Trust me."

The girl said, "I want to do it, I'm ready right now."

IT opened the door and stepped inside Marina's study. She turned from her guests to the doorway and called out, "Steven!"

IT smiled, a sour expression on *ITS* pained face, then turned to look at each of the women, surprised to see the difference in the girl, now that *IT* could see her up close, rather than through the blur of a car window: she wasn't just different inside as he had felt, she was different outside too: unnaturally aged, ripened past her season, like the boy, Luca.

Marina asked what *IT* needed.

Then, *IT* saw what *IT* never expected.

ITS heart pounded, nearly burst through *ITS* chest, at least that's how it felt while thudding through echoes of Boricio Bishop still living inside *IT*.

It was impossible.

It couldn't be.

Unthinkable.

The woman beside Mary once belonged to *him*. The love of his life, Rose.

Suddenly, Boricio Bishop's shadow started to swell within, fighting back for the first time in forever, trying to reclaim its body.

IT could hear Boricio's tormented cries, the anguish of wanting to go to Rose, to talk to her, to tell her he was still there, that he loves her.

IT pushed back, fighting Boricio's will as best it could.

Boricio's internal screams shook like a quake through their shared, intertwined psyche. If *IT* were not careful, the host could expel *IT*.

IT would be exposed, right there in the room, before them all, forced to either find a new host from them, fight them, or flee.

IT had come too far to allow something as shallow as love derail *IT*.

IT pushed several horrible thoughts into the host's mind, an annihilation of the worst images *IT* had collected from *ITS* collective memories — death, decay, murder, mass graves — clubbing Boricio's soul into submission.

It took everything *IT* had to locate a voice, and shove it through the shell's maw with something more than a grunt.

"Nothing." *ITS* smile spread in painful artifice. "I can see you're busy, of course I can wait."

IT left, the shell's heart threatening to burst through skin as *IT* fled the room, quick to put distance between *ITSELF* and the ghosts of Boricio's past.

IT remembered Boricio first seeing her, wiping cheese from her cheek before filling her mouth with eggs, as she ate alone, two tables away. Something spoke to the shell in a whisper — soothing, worming its way into head, heart, and soul, unlike any woman before her: true love, brighter than fire. Playful banter, before she laughed and said, *Boricio? Is that your name?*

He said it was, then held out his hand.

I'm Rose.

Memories of Bishop and Rose that didn't belong to *IT* collided in torment.

Too much.

The shell was brittle, knees weak.

IT fell to the floor.

It was so peculiar, *love:*

Selfish, impatient, insecure, filled with mistakes, too hard to handle.

Beautiful and ugly: a prison.

~

THIRTY

Luca Harding

"*That's* your fist?" Trevor said, his face edging laughter.

Luca stared at his closed hand, which looked like every fist he'd ever seen on TV, comic books, or movies, then back at Trevor. "Yeah, what's wrong with it?"

Trevor held up his hand and showed Luca *his* fist. Even though they were the same age, or close, Trevor's hand seemed so much larger and stronger, at least twice as manly. Other than that, Luca didn't see much of a difference.

"Notice anything?" Trevor asked.

Luca was too embarrassed to say what he was thinking — *I have a girl's hand?* Instead, he shook his head no and tried to keep from looking down.

"Look at my thumb. Notice, it's *outside* of my other fingers."

Luca looked at his own fist, his thumb curled beneath his index and middle fingers. "What's wrong with this?"

"Well, nothing, if you want to break your thumb the first time you hit something hard!"

Luca looked down, ashamed, then back at Trevor's fist, and made his best imitation. He held it up for Trevor's approval.

"Now there you go!" he said, clapping loudly.

Though Trevor was only teasing him, good natured like his dad probably would have, Luca was glad they were far from the skate park or basketball courts, where other kids wouldn't look over and see that he was pathetic enough to need lessons in not just fighting, but also in making a fist!

They were standing under one of the park's several pavilions, littered with picnic tables and hidden among the trees, far enough from where people would see them, and likely laugh at Luca, to keep him from worrying too much about what he looked like to anyone other than Trevor. Though it wasn't yet 4 p.m., the sun had gone missing. Gray clouds hovered above, and a cool breeze blew through the thick clusters of surrounding pines.

"OK," Trevor said, moving out from under the pavilion and into an open area of grass. "Now I want you to hit me."

"Hit you?"

"Yeah, don't worry, you're not gonna hurt me."

"Gee, thanks," Luca joked.

"Hey, just being honest! Hell, you probably won't even land a punch. But that's OK. That's why we're here. I'm gonna make you better."

Luca stepped into the clearing and raised his fists, trying to mimic Trevor's stance. While Trevor looked like a boxer, or as close to a boxer as Luca had ever seen in person, Luca felt like a fraud, like a child pretending to be a boxer.

Trevor began to move back and forth, shifting his weight from one foot to the other, circling Luca.

Luca tried to keep pace, feeling stupid, and bursting into giggling fits.

"Don't laugh," Trevor said, his eyes serious. "Pretend I'm Johnny Thomas."

Luca lost his giggles and tried returning Trevor's serious stare.

"OK," Trevor said. "Now I'm going to move toward you. When I get close enough, I want you to take a swing, OK?"

"OK," Luca said as Trevor moved toward him, fists raised.

Seeing the intensity in Trevor's eyes only made Luca more nervous that one day soon he would be in a real fight with Johnny Thomas, without Trevor around to help him.

Stop thinking about Johnny, and just take a swing.

Luca moved toward Trevor and swung, a halfhearted attempt because he didn't want to accidentally hurt his new friend.

Trevor moved quickly out of the way, and Luca sailed right by, missing him completely. Luca stumbled forward, then felt a sharp jab in his back.

"Ow!" he turned around to see Trevor backing away, his fists still raised.

"Why'd you hit me?" Luca asked, trying not to let Trevor see how much he'd hurt him, especially since he was probably going easy on him with a light punch.

"Because you missed me. Miss Johnny, and he's gonna hit you way worse than that. You need to connect, Luca. You connect, I won't hit you. Deal?"

"I don't want to hurt you, though," Luca said, hearing his dad's voice in his ear, telling him not to sound whiney.

"You're *not* going to hurt me," Trevor said. "But I guarantee: Miss me again and I *will* hurt you."

Their eyes met, and Luca wasn't sure if Trevor was trying to encourage or scare him. It seemed like he was trying to toughen him up so he could be better prepared to face off against Johnny Thomas, but the intensity in his eyes made Luca nervous.

Trevor began bouncing on his feet and jabbing at the air, "OK, Luca, take another shot."

Luca tried bouncing on his feet like his coach, but felt stupid, so instead, he moved in, slowly, trying to find the best angle to approach Trevor.

Luca took a swing, and missed again. Rather than sailing past Trevor, he turned, anticipating Trevor's attack. But he was too slow to defend himself, and Trevor's fist landed in Luca's gut.

Pain erupted through his stomach. Luca doubled over, hoping he didn't look like the world's biggest wimp as he sucked air through his teeth and tried not to cry.

"Did I hurt you?" Trevor asked, his voice suddenly high-pitched and excited.

Luca wasn't sure what to say. He didn't want to seem ungrateful to Trevor for all of his help; no other kid had ever looked out for him like this before. But if he said yes, and asked Trevor to stop, Trevor might not help him become a better fighter. If he said nothing, Trevor might beat the crap out of him during their first lesson.

"Maybe just punch a little less hard," Luca said. "That one kind of hurt."

"Oh, so you want me to fight you like a little baby girl, is that it?" Trevor said, his tone almost mocking. "You think Johnny's gonna take it easy on you?"

"No," Luca said, rising to meet Trevor's eyes again.

"Damn right, he's not. Now let's go," Trevor said, pounding his fists together, then returning to his fighting stance.

Luca began moving, again trying to figure out the best way to hit the kid. He tried to remember some of the moves his father had taught him the other night, but his mind went blank in the moment's heat. If he missed again, Luca would feel like the world's biggest loser, unable to learn the most basic moves. And he'd get hit again!

He balled his fists tight and moved closer, eyes bolted to Trevor's.

Come on: Don't miss, don't miss, don't miss.

Luca took another swing, at Trevor's face this time, giving it his all …

… and missed. Again.

This time, Trevor dodged and closed quickly on Luca before he could turn back around. His fist slammed into Luca, right in his ribcage, so hard he felt like something must have shattered inside him.

Luca fell to the ground, eyes burning as they got wet, wincing through the sharp pain blooming through his right side, while trying his hardest not to cry. Tears painted his face anyway. So Luca stayed hunched on the ground, face buried in his arms, hoping Trevor didn't realize he was crying like a big giant baby.

From nowhere, Luca heard the sound of clapping, from many hands.

Huh?

He wiped his eyes, looking up to see Johnny Thomas, Gus, and Kiyor as all three stepped into the clearing. Johnny and Trevor bumped fists like the best of friends, showing Luca his mistake: Trevor *was* one of Johnny's gang, and the entire afternoon was nothing but a set-up.

Oh no!

Now Luca was alone, in an isolated part of the park where no one could see them, surrounded by nothing but enemies and trees.

He stood, raising his fists, trying to ready himself for whatever was going to come, from whoever was going to deliver it.

Johnny laughed, "Oh, look, Boys, Luca's a boxer now! And it only took one 'lesson.'"

"Leave me alone," Luca said, trying to sound brave despite his streaming tears and knocking knees.

"Or what?" Johnny said. "You gonna kick our asses? You gonna kick *all* our asses?"

"Just … please," Luca said, giving his all to not losing a whimper. "I don't want to fight."

Johnny stepped toward Luca, eyes wild and filled with something between rage and glee that chilled Luca to his bones. "Come on, Luca. Show me your new skills. I want you to hit me."

"No," Luca said.

Johnny smacked him hard across the face.

Luca stumbled backward, his left cheek on fire, though he dared not touch it. He balled his fists, thumbs out, and raised them in front of his face, watching Johnny approach. Unlike Trevor, Johnny wasn't bouncing or weaving or moving his fists like a boxer. He just stood still, staring at Luca, laughing.

"Come on, you little bitch. I *said* I want you to hit me!"

Luca stayed frozen in indecision, trying to determine what he should do. He was surrounded by Johnny and his friends. Trevor met Luca's eyes, giving him that same intense stare he gave him during their "training." Luca shook his head, a silent condemnation for tricking him.

Luca couldn't believe he'd been stupid enough to fall for Trevor's scheme. But he didn't have time to feel stupid or sorry for himself now: he had to fight for his life.

"Come on!" Johnny said, this time shoving Luca back.

Luca stumbled, but stayed on his feet, thinking he should have swung at Johnny when the boy had reached out to push him.

"Come on, Faggot!" Johnny taunted.

Luca kept his fists in front of him, not wanting to make the first move. Some part of him was hoping if he didn't initiate the fight, maybe it wouldn't happen.

Maybe he could still walk away unharmed.

Johnny moved like lightning, his fist striking Luca in the center of his chest, and sending him to the ground gasping for air.

On his hands and knees, Luca reached up and clutched at his chest, as if he could somehow will air back into his lungs. He felt like he was going to die right there, surrounded by bullies. He remembered how Johnny had crushed a rabbit to death. Would he, *could he*, do the same to a person? Maybe rabbits were just the start for a monster like Johnny Thomas.

Luca finally caught his breath and stood as the kids around them began to chant, "Fight, fight, fight."

Luca's heart pounded in his chest, every hair on his body seeming to stand on end, as an overwhelming sense of doom tightened around him.

Johnny moved in to swing.

Luca dodged, managing to bring his fist around to a wallop at the back of Johnny's skull.

Yes!

Johnny stumbled forward, grabbed the back of his head, then turned to Luca, screaming.

Whatever tiny victory Luca might have felt evaporated into Johnny's bellow. Their eyes met, and Luca knew in an instant:

He's going to kill me!

Luca turned to run.

He made it maybe five steps before Johnny tackled him from behind, wrestled him to the ground, and pulled him into a vicious choke hold, twisting Luca around so his belly was facing the dark sky. Luca imagined one of the other kids rushing forth with a knife or something, looking to slice his belly open and leave him to die.

Luca screamed, desperate to wrangle free. Johnny's arm twisted around Luca's neck harder, squeezing tight. Luca kept trying to break free, reaching up to pull Johnny's arm off and digging his nails deep into the bully's flesh, trying to hurt him so bad he'd have no choice but to let go.

Johnny grunted in Luca's ear, "I'm gonna kill you, you little bitch."

He squeezed tighter, despite Luca's fingernails now drawing blood.

Luca flailed, kicked, and elbowed back at Johnny's face,

trying to break free. Nothing worked. Johnny's leg wrapped around Luca's, pinning him in place.

Luca looked up at the others, pleading with his eyes. "He's going to kill me. Help!"

Surely, they don't actually want me dead!

But maybe they did — their eyes were glazed over, like wolves watching a meal stumble into sight.

Luca met Trevor's eyes, pleading. Surely, the boy wasn't faking everything. Someone couldn't pretend to be that nice only to be so cruel, could they?

Please, Trevor!

Trevor turned from him, as if too ashamed to see what would happen next.

Luca gasped for breath as Johnny's vice-like grip tightened on his neck. Luca was certain death would find him in seconds; he thought of his parents and sister, how he would never see them again.

Something flashed through his mind — memories that weren't memories that he'd dreamed: the car crash, his family dying, and the old man, Will, who adopted him. And then there was more ... a sickness that wouldn't go away after his family left him.

The sickness that sent him to the hospital.

Then Luca was cured. His brother had asked the doctors to use this weird, blue, glowing vial. Then in the vision, dream, or whatever it was, Luca writhed on the floor, choking, hoping that each of his breaths wouldn't be his last. Finally, Luca was better. Better than better, able to teleport, away from danger or sadness or lonely, and into ... places. Then his brother ... Boricio was his name ... asked him for a favor.

To go and get another one of the vials.

He needed it to save his girlfriend.

But the old man, Will, wouldn't let him.

So Luca did, and then ...

The vision finished, and Luca was back with Johnny

Thomas's hands circling his neck, convinced that if he didn't break free, he'd be dead. Memories would come true if he let them, if he didn't get up — *now!*

Urgency and anger surged through Luca like fire. It crackled in his veins and nearly exploded, bursting from his body, thrusting him out and away from Johnny's hold. Luca stood upright, staring down at the bully, whose eyes had gone wide with surprise.

"What the?" Johnny Thomas said, jumping to his feet, then falling backward.

Luca barely registered the bully's surprise, as some primal almost *other* part of Luca took control. Luca's eyes seized on the dirt, and a tree branch a few feet away, then blazed toward it so fast, Johnny could barely track his movement.

Johnny had no chance to prepare a defense.

Luca seized the branch, flipped it so its sharp end was pointed out, then brought it forward, driving it through Johnny's gut.

As the makeshift spear pierced him, Johnny's eyes went even wider. He gasped through his final breaths, blood spurting from his mouth. Luca met his eyes, then drove the spear deeper, doing as much damage as he could to Johnny's internal organs.

Screams raged around Luca as the other three kids took off, fear palpable and fueling Luca's rage. From somewhere deep inside, something Luca couldn't recognize, and didn't know existed until it was screaming inside him, demanded that Luca answer as it surfaced to take full control, mind and body.

They can't leave here alive.

Kill them.

Kill them all.

Luca obeyed.

❧

THIRTY-ONE

Paola Olson

There was something … *off* … about the man Steven.

Paola felt something rising inside her, both as he stood in the doorway, and after he left. It lingered in the room like a rotting stench.

She turned from her mom to Marina, then to Rose, none of who seemed to notice anything odd about the man. Paola didn't want to be the only one to say anything, so she didn't. She turned back to Marina and nodded as she settled her back into the fabric and waited for the doors of the machine to close.

As the doors sealed and Paola felt the silence start to grow heavy, a small panic swelled inside her.

Calm down, calm down. It'll be fine.

Paola decided to count down from 100, just like she'd been doing since she was a small child, exactly like her mom had taught her. She didn't want to be scared like a child. She wanted to find a confidence befitting her new body, rather than the mind that was still so comparatively young.

Am I thinking older?

100 … 99 … 98 … 97 … 96 … 95 … 94 …

The Capacitor whirred, the air feeling as if it were

somehow sparking to life with an energy. She thought of a microwave and hoped the machine wasn't about to cook her.

Don't be silly. It's completely safe. Rose used it, and she's fine.

Paola's body rattled, harder than she expected, and banged her back against the machine, shaking her from the inside out: throat humming, hair feeling on fire, tips of her toes feeling like ice; shocks of trauma coiled her ankles and legs, pounding Paola's body with a crackle so sharp she couldn't tell whether it was filled with hellish heat or arctic freeze.

Crackles snapped and sputtered up Paola's body until they sizzled at her shoulders.

Something's wrong!

I've gotta get out!

She wanted to scream but couldn't. The darkness inside the tube went suddenly bright, filling Paola's eyes with more stars than the sky, pinpricking ebony around her. Black got blacker, bright got brighter, and the machine's whir turned into something like a scream.

Paola wanted to meet it with a bellow of her own, but still nothing bled from her mouth but a horrible mocking hush. She tried to reach her hands up to bang on the tube, but her hands disobeyed Paola as surely as her mouth.

Surely they knew she was trying to cry out, they had to know she was dying. Paola expected the doors to fly open but they didn't. She pictured herself collapsing into her mother's wide, parted arms, but her coffin stayed sealed.

Instead, time turned to tundra, and Paola felt a familiar darkness slither inside her.

The same Blanket of darkness that had claimed to itself as her father before claiming her mind outside the Drury. The same darkness that had nested itself inside her, refusing to leave until Luca — a boy she didn't yet know — pulled her from the horror.

The Blanket was back.

This time, the undiluted blackness oozed from the pores of a horrible shape that hovered before her, shifting between the dripping darkness and the man who had been standing in Marina's doorway, just before the machine's doors sealed Paola inside.

"What are you doing here?" The Blanket demanded.

Its voice was dark, heinous, horrible, not quite a voice, more like a rasp of thunder echoing through the tube, caroming against metal walls with a menacing reverb. Paola didn't know if she was inside the machine or her mind, but wherever she was, The Blanket had followed to swallow her *everywhere*.

The world changed, and The Blanket dragged her back to where she'd been before, into the endless hallway past the Drury's kitchen and out onto the neverending road and flattened landscape, over the small gray hills at the front to the larger ones in back, toward what might have been forever, tugging her to the charcoal mountains under churning clouds of cruelty.

The thunder repeated, "Why are you here?" Its voice echoed in ripples around her.

Paola tried to fight, but felt helpless.

Why won't the doors open?

Like before, The Blanket draped her face and threatened to eat her until Paola's memories were molecules belonging to it. Like before, Paola knew death was seconds away.

The Blanket hovered above her, eyes red and lips curled into a snarl. Its skin started to shift as if a thousand bugs were crawling beneath it, changing its face, first to a bald Boricio, then into The Prophet, and finally, into John, Paola's old neighbor.

With endless nothingness around her, Paola tried to run, but just as sound wouldn't come from her mouth, motion wouldn't propel her legs.

Finally, she felt lava in her throat; the heat seemed to make words.

"What do you want from me?" she cried out through déjà vu.

The Blanket laughed, chortles like flame licked Paola's skin. She cried out for Luca, knowing he was her only hope.

If she couldn't find him, all would be lost.

Not just her body and sanity …

… but mind and body for all of the world.

A horrible vision, worse than The Blanket, swung like a curtain in front of her eyes, displaying the plague as it spread like butter across the Earth's bread, swallowing all as it soured the landscape and turned everything into an endless sea of bleakers — just as it had before, on the world that could no longer breathe. And then the vision was gone, replaced by the broken landscape ahead.

Paola cried louder for Luca.

The world flickered, and The Blanket began to flap against a cold wind which pushed it farther above her, threatening to take it away into the swirling clouds, which were alive with crashing blue lightning.

Paola felt its anger as it tried to overcome the wind and reclaim its hold.

A royal blue crackle of sparks surrounded her body, dancing to the machine's whir which she could hear even if it was naked to her eyes.

And then she saw it, a light ahead — a bright whiteness at the end of a long endless brick path ahead of her.

Luca!

She ran toward it, along the long, winding path that stretched into infinity, toward what had to be the boy — it was so, so wonderfully bright — as The Blanket surrendered its chase, thrashing in anger behind her, venting Its rage at having been bested, doing all it could to keep her frightened, though she knew it was only for show: churning clouds and raining acid, the barbed grass swaying from both sides, each blade reminding her it could bite.

The Blanket no longer had shape, losing *ITS* form to the white.

Then, The Blanket got blacker and meaner, determined not to lose.

The blue sparks lost some of their blue as *IT* tried to curl inside Paola's nostrils and seep into her eyes, bleeding into the girl's pores like backward sweat.

"Luca" was a wisp from her lips as the white fought to keep Paola alive.

~

THIRTY-TWO

Luca Harding

Luca wasn't sure where he was, or how he got there, but the sky was ugly and black. He was somewhere in the woods, naked in a stream, washing blood from his body.

Whatever had taken his mind from him, and turned him into a killer, felt like it was gone, leaving Luca alone to deal with an aftermath of fear, guilt, and confusion.

"What have I done?"

Luca whispered over and over to no one, scrubbing so much blood from his skin. He vaguely remembered what he had done: killed them all — Johnny, Trevor, Gus, and Kiyor. It was their blood staining his body. But it was as if he had seen the murders from the eyes of another, watched as it happened, rather than making it happen himself. He heard their screams in his ears, but it was as if the screams were TV, rather than Luca making the show.

Like *someone else* was playing *Transformers*, and *he* was the toy.

What happened after that, Luca couldn't remember. But it seemed late outside, and his parents were probably worried sick. And there was no forest by his house. The only forest Luca had ever seen was the one where they went to for camping in the

San Gabriel Mountains every summer. He had to get home and tell Mom and Dad everything; maybe they would understand what he didn't. Luca's parents loved him, and if anyone could make this somehow better, it was them, and maybe Anna.

Luca finished washing blood from his clothes, then put them back on, soaking wet, before starting to walk, hoping to leave the forest he never should have been in, so he could find a familiar landmark that might help him find his way home.

He walked for a long time, as icy wind bit his skin, through his soaking clothes and freezing scalp until he finally stepped out of the woods and into his neighborhood as trees disappeared behind him.

Most of the houses still had light inside their windows, so Luca didn't think it was too late in the night. That meant his parents should still be up. He was in so much trouble already for whatever had happened — he would probably lose all of his Transformers and Legos, plus TV for the rest of his life — that being up past his bedtime couldn't make it worse.

What if they don't know it was an accident, and I go to jail forever?

Luca stuck to the shadows, avoiding streetlights and alternating between sidewalk and road. He wished he was invisible. He didn't think that anyone had seen what he'd done, but people would probably know he was guilty of something as soon as they saw him. Luca was never good at hiding stuff he wasn't supposed to hide.

His legs were achy, and he shivered nonstop, teeth chattering by the time he finally found his block. As Luca rounded the curve, and saw his home six houses away, he froze on a crack in the sidewalk, staring at the glow of flashing red and blue lights illuminating the street and windows of the houses and cars on the bend.

He slowly approached, peering past the lights as his heart pounded, almost as fast as his chattering teeth. There were police cars, at least three that he could see, outside his house.

They're looking for me! They know I did it.

Luca's family was so close, and yet never felt so far.

There was no way he could go home. The police would grab him, take him away, and throw him in jail. Probably forever. Then he would never see his family again. Luca slunk back into the shadows, safe in the dark under overhanging trees, watching his house, and searching for any sign of his family.

But they were all inside, with the police.

Suddenly, a light went on behind Luca, and a woman's voice, one of his neighbors, though he wasn't sure who, said, "Luca?"

Instead of turning, he ran as fast as he could.

LUCA WASN'T sure how far he'd run, or how far he kept walking after his legs were too achy to race. He was cold, in pain, and felt like he might die if he didn't find a warm place to rest.

Luca had no idea where he was walking, only that he had to put distance between himself and the police who were probably definitely looking for him. He wasn't sure about his next step. Maybe he could find his way back home tomorrow, and the police would be gone.

That seemed like a good idea.

But for now, he had to keep walking.

Luca was in another neighborhood where he'd never been, many miles from his own. Most of the lights were now off, meaning it was late, way way past bedtime. Luca wasn't sure what he was looking for, exactly, maybe a tree house or an unlocked car to crawl inside. Both could mean danger, though a tree house seemed better for the night than a car. Problem was, Luca saw no tree houses.

How come no one has tree houses in this neighborhood? Connor and JT both have one on my street.

Every minute Luca walked seemed like the one when he might finally collapse. He wasn't sure how much longer he could go on, but every movement felt like his ankles were stuck in sludge, and he had to push his body forward with a backpack that was filled with his grandfather's old metal cars, while wearing heavy wet blankets.

Luca began to look longingly at some of the larger lawns, thinking how comfortable it would be to lie down and sprawl on top of them. He imagined the feeling of cool grass against his body as he did. Luca never would've thought of grass as comfortable, like his bed — it was usually pretty itchy — but at the moment, even the smaller lawns looked like his parents' King sized bed.

Luca stopped in front of an old house with an overgrown lawn that looked like no one had cut it in years. The house was small, almost tiny, its windows and doors all boarded. It looked like the sort of house where something bad happened and it had to get shuttered forever. It was the kind of house kids whispered about in warning, "Don't go there!" The kind of house that was always in scary stories at Halloween.

The front yard even had a giant tree with branches reaching like skeleton's arms toward the moon. Yet for all its scary qualities, it had one thing which called to Luca like a lighthouse in the dark — a porch swing.

I'll lie on the swing, and think about what to do next.

Luca slowly approached the house, listening for anything evil that might be lurking inside. He wasn't normally afraid of stuff like ghosts or witches or other things that weren't real, but at night, on his own, in a strange neighborhood, anything seemed possible.

He stepped onto the porch, the wooden, paint-chipped, gray steps creaking under his weight.

A shadow suddenly moved to Luca's left.

He jumped, then realized it was only from the streetlight and wind pushing the swing.

Luca laughed at himself, then sat on the bench, chains pulling tight as he did. He pushed down hard, just to make sure the chains in the roof could support his weight.

Sitting felt great, laying down even better.

He closed his eyes, telling himself that he'd wake in the morning, then find his way home. The police would be gone, Mom and Dad would make everything better.

Luca fell asleep, almost smiling.

IN LUCA'S DREAM, he was on the side of a long road, lying down. It was daytime, and the sun seemed to take up most of the sky.

His skin was itchy-burny hot, his throat was dry and raw.

A dog appeared, carrying a bottle of water in its mouth. The dog was the same one from his earlier dream — Dog Vader. It dropped the bottle of water beside Luca, who grabbed it, unscrewed the cap, and gulped the liquid.

"Where am I?" Luca asked.

"You're on a trek," Dog Vader answered.

"A trek?"

"Yes, you have to find something. Something very important."

"What?" Luca asked, swallowing the last of the water, which tasted like it was from heaven.

"The vials," Dog Vader said.

"What vials?" Luca asked, vaguely remembering something from a dream. No, not a dream, but when Johnny had him on the ground. There had been vials in that dream or vision, or whatever it was.

Dog Vader then thought about the vials, and oddly, Luca could see what the dog was picturing in his head. They were filled with glowing, blue liquid. There were a dozen of them all floating in darkness.

"Wow, how did you do that?"

Dog Vader didn't answer. Instead, he said, "It's time to wake up Luca. Time to wake up and find the vials."

"How will I know where to look?"

"Just trust your head," Dog Vader said, then vanished.

Luca was confused.

Trust my head?

The sun seemed to turn up its heat, like Mom using the stove.

Luca realized, again, that he was dreaming, and remembered his sleeping self on the swing. He had to wake up before morning. A neighbor might see him and call the police.

Luca woke up suddenly, no longer on a swing.

Or anywhere he'd ever been or even seen before.

The sky was a forever sea of blue, and below it, unending rolling waves of bright, hot sand stretching forever in every direction.

Luca knew, with a horrible sadness inside him, that he would never see his family again. He screamed, his voice wafting into the endless empty desert.

∾

THIRTY-THREE

Michael Blackmore

Mike reached the Madrid thoroughly exhausted early in the morning. So exhausted, he was tempted to get a room and sleep first. But he couldn't risk losing Mary if she was already on the road.

Mike approached the front desk with flowers, saying he was leaving them for a guest, Mary Olson.

The receptionist, a pretty young woman with long, dark hair, consulted her computer and looked up, frowning. "Oh, I'm sorry, that guest checked out last night."

"Do you know where she went?" Mike asked, hoping his desperation didn't show.

"I'm sorry, Sir," she said. "We don't have that information."

Mike looked down at the flowers, then back at the receptionist, tossing her the ball. "What should I do? I have to deliver these flowers. Boss said this was a rush job and very important to whoever wanted Mrs. Olson to get them."

The woman looked back at her screen. "I could call the number we have on file for her, if you'd like to leave the flowers here."

Mike sneaked a peek at the screen, saw Mary's number, quickly remembered it like he'd done with who-knew-how-many numbers before, then smiled at the receptionist, confident she'd not seen his theft.

He looked at the flowers again, then sighed, "Well, I can't leave them with anyone but Mary. We've had situations before, leaving them at hotel desks, and the guests never getting them."

The girl looked offended, "What? Here?"

"No, no place as nice as this. But all the same, it's policy."

"I never heard of anything like that."

"Yeah, it's pretty damned stupid," Mike said. "I'll go back to the shop and see what the boss says. If he says I can leave them here, I'll bring them back. Thanks so much for your help."

Mike smiled and headed back to his car.

He sat inside and fired up Mary's laptop, which he lifted from her house, found a Wi-Fi signal and clicked on her money app. He found her recent credit card activity and found the name of the motel she was now at. The Camelot, on PCH in Malibu. A quick Google search showed her about an hour away.

Mike peeled out of the parking lot.

MIKE ARRIVED at the motel in less than 40 minutes.

As he pulled into the parking lot, he spotted a man outside a room kicking a Pepsi machine, cursing.

Mike stared, waiting for the man to turn around enough for Mike to see his face. The man reached into his pockets and shoved more money into the machine, finally getting a can of Coke.

He turned and headed back to his room, and as he did, Mike got a good look at the man who killed his daughter.

Mike stared, snarling. "I got you, motherfucker."

TO BE CONTINUED ...

259

Episode 23

(FIFTH EPISODE OF SEASON FOUR)

"Eye for an Eye"

THIRTY-FOUR

Edward Keenan

Ed Keenan approached the front desk receptionist at Harrison Psychiatric Hospital, then flashed his badge and said, "Ed Keenan, Homeland Security. I need to speak to a patient, Roman Rosetti."

The receptionist, a tired looking mountain of a man, stared at Ed's badge, then turned to the computer screen, and slowly back to Ed, as if trying to decide how helpful he would be. The man picked up the phone, dialed a few digits, and said, "Yeah, we've got someone from Homeland Security asking to see Rosetti."

"Someone will be with you in a moment," the man said casually before returning his eyes to the newspaper unfolded on his desk. He was reading a story about the recent strings of violence. The news media was searching for connections, but at the moment, they were looking in all the wrong places — looking to blame the violence on things like the media, video games, and various political ideologies. None was close to the truth: that aliens had invaded the world and were living amongst us.

"Thank you," Ed said, turning to scan the lobby: large and

sterile, with "artsy" benches rather than couches or anything resembling comfortable furniture.

After a few moments, a thin 40-something, red-headed man in slacks and a button-down blue shirt appeared. He wore no badge, nor offered a name, but was clearly in charge.

"You're here to see Roman Rosetti?"

"Yes," Ed said, producing his badge before the man asked. "Ed Keenan, Homeland Security."

"Martin Gross," the man said. "May I ask what this is regarding?"

"Sorry," Ed said, "official Homeland Security business."

"Come with me." The man led Ed to an elevator, up to the seventh floor, where they stepped off onto polished linoleum. Gross waved a plastic white card over a reader and parted a pair of glass doors leading to the seventh floor reception desk, where a male and female nurse sat. The nurses nodded at them as Gross led Ed down a long hallway of closed doors. Each of the doors had a small square window giving a glimpse into each room.

"This is where we keep the dangerous patients," Gross said.

"Has Mr. Rosetti been violent during his time here?" Ed asked.

"No, he's been a model patient, aside from a few *eccentricities*. We'd have him on one of the other floors if not for the nature of his crimes."

They stopped outside a door at the end of the hallway. The lights were off inside the room, which Ed assumed was Rosetti's.

"What sort of eccentricities?"

"Well, the doctor can tell you in more detail, but in short, he's obsessed about a date."

"What date?"

"Tomorrow. He's been writing the date over and over on whatever paper we give him ever since he arrived. But whenever we ask him about it, he seems confused, not sure what it means. But clearly, it is important to him."

"And is this any more odd than your typical obsessive behavior here?"

"No, and it wouldn't mean anything except ... well, I'm not sure how familiar you are with his case ... but after he shot those people, police went to Rosetti's house and found that he'd written that date, too. So the fear is, he's planning something else ... which is why he's locked on the seventh floor. Is that why you're here? The date? Is he part of some homegrown terrorist cell or something?"

"I can't elaborate on that," Ed said. "It's a matter of national security. May I talk to him now?"

"Yeah, sure." Gross reached into his pocket, then waved a card over the reader beside the door.

The door unlocked and Gross turned the knob, then stepped into the room and clicked on the light.

"Holy shit!" Gross said, backing away before stepping outside the room and slamming his palm on a red emergency button right beneath the card reader, sending a loud alarm screaming through the hallway.

Ed stepped inside, hand on a gun that wouldn't be needed for anything inside an empty room.

The walls were covered in black ink, the same thing scrawled over and over in both tiny print and giant, crazy-looking large text: "It's Here."

Two armed security guards ran from the elevator and through the doors at the end of the hall, approaching Rosetti's room.

Gross snapped, "Rosetti is out. Lock the place down, search every inch until we find him!"

The guards got on their radios, issuing orders. Ed asked, "Who's responsible for overseeing this wing?"

"The nurses we passed when we got off the elevator.

Nobody comes or goes through those doors without the nurses letting them through."

Gross stomped to the reception desk and grilled the nurses, asking them where the hell Rosetti was. Both looked as surprised as Gross to find the patient missing.

"When was the last check-in?" Gross asked.

The man, a thin scarecrow in blue scrubs, punched a few keys on the keyboard, then looked up. "Eight twelve this morning. And he was fine."

Gross barked: "And nobody said shit about the crazy writing all over the walls?"

The scarecrow looked confused. "Writing?"

"Never mind," Gross said. "Who checked on him this morning?"

"Esther signed it."

"Is she here now?"

The scarecrow consulted the computer, and looked up, "She's on break."

Gross grabbed a phone from his pocket, called someone, then yelled at them to bring Esther Greene to the seventh floor immediately.

Gross looked like someone who had shit the bed, and had it smeared all over his body in a drunken stupor. He was probably wondering exactly why Homeland Security was asking about Rosetti, and how much hell he was going to catch for allowing the man to flee his room, and possibly the hospital.

Ed asked the nurses, "Is there any other exit Rosetti could've taken?"

"Not without passing our desk and going through the door," the woman said.

"And were you both here the entire time?" Ed asked.

"Well, aside from bathroom breaks, but even then, we take turns, so one of us is always here."

Ed looked up and down the hall, then focused his eyes on

the camera in the upper corner above the door, one of three in his view.

"Where can I see the security footage?" Ed asked.

Gross said, "Down in the server room, I can have someone pull it up for you."

"Do that," Ed said. "I'll search his room for any sign of where he might've gone."

"OK," Gross said, getting back on the phone and barking orders to his staff, telling people they were going to lose their jobs if Rosetti wasn't found.

Ed stepped back into the room full of lunatic writing. The sheer amount of ink seemed like something that had to take days or weeks, maybe months of obsessive work, not something done in the span of a few hours.

Ed's eyes followed from one "It's Here" to another, noticing that not only were the letters done in different sizes and styles, they seemed almost as if written by many different hands. And though he couldn't determine a pattern, there seemed to be one somewhere within the chaos. He circled the room studying the letters until he found one message different from the others, just above the doorway.

It read, "Turn back, Keenan. Go home now."

Ed stopped, heart racing, cold chills through his body. He looked outside in the hall where Gross was talking on a radio to his security team, making sure nobody was paying attention to what he was looking at.

How the hell does he know my name?

What does this message mean?

Ed thought immediately of the only true home he had, and the girls — Jade, Teagan, and Becca. After Sullivan discovered Ed's safe house in Florida, Ed knew he had to hide his new family better. He found a place in upstate New York, a bit closer to him, that neither Sullivan nor people at the Black Island Research Facility could possibly know of. The girls changed their appearances, stayed off the phones, except for the one he gave them for emergencies, and ensured they had enough supplies to last them a long time.

He wondered if somehow they were in danger.

Sullivan had found him the first time, and said he'd done so thanks to some "power" from the vials. Had Sullivan tracked the girls down? And if so, why? While Ed didn't trust the government, who'd turned him into their hired killer until they no longer needed him, he *thought* he could trust Sullivan.

Ed needed to get in touch with the girls, but couldn't do so yet. First he had to find a secure location to make his call.

Gross interrupted Ed's thoughts: "Esther is on her way up here."

"Good," Ed said.

"Find anything?"

"No," Ed lied. "Just a bunch of crazy chicken scratch. Let's talk to Esther."

~

ED RETURNED to his van with nothing of value. Roman was gone, and Esther knew nothing. All Ed had was a cryptic message that was working to slowly unnerve him.

He called Sullivan and reported Roman's disappearance. Sullivan seemed more upset than usual, asking how the hell Ed could lose a locked up man.

"I don't know what happened," Ed explained.

"Well, you'd better find him, Ed. I don't have to warn you what Bolton will do to you … will do to the girls … if you lose Rosetti."

Ed was surprised. Sullivan had never been so abrupt with him, nor had he ever pulled rank or delivered such a threat.

Ed wanted to blast back, but figured Sullivan must've been in a room with Bolton and was being overly aggressive to save face, and perhaps even *help* Ed in some way.

"I'll find him," Ed said, biting his tongue.

Ed made no mention of the personalized nature of the wall's message, though he imagined someone would find it eventually.

"You'd better," Sullivan said, pressing his luck.

"Where do you want me to go from here?" Ed asked.

"Follow the trail," Sullivan said. "See if Rosetti went back to the 215ers."

"OK." Ed hung up, turned to Brent, still handcuffed and pissed in the back of the van. "Looks like we're going to go visit some of your friends."

"Who?"

"The 215ers. We need to find Rosetti immediately, he's our only lead."

"And how do I know you won't kill them like you killed Lara?"

Ed sighed. He'd played hardball with Brent when he woke in the van, telling him that his family was in danger if he didn't cooperate. That had kept Brent in the van for a while, but if he wanted the man's long-term cooperation, he needed to convince him that he wouldn't pull the trigger on him, or the others. In other words, Ed had to make promises he didn't know he could keep.

"As far as the government's concerned, your friends are conspiracy theorists. They've been spouting nonsense for years, and people have learned to tune them out. They're not a threat. The reporter was. Killing her sealed the leak … the leak *you* created, just in case you forgot."

Brent glared at Ed, not hiding his disgust or fear, only his tongue.

Ed kept selling. "You were a reporter, right? Ask yourself: If you had uncovered a story the government didn't want uncovered, and started naming names, what do you think they would do in order to protect their secrets? How far do you think they'd go to silence you? Think about everyone we came back with. Would you rather I kill a reporter now, or wait until someone has to come clean up and is after us all?"

"You say 'us' like you wouldn't be the one pulling the trigger," Brent said. His tone split between query and accusal.

"You think I'm the only person who does what I do? Why the hell do you think I'm even here? They found me. They found Jade, Teagan, and her daughter. If it's not me, it'll be someone else knocking on doors."

"This is insane. The government shouldn't be killing citizens to keep some fucking secret."

"This isn't just a secret, Brent. This is war. You saw what the aliens did to the other world. We need to find the vials and keep this thing in check before it gets out of hand. If word about any of this got out, the country would lose their minds. You'd have riots, people rushing for safe places, but not knowing where to go, and … well, hell, we can hardly handle hurricanes. You really want to see how we handle an alien outbreak or mass panic? I know you think the government is this big, giant all-encompassing powerful thing, but fact is, there's not a lot standing between us and absolute chaos. Killing a few people to prevent widespread anarchy, it's an easy choice for them, and me."

Brent stared at Ed, seeming to process his words, anger softening.

"So, if I bring you to them, are you going to kill them?"

"I already said they're not a threat. But I think what you really meant to ask was do I plan to kill you, right?"

Brent nodded.

"No," Ed lied.

Order had to be maintained, at all costs, though that was only part of the equation. The other 75 percent were the three lives counting on Ed to do his job, no matter how hard it might be.

∽

THIRTY-FIVE

Brent Foster

Ed finally removed Brent's cuffs when they arrived at Stan's apartment building shortly before dark. He didn't apologize for the cuffing, instead giving Brent a look that suggested apology and a, "Hey, you understand why I did this."

Brent rubbed at his red wrists, venting a deep sigh as he worked up the courage to make a stand, just as Ed was preparing their next move.

Brent hated Ed for what he'd done to Lara. Any thoughts he had of trusting Ed had dissipated in a flash. If he thought he could kill Ed in retaliation, he would have. But, at the moment, he was at the assassin's mercy. Ed decided if Brent lived or died.

Ed decided if Brent's family lived.

Still, Brent couldn't just roll over. He had to make some sort of stand.

He reached for the door to climb from the van.

Brent said, "Wait."

Ed froze halfway out, turning to Brent, "Yes?"

"I'm not going up."

"What?" Ed said, getting back into the van and turning to Brent, not hiding his anger.

"I'm not going up until I have assurances," Brent said, hoping like hell he had a hand to play.

"I already told you I'm not going to kill you."

"I want more," Brent said.

"More? What the hell are you talking about?"

"My wife and child live in the apartments across the street. When we're finished here, I want you to go there with me. I want you to tell my wife I'm not crazy."

"You know I can't do that."

"Then I'm not going up, and you can figure out how to get Stan talking by yourself."

"You think I won't?" Ed said, right eyebrow arching. "You don't think I can convince Stan to talk?"

"I'm sure you can," Brent said. "But Luis already greased the wheels for me, not you. You walk in there, and he's not saying shit."

On the way to Stan's, Brent had called Luis and told him that he needed to speak with Stan immediately; it was a matter of life and death. Luis was hesitant, but finally said he'd call Stan and fill him in. Luis warned Brent that Stan had grown recently paranoid, and might not be eager to talk. Brent figured he could win Stan over, if needed, but didn't think Ed with his brusque manner would have the same chances. As Brent saw it, Ed needed him if he wanted info on Rosetti — assuming Stan even knew anything.

Ed shook his head, "We already discussed this. Black Island sent me to shut you up. Why the hell do you think I'd let you tell your wife? More importantly, why do you insist on endangering her, and your son?"

"Because I can't go on like this, having my wife hate me, and my son not know me. They think I'm fucking crazy. There's gotta be some way to let them know I'm sane without putting them in danger."

"There isn't," Ed said. "End of discussion."

"It's not fair," Brent said, on the verge of tears, months of raw emotions starting to surface at once. It wasn't just that he lost his family, or that his wife thought he'd lost his mind. It was that Brent was alone, with no one to talk to, or help him through this. No one to soothe his pain.

As weird — and pathetic — as it was, Ed was the closest thing Brent had to a friend in the world. Ed had fought the aliens with him. They'd survived a shared hell. And right now, he needed a friend to understand. Even if that "friend" was responsible for Lara's death.

"My family thinks I'm a monster. The last time I saw my son, he was scared of me!"

"We all have to make sacrifices," Ed said, no sympathy in his voice, amplifying Brent's feelings of isolation, alone against the world.

Ed *wasn't* a friend, and couldn't be counted on. For all Brent knew, Ed was still planning to kill him. He'd taken care of Lara. He'd probably "take care of" the 215ers. As far as anyone was concerned, Brent was just one more bit of unfinished business for a trained killer.

Brent felt like a sailor lost at sea, miles from civilization. Being just across the street from his family, without them knowing he was there, cut it deeper.

Brent met Ed's eyes. "If I can't be with my family, you may as well shoot me right now and end my misery."

Ed rushed the space between the bucket seats, into the van's depths. Brent barely had time to register what was happening before Ed had a gun in his hand, pressed hard into Brent's left temple.

"You wanna die, do you?" Ed snarled. "That what you want?"

Though Brent was startled at first, there was comfort in the thought of ending it. He was fighting a battle he couldn't win. There was no way Black Island would let him expose what happened. Why help them? Why not just end it all in the van? *That* would put a wrinkle in Black Island's plans.

Brent met Ed's eyes and he clenched his jaw. He nodded, "Yeah, do it."

Ed stared, as if trying to decide whether Brent was bluffing. He wasn't a man to bluff with — the kind to call your bluff, and make you regret it.

Brent waited for either an angry explosion or a gunshot to end it. He was so filled with rage, and admittedly, self-pity, he didn't care what came next.

Brent whispered, "Please. Do it."

Ed leaned closer, his voice now calm, "I felt sorry for you at first. But you know what? You're a selfish asshole. You would risk the lives of your wife and son just so you can be with them? What the hell kind of *man* are you?"

"What?" Brent screamed, "I'm supposed to be the big, brave super secret agent man who alienates his wife and family so he can run off and play savior? How does it feel on that cross, Ed? Does it get lonely up there?"

Ed got in Brent's face, eyes intense, but voice still surprisingly calm. "You don't know the first thing about me. I don't do this for love of country, or any other martyr bullshit. I do the things others won't to protect my family. I sacrifice my life so that *my family* can continue to live. So don't you lecture me," Ed said, jabbing his finger hard into Brent's chest.

Brent flinched, knowing he'd pushed the killer too far. To make matters worse, Brent knew Ed was right. Brent *was* being selfish. He hadn't thought things through to their logical conclusions. If Black Island had a reporter killed, they wouldn't think twice about killing his family. That was the last thing in the world Brent wanted, and he would gladly take 10 bullets rather than risk his son's life.

While Ed might have been on target with his criticisms, Brent wasn't about to give him the satisfaction of telling him so.

Instead, he looked down at his feet and said, "Fuck it. Let's go."

"You sure?" Ed asked. "I don't need you pulling any stunts up there. If you're gonna play games, I'm not in the mood."

"No, let's get it over with, then you can do whatever it is Black Island wants you to do — either kill me, or leave. Just promise you won't touch my family."

"I promise," Ed said. "Let's go see Stan."

ED STOOD to the side of Stan's doorway, just out of the peephole's range, as Brent knocked on the door. They could hear the muffled sound of a TV blaring from the other side. Seemed Stan really loved 24 hour cable news.

Brent waited for the man's response. While he'd been nervous about seeing Stan, just as he had been about seeing Luis, two people who — on this world — didn't know him even though he felt as if he knew them, Brent now felt nothing. He was numb, wanting only to make it through whatever Ed needed him to do.

Ed reached over and knocked harder.

Still, no response.

Ed waved Brent aside, gun in his right hand, and tried the doorknob with his left. The door swung open slowly, revealing Stan's living room.

Stan was sitting on the couch, facing away from them, staring at the television, broadcasting some story about another mass shooting.

The woman on the TV said, "Authorities say the death toll has risen to 39, the highest for a school shooting in U.S. History. Police spokeswoman Kay Summers, wouldn't say whether reports of … "

"Hey, Stan," Brent called out as they approached the couch, "I knocked, but you didn't answer."

Stan was still silent.

Ed thrust out his hand, palm hitting Brent's chest, stopping him from taking another step.

Brent turned to see why Ed stopped him, when just behind Ed, near Stan's bedroom, he saw two men in Black Island uniforms and closed-face black helmets approaching, weapons raised.

Brent tried to warn Ed with a yell, but Ed must've seen the panic in his eyes, or heard the men. In a few fluid movements, he pushed Brent to the carpet, spun, and emptied his gun at the men.

Gunfire thundered through the apartment as Brent fell, feeling as if someone had slammed bricks against both of his ears. He had no gun, so he scrambled toward the door, fleeing the crossfire.

It was over before he reached the door.

Brent turned around, hoping Ed wasn't dead, glad to see that he wasn't.

Ed dropped to his knees, on top of one of the two fallen men, and yanked the man's pistol from his hand. He tossed it across the floor, toward Brent.

Brent looked down at the gun wondering if Ed was just tossing the gun aside or if he had intentionally given Brent a firearm. He wasn't sure whether he should pick it up, or if Ed would misinterpret Brent's actions as hostile.

Ed looked back at him. "Get the gun, close the door, and lock it. Stand back and shoot anyone who comes through it. *Anyone.*"

Brent nodded, grabbed the gun, and looked out into the hall, checking for more Black Island guards. The coast was clear. He closed the door, locked it, then stood waiting, hoping there wouldn't be any more guards. Brent hadn't shot a gun in nearly two years, and wasn't a match for trained Guardsmen.

Ed ripped the Guardsman's helmet from his head, revealing a young man with a buzz cut, who looked scared shitless. He was shot in the leg and turning Stan's brown carpet red.

"How many more came with you?" Ed asked, calm as if the man and his squad mate hadn't just tried to kill them.

"Fuck off," he said, shaking.

Ed looked at the other fallen Guardsman, groaning on the ground. Ed shot him through his helmet.

Ed turned back to the man beneath him, "I'm going to ask once more. How many others came with you?"

"Just us," the man said, eyes wide, lips trembling.

"What were your orders?" Ed asked.

"To kill Stan, then kill you and … him," he said, nodding toward Brent.

"Who gave the order?"

"Don't ask me that," the man said, still shaking, though Brent couldn't tell if it was from the pain of getting shot in the leg, or from fear of being killed by Ed; probably a mixture of both.

"Tell me," Ed ordered, pushing the gun harder against his head.

The man choked, "Sullivan."

Ed paused, though his face showed no emotion — surprise, anger, nothing. The man was marble, a quality Brent admired in Ed as much as he feared it.

Ed asked, "Why?"

"I don't … don't know," the man said, shaking more now. "Please, don't kill me. I was just following orders."

"Sullivan's orders? You're sure?"

"Y … yes," the man said.

"What were the rest of your orders?"

"W… what?" the man asked.

"What were you supposed to do once you killed us?"

"Call it in, have you picked up."

"And then?" Ed asked.

Brent felt a cold chill. He wasn't sure what Ed was fishing

for, but found it impossible to focus on the door as instructed, instead waiting for the man's next words.

The guard said, "Then we were going to go across the street and get his wife, son, whoever else was there."

"And?" Brent asked, jumping into the questioning.

"Kill them," the man said, looking at Brent, then back at Ed.

"Who else is on your list?" Ed asked.

"Nobody on my list, but we weren't the only ones. They want everyone who knows anything. Everyone who was over there. And all of Stan's little group."

Ed shook his head, sighing.

"What about my daughter?" he asked. "Is she on the list?"

"I d … don't know," the man said. "I only know from some of the others, that the instruction were to g … get everybody."

"Why the hell did they change their minds? I thought they were going to let me handle this."

"I don't know," the man said.

"What *do* you know? Who else is in the field? Have any of the other targets been acquired?"

"I d … d … don't … k … know," the man said, his shaking getting worse.

"You don't know anything else?"

"N … n … no," the man said.

"Then what good are you?" Ed asked, then shot the man in the forehead before he could answer.

Brent fell back, startled.

Ed met his eyes. And for a moment, Brent felt as if the killer was sizing him up, deciding whether Brent was as worthless as the guard he just shot. And while 30 minutes ago Brent was ready to die, that was before he learned that his family was now wearing targets.

Brent felt a fire inside him he hadn't felt since returning to Earth. "They're going to kill us all!" he said.

Ed had yet to thaw, seeming to process their next move. He finally reached into his pants pocket and pulled out a phone, then dialed. After a minute, he hung up and redialed.

Again, no answer.

"She's not answering," Ed said, fear finally creeping into the statue's voice.

"Who?" Brent asked.

"My daughter, Jade. They're in a safe house, no outside contact. They aren't answering the phone."

Brent wanted to suggest that maybe they were out or something, but suggesting anything to Ed always felt stupid. His instincts were razors. If he thought something was wrong, it was.

"What should we do?"

Ed looked at Brent, oddly. He couldn't tell if Ed was offended that Brent inserted himself into the question as a "what should *we* do?" when Brent had pushed Ed so hard just a while before. Brent had intended the "we" as a show of solidarity. They now shared a common enemy. And Brent would rather have Ed on his side than against him.

While Brent wanted more than ever to head across the street to Gina and Ben, to make sure they were still safe, he had to be cautious in broaching the subject. If what the Guardsman said was true, then Brent's family was seemingly safe at the moment. Ed's family, however, could be in immediate danger. Another team could have been dispatched to take care of them, and may have already done so.

"I'm going to my daughter's," Ed said, rooting through the dead men's uniforms, gathering weapons and ammo. He handed Brent a gun and clip. "Here, take this one, instead."

"Should I take a radio?" Brent asked, swapping guns, though he didn't see much difference between them.

"No, they'll either use them to track us or fry it so we can't use them. They're worthless." Ed removed the radio from his belt and tossed it to the ground.

Ed looked up at Brent, "OK, *now* I think you should go get your family and get the hell out of town."

"And go where?"

"Hell if I know, but if they stay there, I can't promise they'll stay safe. Obviously, you can't go back to the room you were renting."

"Then please," Brent said, "come with me, tell my wife what's happening. She's more likely to believe it, and leave, if you vouch for me."

"I don't have time," Ed said. "She was your wife, you ought to be able to find some way to reach her."

"She had me arrested," Brent said. "Things didn't end well. She thinks I'm insane."

Ed looked up at the ceiling and sighed, then back at Brent, "I'm sorry. I need to get out of here now. I don't have time to play marriage counselor. Tell her to turn on the news, though. Tell her all this crazy shit going on, all the violence — it's the alien infection. I don't know if she'll buy it, but it's something."

Brent wanted to argue, wanted to plead, but knew that despite everything, Ed would help if he could. But Brent wasn't selfish enough to ask him to ignore his need to reach Jade as soon as he could.

"You're right," Brent said. "Thank you. I'll figure something out."

"OK," Ed said, "Good luck, Brent. Now get out of here before they send more Guardsmen."

Brent said, OK, looking down at the bodies and hoping he could convince Gina he wasn't insane.

~

THIRTY-SIX

Mary Olson

There was a nightmare inside the machine.

The silence on this side was sickening. Mary could see Paola through the small glass window, her mouth open in a giant O as if screaming, but she heard nothing through the alloy walls. Mary could often feel her daughter, and as her own throat constricted, awful and raw, she *knew* it was Paola's violent pain she was feeling.

"What the hell is happening in there?" Mary screamed at Marina, staring through the window, her eyes large with horror and rage as she stared at her daughter trapped inside the sparking coffin, kicking and thrashing. It looked like she was getting shocked from the inside as she kicked against the metal tube.

"I don't know," Marina said, sounding panicked. "I've never seen anything like this before."

"Can you stop it?"

Without a word, Marina circled to the back of the machine, then disappeared from sight — Mary kept her eyes fixed on the window — as Marina kneeled to what must have been a control panel at The Capacitor's bottom. Two seconds later the whir died, and the sparks stopped. There was a loud hiss, then an ear-splitting release as Marina circled back to the front, flipped a recessed catch on the front of the machine, and opened the doors.

Paola, who looked 13 again, fell from the parted doors, out of The Capacitor, and onto the floor before Mary or Marina could catch her. Mary fell to the floor beside her convulsing daughter, then wrapped her arms around Paola, pulling her daughter tight to her body, smothering Paola with kisses, rocking her back and forth, and whispering that everything would be alright, over and over.

When Paola finally stopped shaking, she looked up at her mother, wearing the same, innocent face Mary had watched evolve from a baby for the last 13 years, the same face she wore before her mother's cut in the kitchen, before she went to the hospital to see what her healing could do, before their mad flight from Colorado, pushing the Volvo across three states to California in a desperate race for help. Paola tried to say something, maybe, Mary couldn't be sure: eyes danced beneath her lids and something like mangled words croaked past her cracked lips.

"Honey?" Mary said, trying to hold herself together, unwilling to let her thoughts unravel and circle the worst.

Marina ran to the wall, slammed her thumb on a button, and screamed, "Dr. Phillips!"

"Honey," Mary repeated, shaking Paola hard, needing her to feel the urgency. Paola stayed silent, lids slightly lifting, just enough for Mary to see how high her eyes had rolled up into her head, showing nothing but white. "Honey," she said again, louder as she rocked her daughter harder.

Paola showed life by licking her lips, drawing a breath, and croaking a whisper. "It's … in … h … "

She tried for what seemed like forever to push another word through her blistered lips, but nothing came. Mary said, "It's in what, Sweetie?" Then, after 30 seconds of waiting: "Just tell me what, Honey, then you can sleep, okay?"

Her heart pounded, waiting for Paola to answer. Finally, Paola licked her lips again, said, "It's … in him," almost in a whisper, then fell funeral silent.

Mary screamed as a man ran into the room. He was sharply dressed in a well-tailored suit, a bright-blue tie looking especially blue against the deep black of his jacket. In his right hand he held a small, leather bag. "What happened?" he asked Marina, ignoring Rose and Mary.

Marina said, "I don't know. The girl went into The Capacitor like two minutes ago, and it all went so … wrong … "

Marina couldn't finish her sentence. Mary thought it looked like she was losing her mind. Still focused on Marina, and ignoring everyone else in the room, the man Mary assumed was Dr. Philips asked, "When did this happen?"

Marina said, "Just now!"

"No," he shook his head. "How long was she in The Capacitor before The Current went bad?"

Marina looked baffled, then after a pause said, "It happened right away … immediately … then her knees wobbled as if the truth was too heavy to hold her, and she sank to kneeling. Looking up at the doctor she added, "She was so much … older … before."

The man frowned, more than worried. He turned from Marina and kneeled toward Paola. Mary screamed at the "doctor" before he made it halfway to crouching.

"You get the fuck away from my daughter!" Mary's arms were snug around Paola. With all her strength she pulled her to a limp noodle version of standing and started dragging her daughter toward the door. "And stay the fuck away from *me*. All of you!"

Rose started to come toward her, apologizing, but Mary yelled at her, too. "No, Rose!"

Mary kept walking backward toward the exit, dragging

Paola while the man and Marina both pleaded for her to stay and let them help.

"No!" Mary screamed.

The man opened his mouth to say something, but Marina shushed him by waving her hand.

Outside the study, Mary managed to lift Paola into her arms — grateful that she was back to her little girl — then used her remaining adrenaline to make it outside. She dropped Paola back to a languid lean against her body, then pulled out her phone and dialed 911 as the valet began to approach her.

"Get the fuck away from me!" Mary screamed before he made it halfway.

The kid, maybe 20, looked like he had been slapped, then slunk off to wait behind a small podium where he probably killed most of his hours working for the same freaks who had brought harm to her daughter.

A single ring, then: "911, what's your emergency?"

"I need an ambulance for my daughter!"

"What is your address?"

"I don't know!" Mary looked around the front porch, panicked, hoping to see an address, or maybe a welcome mat. She looked over to the valet, but realized she had too much bile to say anything civil. "I'm at Marina Harmon's estate, in Malibu! On PCH!"

A brief pause, then: "What is your emergency?"

"I don't know … " Mary felt deeply uncertain, unsure whether she should say anything about the machine or The Church or Marina. She had no interest in protecting them, but the whisper inside her said it was best to say nothing. " … She just lost consciousness, and is completely catatonic."

"We're on the way. Please stay on the line. Tell me, Ma'am, is your daughter breathing?"

"Yeah, she's breathing."

"Do you know if she took any medication?"

"No!" Mary screamed, and was so annoyed with the questions, she hung up.

Mary wondered if she would be able to find Luca, or if Boricio would be able to find him. He had said that he sometimes thought he could feel "a part of the Boy Wonder thinking shit in his head."

Mary tried to think a message to Luca, on the off chance he could hear her, too.

Are you out there, Luca? Can you hear me?

Rose ran out through the front door with Marina trailing behind.

Rose was crying, Marina seemed scared.

"Oh my God, are you okay?" Rose asked Mary through her crying.

"Does it look like I'm okay?" Mary couldn't look at either of them, afraid she would scratch out an eyeball or four — six if the valet dared step toward them.

"I'm so sorry," Marina said. "I have no idea what happened … I've never seen anything like that."

Mary yelled, "Do you even know what your *machine* does — what it did to my daughter?"

"I'm so sorry," she repeated, her face a hot shade of salmon. "We'll do whatever we can to fix this, but you have to let us help you."

Mary said, "You can help by staying away from me, from *us*." Then, through gritted teeth, she added, "Please."

Marina stepped behind Rose, and the three of them — five counting the valet and Paola — waited in silence for the ambulance to arrive.

In less than five minutes the ambulance screamed to the curb, and paramedics poured from the doors. Seconds later, Paola was lying on a stretcher, and the paramedics were asking Mary what was wrong. She said she didn't know, while trying not to sob, still certain that speaking of the machine would do nothing to help Paola, and might even invite Marina and The

Church to say, "Hey, we were trying to cure her. She aged 10 years!"

Marina's gut told her to keep her mouth shut and keep Paola's secret to herself as long as she could.

Mary stepped into the back of the ambulance behind her daughter, lying on the stretcher. Rose tried to climb in behind Mary. Mary wanted no company, but wouldn't have stopped her. Fortunately, the paramedic did.

"Are you family?"

Rose shook her head. "No."

"Then you can't ride."

She stepped back from the ambulance and looked up at Mary, helpless.

Mary, finding a calm spot in her voice, knowing it wasn't Rose's fault, and that she was a link in the chain that might save her baby girl, said, "Take the Volvo. Get Boricio and meet us at the hospital."

Rose nodded as twin doors swung shut and the ambulance brayed, launching away from the wraparound drive and out onto Pacific Coast Highway.

~

THIRTY-SEVEN

Boricio Wolfe

Boricio mashed a green nugget into the bowl with his thumb, flicked the lighter, and pulled in his breath.

For being in a state where weed was legal, if not downright ballyhooed with balloons and streamers, Boricio couldn't believe the Fruity Pebbles, waste of time, barely-oregano he'd managed to score. Boricio had smoked bowls in the best half of the 50 states on the parts of the map that mattered most, and knew how to score without even trying, but he'd had to give it the old college effort to bag crap that would've been weak at Woodstock. Apparently, the good shit in the Golden state was going to the stoners with glaucoma.

After a long night spent ridding the world of bodies that weren't supposed to be a part of his to-dos, Boricio was a cannibal in a mosh pit: hungry as fuck. But he didn't have a car — Rose didn't want to rent one seeing as how they could grab a cab or get a ride wherever they were going, and wouldn't be in L.A. all that long — the only places he could find around the motel were crap shacks where you rolled down your window to grab a bag of food. Weed — even weak-ass crap — made Boricio willing to shove shit in his body he never would've been willing to otherwise swallow, but he was especially sensitive after a purging, sought or not, and would rather gobble cunt from a herpes-pocked whore than order a value meal, with flavors made in a lab.

Boricio didn't want no Walter White wizards waving chemical wands anywhere near his food — snacks or otherwise — and laughed out loud when passing McCrap shacks from Arby's to Zippy's: the biggest drug dealers on the piss-covered planet. Ronald Fucking McDonald may as well have been Rapey Raccoon — made up by marketing parasites to draw kids into their cummy webs from the time the tiny shits could say "Buy me a motherfucking toy," hoping the crack kept itself in their brains, blood, and hankers until after they were old enough to grow out of stupid. Not that they ever did; most assholes' heads were too packed with short and curlies to know any better, partly because their tastes were crude. They could discern sweet and salty, sour and bitter, maybe even astringent, but focused on scent most, which could bend how a fucker tasted. Chewing sent gasses up your smell holes, so shit foods were filled with fake scents and trash that didn't belong, which was why the number one ingredient in a chicken nugget wasn't chicken, but corn.

Right now, Boricio was smoking the weed equivalent of a McNugget, and while he wouldn't settle for inferior food — he would rather eat a banana and wait for something worth chewing — he'd settle for inferior weed since even the feeble shit made Boricio's world a bit better.

Weed slowed his brain enough to think. He usually suffered from juggling too many thoughts at once, but weed gave Boricio the ability to pull one to the front of his mind. It slowed his patterns and calmed his disposition, made it so he could intercept and interpret individual thoughts, then turn them like cubes in a Rubik. Everything was better when weed came first: purging, exercise, cooking, eating, and — no doubt about it — fucking. Rose agreed with that one.

Even sleeping was better, and after the beer-battered bullshit of Boricio's fucked up night, disposing of three bodies when purging hadn't been a line on the day's menu, was exactly what he intended to do. Unfortunately, Boricio made the mistake of turning on the news, which woke his ass up right quick.

The story about the school shootings were barely fresh news when some new bullshit went down — a cop in Chicago went full-on postal, walking into a mall and opening fire with an assault rifle, going from store to store, shooting people until he was finally killed by some dude with a gun. The cop had killed 89 people in less than five minutes.

Boricio knew immediately that it was because of the alien. He was infecting people. While the media hadn't said dick about it, probably covering shit up like they always did, Boricio could feel it in some small part of him that still felt connected to Luca, wherever Boy Wonder was. Though he hadn't heard any of Luca's thoughts in at least half a year, Boricio could feel him out there, feel his concern blooming as shit went down.

Boricio had tried talking to Luca in his head, like Luca had been able to talk to him in the other world, but he'd failed to manage a two-way palaver.

The fan was whirring, waiting for shit to hit it. As Boricio watched the news, he felt an overwhelming responsibility for the women in his life, Rose, Mary, and Paola. He didn't know where they were going, but he wasn't gonna let any of them out of his sight until shit had dimmed.

It looked like the Brady Bunch would be getting back together for a very special episode, and Boricio would be looking for Little Man Luca — just as he promised Mother Mary — in no time at all.

But first, he needed some sleep.

Boricio pointed the remote at the TV, flipped it to black, then dropped the remote to the carpet and closed his eyes.

Worry — for people other than himself — was new for

Boricio. Boricio had spent nearly all of his life concerned about Boricio, and on Christmas and other such charitable days, a bit more Boricio. After Luca got to "fixing" him, he realized life was more than Boricio squared, and that there was something primal in knowing there was more than your lonesome — a reassurance in being touched, in feeling the brush of someone wanting to touch you, and not just on their way to your yogurt.

That's what had happened with Boricio and Rose: He knew it the second he saw her, not too long after crossing back into this world from the other, seeing her smile and somehow knowing they were destined, even though Boricio didn't believe in shit like that.

Rose was the flower in his garden, worthy of all the shade and sun and food he could find, deserving of shelter from every instinct Boricio would squash to give her succor.

Though the shit wasn't as Shakespearean, it was also how Boricio felt about Mary and Paola, as if they were connected, and *his* responsibility, maybe a cosmic duty, to keep them from harm. He saw it when he opened the hotel room door to Mother Mary smiling, saw it when a too-young-for-titties looking Paola stood awkward behind her mama, and knew it like he knew the swing of his own sack while standing beside Mary in the garage, sniffing danger around them.

It was odd enough, giving a shingle of shit about one person, let alone three, and now added to that Boricio felt a sudden and indefinable worry for the entire goddamned planet. He shouldn't have: Boricio was a hunter, not prey. If the world circled the shitter, he'd survive, same as always.

When the meek got fucked, the wolves did fine.

Boricio was top of the food chain, and loved his crown, but it was a lot harder to stay at the peak when worried for others — what they were doing and what you had to do to keep them breathing.

FUCK!

Sleep was impossible: too much on his mind. Boricio swung his legs from the bed, planted his feet on the floor, then launched himself to standing, and started pacing the room.

He wanted to tell himself it wasn't time to worry, but predator's guess said it sure as fuck was. He wanted to turn the problem like a puzzle in his hand. He had to do something, figure shit out, couldn't allow himself to stay clueless. Too much depended on him making the right move, though Boricio didn't know what the right move was beyond some vague notion of first finding Luca.

Beyond that, he didn't know what they should do, where they should go, whether they should sit back and stay quiet, wait out the evil, or strap bombs to their chests and get the ticking to going.

Boricio reloaded his pipe, lit the bowl, and inhaled the skunky cloud into his lungs. He held it long enough to hurt, then blew the plume against the glass, losing himself to a laugh as he realized he was smoking in front of the window for all the world to see.

Fuck them, they can probably smell it out in the parking lot, too. I got glaucoma, bitches!

Boricio opened his window, took another puff, blew it out into the Malibu air, then collapsed on the bed, wondering if there was anything he could do about the dread he wasn't used to feeling in his brain, like rats nesting in an attic. He lay in bed, breathing slowly in and out, circling idiot worries that would do him no good until his eyes finally grew heavy and he heard himself snore.

Boricio smiled, glad that sleep was finally coming.

He would rest, gather his strength, then after waking recovered, Boricio would start looking for Luca.

BEHIND BLACK LIDS, Boricio's world went suddenly white.

He blinked for minutes, searching for focus until his eyes were clear enough to see that there was nothing but sand all around him. High, white dunes and nothing else: no cacti, no water, no oasis in the desert, just endless miles of tiny grit, which for some reason made Boricio think of the countless stars peppering infinity and space.

Like the universe, Boricio could see but a wink of the desert, and knew it went on forever. And even though he knew he was dreaming, Boricio also knew he'd never be able to cross, or track his way through the expanse. Like the universe, the desert was endless, an infinite number of grains, each a bottomless pit of possibility, with limitless ways to die.

In the distance, Boricio saw a dot. He followed, chasing the dot until it grew larger after what felt like an hour of trudging; still tiny, but maybe twice its size. The sun grew hotter and dunes climbed higher as the dot ahead seemed to mock him by growing only farther in distance. Only after Boricio had been chasing the dot for too much of forever did he finally realize what it was:

Luca.

Boricio trudged harder, ignoring the pain in his legs and back, blinding himself to the torment in his shoulders as he pushed through the desert, lurching his body in pursuit of the boy.

"Wait!" he called. "You didn't fix shit! You owe me a proper healing!"

But the dot kept going, Boricio moving behind it.

He followed for more of forever, until he felt someone or something behind him, quickly gaining, faster than he was gaining on the dot, which was closer now, enough for Boricio to see him clearly.

The boy wore a backpack, and a determined look, face shifting as if things were crawling beneath his skin, reordering muscles as he went from a small boy of maybe 8, to an old man near dying. His shirt was the constant: a husky, snout turned to the moon in a probable howl, though it was hard to see from behind its mask: Darth Vader, but white instead of black.

Boricio felt the something behind him closing in, but he could not turn around to see what it was. Not out of fear, but he just wasn't able to turn. He didn't know what it was, but knew with certainty that if it caught him, it would end him.

Boricio ran, losing his balance and spilling his body to the sand. He scrambled back to his feet and found himself back in his hotel room, which was now the size of a planet. He was still dreaming, running away from the bed and toward the door a thousand miles away.

The thing behind him came closer, its shadow draping Boricio, sending a cold chill through him as it grew larger. Boricio knew he could flee it if he could only wake up, open his eyes long enough to grab hold of the real world.

His phone suddenly rang, a shrill screech like screaming from the sky, loud but far enough to mock him.

He couldn't wake up, or answer the phone.

That meant he couldn't escape.

And if Boricio couldn't escape — he knew because the scream inside him swore it was so — then he would surely die.

Then the world would follow: meek and wolves, no difference between them.

~

THIRTY-EIGHT

Brent Foster

Brent returned the gun to the back of his waistband, pulled his shirt over it, and waited for the elevator to ding.

He'd spent the entire run from Stan's place to his old one trying to come up with a pitch that Gina might buy. It was 3:35 p.m., so Brent figured he had a while until Jack came home to open the door that used to be his. Brent prayed that Gina was, in fact, in the apartment, and not out somewhere.

If Gina was gone, Brent wasn't sure what he would do. It wasn't like he could hang around and wait for her to come home. There was no telling how long it would be before Black Island would send reinforcements to finish what the first Guardsmen failed to complete; he was certain they were living on borrowed time.

The elevator parted, and Brent stepped through the doors into the hallway, approaching the lock his key no longer fit. He was now a tourist instead of a citizen, forced to knock like a stranger.

He rapped his knuckles on the wood, waiting for Gina, hoping she was there.

Moments later, he heard Ben on the other side. "Who is it?"

"It's Daddy, Ben."

Seconds later, Brent heard Gina. "I told you not to answer the door, Ben. Go watch TV."

"It's Daddy," Ben said.

Brent couldn't hear Gina's response. He hoped she wasn't telling him to go hide from Scary Daddy, or worse, calling 9-1-1.

"What do you want?" Gina asked, peephole going dark as she stared through it.

Brent hoped he didn't look like someone running from the government, as his worst fears suggested. He tried to seem calm, but doubted he was coming anywhere close with his awkwardly plastered smile.

"I need to talk to you, can you please open the door?"

"I don't think that's a good idea," Gina said. "I can hear you fine; say what you need to say."

Brent shook his head. This wasn't boding well for the remainder of their conversation. He had to see Gina face-to-face — it was impossible to convey the importance of his message through a closed door with a barely willing listener on the other side.

"Please, Gina," Brent said. "I'm not going to cause any trouble. I just want to talk to you. It's important."

"Are you drunk again?"

"No," he said, trying to hide his annoyance at her accusation.

Gina paused, as if deliberating — or maybe calling the police. Brent was screwed if arrested. Black Island would find out, send someone to spring him, then take him somewhere private to pull the trigger.

"Just say whatever you have to say," Gina said, not opening the door, clearly growing impatient.

"OK, I didn't want to say it through the door, but it looks like I don't have a choice. You're in danger, Gina."

"What?" she said, her voice rising like it did — and always had — when she thought Brent was being ridiculous.

"Remember what I told you about Black Island? Well, they sent someone after me today. Me, and one of their own agents, a guy named Ed Keenan. They tried to kill us, Gina."

He could hear her sigh from the other side. "Please, just stop." A pause, then, "I really hate this part of you."

"I'm telling the truth, Gina. They said they're coming to kill you and Ben next."

"Stop," Gina repeated, raspy. There were a few seconds of silence, then Brent heard her start softly crying. "You're sick, Brent. You need help. Please, just go away and leave us alone. I don't want to call the cops."

"Daddy?" Ben said, far off.

"Go," Gina yelled at their son.

"I want to see Daddy," Ben whined, then started to cry.

Gina yelled, "Are you happy, Brent? Is this what you want? You're upsetting your son! Please, just go."

"Daddy!" Ben screamed, his voice shrill enough to shatter Brent's heart into even smaller pieces than the shards he already carried.

"Dammit, Gina," he yelled, louder than his intention. "Open the door!"

"Go away! I'm calling the cops, Brent!"

He heard her footsteps fading from the door, and with them Ben's crying as she carried him away. Brent could picture her lifting their son like a sack of potatoes, removing him from the situation before he erupted in tears.

Brent's blood boiled, frustration turning to panic. He couldn't let Gina call the cops; he had to stop her.

Brent stepped back and kicked at the door, just below the knob.

Gina screamed, "I'm calling the cops!"

Ben screamed louder.

Brent backed up, took a run at the door, and kicked again, this time separating the door from its frame, popping it open.

Gina stood in the living room, holding her phone in one hand and Ben in the other. She was about to bring the phone to her ear when Brent surprised her.

He pulled the gun and aimed it straight at Gina. "Put the phone down."

She stared at Brent, green eyes soaking wet beneath her dark bangs, body trembling. Ben reached out for his daddy, fingers opening and closing, wanting Brent to hold him.

Brent clarified his order, "Hang up and put down the phone."

Gina obeyed, lowered her shaking hand, and set the phone on the couch as tears slowly fell from her eyes. "Please, don't hurt us," she said, her voice low as if she were afraid volume might set her intruder on a rampage.

Brent stepped toward them. "Let me hold my son."

Gina set Ben down, slowly, and said, "Please, don't hurt him."

Brent scooped Ben up into one arm, hugging his crying boy as he moved the gun from Gina, hoping she wouldn't do something stupid.

"It's OK," Brent said to Ben. "It's OK, Daddy's here."

Ben kept crying as his small hands closed around the back of Brent's neck. It felt wonderful to hold his son again. Ben looked so much older than the last time Brent saw him. So much time had slipped away, stolen by Gina. As he met his ex-wife's eyes, Brent couldn't hide his anger. A part of him — most of him — wanted to take Ben and run.

Screw her if she doesn't believe me.

Let her and her fucking lover, Jack, deal with Black Island.

"What do you want, Brent?"

"I want you both to come with me. I want to protect you."

"Protect us from whom?"

"Black Island Guard, they're killing everyone who knows anything about The Event. They're cleaning the mess."

"Do you know how crazy this sounds?" Gina asked, her voice still low and eyes wide, like they would always get when she was trying to reason her way through one of their arguments.

"I know," Brent said. "I don't have time to make you believe me. They could be coming at any minute."

"You said someone else was with you? Where is he now?"

"He had to go, to protect his own family," Brent said.

"Of course," Gina said, rolling her eyes.

Ben was finally starting to calm down, leaning against Brent and listening to his parents talk. Brent tried not to say anything that might scare his son, and kept his voice as calm as Gina's.

"I'm not crazy, or making stuff up. I'm trying to save you both. This is real."

"I don't know what's happening," Gina said. "I've been seeing reports on the news about a bunch of people all over the place going nuts, doing horrible things. There's gotta be something in the air, the food, the water, or *something*. You're sick, Brent. You need help. No one is trying to hurt you."

Brent shook his head, "Those people on the news, they're infected."

"Infected?" Gina repeated, as if he'd just told her he spent the weekend with Santa Claus and was now off to market to buy a fat pig and play poker with Jesus. "Infected with what?"

Brent laughed, knowing as he did so, it only made him look crazier. "Sorry, he said. But if I tell you, you'll say I'm nuts."

"Try me," Gina said.

"Infected by aliens."

"Aliens? Ah, of course, the aliens! The ones from the other Earth, right?" she asked sarcastically.

"Jesus, Gina, can't you just … "

He stopped talking when he noticed her attention shifting to something behind him.

Brent felt something in the small of his back, as a man's voice inches behind him said, "Get on your knees and lower your weapon or we'll shoot!"

We'll?

Shit.

Police or Black Island?

Brent half-turned to see who he was dealing with as Ben returned to his tears.

The man shoved the gun — Brent presumed — harder into his back.

"On your knees, Sir, or we will shoot."

And if they shoot me, they'll hit Ben.

Shit.

Brent slowly kneeled, and set his gun on the ground, knowing he was surrendering his only defense if there were Black Island Guardsmen behind him.

Ben cried louder, and Gina came forward, ignoring the men with the guns, and pulled Ben from the monster, hugging him hard, crying, as she glared at Brent.

He felt his arms yanked behind him, hard, and seconds later, Brent's wrists were in plastic restraints.

A man stepped from behind Brent, a tall, pale man with a face like a shovel, and a Black Island uniform.

"Where's Keenan?" the man asked.

"I don't know," Brent said. "He told me I was on my own. I came here as fast as I could."

The guard looked up and nodded to whoever was behind Brent.

Brent turned and saw a second guard start to close the door, as best he could with the broken frame.

Better to hide their actions from the neighbors.

They're going to kill us.

Brent pleaded, "I swear, I don't know anything about Ed. And I won't say anything about Black Island! Please … "

Gina's eyes suddenly shifted from glaring at Brent to unbridled confusion, then to understanding, all in seconds.

"Who are you people?" she asked, her voice sharp, under the illusion that she had civil liberties.

Shovel Face turned to her and fired a single shot straight into her head.

~

THIRTY-NINE

Marina Harmon

Marina was so distraught over what had happened to the girl that she had no idea what to think or do, didn't even know how she should feel. Rose had left a few minutes earlier, leaving Marina at the house to wait for news.

There would be torture inside her until she heard something back.

It was awful, watching the girl thrash inside The Capacitor like she had. Marina had never seen anything like it, but worse, she had never even imagined something like that was possible.

The machine was supposed to be — and always had been — pleasant: It made you better when you left it than when you went in. Marina had never known, or heard of anything different. But that definitely wasn't the case with the girl. The Capacitor had nearly killed her, and Marina had seen it with her own eyes.

More than that, it had also stolen years from her body, turning her from a woman into a girl. The mother, Mary, was hysterical.

Maybe that's what she had been before.

Marina hadn't considered the possibility that the premature aging was what was wrong — why mother and daughter had sought her help in the first place — until after the ambulance pulled out from the drive. But once she had, Marina wondered if something like that were really possible. She had heard of cases of Progeria before, from Daddy, of course. When you grew up with a man like J.L. Harmon, you — like him — tended to know a bit about this, that, and everything else.

Progeria was an extremely rare genetic disease that fascinated her father because he believed it held clues to the *normal* process of aging. He had even been involved in some clinical trials about 10 years back, trying to get kids suffering from Progeria — their average life expectancy was under 13 years — to elongate their life span through additional weight gain, improved hearing, and an increase in their blood vessels' flexibility. Marina had seen plenty of pictures, but none looked like the girl — or woman — Paola. Progeria sufferers looked ... not normal: usually hairless, with tiny faces and shallow jaws. Their skin was usually wrinkled, with larger heads compared to their bodies. If anything, the girl — woman — Paola was beautiful.

As horrible as it seemed and felt and looked to see her inside the machine, thrashing around as if attacked, if Paola *had* been a child — somehow, Progeria or not — then The Capacitor had corrected her Current and done what it was supposed to do, no matter the horrible cost.

They couldn't be mad if they got what they wanted. Except, they hadn't expected Paola to fall unconscious.

But that has to be a temporary thing, right?

Marina was only guessing, and until she heard from Rose, she would stay confused. She started to pace, flirting with the idea of pouring herself a stiff drink before deciding it was too early. She looked out the window, hoping there was some sort of answer hiding outside, saw nothing, then went to the sofa and collapsed onto the soft cushions, just as the door opened and Steven stepped into the room. He closed it gently behind him, and in his soft voice with his typical care said, "Are you okay?"

Marina turned to the door, feeling better like she always did when she saw Steven. She shrugged. "I'm not sure. I feel scared, mostly for those poor girls, but I'm also afraid because I don't understand. Something tells me Dad wouldn't even know what all of this means, even if he was here."

Steven didn't ask what it was that Marina didn't understand. Instead, he sat across from her on the white sofa, propped her naked foot into his lap, kneaded Marina's skin with the balls of his thumb and said, "Tell me what happened."

She shrugged again. "I'm not sure. I didn't do anything different from what I would usually do. Rose brought her friend Mary in for help; we fixed her migraines after Veronica brought her in — she introduced her because of the Maris Brothers. Mary wanted help for her daughter, but she wouldn't say what for. The only thing she seemed sure about was that she didn't want to do it at all, but her daughter, Paola, did, and insisted that she go inside. As soon as she did, everything went wrong. The Capacitor whirred like always, but it was the wrong kind of whirring, and it sparked like usual, but the sparks seemed … angry."

"Angry?"

"Yes, they were too fast and too many."

"Hmmm," Steven stopped rubbing Marina's foot, and leaned back into the sofa, stroking his chin, as if he'd fallen into thought. After a moment of quiet he asked, "And they didn't tell you what the girl's problem might be?"

"No," she shook her head.

"And do you always know what the problem is, before you put someone into the machine … into The Capacitor?"

"Well, yes but … "

Steven cut her off. "Well then, couldn't *that* be the problem? Maybe The Capacitor understands intention, maybe it's somehow able to read the operator, in this case that would be you. Maybe because you didn't know, it couldn't do its job."

"I think maybe it *did* do its job. I think maybe the girl was *supposed* to be younger."

Steven frowned, confused.

"I know that sounds weird, but ... well, The Capacitor turned her young, by a lot of years, Steven. She came in as a woman and left as a girl."

With a shocking absence of emotion, Steven said, "I know. I saw her from the window."

Marina looked at Steven, then, not knowing what to say, continued.

"If it could make her young, then maybe something else made her old — before they came to us. Maybe that's *why* they were here. I don't know ... " Marina shook her head, getting upset. She needed a drink. " ... Maybe I was wrong about The Capacitor, maybe my father was wrong. Maybe the machine ... isn't good, or at least not what I thought it was."

Steve stood from the couch and headed toward the bar to make Marina a drink. "Relax," he smiled, "you're all over the place. You just said you thought that The Capacitor *did* do its work, and now you're saying your faith might be misplaced? In practically the same breath? Your faith is correct, Marina, and it's one of the things that gives you your strength. It would be best not to lose it. True belief doesn't mean the world will give you what you want, it means knowing the world will give you what's right."

Marina stared at her man, grateful for him being right so often.

"Don't worry," he said, crossing the room to hand her a tumbler of scotch. "We'll look into The Capacitor, starting right now. I'll talk to Dr. Phillips as soon as you finish this drink, okay?" Marina took the drink, trying to smile. "I promise, all of this will be fine."

She thanked Steven, told him that Dr. Phillips was with The Capacitor already, then started sipping scotch as he left, hopefully on the way to deliver his promise.

As Marina sipped, she kept feeling worse, wishing that Rose had never brought the two women into her house to give her a scare and question her faith. As the alcohol started to buzz inside her, Marina decided she could wait no longer. With every second feeling like a minute, and every minute something like an hour, it would take a year to muffle discomfort.

She stood, went to the desk, picked up her phone where she'd dropped it an hour before, scrolled through the contacts, found Rose, and hit the number for her cell.

Marina let the phone ring seven times — no voicemail — then hung up and let it ring for another seven. She tried again after that, hoping that the third time would be charmed, then hung up feeling worse than ever.

Marina dropped her cell onto the desk, wishing she could hurl it through the window without having to wait for a new one, then slammed her ass back to the couch and sipped her glass to empty, hoping to dull more shitty feelings with every fresh swallow.

But she didn't. Somehow, every sip seemed to make Marina feel worse, from the first glass from Steven to the second prepared by herself. Then, by the end of her third glass, Marina was thoroughly drunk.

Her empty glass landed on the carpet, spilling the final few drops into the fibers. Marina's head drooped as she started losing herself to sleep.

And as she slept, she dreamt.

Marina didn't fall into the casual dreams she was used to, threaded thick with loose ends and nuggets from her day. These were horror incarnate; things Marina didn't understand but longed to; things her mind was trying to say; starting to whisper, rolled into screams when she failed to listen.

Something inside Marina clicked, rinsed her resistance and left her world in nothing but white.

As the empty settled around her, she saw something surface from the dark: the girl, Paola, even younger than she had been when falling out of the machine, maybe by a couple of years.

The girl ran from the light and into the dark, racing as if chased. Marina raced after the girl, away from the light and into the black, ignoring her hammering heart.

She crashed into darkness and infection plagued her mind; a virus seeping from Paola's dream into hers, making Marina somehow certain that what she could see through the girl's eyes was true, that wherever she was, every molecule around her, though dreamlike, was absolutely real.

She had to escape, but couldn't.

Escape was flight, and that meant leaving the girl, abandoning her to the blanket of darkness.

Marina couldn't do that, so she crept forward instead, stepping timid yet bold into the black, until she saw the horrible truth: what that darkness was and what that meant.

It snarled, and Marina woke screaming, heaving and panting as she fell from the couch, rolling from the sofa and the man sitting, his arms draped across it from either side, smiling like a demon as he stared into her eyes.

"Oh, I really wish you'd not seen that," Steven said, then leapt from the couch, circled his hands at Marina's neck, and began to squeeze the ragged breath from her body.

~

FORTY

Luca Harding

It was impossible, but the sun swallowed the entire sky anyway.

It was too hot. Luca felt like he might pass out, if not die from the weight of a 100 summers at once.

He wasn't sure how long he'd been walking the desert, but it felt like two forevers. His body was soaked in sweat, his skin red and peeling and sore.

His lips were cracked and dry, starting to bleed.

Luca felt like one of the astronaut chickens Mom bought from Albertson's, their skin all wrinkly and crinkled under the plastic dome. He wasn't sure he could last much longer, but felt so tired he thought he might die if he slept.

Something inside Luca kept telling him to look for a rainbow, promising that if he found it, that colorful arc might tell him where to go. But he couldn't see any rainbows, no matter how hard he looked, and so he had no idea how to get home, or how he had gotten to wherever he was in the first place.

Luca had tried telling himself he was inside a dream, or rather, a nightmare. He had said it over and over, but couldn't get himself to believe it. No nightmare was so relentless or unending. He wondered if he had been kidnapped while he was sleeping, then driven far, far away. The only other thing that made any sense was that Luca had died in his sleep and was now walking through hell.

No, this wasn't like the Hell he read about in the Bible, though Dad had always said the Bible wasn't exactly true (even though Grandma said it was), but rather stories that were supposed to represent God in a way that made it easy for grownups and kids to both understand. "Man's best guess," Dad had said.

Maybe hell was really just an endless desert, and Luca was there because he deserved it for murdering Johnny Thomas and Trevor and Gus and Kiyor.

~

THE WIND CAME AND WENT, but each time it did it whipped Luca in the face with gritty sand that stung his eyes and bit him all over his skin.

Luca had cried and cried, until he ran out of tears; he had hoped and hoped that he would wake up, until he surrendered, knowing he wouldn't; and he had walked and walked for so far, that he had finally given up the idea of doing anything else, maybe ever again.

Until he finally slept.

And that, of course, would come with death.

Unless that had already happened, which Luca figured it probably had.

He kept walking his endless walk that felt somehow oddly familiar — like he'd done it before — like when Johnny Thomas was choking him, and he thought he could see his entire life like a movie played fast, except it wasn't his, even though it felt like it, because the new one that felt as real as the old one had his family dying in a car accident, some old man adopting him, and a brother whose name just sat there on the tip of Luca's tongue.

The movie didn't feel like imagination, it felt like something that had happened; a memory as impossible as him walking; a memory like the one that told him to look for the rainbow.

But Luca had never gone on a walk through the desert, or lost his family, or had a rainbow tell him where to go.

Even though the stuff inside him swore that all of those things had happened.

Luca kept forcing himself forward, a step at a time, each more painful than the one before it, every step growing more certain that nothing would feel better than if Luca were to simply lay down and die.

Maybe if I lie down, like I did on that porch swing, I'll wake up back there.

Yeah, that's it.

I just need to rest.

He fell to his knees, but the moment his hands touched the white sands, Luca jumped back up, palms like lobsters from the lots of hot on the ground.

He would have cried if he had any wet in his eyes, but it was all dried up or gone. So instead, Luca kept walking.

SOMETHING DARK DRAGGED shadows across the sand. Luca, startled, looked around, but saw nothing. He realized with a chill that the something wasn't on the ground, but rather above him, hovering with the promise of death.

Luca looked up to a large dark bird, circling.

A vulture, waiting for me to lie down ... or die.

I can't stop.

Must go on.

Luca wondered if the bird would attack him if he wasn't dead. From what he could remember, vultures only fed on bodies. He didn't think they actually killed anything. But he wasn't sure about that, and didn't even know if the bird was a vulture. It might've been a predator, maybe waiting for Luca to get even weaker.

Get weaker, or in the sun.

Luca laughed: the irony of a bird waiting for *him* to finish roasting. He thought again of the astronaut chickens, and couldn't stop laughing.

The more Luca thought that the chickens weren't funny, the louder he laughed.

Oh, God, I'm losing my mind.

Luca kept walking, trudging through the sand, ankles burning as he tried to pull himself from his ugly whirlpool of thoughts. If he could somehow remove pain from his movements, he might be able to go on, like a robot without feeling.

Just. Keep. Walking.

Eventually, I have to find something.

Luca continued, ignoring shadows from the circling bird.

After a while, the shadows left, when the bird gave up and disappeared. Luca felt relief that he could surrender his guard. And at the same time, felt an odd sense of loneliness with his only companion gone.

This, of course, made Luca think of his family.

He thought of playing Legos with Anna. He thought about the last time she'd asked him to play with his Ninjago pieces, after he'd put them with his *Legends of Chima* and used them to build a super fortress. Anna wanted to build a house for Boo, since Boo was so small, but Luca told her no. He didn't want her ruining his super fortress like she always did. She said that Luca was mean and he said she was stupid, just like Boo. Now that he was in the desert, Luca realized that she wasn't right until he answered.

That made Luca want to cry.

But, of course, he couldn't.

~

LUCA KEPT WALKING, his skin blistered and sore, throat raw, and body feeling seconds from collapse.

The sun went hiding behind the horizon as the sky turned from blue to purple, on its way to black. Luca touched the sand, wondering if it was safe enough to lie down on yet, then jerked it back when it was still burning to the touch.

He kept on, until the sun was gone. Purple turned to black as expected, but darker — blacker than anything Luca had ever seen. The desert was so wide open and giant that it seemed claustrophobic in the dark.

He reached out, hands in front of him, hoping not to bump into anything — not that he'd passed anything he could possibly bump into so far. Luca hadn't seen a single cactus. Every step was timid, and since the wind had died, it was replaced by a silence so deep it was deafening, like a high-pitched whistle, constant in his head: one more hurt to pile on the many.

Luca couldn't shake the feeling that at any moment, something would reach out from the darkness and grab him.

He kept walking. Slow but steady.

Suddenly, he heard something move behind him.

Luca froze, his heart pounding as he tried to hear above the quiet's high-pitched whine.

Something brushed by him, bumping against his waist. Luca screamed, and stumbled forward. Momentum carried him forward and he ran — faster than he would have thought possible since every inch of his body was crusted in pain.

He kept racing into the darkness, hoping that whatever pursued him was as blind as he was. He didn't dare stop to listen, or see if he'd lost it.

Luca had to keep running, or he would be dead.

As he ran, Luca's mind raced over the possible things that might have bumped into him. There weren't many; how many predators called deserts their home?

Some sort of hyena? A giant, poisonous lizard? A wolf?

Luca's feet gave out from beneath him. He lost a scream as he plunged forward, down into the darkness. His body hit the black sand hard, rolling, tumbling, out of control down a seemingly endless hill until he came to a sharp and sudden stop, gasping for air and peering into the black, ears perked to hear whatever he'd bumped into.

Seeing nothing, and hearing nothing, Luca curled into the sound as if it was Mom, feeling Alaska in his bones. The ground was still warm, unlike his insides, and felt relief against the evening's cool air.

Luca laid down, pulling himself into as tight a ball as his body allowed, making himself as tiny a target as possible so that whatever was waiting in the dark might not find him.

Finally, after thinking he would probably die if he fell asleep, Luca could hold his lids open no longer. He closed his eyes and started to snore.

LUCA WOKE to something licking him.

He opened his eyes, blinded by daylight as soon as he did. He threw his hands in front of his face, protecting himself from the bright light and whatever was licking him.

A familiar voice said, "It's OK, Luca."

Luca saw Dog Vader. The dog looked down at his feet, where four bottles of water were lined neatly in the sand.

Luca grabbed the bottles, unscrewed the caps, and gulped them down, one at a time.

"Whoa, slow down there, Luca. You'll puke. And the last thing you want to do in the desert is puke."

Luca slowed, and swallowed, water stinging his dry throat and cracked lips.

"Where am I?" he asked.

Dog Vader said, "You're close."

"Close to what?" Luca's throat hurt worse with every word.

"Save your voice," Dog Vader said. "You'll need it to speak with him."

"Who?" Luca asked.

Dog Vader nodded with his snout toward the distance. Luca saw a dark shape like an igloo, maybe made of dirt, with a small trail of black smoke spiraling into the sky above the igloo.

Luca asked, "Who is that?"

But Dog Vader was gone.

Luca grabbed the remaining bottles, shoved them into his pockets, and stood. His body ached, every movement felt as if he were breaking scar tissue, but he had to move forward. Not only had Dog Vader told him that he had to, but it was the first creature he'd seen in forever.

As Luca forced himself forward, the sun returned, then climbed in the sky, cooking his flesh as the igloo drew nearer. As he got closer, Luca felt it harder to continue. But he kept on, despite the pain, until the trail of smoke pluming above the igloo had vanished.

Luca hoped whoever was there hadn't left.

He pushed himself to move faster, even though faster was a crawl. As Luca moved closer, he saw that the igloo wasn't made of dirt, but something darker, which he couldn't yet untangle with his eyes.

He finished another bottle of water and shoved the empty into his back pocket as he came within a hundred or so feet of the igloo.

He was immediately met with a wall of stench that overwhelmed his senses.

Luca turned, trying not to puke. He remembered Dog Vader warning him not to. He wondered if this was why?

Luca now knew that the igloo was made of poop.

I can't go in there.

I can't.

Luca forced himself to duck down and look through the entrance at the someone inside.

He dropped to the sand and scrambled into the igloo, despite the reek. The man inside was older, with dark hair hanging in his face. He was also naked, except for the gloves made of poop. His eyes were closed, and he was sitting cross-legged in front of an iron pot. Beneath the pot, a fire's ashen remains.

Luca stared, shaking and afraid, wondering why he was supposed to talk to this crazy man. The man hadn't even twitched since Luca had entered the igloo. He wondered if the man was dead.

His eyes flicked open, blue eyes, bloodshot and tired.

"It's you," he said.

"Who are you?"

"My name is Roman, and I've been waiting for you."

~

FORTY-ONE

Boricio Wolfe

Boricio woke up, shocked to find himself in a peculiar situation — tied to his bed, and not in a good way.

His lids weren't gummed, and he wore no blindfold, but he kept them closed while sussing his surroundings, as best he could with his lids still drawn: metal cuffs biting into his wrists, thick clothesline or something pulling his ankles and wrapping them tight, and a twitching nose said prey in his room, waiting for a purge. Only this prey made the mistake of thinking itself a hunter.

Must've come in through the open window, Boricio figured. Some people would do anything for weed. Boricio knew it wasn't related to the people who'd tried to kill him and Miss Mary. Otherwise, he'd already be six feet under. No, this was someone with a fucking death wish, eager to take the Boricio Express to the Pearly Gates.

Somebody's going to die, and I'm going to wear that somebody's face as a mask, while I shit on their body.

Whoever had Boricio was watching him, his prickling ears said so, inches from the short hairs dancing at his neck.

Boricio finished figuring as much shit as he could with his eyes closed, then opened them to the man sitting a few feet away in the room's only chair. It was an old dude, overweight, who looked like, and smelled like, a cop.

He met the man's eyes, then curled his lip and said, "You wanna let me go now so we can play chase? I'll be *it* first, you'll get a one hour head start. Of course, when I catch you I'll carry your bones in a backpack, maybe wear your fingers around my neck."

The man said nothing, keeping Boricio wondering on his identity as he sat in the chair, running his hands along five inches of blade from his nine-inch, high-carbon stainless steel knife. The man had taste.

He stared down at Boricio, still silent, his only broadcast a gesture, ever so slight: a tilt of his head toward a folder at his feet; manila, closed, contents a mystery. Of course the folder had something to do with why the man was in Boricio's room, maybe everything, but Boricio sure as hell wasn't going to ask about it, or even open his mouth — not after the pile of cock hairs had refused his generous offer of being *it* first.

"Ah, you're awake," the man finally said, still staring at Boricio, face so void of emotion that Boricio had to wonder if he practiced at keeping it blank. Boricio nearly asked him, but kept his trap tight since he knew the fuckface wanted him to talk. Another several minutes of silence, then, "You've got nothing to say?"

Boricio smiled: *The guy was already losing and too stupid to know it.*

"Well," Boricio was ballsy enough to laugh, "It would be nice to make your acquaintance since I never like to tear the life from a man's throat, or intestines from his belly, without knowing his name first. No need to be proper, a nickname will do. What do they call you at the rest stops, Ass Vandal? Hershey Murial? Mr. Butterworth on account of your colita being so rich and creamy?"

The man's already sour face turned to vinegar. "My name is Michael Blackmore. Four years ago, you raped and murdered my daughter. I've come to claim justice in her name."

"Ha," Boricio laughed, repeated the man's words, but three octaves higher, then went back to his swaggered baritone and said, "I probably came for justice in her mouth."

The man's nose twitched, and the way it did, Boricio realized this particular purging and subsequent escape would be a fuck ton more work than the usual, and more than he had time for, considering Rose, Mary, and Paola were due back from their meeting with the Flux Capacitor at any goddamned minute.

He'd have to hurry shit, not just because he'd want to eliminate the threat to himself, and bury the evidence afterward — *tic-tac-toe, three in a row* — but because Boricio didn't know what the man might do when three women came into his room and interrupted his Count of Monte Cristo.

"Look man, I'm just fucking with you," Boricio said. "I'm sure what we have here is a case of mistaken identity. I was busy the night your daughter was raped and murdered, it couldn't have been me. Have you checked with O.J.?"

The man looked like he wanted to spit on Boricio. Instead, he reached down, grabbed the folder from the floor, opened it, then scooted closer to Boricio. He pulled photos from the folder, one by one. The first few made Boricio feel like he was watching some Hallmark After-School Saturday Morning Special: *Before Your Bitches Start Bleeding*, with one photo after another of some rug rat with pigtails, then braces, then grass on her patch, which Boricio couldn't see, but knew by the tits in her sweater. The man looked like he was teetering near losing it, so Boricio didn't push, though he could think of a dozen things that might make the fucker fall right over. Problem was, the man had a nine-inch knife, and Boricio wasn't sure he wouldn't take the rapist and murderer with him when he went.

They reached the end of the Hallmark part of the presentation. The man pulled out the photo of a crime scene and his daughter's mutilated corpse.

The first picture had the girl's body sprawled across a filthy motel mattress, with some of Boricio's funnier sketches scrawled on her skin in blood: a cat; a walrus; the Applebee's logo with a line through it. The second picture wasn't of the girl, so much as her head, all by its lonesome and resting on the dresser, hair pulled into pigtails — a lot like in one of the first few pictures the man had showed like shit from his wallet. Boricio wondered if Daddy saw the resemblance.

Of course, he remembered the girl, Boricio wasn't kidding about knowing names. That somehow improved the purging, though back when he split Amber's head from her body, it wasn't purging so much as an excellent way to spice up a night. But Boricio remembered everything about that partic-ular evening: He remembered meeting Amber at the Lucky Puck; remembered her looking right into his eyes and knowing she'd be eager for all the things Boricio wanted to do, except for the last one, of course; he remembered driving to the motel, in separate cars; he remembered every minute of the two hours spent filling each of her three holes — no persua-sion needed; and he remembered decorating the room in honor of Heath Ledger, whose excellent performance deserved to be commemorated after the sad man lost his sad, little life one year prior.

"I remember Amber."

Boricio saying his daughter's name seemed to shake the man from his fugue. "You knew her name?"

"Of course, I knew her name," Boricio said, as if it were no different from knowing how much the Astros lost by the night before. "I never get business finished without knowing a name. My way makes it better for everyone."

The man was clearly shocked, staring at Boricio, clearly clueless as to what he should say. Boricio figured the man had never met anyone so honest, and was probably expecting the old back and forth: *I didn't do it, it wasn't me; please, I'll do whatever you say, just don't hurt me; I didn't mean to, now I've seen the error of my ways.*

But that wasn't Boricio.

The man gathered his composure, then leaned down from the chair, lifted Boricio's shirt, then dug the knife's tip into his skin, starting at the shoulder and dragging it all the way down, nearly to his wrist.

Blood soaked the carpet as Boricio screamed, inside. Outside, he stayed silent, chewing his lip and vowing on mute that he would end the man in the most painful way his minutes allowed; splitting all 20 of his digits wide, peeling them back to shred tendon from bone, blooming pain and making sure the fucker felt raw hairs of torment with every flay.

"I've had a lot of time since you took Amber from me," he said. "I've spent most of it searching for you, and when I wasn't looking, I was dreaming of the day I'd finally find you. And I'm a man who likes research. Once upon a time I was a cop, now I'm a writer. I research what I don't know. I get online and sift through mediocrity until I find the meaty stuff. If I'm writing about a city, I make sure I know everything about that burg, from who has the best chili-dogs to the layout of its award winning parks, before typing the first word on that first paragraph. If I'm writing about a mechanic, I make sure I know all there is to know about the Dodge Charger sitting on blocks in his driveway. If, however, I'm not writing, but say, looking to find someone deserving of torture, I make sure I know all there is to know about various torments and agonies, enough to elongate the pain and suffering, misery and anguish, so I can keep a fucker like *you* in purgatory, just long enough to get you begging for hell."

"That's so purty, I think I might weep," Boricio said, daring to push him.

Time is not on ole Boricio's side.

"You won't be brave once I start showing you what I can do," the man said, ignoring Boricio. "You'll be screaming."

"Well, Señor Sorrow, I'm not sure you've thought this through. I'm sure you're a smart enough Officer Friendly to keep yourself from getting caught, despite the blood on the rug, but I start screaming and you're trapped. You'll hit traffic on PCH, soon as you leave the lot."

"You won't be screaming for more than a second."

Boricio smiled, liking Señor Sorrow in spite of himself. "What's with all the bullshit? Why not just kill me? You want me dead, why not just slice me up and get it over with, then run off into the night and cut your own wrists so you can join your daughter and the two of you can ever-after together?"

Señor Sorrow started to cry.

"Because," he said, tears spilling from each eye and slopping down both sides of his face. "I want to know why. I have to know why you did what you did to Amber; I have to know why you took my daughter away!"

Boricio fell uncharacteristically quiet, doing what he rarely did — thinking about what he would say before it spewed from his mouth. He'd rather die than plead, but Boricio would rather live than die, and truth was, he felt for the guy, Señor Sorrow or not. Boricio could see the man's grief in a way he never could've before, on the old world, or this one before his visit to that one; he could see things in a way he never had prior to Luca's fixing. Boricio wanted to slip out of the danger, but he also wanted to explain things to the man, and maybe, he realized, to himself.

When Boricio finally spoke, he met the grieving father's eyes and held them, staring into his anguish, owning it in a way that made his heart beat faster, his throat go drier, and covered his palms in a thin slick of sweat.

"Evil isn't action, man. It's a point of view. It's perspective. God kills, so do His hunters. We're random, indiscriminate. We take rich and poor, pretty or not. I was a different man when I met your daughter, and right this second I'm sorry about that, truly. I'm still a hunter to the bone, but now I'm more selective. I see evil and purge it, using my need to scrub the world one shit-stained tile at a time. But I didn't do that with your daughter, because she wasn't bad, and I didn't know this version of me. I can't give you a *reason* why I did what I did, but I won't insult you by saying I didn't do it, and I won't beg you to spare me. Use that knife how you want to, the way your hand's itching to start carving, then soon enough you'll be no different than me. See, you're already a hunter, that's why you're here, that's how you found me, but you're not a predator until I'm dead. So decide, Señor Sorrow, how much hell you want to live with for the rest of your life."

Boricio braced himself, having no idea whether the man would go through with what he could do without blinking.

His face was wet, his hair sweaty, hands shaking with doubt. Then, Señor Sorrow found his resolve. Determined, he kneeled to Boricio, grabbed him by a thick clump of hair, yanking his head back with his left hand, and drawing the blade with his right.

"Any last words?"

Boricio had plenty, but before he could get a single one out, the door clicked with a key card, then opened to Rose.

She gasped, and froze.

Señor Sorrow dropped Boricio's head and leapt for his gun. Before Rose could move he had the barrel aimed at her heart.

"Get in here," he said.

Rose stepped inside and closed the door behind her, pale as she entered, as if already scared or bothered or upset by something that had nothing to do with the Tarantino going down in the room. Now she had piled terrified atop her pallor, body shaking and eyes bloodshot, skin so pale Boricio thought she seemed nearly see-through.

He wanted to comfort her, reach out and touch her, he

wanted to tell Rose that everything would be fine if she could just trust him. But he didn't say a word, not wanting Señor Sorrow to know he could wound Boricio without touching him.

He looked from Boricio to Rose and back, several times, calculating, knowing what Boricio didn't say.

Still aiming his barrel at Rose, he sat and growled, "An eye for an eye. Now it looks like I have four."

TO BE CONTINUED...

Episode 24

(SIXTH EPISODE OF SEASON FOUR)

"By Any Other Name"

FORTY-TWO

Luca Harding

"What do you mean you've been waiting for me?" Luca asked, stepping back from the weird naked man sitting cross-legged in front of him.

Roman didn't stand or try to stop Luca from leaving. "I was a friend of Will's. He told me in my dreams that you'd be coming."

"Will?" Luca tasted the name and its familiar confusion. "Who is Will? I dreamed about him, but don't know who he is."

The man's head turned sideways, as if struggling for recall. "You don't remember Will?"

Luca shook his head, "Only from my dreams. Who is he?"

"He's an old friend of mine. Gone now. But he came back long enough to show himself in my dreams; he wanted to let me know you were coming, that you were pure, and that I could trust you. So … can I, Luca? Can I trust you?"

Luca was more confused than ever, not understanding what Roman meant about "pure." But as the question of trust settled, Luca started to vigorously nod. He had always prided himself on his ability to stick to his word. If Luca said something, he meant it, and always did as he said.

"Yes, Sir, you can trust me." A slight pause, then, "But trust me for what?"

"To be a custodian, Luca."

"What's that? Is that like Mr. Randall at school?"

Roman laughed, shaking his head, "Not that kind of custodian. No, Luca, this is much, much different. You've been chosen as a guardian, a protector. This is a huge responsibility, and if I'm being honest, you look … young."

"I'm 10!" Luca said, wanting responsibility, understood or not.

"Will said you've been touched by The Light."

"The Light?" Luca asked.

"Yes, some of us have been touched by The Light. Will was. I was. A few of our friends from back in the day were. We've all been chosen. For a long time I didn't know why or what for. I thought I was cursed. But now … now I see the blessing."

"I'm confused, Sir, but OK."

Luca felt certain that the crazy-looking man was in fact crazy. He remembered once when he was 6, walking with his family on the boardwalk after getting ice cream at Moosy's. A weird, dirty-looking guy approached them and started saying wacky things about how the government was using mind control rays and adding stuff to our water. For a moment, Luca thought the man might hurt them, but his dad handled the situation, talking to the guy in the same voice he used when trying to talk Luca down from a tantrum, and using some of the same words, until they got away without having to fight. He dreamed of the crazy guy for months after it happened. Roman reminded Luca a lot of that man. Though he wasn't making any threats, Luca thought the old guy might turn violent at any moment. He decided to follow his father's example by using the "no-more-tantrum" voice and saying whatever was needed to find his way home.

Roman looked Luca up and down, "Are you pure?"

Luca tried to keep his fear from showing. As long as the guy stayed seated on the ground, Luca figured he was OK. If he stood, Luca might have to run.

"Yes," Luca said, though he still didn't know what the man meant by pure. "Can you tell me how to get back home?"

"The Light will return you," Roman said.

"Good," Luca said, hoping the man was right about that much, if nothing else.

Roman pointed at a spot in front of Luca where the sand piled slightly higher.

"They're in there," Roman said. "Dig them up."

Luca dropped to his knees and started scooping sand from his body, not sure what was buried. He had so many questions:

Is this a dream?

How did we get here?

Why are you covered in poop?

But Luca dared not a word. He wanted to get whatever the man had to give him, then go home. Luca didn't even care if the police were waiting. Anything was better than getting baked in the desert.

Luca's hand found something hard in the sand, about a foot down. He swept grains aside until he could pry the object free. He pulled it from the ground and saw it was a black, metal box of some sort, about the size of the final Harry Potter book. It felt cold and weird on Luca's fingers, more so once he realized it was vibrating.

"Weird," he said, staring at the box. Luca looked closer, wondering if it was, in fact, a box, or some sort of meaning-less metal rectangle, empty inside. It had weight, maybe like a bag of apples, but Luca couldn't feel anything shifting inside. The box looked both new and somehow ancient, with no hinges, buttons, or clasps. Naked: black metal, smoother than anything he'd ever touched.

Pure.

"What is it?" Luca asked.

"That is The Light. Which you must protect."

"Protect from what?"

Roman leaned closer to Luca and whispered his next words as if volume might invite nightmares. "The Darkness."

Luca's mind flashed on something, dark and ropey, moving fast, and gaining speed as it spilled across the streets of his hometown. He couldn't tell if it was another one of his growing number of unexplainable memories, a dream, or just his imagination working to unknot the old man's whispered words.

"How do I open it?" Luca asked.

"Put your palms on the top and bottom. It will do the rest," Roman said. His face was pinched with wonder, waiting for Luca to open the box.

Luca placed his palms on what seemed to be the top and bottom, and felt the box vibrate, tickling his hands and wrist. Luca laughed. The box clicked and opened onto his palms like a book.

Inside the box, Luca stared at six glass tubes on the right side, inserted into a sticky looking blue strip of what looked like wet plastic. Each of the vials was filled with glowing, bright-blue liquid. Its glow lit his skin and, to Luca's shock, eased the blisters from burning to gone.

"Wow," Luca said, watching his knitting flesh repairing the sun damage. "What are these?"

"Vials of The Light. Notice: Six are missing."

On the left side was a similar strip, but dried and gray. Luca saw spots for another six vials. "Where did they go?"

"I realized early on that I could never keep them all to myself. It was too dangerous. So I gave them to people I could trust, people who promised to never open them unless something bad happened in the world."

"Bad?" Luca asked.

"Just … something bad I've been dreaming for a long time."

Luca felt warm in a wave through his body, erasing the sun's damage. He said, "This is amazing."

"Isn't it?" Roman laughed. "We've been blessed."

Luca asked, "But why are you giving these to me?"

"Because I can't open them. I'm tainted, not pure. Will said if I open them, bad things will happen. *Very* bad things. So it has to be you, Luca. You have to save the world."

"Save the world? From what?"

"The Darkness is here, Luca. It's been spreading. People going crazy, murdering one another. War, famine, chaos, it's about to get so much worse."

Luca was done with Roman's crazy talk, and wanted to find a polite way to thank him, then find his way home.

"How do I get back?" Luca asked. Direct was best, while the man was still in such a good mood.

"You will … " Roman stopped talking. He held a hand to his ear.

"Wait … do you hear that?"

"What?" Luca asked, hearing nothing but wind getting angry outside.

Roman stood and moved with surprising speed toward the igloo's exit. "Who are you?" he asked to something outside.

A chill through Luca made him think that one of the things he had bumped into earlier had followed him. He closed the black box, clutching it tight as he stepped from the igloo. Dog Vader was outside, growling at Roman.

Roman put his hands in front of Luca. "Be careful, he's evil."

"No," Luca explained, walking past Roman's outstretched hand toward Dog Vader. "He's my friend, Dog Vader. He's a talking dog."

Dog Vader looked up at Luca, and stopped growling, as Luca stroked him between his ears.

"You brought him here?" Roman yelled, angry. "You brought the evil here?"

He ducked back inside the igloo.

"Come on," Dog Vader said to Luca, nodding toward a large, glowing, purple rectangle; a door of light sprouting from the ground just yards away. "It's a portal, to get home."

Luca smiled, glad to see a way home, but feeling bad because Roman got scared off by Dog Vader. He called into the igloo, "Hey, Mister. You can come home with us. Dog Vader found a way back."

"Is that so?" Roman said, crawling back out of the igloo. His left hand was behind his back as he stared at Luca, crazy-eyed.

Luca started to step back, nervous, wondering what Roman was hiding behind his back.

The crazy, old man walked faster, quickly closing the distance between them. Dog Vader growled, stepping between Luca and Roman.

Roman revealed his hand, holding a pistol, aiming it at Dog Vader and fired, twice. Bullets whistled past the dog and slapped the dirt.

Luca was confused, his heart pounding in his chest, fear coursing through him, telling him to run.

Dog Vader turned and growled, "Run, Luca!"

Roman raised his gun and aimed it at Luca. "Stop!"

Dog Vader barked louder, viciously snapping at the man, and rising his rear as if he was about to jump Roman at any moment.

Roman laughed, ignoring Dog Vader. He said, "You're not real," then stepped through the dog and fired a shot past Luca.

"Give it back, Kid!"

"Run, Luca!" Dog Vader yelled.

It was impossible for Luca to reach the portal, unless Roman was a horrible shot. He had to return the box. As Luca turned, about to hand the box to Roman, Dog Vader yelled, "Don't give it to him. He's evil. Run, Luca!"

"Shut up!" Roman screamed back, firing a shot at the ghost dog.

Dog Vader rattled his body, like he was trying to shake water from a soaking coat. Luca stared, confused, watching as his fur darkened, then sloughed off in fluffs, floating at first, then gathering around the dog in a tiny tornado of fur. The fur multiplied, spreading upward, spinning a 12 foot by 12 foot wall between Luca and Roman.

Dog Vader, whom Luca could no longer see through the black tufts of swirling fur, called out, "Run, Luca!"

Luca ran to the portal, clutching the box tight in his fingers as Roman screamed, "Come back!" firing shots.

Luca reached the portal and was about to step through when he felt an eruption of agony, starting in his left shoulder and shooting through his entire back.

I'm shot!

He tumbled forward, inches from the portal's shimmer. The pain was so intense, Luca couldn't move. He wanted only to fall. But he dared not stop. Roman would keep shooting until he finished the job.

"Go!" Dog Vader screamed.

Luca forced himself to focus on moving forward, despite the pain. He fell to his knees, and heard more gunshots erupting behind him.

"Go! Go! He's coming!" Dog Vader screamed.

Luca somehow pushed himself in a crawl toward the purple light. As it bathed his skin, Luca's flesh began to ripple.

Keep moving! Into the light!

Luca continued crawling until the purple consumed him.

∾

FORTY-THREE

Edward Keenan

Ed was preparing to leave Manhattan in a stolen Camry when he saw the black vans barreling toward Brent Foster's street. He tried telling himself they were heading to Stan's, following up on what happened with their fallen agents, but even if that was true, they'd still hit Brent's next.

And if they got to Brent, there was no way they'd let him, or his family live.

Screw it. Brent made his bed when he started talking.

Ed kept driving, dialing Jade's cell repeatedly, hoping she'd answer, and that she, Teagan, and Becca were safe. If Sullivan was compromised, and it seemed he was if he'd given the order to kill them, Ed had to assume his family was in danger. Sullivan said that he had been affected by the vials, that his abilities allowed him to track Ed to his Florida safe house. Ed wasn't sure how Sullivan had managed, if it was some sort of psychic connection they all shared that he could track, or if Sullivan was lent some supernatural ability to home in on them. Ed would assume the worst unless Jade picked up the phone.

But she didn't answer.

He hung up, cursing again.

As Ed drove faster, away from the city, he couldn't push Brent from his mind.

He had no way to know if Jade was in danger. He guessed she was, based on shit and the fans it was likely to hit, but he didn't know. Maybe Jade's phone was dead, or they were out of the house. Maybe she left the phone's ringer off while sleeping. Plenty of scenarios saw Jade, Teagan, and Becca all still safe.

However, there was only one possibility for Brent Foster and his family if Ed didn't go back. While Brent might have been stupid, talking to too many people, his wife and child had done nothing wrong. And though Brent was being selfish in his pursuit of a family reunion, Ed understood. The man had lost everything; it was difficult to expect someone like him to embrace sacrifice when it was shoved down his throat.

Ed had made a choice to work for the government. He knew what he was signing up for, even if he could never have known the depths of what he was getting into or what he'd be forced to surrender.

Brent was thrust into hell without any choice.

He lost his job, wife, and son. Sure, Brent could have — *should have* — handled things better, but Ed didn't know many people who would've played their cards differently.

If Ed didn't intervene, Brent would pay the ultimate price.

Fuck!

Ed pulled into the left lane and spun the car, heading back into the city.

ED ARRIVED at Brent's apartment as the sound of gunshots echoed through the broken door and into the hallway.

Too late!

Ed rushed through the door, scanning the room. Two

Black Island Guardsmen stood over Brent, cowered on the floor and begging for life, arms around his son.

Brent's wife was sprawled on the floor, motionless, blood spilling from a gunshot wound to the head.

The Guardsmen whirled, guns raised. The taller of the two had an M-16, the second a Glock-17, like Ed. Neither was Ed's match for speed or the element of surprise. He already had the larger man in his sights. Ed fired two shots to his helmet and one to his groin, dropping the man in an instant. He rolled to the ground, avoiding the second guardsman's shots, then sprang to his feet and fired into the man's crotch, gut, and face in three successive shots.

Ed stood steel bar straight, tensed as he made sure the men were dead. Once certain, he kicked their weapons away, and reloaded his Glock.

He turned to Brent and his son, both huddled over Gina's dead body.

"Mommy! Get up, Mommy. Please," Ben cried, hugging her.

Ed couldn't stand to look. If he allowed their grief to overwhelm him, he wouldn't be ready. He'd seen two vans, not one. There were more Guardsmen nearby — maybe across the street at Stan's. If so, it was only a matter of minutes before they came to Brent's, called in reinforcements, or both.

"We have to go," Ed said, leaning down. "There's more on the way."

Brent was crying, holding his son, rocking him in his arms, ignoring, or not hearing, Ed.

"Come on; it's not safe here!" Ed yelled, his eyes back on the doorway.

"She's dead," Brent said, staring at his wife, still in shock, unable to see the situation's urgency.

Ed didn't have time to earn Brent's attention. He leaned over, grabbed Ben, and started to pull him from his father.

Brent jerked his son back, looked up, eyes angry, "Hey!"

Ed had his attention. He let Ben go, and met Brent's eyes. "Grab some ammo for your gun, we need to get out of here! Now! Or they'll come back, and they will kill us — all of us."

Brent swallowed, looked down at Ben, who was back on the floor beside his mother, begging her to "wake up," then looked down and picked up the M-16.

Brent pulled Ben from his mom. The boy screamed, "No, Daddy!"

"We've gotta go," Brent said, his voice more soothing than he could have possibly felt.

"No!!" Ben screamed, his face red and swollen as he tried to push free from his father. Pushing turned to hitting and scratching, desperate to stay with his mom. "We can't leave Mommy!"

"Mommy's dead," Brent said, hugging his son closer. "She's gone to heaven, buddy. We need to get out of here before more bad men come."

Ben collapsed against his father, crying into surrender.

"Come on," Ed said, fighting back the tears in his welling eyes. He couldn't allow the boy's pain to dull his senses. If he didn't stay sharp, the boy, and his father, would die.

～

FORTY-FOUR

Steven Warner

IT tightened *ITS* grip around Marina's neck, digging long digits deeper into her flesh, allowing *ITSELF* to enjoy the fear pouring from her shell's sweating skin.

IT enjoyed her confusion, and her desperation to try and make sense of the situation. Wondering why *IT* was killing her.

Just as *IT* was about to crush her throat, *IT* felt a scream somewhere out there.

Something was wrong with Rose — the human woman *IT* somehow couldn't see with the same indifference *IT* felt for the rest of the planet. Her *love* once belonged to Bishop, and *love* made ridiculous trade: He owned a piece of her, and she of him. Owning a piece of Bishop, therefore meant she owned a piece of *IT*.

Rose was in trouble, maybe near death.

IT homed in on the vision: Rose being held by a stranger at gunpoint. *IT* could feel her fear and confusion, her racing heart as she worked to absorb her surroundings, flitting terrified eyes from the stranger to her man, the other Boricio, the hunter, incapacitated and tied to the bed.

The stranger had come for the hunter: Bishop's *love* was in the way, and therefore in danger. If *IT* did nothing, her death was imminent.

Suddenly, *IT* realized that *IT* had let go of Marina's throat.

She squirmed, wiggling away as she whimpered. *IT* grabbed her by the hair and jerked her head back harder, dragging Marina toward him as she cried out.

IT had to go. *IT* could take Rose and rid *ITSELF* of the hunter, whom *IT* somehow knew was more than a threat: maybe *the* threat, growing stronger through every unattended minute.

IT looked down at Marina, who stared up at her lover, defiantly, unwilling to surrender because she was stupid. Marina saw *IT* as a monster, rather than humanity's hope: a promise a species as putrescent as man was lucky to get.

IT looked into her mind, seeing Marina remembering her father's warning that, "The Darkness was coming."

IT wanted to laugh.

IT wasn't used to — or comfortable with — indecision.

IT should kill her.

IT should leave her to nothing.

IT should punish her for wasting *ITS* time, for never revealing the vials' location, or the machine's truth, despite months in her presence.

But *IT* suddenly couldn't. It felt … wrong.

Marina had not yet finished serving her purpose. *IT* had been drawn to her bed for a reason. She had been touched by the vials, and would lead *IT* to them if *IT* waited long enough. But even if she never found the vials, Marina gave *IT* unprecedented access to a potential army of millions of hosts.

She might be *ITS* best tool, after the next phase.

Her heart beat faster, as Marina grew more desperate to escape.

"What are you?" she asked, her voice full of disgust.

"I am the true All Seeing," *IT* said, mocking her faith.

"You and I have so much work to do. But first, I have a matter to tend to, I hope you don't mind."

IT tightened *ITS* grip on Marina's hair, pulling harder as it reached down, slipped *ITS* hand under her skirt. She screamed as *IT* yanked her panties down over her knees and past her ankles, then balled them up, and shoved them into her open mouth to muffle the screaming.

IT threw Marina over *ITS* shoulders and marched from the room and to the elevator, not caring who saw *IT*. If anyone got in *ITS* way, *IT* would kill them.

Marina screamed, punched, kicked, and tried breaking free, but she was no match for *ITS* strength. *IT* brought her to the basement, then pressed two buttons together, the first and third floor buttons, which brought the elevator one more floor down, to the secret room that Marina didn't know *IT* knew about — the crypt where her father's body was. Where she came to pray for advice from a dead man.

A panel slid open on the elevator showing a digital screen with blue digits. IT punched in the code, 5115, and the elevator doors opened.

Marina, realizing where they were going — a room nobody would hear them in — kicked and screamed louder until she coughed and gagged on her panties.

IT walked into the room, which lit at their entrance, and dropped her hard to the ground.

She jumped up and took a swing.

IT swung *ITS* fist hard into where her neck met her head, dropping her to the ground in an instant, cold.

IT left the room and sealed the crypt, leaving the acting head of The Church of Original Design locked inside a room where only two knew the combination: one bound inside it.

Now *IT* had to go save Rose, and finally finish the other Boricio.

~

FORTY-FIVE

Mary Olson

Mary stared at Paola, thinking about the storms inside her comatose daughter, lying in the hospital bed. Paola was hooked up to more machines, as if the one she'd been in hadn't done enough damage. Tubes going into her, electronics monitoring her vitals, and God-only-knew what sorts of medications (and how many) pumping through her system.

The doctors and nurses had asked Mary a battery of questions, both about Paola's medical history and what happened prior to her arrival. Mary felt like her head was about to explode. She couldn't keep lying, especially if her lie might mean the difference between Paola living and dying.

She finally told them about Marina, about the machine, and what happened. She told them everything except why Paola had gone into the machine. Mary lied, saying the girl had been having headaches lately. Nothing horrible, but their friend had claimed the machine cured her migraines, so Mary didn't see the harm.

She was surprised that Dr. Thomasson didn't look at her like an idiot for turning to a cult for medical help. Perhaps The Church was well known in these parts and actually seen as semi-legitimate.

The doc said he'd need to call Marina and ask her some questions, find out what he could about the machine. Mary had freaked, wanting to call Rose to tell her to call Marina and lie, but she couldn't make a call without being discovered by one of the several staff members coming in and out of Paola's room.

The doc came back and announced that he'd left a message but had yet to hear anything.

Following tests, X-Rays, and an MRI, none of which showed anything to explain Paola's state, everyone was playing it by ear.

Mary sat at her daughter's bedside feeling more alone than ever.

She kept flashing back to when Paola had nearly died at the Drury. How she was lying there, dead to the world, until Luca came to save her.

Mary always felt her daughter, like a spirit she could sense no matter where the girl was. The only times she had ever felt disconnected was at the Drury, and now. Both times she felt nothing: Paola might as well have been dead.

She couldn't lose another child.

No, don't think about it.

Mary had tried not to think about her miscarriage after returning to Earth. Tried not to think about losing Desmond's child. No good could come from it. Just as no good could come from thinking about Desmond, or even Ryan for that matter. Thinking about things that could not be, that would not be, was holding court with ghosts and only attracting more death.

She stared at Paola, afraid that even thinking such things was somehow draining her child even as she thought them.

No, no, stop. Think of something happy. Something—

If the worst happened to Paola, Mary would join her.

She already decided. The only question left was how she'd do it. Pills, gunshot, or maybe something else?

She was too tired if fighting the inevitable. Too tired of trying to dim the pain.

A child's death mocked logical order. A mother was *supposed* to precede her child's passing, not be forced to adapt illogical reality. *She* was protector and provider, not a survivor … not over her child.

She brushed a thumb across her daughter's too-cool skin. Mary felt lost and sad; fatigued, her thoughts cloudy. She had no idea what to do to pass the time, so did as she had been every few minutes since reaching the hospital.

Mary pulled the cell from her pocket, dialed Boricio, and again got his voice mail. Like every other time, she listened because it made her feel ever so slightly less awful:

"Howdy there, you've reached Boricio's Center For Mental Fitness. Please listen to the following options: If you're obsessive compulsive, press #1 over and over, 47 times or your mother will die. If you're co-dependent, turn to the nearest asshole and ask them to press #2 for you. Multiple personalities, I will direct you to buttons #3, 4, 5, and 6. Press them all, one at a time. If you're paranoid, we know who you are, and we will motherfucking find you. Delusionals press #7, then patiently wait for your transfer to Planet Zebot. Schizophrenics, listen for your inner assholes. Sufferers of short-term memory loss, try again later. And those afflicted with low self-esteem: Fuck you, no one wants to talk to you."

She laughed, even after hearing it so many times. Only Boricio could leave such a long message which not only tested your patience but taunted you, daring you to hang up.

Mary ended the call and phoned Rose — still no answer — then grabbed the TV remote from a tray, aimed it at the room's corner screen, knowing it was a mistake before the TV bled with color and filled the room with tragedy.

The nation's news had been growing worse by the week.

The worst school shooting was followed by the worst mall shooting in U.S. History, as if the monsters committing the crimes were trying to outdo one another in gruesomeness. "Experts" were on TV blaming everyone from the president to the decline in morality and family values, to the lack of religion in schools, to bad parenting.

Mary wasn't one to personalize the news. But it was impossible not to. Part of her could feel the truth, even before standing in the garage with Boricio, before their drive from Colorado, and — if Mary was being honest with her whisper — before the blade bit into her finger.

Something *big* was happening; a darkness gathering like pregnant clouds. Earth's horizon was collapsing, reality turning into something terrible. Whatever had happened *over there*, was on its way *here*. Mary could feel it like she could often feel it was about to rain. This storm would be endless.

The world wasn't prepared for such a flood.

Mary and the others had survived once, on the other Earth, again saved by Luca. But Luca wasn't around to save them this time. And there was no safety net of an uninfected Earth waiting for their return. If Boricio was right, and the aliens had come here, this was it.

Mary didn't know if she could make it this time — especially without Paola by her side. But so long as Paola was alive, Mary would have to be strong, would fight with everything she had left, tired or not.

That was her job.

While Sullivan hadn't warned her of any specific dangers, Mary hadn't felt safe since losing Ryan and then coming home. She could never allow herself to be in a position of weakness again, waiting for others to help her.

She had to be prepared for when shit hit the fan.

It was one of two reasons they had moved to Colorado. Paola's art school was fantastic, and made selling the move easy for Mary, but the real reason she wanted to move to Colorado was because of the Boulder Outdoor Survival School: the world's oldest and largest. One week into their new address, Mary was enrolled in her first course with many to follow, testing her skills — and sometimes Paola's — everywhere from southern Colorado up into Utah. It was why Mary continued Desmond's training without him, joining the Boulder Rifle Club and refining her excellent aim by the week.

She never would've imagined herself a survivalist type, but there was something comforting in being able to take care of yourself when things went to hell. Living through the nightmare that had happened on the other world opened Mary's eyes to realities she could never close them to again. Even if the aliens weren't a threat, they were living in an increasingly unstable global economy: Countries went bankrupt, terrorism was at an all time high, political tension hung like a fog over the planet. Races, religions, and classes were clashing, making the news nearly every night, well before and unrelated to — Mary was certain — the recent horrors.

It was easy to see that *something* was brewing.

The world was a pressure cooker, and it was only so long before something exploded. When it did, the unprepared would be punished as everything man-made started to fail. Mary had seen it happen on the other side already, how destruction was swept into horrifically tidy piles. Planes would crash, dams would burst, pipelines would blow, and grids would fail. Society was a luxury, and learned skills essential: Know-how requires no wires or batteries.

Despite her training, Mary didn't feel ready yet.

She let Boricio take on three freaks while she hid behind a car. Mary tried to tell herself she was playing it smart. She was unarmed — *a stupid error, by the way* — but also, Boricio was so damned good at what he did. And he *had told her* to get back.

Still, Mary felt like she should've done more.

The weird thing was, that as they came under attack, the very thing that gave Mary strength — Paola — had weakened her. As she crouched behind the car, she found herself worrying what if she were killed? Who would take care of Paola?

The fear had paralyzed her.

She'd been fortunate that Boricio was there. But fortune didn't usually favor the weak or unprepared. Next time, she had to act in spite of the fear.

She looked at her daughter again, wishing she could reach into the girl's head and wake her.

"I'm still here, Honey," she whispered. "We're all waiting for you to wake up. Everything's gonna be OK."

As Mary promised that everything would be OK, two old, white men on the news were arguing over whether there should be more guns, or less. They each used the same evidence to support their theories, citing the recent tragedies. Their explanations were so vapid, Mary had to kill the TV.

Paola didn't need to hear that crap, assuming she could hear anything in her state.

"Everything's going to be OK, Baby," Mary said, squeezing her daughter's hand gently.

Mary wondered what she had done to upset karma like she had, wondered why things couldn't be normal for her or Paola — why her daughter couldn't have a normal childhood filled with school, puberty, a reluctant boyfriend, or a stupid cover song posted to YouTube.

She leaned onto her daughter's bed, resting her head against Paola's side. As she settled, a shock of thunder sent her leaping up and out of her seat.

Mary had probably heard more gunshots than any greeting card artist in history, and knew the sudden thunder wasn't a car backfiring or fireworks lighting the sky: six even shots, followed by thick silence garnished with screams after it settled.

She heard another pair of shots, closer, definitely in the hospital. They sounded right outside the hall. Mary couldn't afford to panic, so she didn't, thinking about her bag of guns in the Volvo — *again unprepared!* — knowing she couldn't get them and abandon Paola to whatever danger lurked in the halls.

Mary dipped her hand into her purse, wrapped her fingers around the knife's handle — *Well, I've got this, at least* — then closed her eyes, drew three successive breaths, and drew the blade from its sheath.

She went to the door, opened it a crack, then slipped her head through the opening. She looked left and saw nothing, then turned her head right, let out a scream as a zombie stumbled down the hall, toward her room.

Mary knew no other word for someone so vacant, drenched in blood with his mouth drooped open, more plasma oozing from his low-hanging lip. While his expression was empty, his eyes were not. They were entirely black, yet seemed to be focused on her. As the creature drew closer, he reached out for her.

Mary managed to scream, "HELP!" before slamming the door and planting her back against it, bracing for the worst as she looked over at Paola, still oblivious to the world, inert in her bed.

The zombie slammed into the door, the heavy thud followed by an inhuman growl. While Mary wouldn't have been surprised to see bleakers, the all-black, alien things that had hunted them on the other world, or even an infected person who was part human, part alien like Ryan had been, she didn't expect this — a deceased man so obviously walking, trying to break down the door.

Mary pushed her shoulder harder against the door, staring through the small window at the top, which reminded her — horribly — of the small window at the top of The Capacitor — and saw the dead man's face in the window, mashing his cheek to the glass and smearing drool in a rainbow of red.

The lever that served as a doorknob lowered with no way to lock it.

Mary's mind raced trying to decide how to handle the thing once he broke through and into the room if someone didn't come and shoot him first. Might be best to open the door and let the creature spill into the room, carried by momentum and falling to the ground. Then she could stab him in the neck.

Mary was probably fast enough, but what if she wasn't? Or what if the creature didn't stumble and fall? What if he just broke through and stayed perfectly upright?

The thing on the other side slammed the door harder, managing to nudge Mary a few inches. Before thinking, she threw her body back at the door, forcing the creature away. He hit the door harder, opening it an inch — just enough for the dead man to jam his fingers inside. Mary threw her weight against the door and crunched the zombie's fingers with a loud snapping.

The dead man cried out, sounding almost alive in his rage.

He slammed harder into the door, forcing Mary back an inch before she could manage to reclaim the loss in some sort of unholy tug-of-war.

She tried to hold steady, but her shoes slipped along the slick linoleum, slowly losing the battle.

She let go of the door and jumped back, managing to stay on her feet and put a few inches between herself and the dead man, waving her knife in arcs before her.

The creature, ignoring the knife, moved forward to attack.

Mary swung, aiming for his left hand, but before she could connect, two more gunshots echoed through the room.

The man still stood, slowed and stunned, but not yet dead, until three more shots sent him to the ground.

An officer stepped through the open doorway, waved his gun through the room, left to right before letting it fall and offering a hand to Mary. "Are you OK?"

"No," she said. "What the hell is happening?"

Mary looked at the mess of a man, twitching as blood poured from his wounds.

"No idea, Ma'am," the officer, a young man with piercing, green eyes, said as he stepped in front of the dead man, away from the pooling blood. "Are you OK?"

"Yeah, yeah," Mary said, turning quickly to Paola to make sure she wasn't shot by the officer.

She leaned close to Paola, looking her up and down, but saw no sign of injuries.

"It's OK," she said, leaning forward and kissing her daughter's head. "Everything's OK, Baby."

Mary turned back to the cop, just in time to notice something black hanging in the air behind him, floating almost like smoke.

"What the?" she said, confused.

"What?" the cop said turning around and looking into the hallway.

The smoke moved fast, three ways at once — toward a second cop just behind the first, and then right and left down the hall.

Mary's eyes were fixed on the second cop, watching as his face shifted — like a hundred bugs beneath the skin — then settled. His eyes drained until they looked as empty as the creature kissing blood on the floor. Before Mary could do anything to stop it — though she should have seen it coming — the hollow-eyed cop lifted his gun and fired twice at the one in front of her.

The officer fell to the already-bloody, sticky floor as his partner pulled the trigger again, blasting him in the face.

The possessed cop's gun clicked three times, ammo empty, and Mary found both heartbeat and breath. She used it to scream on her way toward the door.

She jumped over the two dead men, slammed the door shut, then held her shoulder to it, again, muttering prayers, and begging any god from either world to hear her.

FORTY-SIX

Paola Olson

Paola was confused.

She woke in warmth, wondering how she got outside. Then, as her eyes adjusted, she realized she was no longer in Malibu. The streets, mansions, and oceanfront land had exploded in a million tiny pixels, then settled into endless miles of sand.

Something was wrong.

Why aren't I awake yet?

Am I still in the machine? Still dreaming?

Paola turned in a circle searching for any sign of anything. She wanted to call out, "Hello?" But a cold chill ran through her, warning her of The Darkness still behind her.

Is it here, too?

Endless sky mirrored the sand below, not a single cloud to mar its blue.

Paola's shoes had gone missing, warm sand slipped between her toes with a pleasant burn.

Not knowing what to do or where to go, she began walking, figuring things would make sense soon enough.

This is a dream, right? Things always work out.

Paola trudged through the desert, walking for what felt like hours before she saw something dot the horizon.

Luca!

She wasn't sure how she knew it was him, but it had to be.

Paola pushed herself to walk faster, despite the heat bearing down hard enough to soak her shirt.

Luca will help me get out of here.

I have to catch up.

Paola smiled as she ran after Luca, burning her ankles as she closed the distance between them. She was surprised how much of the gap she had managed to narrow in only a few minutes, and used the wonder to fuel herself faster.

Just as she was near enough to call for Luca, a second Luca appeared in front of her, bathed in brilliant light.

The Light looked less like the Luca trudging ahead, and *felt* more like the Luca who saved her the first time. He was an old man again.

He spoke in an almost musical hum, "No, Paola."

She froze.

"He's not who you're looking for," The Light told Paola what she suddenly already knew. "He's an impostor."

"I know, but what can I do?" Paola leaned into The Light, wanting its warmth, despite the hot blazing keeping them under its heel. "Can you help me?"

"You don't need me, you need The Light."

"But you are The Light!" Paola knew it was true because she saw it in her dreams.

"No," The Light said. "You have misunderstood. Your dreams show you The Light, not where it shines."

Paola knew what was coming; felt it inside her before The Light said it.

"*You* are The Light now, Paola, only you can shine for us all."

The desert disappeared and took her with it.

Paola found herself on a dark street along the shoreline,

though whether it was real or imagined she did not know. For some reason, everything was bathed in an odd and ugly red. She looked up and saw it was because of the moon.

A cold breeze forced her farther inland, near a cluster of houses. A light was on in one: a beacon for just her.

She raced forward, eager to reach it.

He's in there. Waiting for you.

She wasn't sure who *he* was, but the voice seemed more promise than threat.

Somewhere in the distance, a shriek — the all-too-familiar voice of a bleaker.

Paola picked up her pace and raced ahead, finally reaching the house. She saw that while the window was lit, there were black, iron bars over it. And several claw marks in the rotting wood around the window.

Shelter for someone: a survivor.

Paola walked up three stairs and knocked on the door, hoping she was making the right choice, and not walking into her enemy's camp.

The door opened. Paola fell back two of the stairs.

"You?"

∾

FORTY-SEVEN

Edward Keenan

Avondale, New York

IT TOOK NEARLY seven hours to drive from Manhattan to the Canadian border where Ed had a safe house nestled in the tiny town of Avondale.

They arrived at night. Ed stopped the car in front of a diner and turned to Brent and Ben in the back seat. "I want you guys to go inside and eat. I'll head to the house on foot. If I'm not back in an hour, things went bad. Take the car and go."

"Then what?" Brent asked. "Where do we go? Who do we trust?"

"I don't know," Ed said, wishing he had a better answer. "Find somewhere safe and live off-grid. Use false names. No phones, no Internet except in public places, and nothing that can be used to trace you specifically. Don't give the government anything they can use to track you. Hell, you're resourceful, Brent. I'm sure you'll manage. I've got some cash in an envelope in the trunk. If I don't come back take it. Use it to set yourself up somewhere."

"Do you think they're waiting for you here? Do you think it's a trap?"

"Only one way to know," Ed said. He got out of the car, grabbed a bag from the back seat, stashed with weapons taken from one of the Black Island vans before leaving the city.

"Be careful," Brent said.

Ed looked at his watch and made sure the time matched the car's — two minutes off at 8:20 p.m. "It's 8:20. If I'm not back by 9:20 p.m., get out of here. Got it?"

"Yes," Brent nodded. "And thanks ... for coming back."

"Yeah," Ed said, wanting to add that he wished he'd come sooner, but knew it wasn't necessary.

He left Brent and his son, attempting to stitch their family of two together in the long shadow of Gina's death.

THE GIRLS' car was in the driveway and lights were on behind the blinds: good signs, though far from any sort of guarantee.

Ed slowly walked the roadside, like a neighbor strolling, carrying a big bag of weapons. He'd thrown a red and blue Bills jacket over his Black Island Guardsman shirt and Kevlar vest, though he didn't bother to disguise his black pants or boots.

So far, Ed had only passed a handful of people. He pretended to be on his phone to avoid conversations and eye contact. So far, none of the people he passed seemed like agents of either Black Island or his former agency, and he saw no sign of surveillance vehicles.

If Ed was stepping into a trap, it was the most low-profile trap he'd ever seen.

Ed passed his daughter's house once, keeping an eye on the blinds to see if they fluttered. They didn't. He also watched the neighboring houses and cars in the driveways. Four of the five closest houses had lights on inside, two with curtains or blinds drawn. One house was dark, which could have meant his enemy waited there, or, just as likely, nobody was home or already asleep.

Ed kept walking to the corner, then turned down a side street to head back up the next block. He would hit his daughter's house from the back, cutting through neighboring lawns.

Ed found the third house from the end of the street and cut through the yard, approaching Jade's from behind. The rear had a back door and kitchen window that looked into the yard. Both had curtains drawn over their windows.

He looked back to see the house that backed up to Jade's, two stories, also lit with shades drawn. No one could see him unless there was someone upstairs in one of the darkened windows looking down. If that was so, there was nothing Ed could do to stay invisible, except hope for the best and prepare for an ambush.

Gun in hand, he approached the back of Jade's house, ears perked. He heard the faint sound of a television, but not the girls or Becca. Maybe Becca was already in bed, and the girls were relaxing, watching the glow.

Ed grabbed his phone again and dialed Jade.

He couldn't hear it ringing inside the house, and she wasn't answering.

Ed softly reached for the knob on the back door, not sure what to expect. He was surprised when it twisted in his hand.

No way they leave their back door unlocked!

My daughter isn't that stupid.

Rather than step through the doorway, Ed fell back, reconsidering his next move. A gun pressed to his head.

Shit.

"We've been waiting for you," Sullivan's voice said from behind. "Drop the bag, and your gun."

"You better not have hurt my family," Ed said, dropping both gun and bag of weapons to the cold ground.

"Inside," Sullivan said, pushing the gun against Ed's head for emphasis.

Ed began calculating escape the second he felt the muzzle pressed to his head. There were ways to counter your enemy, distract them, gain the upper hand and wrest the weapon away, even when the gun was barrel to head. However, there were too many variables, chiefly what kind of backup Sullivan had behind him. There was also the question of whether the girls were a) still alive or b) still here. Maybe they'd already been taken off site, which meant Ed's escape would bring him no closer.

He had to assume that Sullivan didn't want him dead, or he would've simply shot him. So Ed would play — for now.

He stepped into the house, relieved to see Jade and Teagan sitting on the sofa, surprisingly not bound or gagged.

"Daddy!" Jade said, looking like she wanted to jump from the couch.

"It's going to be OK," Ed said to the girls, both crying. "Where's Becca?"

Teagan said, "Upstairs, sleeping."

Ed tried to divine their stress level from expression, body language, and voices, hoping to determine what Sullivan had done or threatened already. They were scared, but didn't seem traumatized.

"Have a seat with your girls," Sullivan said.

Ed was surprised he wasn't trying to tie him.

There must be others, upstairs or on their way.

Ed took a seat as instructed, while Jade and Teagan covered him in hugs. He wanted to cry, grateful that they were alive. He sank into the comfort of their hugs, but kept emotion from leaving his body. First, he had to see what he was dealing with.

"What do you want?" Ed asked.

Sullivan looked different. Normally, the young man was impeccably dressed, pinstriped, and tidy, hair slicked back.

This Sullivan looked like he was barely surviving after a three-night bender — hair unkempt, white dress shirt untucked and wrinkled, tie unknotted and limp. His eyes had dark circles beneath them, and he wasn't wearing his black hipster glasses.

Ed wasn't sure if the man sometimes wore contacts, if the glasses were misplaced fashion statement, or if something else was happening entirely, though just *what* that might be, Ed had no idea. But *something* was definitely wrong with Sullivan.

He took a seat in a chair opposite the couch with only a coffee table between them. Ed considered ways he could use the coffee table to his advantage, but kept his eyes on Sullivan while waiting for his answer.

"I like you, Ed," Sullivan said.

"I'd hate to see how you treat people you don't like."

Sarcasm seemed lost on Sullivan.

"There are few humans we see as worthy of joining us. Accessing Sullivan's memories, and archives of our experience going against you, we see you as a formidable enemy, and a possible ally in this new world."

"What the hell are you talking about?" Ed said, his mind already guessing. "Wait? You're *infected?*"

Sullivan smiled. "Infected is such a pejorative term. We prefer *evolved.*"

"How long have you been *evolved?* Did you come to this world like this?"

"No, Sullivan is one of our more recent acquisitions. A good one. A heightened human, like yourself. We appreciate humans who can benefit our species, rather than bleed it."

"What do you mean?" Ed asked, using curiosity to buy minutes.

"We made a mistake on the other world, attempting to assimilate your species all at once. Yes, we won, but it was messy, and missed our purpose. It was chaos, destroying us as much as you. This time, we are looking to keep you alive, as hosts."

"Hosts?" Ed repeated, unable to hide his disgust. "You want to nest inside us like parasites?"

"I believe your word symbiosis is closer. Mutual existence, both of us better for the union."

"I'd like to ask Sullivan what he thinks about this arrangement," Ed said. "If he's even in there anymore."

"I'm still here," Sullivan said, though Ed couldn't be certain he was hearing Sullivan at all. For all Ed knew, the only thing left of Sullivan was his flesh.

Ed asked, "You like having this thing in you, Sully?"

"You humans are such hypocrites," Sullivan said. "Your body teems with bacteria and tiny bugs which allow you to live as you do, and digest foods that you eat. Without other life forms, you'd cease to exist. If we didn't come along now, you'd surely annihilate yourselves in a matter of time. You put on such a benevolent face for such a hostile species."

"I've seen what your kind did on the other world," Ed said. "How do you expect me to see you as anything other than a threat?"

"I told you, you're among the chosen who will evolve. You, *and* your family."

"And what about everyone else?"

"Let me ask you this, Ed. If you were growing a garden and weeds started to sprout, would you nurture those weeds the same as you would the plants you wanted to thrive? Or would you eliminate them?"

"Eliminate them," Ed said. "But in my version of this hypothetical, you're the weeds."

"Oh, come now," Sullivan surprised Ed with his casual tone, "you've seen the worst of your species. How you treat one another, with no regard for life — how can you see humans as anything but parasites? Your societies are based on destruction — of one another, and your resources. I know you see this as true, which is why I'm inviting you to be a part of something better. Something better than either of our species could ever be on our own. We're gathering numbers and strength, preparing for our day. I promise you, Ed, it will be glorious: no death, starvation or destruction; only life forever."

Ed pretended to contemplate the monster's offer, buying time, mulling options. Sullivan seemed to be on his own, so Ed could defeat him if he could gain the upper hand. As his mouth moved, his eyes scanned the room for something he could use. "Why should I trust you? This isn't exactly something people will sign up for — 'Oh yes, please, infect me, take over my body.' "

"You only fear this because you've not yet seen the good we are capable of when you're one of us. We exist as one, each caring for and knowing what the other thinks, wants, needs — because we all think, want and need the same thing. There's no distinction between one and all. There's no need for the barriers of language. We communicate here," Sullivan pointed to his head. "How long have humans been here, and this is the *best* you can do?"

"Can't argue that," Ed said. "Humans suck, yes Sir."

"It's your choice, Ed. Join us and we can usher in a new world together … or die with your family."

~

FORTY-EIGHT

Rose McCallister

Rose stared at the man holding them hostage, confused, afraid, and feeling as if the world had been pulled out from under her the moment she entered the hotel room. "Who are you?"

Rose looked to Boricio, frantic with questions, hoping she would see something in his eyes that might explain the impossible. But his face was uncharacteristically absent. He was smiling, but it wasn't any sort of smile Rose had ever seen. His eyes looked odd, too, like he wasn't there — or perhaps was maybe drugged, something more than his pot.

She turned to their attacker. He looked like a retired cop more than a psychopath. "What do you want with us?"

The man's lip peeled back in a horrible smile. Off-white gleamed under the ugliest grin Rose had ever seen.

"My name is Mike Blackmore," he said. "As for what I want ... I suggest you ask *your boyfriend.*"

Boricio said nothing. The man she loved was buried behind a smile so sour and stripped from its usual confidence, she could barely stand to see it. He looked equally stoic and crazed. Seeing the stranger above him holding the gun made

Rose think of a cat and a snake, but she had no idea which was which.

Rose kept begging Boricio for an answer, her eyes to his, but his silence only got louder. Finally, Mike stepped into its middle.

"Cat got your tongue, Boricio?" He waved his gun from one captive to the other. "You were writing books with your filthy mouth a few minutes ago. Clearing years of work from my desk, writing lines for psychos in every novel or novella I'll ever write, and *now* you're playing mime because we have company?"

Boricio stared at Mike, muscles bulging as he flexed against his restraints. "Leave her out of this!"

"The world will never stop surprising me," Mike said, turning to Rose. "I wouldn't have thought a monster could feel what this one seems to feel for you."

"What are you talking about?" Rose dared a step forward, hoping the stranger wouldn't pull his trigger in a packed motel. She needed Boricio, and had to get nearer even if only a step at a time.

Mike reached down to the bed, picked up a manila folder and thrust it at Rose. "See for yourself."

Rose grabbed the folder, heart racing as dread spilled through her gut. Whatever had brought the man here would be revealed in its contents. She imagined that he was some conspiracy theory nut who was about to hand over a whole bunch of documents which would prove that the world was out to get him. Boricio happened to be in the wrong place and time, crossing paths with a lunatic.

What could have unraveled him like this?

Rose opened the folder to faded photos of a young girl — the kind parents had, baby photos and school portraits. Pigtails, freckles, uncertain smile, crooked. The pictures then went evil: a desecrated body, almost cartoon in its defacement, with crude drawings that looked … at first the word in her head was *familiar*, until *familiar* grew meaning and Rose found a sudden and soul-raking horror. A scream caught in her throat, then slowly clawed its way out as her eyes found the Applebee's logo with a line through it, then blew from her lips as she hit the final picture: a head like a jack-o'-lantern sitting atop the dresser.

Rose was mush, her legs weightless. She wasn't sure how she managed to stay on her feet. Her head was dizzy, stomach churning, heart beating out of her chest. "What is this, and why are you showing me?"

Her eyes were on Mike.

Mike moved his to Boricio.

Oh, no.

"That was my daughter, Amber. Last time she was seen alive, she was in the company of your animal, here. Why don't you ask *him* what he has to say about *her*? Already said plenty before you got here."

Mike pitched his voice into a reasonable approximation of Boricio. "What do they call you at the rest stops, Ass Vandal? Hershey Murial? Mr. Butterworth on account of your colita being so rich and creamy?"

He lost his Boricio, went back to a barely controlled Mike.

"Before that, your boyfriend said it was nice to make my acquaintance since he never likes to tear life from a man's throat, or intestines from their belly, without knowing a name. He said there was no need to be proper, nicknames were fine. Your monster also said he 'came for justice' in my murdered daughter's mouth."

Rose heard every word like the song it would have sounded like, sung by Boricio. She could hear a sick glee in the words.

Boricio finally spoke: "This is between me, you, and the four balls between us. She ain't done nothing but be here. You do what you have to, and I'll make it easy. But you've gotta let her go."

"Like you didn't for Amber."

"Apples to oranges. I was doing what I did, but you're only doing what you *think* you have to. You're better than I am."

He admits it. He did do it!

Oh, God!

The stranger shook his head, then waved his gun at Rose. "Being with someone like you makes her a monster, too. I'll be doing the world a favor, putting both of you down like the mongrels you are."

"That's the thing, Señor Sorrow, you've already broken the dishes. This shit is for real and forever. She don't know the Boricio you know, and never did. She knows the Boricio *she* knows, the one who deserves her, instead of the one who deserves you. Both Boricios were always there, you showed her the one she didn't know about. Now she'll wake up screaming through the rest of her life. A bullet's mercy would be best, but I'll beg you not to anyway, because I'm a monster to the end, selfish enough to not want a world without my Rose, even if she's miserable inside it."

Mike leaned into Boricio. "Tell her what you are, maybe I won't kill her."

Boricio turned to Rose, and gripped her eyes like fingers on a cliff.

"I'm every bit of the Boricio you know, and what I'm about to say won't alter an apostrophe on our covenant, Rose, but there's a side of me you've not met. I'm a hunter. Simply put, I end lives to keep mine strong, and sometimes to make it stronger. At least I used to, before all that happened did. After Boy Wonder, I've only purged the deserving. Like that pile of shit preying on Paola."

Rose gasped.

"The bodies from last night, that wasn't purging, Rose, that was saving my life and Mary's. Someone was obviously after us. This here," he nodded up at Mike, looming above him, "has nothing to do with that."

"You murder people … just … *because?*"

"There ain't no just because … "

"Answer the question!"

"I purge because I have to."

"What do you mean, Boricio? No one *has* to kill anyone else!"

"It's them or me," he said, simple, like he'd decided on chicken. "Purging pushes my darkness to the bottom. If it rises too high, it'll spill out and kill me. Too long without, I'll put a gun in my mouth and pull the trigger, like flushing a shitter."

Rose didn't know what to say. Or think. Or feel. Or do. Part of her wanted to say that maybe he should've put the gun in his mouth. He was a monster, and didn't deserve to live. She wanted to say that and a hundred other things, but her tongue was too thick in her mouth, unable to find will or words.

More than anything, Rose *wanted* to run.

If there wasn't a man holding her in place with a gun, that's exactly what she'd do. Rose was mortified. If this was her scene she would have to rewrite: It wasn't believable for her heroine to be with a man like Boricio and not *know*.

How could I have been so stupid?

Part of her wondered how she could ever believe in anything again. Another part, the part who loved Boricio in ways she couldn't explain, wondered if there were pieces of herself that knew all along, and stayed in denial.

Boricio.

She loved him. Not just the man she *thought* she knew, but the man she did. The man who knew it was him or the world, and was strong enough to keep himself breathing inside it.

But loving Boricio was horrible: Thinking on it for longer than a blush was too awful to stand.

Anger bubbled inside her. She ignored Mike's gun, stayed in its aim as she marched to Boricio and slapped him hard across the face. She drew back her hand, swollen and throbbing and stared at the red welt. Boricio stared at her, eyes welling up with tears, silent.

Boricio had held his tongue for longer than Rose had ever seen.

She wanted him to talk, to say something — *anything* — that might help her understand *why*.

She knew he could somehow make sense of this if he would try.

They held their stares, neither blinking forever. Rose knew — because she knew Boricio — that it would break something inside him to open his mouth.

His breath reminded her of an animal pawing dirt, getting ready to run. Her pulse quickened, knowing Boricio was seconds from speaking. He opened his mouth. She tipped her body toward him.

Mike's attention prickled behind her.

Boricio spoke, but before Rose heard a word, the door behind her ripped from its hinges. She spun around, and found herself staring into the eyes of the man who had inter-rupted something else before, at Marina's, a second before Paola stepped into The Capacitor.

Steven was his name.

His eyes found Rose, held her stare, and told her without words that she was his reason for coming.

~

FORTY-NINE

Edward Keenan

Sullivan watched them on the couch, waiting for Ed to accept his proposal: Join the aliens or die.

"I'm not letting those things inside me," Jade said, vehemently shaking her head, glaring at Sullivan, not seeming to care if he saw her disgust.

Crying, Teagan said, "If they're going to kill us anyway, why not join them? I mean, it seems like he's still human."

"Looks are deceiving," Jade said. "You saw what they did on the other world! You saw them kill your Ed! How can you trust them?"

"He said it was different this time." Teagan desperately wanted to believe whatever bullshit Sullivan was selling. Ed felt sorry for her, but at the same time, he couldn't blame her. She was looking out for her daughter. Given the choice to live, even if it meant a parasite inside you, or die, most people would choose life. That was everyone's ultimate goal, after all, to live, no matter what.

Ed stayed out of the argument, letting the girls talk it out as he studied Sullivan's responses. At times, his face seemed to flirt with emotion, though Ed could never be certain what emotion it was. At other times, the man's (alien's?) face was blank. Ed wondered how much of Sullivan had stayed inside the body. If "Sullivan" had any control over the alien's actions, or if he was forced to sit, mute witness to whatever the alien wished to do with his body.

Teagan must've been wondering the same thing. "Sullivan, if you're still in there, tell me something about yourself. Give me a reason why I should believe what the alien's saying."

Sullivan's face shifted ever so slightly. He cleared his throat. "When I was 13, my father found out he had cancer. My mother was scared to death, didn't know what to do. He told her everything would be OK, that not only had he taken care of all the financial stuff and paperwork, the doctor also said there was a chance he could go into remission. It wasn't much hope, but enough for my mom to hold onto. My mother was a devout optimist, and *needed* that ray of hope. A few weeks later, I was sitting outside on the porch swing, daydreaming, when the front door slammed and my dad came out and sat beside me. He told me he was going to die. I said I thought the doctors told him he had a chance. He said he'd lied to my mom. While he knew there wasn't any hope, he didn't want *her* to know that because of how much it would harm her. He needed her to believe, not for his sake, but hers."

Sullivan started to choke at the memory, though Ed wasn't sure if it was genuine emotion, or some guise of humanity broadcast.

Sullivan continued, "So I asked my dad why he was telling me. Why not lie to me, too? He asked what I preferred, a lie or the truth. I told him I'd always rather have the truth. He said he knew that about me, because I was just like him. We were realists, prepared for when the world pulled the carpet from under us, especially when compared to idealists, like Mom, whose worlds crumbled when reality crashed. He said it was up to me to make sure Mom didn't lose faith. There was nothing more important than keeping her hope as high as I could. I asked why, especially when there was none? He looked me in the eyes and told me that he didn't choose not to believe. That's just how he was wired. But for those who could believe in things like hope, God, and whatever was better than that, he felt it necessary to maintain the illusion, because sometimes belief paid off and offered a salve that indifference never could."

Teagan swallowed, her eyes welling with tears. "What does that mean?"

Sullivan answered, this time his voice bleached of emotion. "I believe that was Sullivan's way of saying what you needed to hear, but that he himself doesn't appreciate his role as host."

Ed had to make his move.

Sullivan sat, Glock in hand, somewhat on them, but not directly. If Ed could get Sullivan — the real Sullivan — thinking again, he might be able to strike while the alien was preoccupied.

Ed said, "I would like proof that Sullivan's still in there somewhere."

Sullivan looked up, "What proof?"

"When we first met, you were questioning me in an interrogation room, do you remember?"

Sullivan's face softened. His eyes looked up and to the left as he searched for recall.

"Yes," Sullivan said. "I remember."

"I told you about something back then, something important about my job, do you remember what it was?"

Sullivan looked up, trying to remember. Ed launched himself forward, over the coffee table, both hands reaching out for the gun. He grabbed it by the barrel, but couldn't pull it from Sullivan's hands as the two men fell to the ground in a tangle. Ed pressed both of Sullivan's hands to the ground, facing to the right, and shouted back at the girls, "Run! Get Becca and get my guns in the back yard!"

Teagan jumped from the couch and raced upstairs while Jade ran out the back door to get the guns Ed was forced to drop. All he had to do was make sure Sullivan stayed down until Jade was back.

Sullivan's eyes met Ed's, as they fought for control of the gun. His eyes looked like a scared man's, though Ed wasn't sure if it was the alien's fear of Ed or Sullivan's fear of what the alien would do if it wrested control of the gun.

"Let go!" Sullivan grunted.

Ed said nothing, pressing his body harder against Sullivan's, keeping him down.

Hurry up, Jade!

Ed felt something slipping around his neck and tightening, black and slippery, like twisted, fleshy vines slithering up from Sullivan's ribs. An alien appendage ripped through his clothes, threatening to strangle Ed if he couldn't stop it.

If he let go of the gun, Sullivan would be back in control.

If he didn't, the alien would crush his windpipe and kill him.

Ed pushed with his feet, head butting Sullivan in the face as hard as he could, repeatedly, despite the pain to his own skull. He heard Sullivan's nose crunch and break. Hot blood streamed over them both as the black ropes loosened from his neck. Before Ed could use momentum to gain the upper hand, more ropes wrapped him at the fingers, pulling them back, and away from the gun. Ed screamed as his left index finger snapped.

He let go of the gun, and Sullivan seized both moment and pistol, grabbing it as he turned and fired a shot, barely missing Ed, bursting his eardrum as it did.

Ed heard a muffled gunshot, and turned to see Jade behind them, aiming a pistol into their tussle. She screamed, "Let him go!"

Sullivan put his gun against Ed's head and held him tight. He said, "You all get one final chance: Join us or die."

FIFTY

Rose McCallister

Mike pointed his gun at Steven. "You need to turn around and get the fuck out," he said. "Nothing to see here."

Steven paused, smiling. His entire body seemed to soften, bones going mushy as he looked around the room, from Boricio to Mike, before hanging his stare again on Rose, smile still shining. She felt it, like fire on ice as the man stepped toward Mike, ignoring the waving gun.

Mike raised his voice and yelled, "Get out!" probably hoping louder would work.

A few feet from Mike, Steven curled his palm into a fist. Mike's shirt wrinkled at the collar, and his body rose in the air, levitating along with the man's raised arm. His fingers shot open, dropping the gun, and his feet wiggled, brushing the carpet with his toes. Steven held his smile, wrenched his arm like he was hurling a ball, then watched as Mike crashed into the wall and dug a melon-sized scoop from the drywall.

Steven laughed, laying his hand so it hovered horizontal and parallel to Mike, while Mike struggled for breath.

"What's happening?" Rose cried out, unable to believe she had landed a BINGO of crazy: the machine turning on Paola; finding out her true love was a homicidal maniac; Marina

Harmon's man — a guy with super powers — had come to (maybe) save her and now her attacker was being murdered by that same man, with an invisible hand.

"What's happening?" Rose repeated more than once. Steven ignored her, keeping his focus on Mike, squeezing his right fist tighter as Mike struggled harder, until after turning purple and bloated he struggled no more. Seconds after Mike's foot twitched for a final time, Steven turned to Rose. He stood beaming, like he was waiting for a kiss.

Rose said, "What's going on?"

Steven looked surprised, maybe hurt. He stepped toward her. Rose held her ground, knowing a fallen step meant surrendering all she had.

The man's face darkened. He said, "You don't remember me?"

"No," Rose admitted.

His face shifted. Tiny waves rippled across the surface, reminding Rose of rolling dough beneath a pin. It stopped as Rose screamed.

The new face was mostly Boricio's, though kinder and gentler, less hardened. His eyes were still intense, but not as angry.

"Boricio?" Rose whispered, holding out her hand, knowing this other Boricio was somehow different from the first.

The true Boricio found his voice and screamed. "You have to get out of here, Rose!"

He thrashed on the bed, yanking restraints as muscles bulged on his neck and biceps.

"It's not human! Run, Rose, run!"

Rose turned toward the door, and tried to run, but only managed three steps before something snaked her ankle and yanked, sending her face first to the carpet. She turned over, looking back to see a large, black, wet tentacle-looking appendage coming from Steven's ribs through a hole in his shirt and holding her by the ankle.

She screamed. She immediately thought of the aliens Boricio had battled on the other world. *Now they're here.*

"Don't scream, Rose, I'm not going to hurt you. I'm here to save you."

"She don't want you, you limp dicked alien fuck," Boricio screamed, shaking the bed hard again. A loud splintering crack grabbed both Rose and the alien's attention. The black tentacle let go of her ankle.

Boricio broke the headboard, and was desperately trying to squirm free, hands cuffed, one to another.

Rose backed toward the door as Boricio jumped from the bed, legs still bound, and knocked the alien down.

Boricio looked up at Rose, eyes wide and scared — the first time she'd ever seen him scared — as he screamed, "Run!"

The alien turned back to Rose. Eyes narrowed, he said, "Move and I'll kill you!"

Rose was frozen, paralyzed by fear, imagining the black tentacle racing toward her and grabbing her at the throat.

Boricio brought his cuffed hands up and drove his thumbs into the alien's throat, choking him. The tentacle snaked up and twisted around his throat, the two Boricios engaged in an attempt to choke one another to death.

Boricio looked up at Rose, and widened his eyes as if to say: *Go, now … while you can.*

"Die!" Boricio grunted as he dug deeper into the alien's throat.

The alien's tentacle pulled Boricio up by his neck, until Boricio was forced to let go of his hold. The tentacle lifted Boricio like he was a bag of trash, and tossed him onto the bed.

The alien turned to Rose. She froze.

Boricio grabbed a broken piece of headboard and raised it above his head, about to strike.

The alien must've noticed the change in her expression, as he turned back on Boricio, his tentacle grabbing him by the wrist, and shoving him down onto the bed.

The thing that wore Boricio's face leaned into the thing that was born with it and hissed, "I should have killed you over *there*. I've been waiting for this. I wasn't ... pleased ... with what happened last night, but am ... happy ... it turned out as it has. Now I've found my Rose, again."

"Well I've gotta warn you, I ain't done a dookie douche in a while, so there's like a 100 percent chance you're gonna get muddy."

"You are a cat," the man said, "in constant need of scratching, a dog who must beg for attention."

Boricio cackled: "I thought you said I was a cat."

"*You* are a child."

"Well whatever you are, it sure as shit ain't Boricio."

Boricio kept mouthing off to the man as Rose made slow steps backward toward the door. Boricio was no match for the alien, and he seemed to be running thin on patience. If she was going to run, she had to do it now.

Her heart galloped, certain the impostor would turn and see her at any second, but Rose made it to the open door. She stepped through the doorway, suddenly not wanting to leave Boricio with the impostor.

Yes, Boricio deserves to die. But not like this.

The impostor turned to her and their eyes locked. He smiled, then turned to Boricio, giving Rose silent permission to leave.

But then what?

He murders Boricio and comes after you. You think you're really going to get away? And go where?

Rose didn't know if it was because she loved him, or her life, but it was impossible to leave Boricio to his fate. Leaving the room meant running forever, and knowing that *thing*, whatever he was, would kill Boricio, and would probably never stop looking for her.

She was six steps from the door, into the parking lot, when she looked back and saw the thing choking Boricio with his tentacle. Boricio's face was turning blue, and he looked seconds from death.

Rose saw Mike's gun on the bed where he dropped it when the impostor grabbed him. She ran back into the room, leaned onto the bed, grabbed the gun, twisted around from the mattress and landed flat on her back, then pulled the trigger three times.

Rose fell back against the wall with the gun raised, poised to shoot again. The one on the left missed him by atoms. The third bullet slammed into the monster's face and sent him writhing to the ground. Rose had already made enough noise to bring sirens, so she lowered the barrel to the fallen monster's head and pulled the trigger again, killing him for good.

She turned to Boricio and said, "We've gotta get out of here."

~

FIFTY-ONE

Boricio Wolfe

Boricio's heart barely ever raced. Notes climbed, sometimes before the kill, but that's because good murder was a symphony in tune, with no motion an accident. His heart raced, but never ran. Few got far running from Boricio.

Yet, his heart was away from him now. Gone, and if he got it back it would be inside out and stomped on. He had melted her face, his confession pouring acid on their every shared moment. He had destroyed their trust and her faith in him.

For all the horrible things he'd done in his life, and some he actually felt bad about, nothing matched breaking Rose's heart like this.

"Let me explain," Boricio smiled for Rose, knowing the one thing that always worked would never work again.

She turned from his smile. "You're a monster."

"No," Boricio said, reaching down and untying his feet, desperate to make Rose see what logic couldn't. "I'm not like that, Rose. I was, before you. You changed me, even more than Boy Wonder. I purge to breathe, Rose, but I do right by it. I keep us safe."

Rose shook her head. She looked like she wanted to spit on him. Boricio wished she would, it would've been honest, rather than suffer the hush, wondering each second what she was thinking, and living through a hell of waiting to know.

She clawed his heart, calling him a monster, then slammed it with her heel when she said it again. "You're a monster ... I can't believe I trusted you ... can't believe I loved you!"

The something bubbling in Rose erupted: She ran at Boricio and beat at his chest with the butt of the gun. Then she lifted it, nudged the barrel against Boricio's temple and pushed. He looked up at her like a beaten puppy, waiting for a kick.

"I should kill you!" she screamed.

Boricio was silent.

"I'd be doing the world a favor, I'd be doing *me* a favor."

Before she could say finish, Boricio said it for her: "You'd be doing *me* a favor, right, Rosie?" The gun shook against his temple. "You're right, Rose, that you'd be doing me a favor, *and* that I'm a monster. But nothing in this world is worth a smear to you, and I can't stand knowing you're thinking all the things you are about me. So no, I don't wanna die, but I won't stay if you want me to go. I figure if the door that ain't death means living without none of your sweet miss near me, maybe Door Zero ain't so bad."

Rose held the gun on Boricio as he looked up, forgetting how to blink. He saw straight to her insides, and knew she wouldn't — couldn't — pull the trigger. She wanted to see him dead, but didn't want to kill him.

Her eyes flickered, and for a second Boricio wondered if he was wrong, if he had misjudged things, if Rose really would shove the gun deeper and paint the wall behind him in red. She drew the metal from his skin, took two steps back, held the gun to Boricio, and pulled her phone from her pocket. "No," she said, "you don't deserve mercy."

"What are you doing, Rose?"

He watched as her fingers dialed 911.

His instincts to live crackled to life. Boricio had no

problem being killed by Rose — it was almost poetic — but there was no way Boricio would let a donut diddler curdle his milk.

"What are you doing, Rose?" *Rose* snarled out from his mouth, mocking him.

"I'm calling the police, Boricio. *That's* what you deserve: not an easy way out."

Boricio heard a woman on the other end of the phone, "Nine one one, what is your emergency?"

Boricio pleaded, "No, baby — you've gotta listen to me. You'll regret turning me in forever; it'll keep you up at night; you'll want to die. You can forgive yourself for killing me, but you'll never be able to do the same for turning me in, Rose. And you know it, because you know me, the *me* that's got nothing to do with this."

Boricio's whisper kept his words from the operator.

Rose held her eyes to Boricio.

"Nine one one, what is your emergency?" the voice repeated for the third time.

"Hang up and shoot me, Rose."

Shots were fired. Someone in this hell hole must've heard it. The police will be coming, even if she doesn't call. We don't have long.

"No," she steadied her aim and took another step backward toward the door. Her lips to the receiver: "I need help. I'm being held against my will."

Rose gave the operator an address as black liquid puffed like smoke from the fallen impostor's nose, then plumed over the floor, and raced up Rose's ankles, enveloping her body on its way to her face. It happened so fast that Boricio barely had time to register movement before the alien was seconds from overtaking her.

"Rose!" Boricio yelled, waving his hands, then moving toward her. "Rose! Look out! It's getting inside you!"

He was too late.

The Darkness curled into her nose like cartoon scent, the rest of its body quickly following.

She dropped the phone, and her body began to shake, either a process of invasion, or her trying to fight it, Boricio couldn't be sure which.

He watched in horror, helpless, as The Darkness settled, hating *It* for everything *It* had done and everything *It* likely planned to do.

Boricio stared, knowing his Rose was gone and could never come back; a trip through evil would ruin her if she tried. *It* turned, shocking Boricio with a glimmer of his Morning Rose still in her eyes.

It reached down and tore the cuffs from Boricio with inhuman strength.

"GO," Rose cried out, her voice even less her than the tormented face. "I don't know how much longer I can hold it back."

"No," Boricio said, flexing his freed wrists and grabbing Rose roughly by the arms. "I'm not leaving you."

With the same inhuman strength that had freed him, Rose leaned into Boricio, grabbed him by the arms, yelled "Go!" then sent him flying through the doorway and out into the parking lot.

"Get out!" Rose screamed.

Boricio stared back as Rose's face made tormented ripples. He snarled at the creature who had taken so much, including all that mattered. Boricio vowed that he would grow strong enough to kill the monster, no matter what it took, or what surrender was required to make things right.

Then Boricio did something Boricio never did: He ran.

~

FIFTY-TWO

Sullivan

Sullivan held the gun to Ed's head, watching as the girl, Jade, aimed hers at him, demanding that he let her father go.

The alien part of Sullivan had tried to reason with them, was honest with *Its* purpose. While one of them, Teagan, seemed to see sense in his offer, the rest could not, too polluted by fears.

Sullivan's human side tried to be cryptic in his warning to the girl, as if the alien side would not realize his intentions. Truth was the alien didn't care to lie. *It* was confident that *Its* offer was death's superior alternative. Who wouldn't want to evolve? Who wouldn't want better? Apparently, *It* had overestimated the intelligence of these humans.

It would have to kill them, or settle for a hostile invasion.

The problem with taking humans who fought it, was living with lesser control, weaker integration. An inferior host wasn't as useful to the Collective. And a host as strong-willed as Ed might prove damaging. If *It* couldn't convince them to surrender, *It* would have to kill them all.

But even as *It* thought that, *It* could sense Sullivan's hesitation, he too a reluctant host. Sullivan was different from others because he had been touched by *Its* counter, The Light, enabling Sullivan to mount a better defense, and prevent an outright takeover.

Even as Sullivan held the gun to Ed's head, his human side resisted, trying to seize control. It was all *It* could do to maintain Sullivan's hand on the weapon, making it all the more difficult to keep an eye on Jade.

"Put the gun down or I'll kill your father!" Sullivan commanded.

"Kill us, kill us both, Jade!" Ed yelled.

"No, Daddy!"

"If you don't, he'll kill us all! Shoot him in the head!"

It had tolerated plenty. It was time to end this, cut *Its* losses. *It* sent the command to *Its* host to squeeze the trigger: *Kill Ed.*

The host's hand started to squeeze, but froze, gun shaking in Sullivan's hand.

Do not resist me! It commanded. *I will hurt you.*

Sullivan's human side resisted, apparently not learning the lessons *It* had already taught him. Or perhaps the human side could tell *It* was bluffing. *It* couldn't send a blast of pain to Sullivan, not now. If *It* impaired Sullivan, Ed or his daughter might get the upper hand and kill *It*. While *It* could find another host in one of the others, there was also a chance they could fight *It* off enough to stop *Its* ability to find another body.

It pushed *It* thoughts harder: *Shoot now.*

Suddenly, *Its* connection to *Itself* in Steven Warner's body, thousands of miles away, dropped.

Something had happened to Steven. Someone had killed the master organism. *It* was stunned, weakened, trying to focus on Sullivan, but unable, *Its* power crippled.

~

SULLIVAN WAS BACK IN CONTROL.

He wasn't sure what had happened to the alien, but he could feel it inside, already trying to reassert control. Sullivan's mastery of his body was likely short-lived. He leaned toward Ed's ear, and said, "I'm sorry, Ed. Sorry, I couldn't stop it. I want you to take the girls and run, run before it gets into you."

Sullivan put the gun to his head and pulled the trigger.

~

FIFTY-THREE

Edward Keenan

Ed jumped at the gunshot, turned back, and saw Sullivan lying on the ground, bleeding out, dead eyes staring up at him.

Upstairs, Becca cried out, surely startled awake by the thunder.

"Dad!" Jade shouted.

Ed turned to his daughter, saw her pointing behind him. Dark strands of alien matter stretched from Sullivan's open mouth like strings of rope in search of a host.

"Get my bag!" Ed yelled at Jade, keeping his gun on the dark strands as they poured faster, gathering speed and strength.

Jade ran to the back yard and dropped her black bag on the ground. Ed raced to the bag, grabbed an incendiary grenade, then pulled the pin while holding the lever.

Teagan ran downstairs, Becca in hand. Ed turned to the girls, "Grab my bag and go out the back! Both of you."

They ran as Ed backed away from the alien, gun still on it, looking for the spot where mass was mostly gathered. Ed released the lever, counting backward to three, then tossed the grenade at Sullivan's body, turned, and flew out the back door.

The explosion was immediate, shattering glass along the home's back windows.

Ed grabbed the bag from Jade as fire swallowed the house that was home for months. "Are you OK?" He asked Jade, over Becca's wailing.

"We're OK," she said, looking around at the houses behind and to their sides, neighbors peering through windows. "We better get out of here."

Ed glanced at his watch: 8:58 p.m. "Come on," he said. "We're gonna meet a friend of mine, then get out of town."

~

FIFTY-FOUR

Mary Olson

The door at her back shook in its frame as Mary's feet again slipped on the floor.

She wasn't sure how long she had before the door exploded, and she would have to fight another infected.

The banging stopped, something on the other side of the door dropped.

Mary froze, listening for sounds of someone coming to her rescue.

Did someone shoot the cop?

Suddenly, she saw something she wished she hadn't — dark smoke pouring under the door.

No, no!

The smoke poured in a thick, undulating fog, crossing the floor as if searching for something.

Her first thought was Paola, in the bed, helpless. Mary's heart slammed in her chest as she tried to decide between letting go of the door and running to her daughter, and staying put, just in case leaving the door would allow however many zombies out there to rush in.

Even if she reached the bed, she wasn't sure how to fight something as mercurial as an alien fog.

The dark cloud puffed and swelled in size, taking form, almost bleaker-like, and walked toward Paola's bed.

"You stay away from her!" Mary screamed, letting go of the door and throwing herself at The Darkness. As she swung her blade, it dissipated, and then reformed behind her.

The Darkness stood there, still in front of her, as if trying to figure out what it should do first — kill Mary or take Paola. Just then, the door burst open, several zombies standing in the hall, moving toward them.

Mary had to ignore the alien fog. She dropped the blade, grabbed the dead cop's gun from the floor, and fired shots into the closest of them as she raced back toward the door. She slammed it shut, again, but not before seeing the entire hallway filled with walking dead. She threw her back against the door, crying out as it rattled her spine, again.

She stared at the alien fog, standing there, staring at Paola, but not yet trying to go into her.

"Get away from her!" Mary screamed.

On the other side of the door more zombies piled up, banging on the door. The pounding carried to the wall beside her, over and over. THWAP, THWAP, THWAP.

The THWAPS grew louder and closer together, one after another, THWAP ... THWAP ... THWAP ... THWAP. It sounded like dozens.

Mary screamed, "Leave us alone!"

THWAP

THWAP

THWAP

"Stop it!" Mary screamed.

A collective gust, exhaled from many mouths, muffled through the door, just loud enough as it seeped into the room:

"Give us the girl ... "

The door exploded open, throwing Mary to the floor. Two and three at a time, zombies poured through the doorway.

Mary backed up toward her bed, aiming and shooting,

taking them down until the gun was empty. The undead circled her, with the dark smoke standing in front of them as if leading their assault.

Once her gun was empty, they raced forward, all at once, clawing and tearing at Mary's arms as she punched, kicked, and tried to fight them away from her daughter. There were too many. Hands pulled her from Paola, dragging Mary from the bed, helpless as they circled.

"No!" Mary screamed, kicking, biting, clawing a mass of flesh.

Suddenly, the room was awash in an icy-blue light.

The assault stopped. Everyone's attention went to the shimmering air and light beside Paola's bed. A seam in the room's reality split, as if the air was smiling, then parted wide enough for a man to step through.

Then, a man did. A dead man.

Mary's heart nearly stopped as Desmond stepped into Paola's room, holding an M-16. He opened fire, taking down the undead in a surprising display of military precision.

Mary scrambled to the ground, grabbing her knife, and stayed down, out of the way of the gunfire.

The room rained in red, almost humid, so suddenly hot, sticky, and wet. The gunfire stopped, and the black alien smoke was gone.

Mary wiped a slick of blood from her face and out of her eyes, staring in disbelief at the living breathing ghost. The only man other than Ryan she had ever loved.

"How?" was all she could finally manage. "You died."

"Not now," Desmond said, waving his gun at the blackness oozing from the corpses and slowly fogging towards them. He reached across Paola's bed, unhooked her from the monitors and IV, and scooped the girl into his arms. "Paola found me and told me to come save you."

"Paola? She's OK?"

"Come with me," he said stepping toward the light.

"Where?"

"Just come," Desmond stepped into the light and vanished with Paola.

Mary followed.

~

FIFTY-FIVE

Marina Harmon

Marina woke in the bright room, head splitting and throat on fire. She remembered Steven choking her, dragging her down to the room and locking her inside. She banged for hours, begging at first for him to let her go, then for someone — anyone — to hear her.

But nobody could.

This was no ordinary room. It was a soundproof, steel-reinforced fallout shelter/safe room her father had designed years ago for when "the end" came. He had designed it to serve as either his headquarters to operate from post-resurrection if people were hounding him, or as his crypt, his body entombed in a casket in the room's center for as long as The Church owned the estate.

The shelter's problem was that it served its purpose too well. No one could hear Marina. When she tried opening the door, she was unable. The codes had been changed. When she tried making a call or using computers to reach the Internet, she quickly reached no one. Steven had *planned* to use the room as her prison. For what, she had no idea.

The shelter was in the basement, an area few people ever

had reason to go. Marina could bang for a week and go unheard. Even if someone did, no one else knew the elevator or door codes.

She sat at a desk, trying not to look at the casket holding her father's remains. It was steel, fused shut after his death to prevent anyone from tampering with his body. There was a small bed, a second chair (where Marina had sometimes come to sit after his death, praying beside him), and a small closet filled with food, water, and medical supplies. There was also a shelf with books and a scattering of other items that might occupy someone for a few days, but nothing Marina could use to reach the outside world.

Why didn't you think to stash a cell phone?

Not that it would've probably done any good. Considering she got shitty phone reception in certain parts of the house, Marina doubted there was anything close to a decent signal underground.

There was a line of monitors along one wall, all showing static. And Steven had seen to it that the closed circuit television feeds were cut.

He'd thought of everything.

Marina spent much of the first hour after waking cursing herself for being so damned stupid — for not seeing Steven for what he was. Marina wasn't sure what that meant just yet, but he was clearly making some sort of play — for her money? Fame? For The Church?

Then there was the dream. The dark thing chasing Paola. The dark thing that *was* Steven. When she woke, he was there, watching her like a creep.

"I really wish you hadn't seen that," he said.

Seen what?

Did he see into my dream?

If so, what the hell is he?

Marina thought of The Church's more arcane teachings,

things only taught to those who had reached Level: Enlightened Master. The Church, or rather, her father — who knew how many in The Church truly shared his oddest beliefs — believed that negative energies lived among us. They were called Nebulons, and were made real by things like fear and doubt. One spent thousands of hours learning to meditate and fight them. Nebulons were strongest among addicts and people without faith. Sometimes, it was said, they grew powerful enough to possess a soul.

Marina had never believed those parts of her father's religion. It seemed like one of those things some people used to personify weakness and fight it. As a self-help tool it worked wonders, so Marina never saw reason to try and change people's minds when speaking of Nebulons. Once she finally stopped arguing with her father, Marina decided not to battle over beliefs she saw as ridiculous or misinterpretations of her father's true work.

If it works for people, let it work.

As Marina remembered the dream and seeing Steven's dark form, she wondered if maybe her father hadn't been onto something after all.

If she'd just had the dream then woke, she never would've given it credence. She would've seen the dream as more of her own fears, past relationships twisting her sleep. But when Steven was beside her, saying he wished she'd not seen it … she knew there was something more.

MARINA WASN'T sure how long she had been asleep when she was suddenly woken, startled by whispers.

She stood from bed and looked around the room, stopping at various spots, such as under the air ducts, and by the door, ears perked. She heard nothing outside the gentle whir of air conditioning. She assumed the whispering was fragments of a dream she'd yet to swim from.

Marina wondered how long lights would last in the shelter, and whether they were wired to the house's electricity, or ran on the solar panels installed on the roof.

Whispers grew louder. One of the loudest rasped, "Marina."

The loudest came from the casket.

Marina stepped closer, unable to believe her ears.

"Marina," the voice repeated: her father.

Her heart pounded, goose bumps pimpled her skin. It couldn't be Daddy. He was dead and buried, for nearly two — *impossible* — years.

"Marina," the voice repeated.

"This isn't funny!" she shouted, imagining Steven laughing as he watched. She searched for a camera, and found one on top of the computer monitor, apparently off.

"Marina ... "

She approached the casket, and reached out to touch it, slowly, ready to pull back her hand, half-expecting the coffin to pop open and a skeleton to reach out to grab her.

She touched the casket, and felt a vibration: warmth from within.

What the hell?

The vibration turned into a low and steady hum. With it, whispers grew louder.

"Marina, Marina."

I must still be dreaming.

She tried telling herself to wake up, she was dreaming. Usually, once Marina realized she was dreaming she'd open her eyes, even when she didn't want to wake up, like every now and then when she was inside the dreams that kept her wet.

Something clicked inside the casket, a loud clicking, like an opening vault.

Marina stepped back, expecting the casket to swing wide, even though it was fused shut.

Instead of opening, it sank into the ground.

Marina stared in shock.

Whatever was happening wasn't otherworldly. It was, instead, mechanical, and what seemed like an automated response. Marina wondered if her father had set something in the room to recognize if she were trapped. She didn't know the casket sank into the floor, so God only knew what other surprises there might be.

The casket stopped, and a light came on, revealing a second room under the shelter.

"Marina," the voice repeated, louder, wafting up from a speaker below.

She stepped onto the casket, carefully, keeping one hand on the floor above in case she had to pull herself up.

Marina looked around and saw a small hallway with a door at the end. On top of the door was a video camera, and a speaker.

"Marina … Marina," the voice brayed; no doubt her father through the speaker. The voice was recorded, same thing each time in an automated loop.

Marina had to know what was behind the door.

She let go of the floor, dropped into the hallway, and approached the door. There was no knob. Instead, a keypad that looked like it belonged on a decades old phone.

"What am I supposed to do? Dial a number?"

The door clicked partly open.

Marina stepped toward the door, seeing blue light bleeding from the black.

"Hello?" she called, hesitant to step all the way inside the room.

"Marina, is that you?" a voice said — her father.

She stepped into the room and saw him, lying in a bed,

looking as dead as the last time she saw him. His eyes were closed, so was his mouth.

"Marina?" he asked, though she couldn't see how he was speaking when his lips weren't moving.

She longed to run.

But where can I go? Back up there? And face Steven?

"Yes, it's me, Honey. I've been waiting for you."

"Where are you?" she asked, looking around the small 10 by 10 room. The box held nothing besides her father, the bed, and another door on the opposite side. There wasn't even hospital equipment or anything that looked like it might be keeping him alive.

"I'm here, in front of you."

"You're not moving," she said. "You look dead."

"I am, Honey. But as long as my body is here, I'm connected enough to reach you. Did you hear me calling?"

She wasn't sure if he meant now or in her dreams. "I think so," she said. "What's happening?"

"Bad things, Marina. This is what I warned you of. What I dreamed. The moment. I need you to do something very important."

"What's that?" she asked, stepping toward him and putting a hand on his icy arm. She pushed on him to see if he'd say anything, see if he noticed. Of course, he was dead. That didn't keep him from speaking.

"I need you to go through this door. Inside, you'll find something very, very important. A box."

"What's in the box?" Marina asked, staring at the door as if it might burst open at any moment.

"There are two vials, Marina. You must guard them with your life."

Behind Marina, a motor churned. She looked outside the door to see the casket rising, locking her down here.

She cried out, "The casket is locking me in."

"That's OK, Marina. Because you're going to go through

the door, and take the tunnel until you reach a second door that will open into a monastery cellar two blocks away. There's a man there I want you to find, Father Thomas Acevedo. Tell him who you are. He will help you."

"Help me what?"

"Save the world."

Epilogue

Luca stepped through the portal.

He fell to the floor, inches on the other side, head swimming from the enormity, not just from the largest house he'd never seen, but from reality's fabric stretched like taffy.

He tensed, anticipating the crazy man following him over, but the portal closed, leaving just the blue sky above him.

Luca shivered as he crawled forward in the grass, trying to reach the house. His entire back was numb, blood soaking his shirt. He felt dizzy, maybe like he was going to run out of blood and die.

He struggled to call out, "Help!"

He fell to the grass, barely able to keep his eyes open.

There were footsteps, someone approaching. He tried raising his chin, wanted to look up, but he may as well have tried to sprout wings.

Luca tried harder, then passed out.

~

LUCA WOKE IN A LARGE, white bedroom, to see a woman sitting in a chair beside him.

She was friendly looking, with long, brown hair and a giant smile. She was beautiful, and … somehow familiar.

A name bubbled to Luca's mind. His lips parted as if to whistle the sound and fill his air with a memory.

"Rose?"

"Yes, Luca?" The woman widened her smile as she reached out to touch his head, like Mom did when he was sick. Rose reminded him a lot of his mom; she had once taken care of him.

Luca's mind flickered through more memories of a life he lived but didn't. Memories of that other Luca whose family died in an accident. In that life, Luca's brother, Boricio, was in love with this woman, Rose. She was like a big sister to Luca.

"How do I remember you?" he asked.

"Because you knew me," she said. "Before someone took your memories."

"You mean my family is … really dead?" Luca sat too quickly, his head was immediately dizzy. "That really happened?"

"I'm afraid so, Luca," she softly said.

He began to cry, sad and confused. Nothing made sense, everything was wrong and upside down.

"But I was with my family, and they were alive."

"Someone lied to you, Luca," Rose shook her head. "I'm your family, now. I'm all you have."

"No," Luca cried. "They're still alive."

"Those people aren't your family, Luca. They don't know you. Or love you."

"Stop it!" Luca cried, swatting at her hand. "Why are you doing this?"

"I'm trying to help you remember. You've felt different for a while, haven't you, Luca? Like something was wrong, but you just couldn't place it?"

He nodded.

"And you may have even felt like you did some bad things, right?"

"I *did* do bad things," Luca said, thinking of the dead bullies. "Didn't I?"

"Want to know the truth, Luca? The truth they've been hiding from you?"

Luca nodded again.

Rose reached to the floor, then picked up a black, metal box and set it down on the blanket. Luca looked at his lap, vaguely remembering the box that looked like a book.

The box, the vials, and the crazy man.

"What is this?" he asked.

"It's the truth, Luca. Open it, and set yourself free."

Luca opened the box to six, blue vials glowing bright.

"Go ahead," she said. "Take one out. Open it."

"Open it?"

"Yes," she said, smiling.

"And do what?"

"You won't need to do anything other than open it."

Luca's hand was shaking, and he felt weird, like maybe he shouldn't open anything at all. A vague memory flashed, another weird one he couldn't place — of him handing a vial to his "brother" Boricio. Bad things happened, maybe in a dream, maybe reality, Luca was certain of nothing.

Except that Rose wouldn't lie to him. She was too sweet. Luca could tell just by looking. And feeling. Luca felt it more surely than he'd ever felt anything. If Rose were his age, he would've thought the feeling was love at first sight.

"Open it?" he asked again, just to make sure. The smile on his face felt good.

"Yes, Luca."

Luca looked down at a black, rubber-looking stopper sticking out partly from the tube.

"Just pull this out?"

Rose nodded, her eyes giant, like she couldn't wait for

Luca to pop the vial. He wondered what she knew that he didn't, and wondered if it was some sort of magic potion that would make everything OK again.

Or at least get things to make sense.

He pulled the top.

As the blue liquid crept up the sides, Luca jerked his arm from the glass and dropped the vial on his blanket. Blue light blew wider, like melted plastic, then turned dark.

Luca screamed, trying to jump from the bed, afraid of what he had spilled.

Rose held him down, shoving him against the bed with shocking power.

"It's OK," she said, leaning closer, again like Mom, but with something that was nothing like his mother's never-flinching love.

Rose shoved her fingers into his mouth. Luca gagged, nearly puking. He didn't because she held him down and told him not to.

"Open up and let US in," she said as black stuff rose in soupy strands around her and inched toward his open mouth.

Luca screamed as he inhaled a Darkness that promised death to the world.

A Note from the Authors

Thanks for reading *Yesterday's Gone: Season 4*

If you enjoyed this book please write a review on your favorite bookselling site so other readers can enjoy it too. Just a couple of sentences would mean a lot to us.

Thank you!

Sean & Dave

About the Authors

Sean Platt is an entrepreneur and founder of Sterling & Stone, where he makes stories with his partners, Johnny B. Truant, and David W. Wright, and a family of storytellers.

Sean is the bestselling author of over 10 million words' worth of books, including the Yesterday's Gone and Invasion series. Sean is also co-author of the indie publishing cornerstone, Write. Publish. Repeat. and co-host of the Story Studio Podcast.

Originally from Long Beach, California, Sean now lives in Austin, Texas with his wife and two children. He has more than his share of nose.

~

David W. Wright is the co-author of edge-of-your seat thrillers including the best-selling post-apocalyptic series *Yesterday's Gone*, the paranoid sci-fi *WhiteSpace* series, and the vigilante series, *No Justice*, as well as standalone thrillers *12*, and *Crash* which was recently optioned for a movie.

David is an accomplished, though intermittent, cartoonist who lives in [LOCATION REDACTED] with his wife and son [NAMES REDACTED.]

He is not at all paranoid.

He is "the grumpy one" on the *The Story Studio Podcast* with fellow Sterling and Stone founders, Sean Platt and Johnny B. Truant.

David writes about books, TV shows, movies, and video games he enjoys; his struggles with anxiety and OCD; writing; and posts the occasional drawing at his personal blog at davidwwright.com

You can email him at david@sterlingandstone.net

We swear, he almost never bites. Unless you feed him after midnight.

For a full list of his most recent books visit sterlingandstone.net.

Karma Police Series

Jumper

Karma Police

The Collectors

Deviant

The Fall

Homecoming

Yesterday's Gone

October's Gone

Yesterday's Gone Season One

Yesterday's Gone Season Two

Yesterday's Gone Season Three

Yesterday's Gone Season Four

Yesterday's Gone Season Five

Yesterday's Gone Season Six

Tomorrow's Gone

Tomorrow's Gone Season One

Tomorrow's Gone Season Two

Tomorrow's Gone Season Three

Available Darkness

Darkness Itself

Available Darkness Book One

Available Darkness Book Two

Available Darkness Book Three

WhiteSpace

WhiteSpace Season One

WhiteSpace Season Two

WhiteSpace Season Three

Stand Alone Novels

Burnout

The Island

Crash

Emily's List

Pattern Black

Devil May Care

The Secret Within

Also By David W. Wright

Cold Justice

Cold Justice

Cold Reckoning

Hidden Justice

Hidden Justice

Hidden Honor

Hidden Shame

Hidden Virtue

No Justice

No Justice

No Escape

No Hope

No Return

No Stopping

No Fear

Karma Police

Jumper

Karma Police

The Collectors

Deviant

The Fall

Homecoming

Yesterday's Gone

October's Gone

Yesterday's Gone Season One

Yesterday's Gone Season Two

Yesterday's Gone Season Three

Yesterday's Gone Season Four

Yesterday's Gone Season Five

Yesterday's Gone Season Six

Tomorrow's Gone

Tomorrow's Gone Season One

Tomorrow's Gone Season Two

Tomorrow's Gone Season Three

Available Darkness

Darkness Itself

Available Darkness Book One

Available Darkness Book Two

Available Darkness Book Three

WhiteSpace

WhiteSpace Season One

WhiteSpace Season Two

WhiteSpace Season Three

Stand Alone Novels

12

Crash

Emily's List

Threshold
The Secret Within